T0244142

BLIND FAITH

BLIND FAITH

A Novel and Screenplay by
Patrick Girondi

Skyhorse Publishing

Skyhorse Publishing books may be purchased in bulk at special discounts for sales promotion, corporate gifts, fund-raising, or educational purposes. Special editions can also be created to specifications. For details, contact the Special Sales Department, Skyhorse Publishing, 307 West 36th Street, 11th Floor, New York, NY 10018 or info@skyhorsepublishing.com.

Skyhorse® and Skyhorse Publishing® are registered trademarks of Skyhorse Publishing, Inc.®, a Delaware corporation.

Visit our website at www.skyhorsepublishing.com.

10 9 8 7 6 5 4 3 2 1

Library of Congress Cataloging-in-Publication Data is available on file.

Cover artwork: *Blind Faith* by Megan Euker (wood, acrylic, bronze, rock on panel)
Cover design by APOTH Creative
Photo of cover artwork and author by Jon-Patric Nelson

ISBN: 978-1-5107-7830-6
Ebook ISBN: 978-1-5107-7831-3

Printed in the United States of America

Dedications

I dedicate this book to my spiritual mothers and fathers:

To my own mother, who never gives up. I also will never give up.

To Zia Rosa, who, after all she has been through, remains a guiding light to me and many more. I will always be your *scirompolato*.

To Don Mario Paciello, whose wisdom has carried me through a few storms.

To Father John Frawley: You lived during the turbulent scandals of the church. Thanks for never bending.

To my three sons, the Skyhorse Publishing team, and to Megan Euker, my agent. Thanks for the confidence and support.

Contents

Character List

Aaron Abbott	Elitist businessman, son of Howard Abbott
Abbott Electronics (AE)	Largest, best-run corporation in the state
Adele	Customer at Anthony's expensive hair salon
Albright (Mrs.)	Socialite, customer at Anthony's Hair Salon
Andrew Industries (AI)	Company owned by Melissa's father, Blake Andrew
Andrew Schwartz	Distant cousin of Lawrence Barr; big guy in D.C. office
Angelo "The Hook" LaPietra	Chicago mobster that ran Bridgeport
Anthony Cristiano	Owner of Anthony's Hair Salon
Anthony Santis	Hat's brother
Arnold Cohen	Unwed upstairs neighbor of Lubuskus family
Arnold (Dr.)	Psychiatrist in defense of Trisha Abbott
Arthur	Mrs. Kittle's son
Aunt Agatha	Aunt of Aaron and Trisha
Baby-face	Bridgeport neighborhood guy
Benny	Short Italian-looking man, works at Franco's restaurant
Beyoncé	Employee at Anthony's salon
Blake Andrew	Owner/CEO of Andrew Industries
Brabec (Dr.)	Trisha's doctor
Bradford Abbott	Founder of Abbott Electronics and late husband of Luellyn Abbott
Chester Chowaniak	Lawyer specializing in getting court delays
Chucky	City worker
Colletta	Funeral director
Cristina	Employee at Anthony's salon
Daley Family	Chicago political family
Daniel Abbott	Abbott ancestor
David	Guard at court building
David Lubuskus	Judge Cohen's father

Debbie	Trisha's childhood classmate
Dominic Santis	Hat's father
Doris	Maid for the Abbott family
Duff	Retired policeman
Eve	Dr. Arnold's secretary
Father Gondolfo	Priest that knew Hat
G	The Government
Georgia Santis	Hat's mother
Glum	Bartender at Punchinello's
Griff	Sheriff at the courthouse
Harmon Bicks	Lawyer from Tillerson and Bick's law firm
Howard Abbott	Head of Abbott Electronics; father of Aaron and Trisha
Ingrid Abbott	Mother of Aaron and Trisha; elitist socialite
Irene	Cousin of Rebecca
Irving Cohen	Trial judge; formerly named Irving Lubuskus
Irving Lubuskus	Judge Irving Cohen's original name from birth prior to his name change
Jackie	Secretary at Tuesday's Child
Jackie Cerone	Possible relative of "C"
Janet Yellen (Hollerin as referred to mistakenly by C)	US Secretary of Treasury
Jebson	Clerk for Judge Cohen
Jennings (Mrs.)	Employee at Tuesday's Child
Jesse	Sheriff at the courthouse
Jimmy	City worker
Joan Coullane	Funnies columnist
Joel	Irv Cohen's older brother
Joey Pitasi	Neighborhood "wiseguy" from Bridgeport and a follower of "C"
John Tillerson	Partner of Tillerson and Bick's Law Firm, and brother of the Secretary of State
Jonathan	Attorney Sebastian Sherwin's secretary
Juan	Waiter at Franco's restaurant
Judy O'Brien	Owner of Judy O'Brien Public Relations
Kathy	Assistant to *Chicago Tribune* reporter Lou Sherman
Kevin	Special needs boy at Tuesday's Child

Kittle (Mrs.)	Socialite, customer at Anthony's salon
Lauren	Estranged wife of Patrick Danahy
Lawrence Barr	Attorney of Luellyn Abbott
Liz Madia	Trisha's co-worker
Lou Sherman	*Chicago Tribune* Reporter
Luellyn Abbott	Widow, owner of the Abbott estate, grandmother of Aaron and Trisha
Marianne	Dispatcher of court security staff
Marva ("soon to be counselor")	Judge Cohen's daughter
Mary	Judge Cohen's wife
Maxine	Sebastian's law office receptionist
Megan	Aaron's secretary
Melissa Andrew	Aaron's ex-girlfriend; daughter of Blake Andrew
Mikey Passarelli	Bridgeport neighborhood guy
Molly Deere	Attorney Patrick Danahy's secretary
Mullen (Mr.)	Rich perverted man
Mush	Bartender at Kelly's
Nets	Neighborhood cop
Patrick Danahy	Attorney for Trisha
Patrick Jr.	Son of attorney Patrick Danahy
Perkins	Detective that surveilled the Cabbage House
Peter "C" Cerone	Gangster involved in legal and illegal matters
Porky	Neighborhood guy, customer at Punchinello's Bar
Pritzker (Miss)	Socialite, customer at Anthony's Hair salon
Ramon	Waiter at Franco's restaurant
Rauner	Governor
Rebecca Riley	Irish immigrant, nanny of Trish a Abbott
Rihanna	Employee at Anthony's salon
Rob "Hat" Santis	Trisha's fiancé who was killed in car accident
Robbin	Attorney in Sebastian Sherwin's firm
Rose (Mrs.)	Mourner at Luellyn's wake
Samuel Behren (Dr.)	Certified psychiatrist/expert witness; testified against Trisha Abbott
Schultz	Rabbi

Sebastian Sherwin	Atheist Jew, attorney for Aaron Abbott
Sharon	Judge Cohen's younger sister
Sheldon Sparks	Luellyn's attorney
Stern (Mrs.)	Socialite, customer at Anthony's Hair Salon
Susan	Political aide
Susan	An assistant to *Chicago Tribune* reporter Lou Sherman
Taylor	Manicurist at Anthony's salon & paramour of Aaron
Ted	Sebastian's brother
Toad	Patron at Kelly's Bar
Tony	Judy's assistant at Judy O'Brien Public Relations
Tounch	Neighborhood guy that got fired from the CTA
Trisha Abbott	Girlfriend of Rob "Hat" Santis; Aaron's younger sister
Vincent Walker ("Walkin") Foster	American attorney who committed suicide after serving in the Clinton administration
Washington	Chauffeur of Howard and Ingrid Abbott
Zold	Editor of *Chicago Tribune*

Chapter 1

Here Comes the President

Since Anthony Cristiano's salon opened in the Trump Tower on the Chicago River at Wabash Ave., few elitists trudged down to Kiva's in Water Tower Place. It's true that a haircut in Anthony's could cost $600, but it was worth not having to mingle with the common folk. At least that's what Aaron Abbott believed.

Daniel Abbott, Aaron's direct ancestor, landed in Providence, Rhode Island in 1630. The griffin, a legendary creature with the body, tail, and back legs of a lion, the head and wings of an eagle, and eagle talons as its front feet, sits at the top of the Abbott coat of arms. In Aaron's unpretentious opinion, it epitomizes the strength and splendor attributed to his blood dynasty.

Of course, the Abbotts should not be confused with the Abbotts of Dublin, Ireland, whose lineage has been polluted with servants and the like.

The Abbotts live in a thirty-thousand-square-foot mansion at 7 Fox Hunt Road in Barrington, an elite suburb northwest of the city of Chicago. Next to the manor is the Cabbage House, where Aaron's little sister lives with Rebecca Riley.

Aaron skipped past the concierge desk, nodded and hit the up button. In a reflection, he sees a slender six-one figure, elegantly dressed in a brown suit, beige shirt, large blue tie, and large gold cuff links. Aaron smiles tightly. He's gorgeous.

Anthony's is on the mezzanine. Aaron was grateful that there was no escalator or stair access. The elevator worked as a populace filter.

It was a stressful period for him. He was trying to return his life to some sort of normalcy. He had lots on his plate, and a manicure and haircut was the perfect way to get back into the swing of things.

He got off the elevator and walked into Anthony's. Beyoncé, the receptionist, smiled. "Good morning, Mr. Abbott. Anthony is waiting for you and, of course, Taylor will be doing your nails."

Aaron smiles and gazes at the men and women sitting under dryers, getting their nails done and their hair cut and highlighted. While Aaron is walking toward Anthony Cristiano, his phone beeps.

Anthony is fifty. He's working on the hair of an eighty-year-old man. The style and hair color is like Donald Trump's. In fact, Donald asked Anthony to slow down on the look-alikes when he became president. Now that he has been impeached and is no longer president, there are far fewer imitators.

"Adele, come finish here please." Anthony passes a few regulars heading toward Aaron. "Oh, Mrs. Stern, it's perfect. Red is your color."

"Really? We have the opera tonight. I'd just die if I didn't look perfect," Mrs. Stern says.

"Mrs. Stern, when they see you, they'll put you on the stage."

She croons as Anthony sails forward.

Aaron reaches for his phone, and it dawns on him: it's lucky that Anthony charges for service and not results. Most customers would still be ugly after they spent $1,000 to get their hair and makeup done.

Aaron is staring at his phone: *Andrew Industries loses investor confidence.*

Anthony arrives and whispers in Aaron's ear. "Do you have a tip for me, Mr. Abbott? The three stocks you gave me are working like a charm. You're the best."

Aaron's face is suddenly drawn. He looks through Anthony in shock. One by one, clients watch and a few begin to whisper. Anthony takes out a comb and picks at Aaron's hair. "These blond highlights turned you into another Brad Pitt."

Taylor approaches and takes Aaron's fingers in her hand. "Mr. Abbott."

Aaron reaches into his pocket and hands Taylor a ten-dollar bill then creeps forward in a walking coma.

"Mr. Abbott, are you going to return for your haircut and manicure?" Anthony asks.

Seemingly, the whole salon watches Aaron walk out.

Anthony claps, "Beyoncé, call the mayor's wife. If she's still in the building, I'll take her."

Anthony looks at Taylor. "He likes you, honey. What a catch, he's one of America's most eligible bachelors. His father, Howard Abbott, is at the helm of Abbott Electronics, one of the largest, best-run corporations in the state, maybe in the country. One day Aaron will command that ship."

She whispers something to Anthony. His eyes open wide in disbelief. He captures his composure and claps. "Pull Miss Pritzker from under the dryer or she'll roast."

Anthony continues to float forward. "My own salon and I'm still the last one to know the dirt," Anthony whispers to himself.

Aaron is scrolling on his phone. Two old socialites, Mrs. Kittle and Mrs. Albright, step off the elevator. Aaron notices them but looks the other way hoping that they'll spare him.

Suddenly Mrs. Kittle bubbles, "Aaron, Aaron Abbott."

"Oh, hi Mrs. Kittle, Mrs. Albright." Aaron nods his head slightly.

As always, Mrs. Kittle is sporting a mammoth, fake smile. "Aaron, remind Mum about the Mid-America Auxiliary meeting on Friday," she says.

"And do tell Melissa that we said hello," Mrs. Albright says.

The pair mechanically raise their right hands and wave. Aaron smiles reluctantly and nods.

Mrs. Kittle turns to Mrs. Albright, speaking in a low tone. "He's not with Melissa Andrew. He disappeared a few days before the wedding."

"*I know*," Mrs. Albright says, "I just couldn't resist. I hope he tells Ingrid, that witch of a woman he calls his mother."

"He's a cad, and everyone knows it," Mrs. Kittle says, "My son, Arthur, told me that he left her because Andrew Industries is in financial trouble."

Mrs. Kittle and Mrs. Albright turn in to Anthony's salon.

"Mrs. Kittle, Mrs. Albright, what a pleasure to see you. "Cristina, Rihanna, Beyoncé, "Anthony says in a loud voice, "the Albright and Kittle girls have arrived."

All eyes in the shop turn except for those who loathe Mesdames Albright and Kittle or those who object to the announcement of customers as if they were royalty arriving at a ball.

⚘ ⚘ ⚘

Less than a mile away, Attorney Sebastian Sherwin and Attorney Lawrence Barr are together in Sebastian Sherwin's office and reading the same article that startled Aaron. Sebastian is a neatly dressed attorney of thirty but looks every bit of thirty-five. He'd be smiling from ear to ear, but his paper-thin lips would snap.

Sebastian is a self-proclaimed atheist of the Jewish faith. He's a member of the Society for Humanistic Judaism and a big fan of Baruch Spinoza, a Spanish philosopher of the Age of Reason.

Attorney Lawrence Barr is twenty-five years Sebastian's senior and also carries his age like a hog carries a tune. "I doubt if Aaron's old man knows how much Andrew Industries stock Abbott Electronics is holding."

"It's not something I'd volunteer," Sebastian says. "If it comes back, he's a genius. If not, he's an idiot."

Sebastian shakes his head gently.

"What was he thinking?" Lawrence Barr asks.

"The share price kept falling. He kept doubling up; greed's my guess," Sebastian says.

"He was engaged to Andrew's only daughter. Why didn't she warn him?" Barr asks.

"I think that's why he dumped her. He thought that her family double-crossed him," Sebastian says.

"And did they?" Lawrence Barr asks.

"Lawrence, how long have you been Luellyn Abbott's puppet?" Sebastian asks.

"Counselor," Barr returns.

"Yeah, right," Sebastian slithers, "that feisty old hag doesn't take counsel from anyone. It's a shame her grandson, Aaron, doesn't have some of her astuteness."

"She'll be gone soon enough," Lawrence adds.

"Why do you dislike her so?" Sebastian grins pleasingly. "She must have kept you under her heel."

"I'll finally get mine when she's gone," Lawrence adds with a high degree of satisfaction.

"I've been waiting seven years myself," Sebastian says.

Lawrence looks at him cautiously.

"Sebastian, I'm divulging privileged client info here. How's this going to help me?"

"One hand washes the other . . . one hand washes the other. Besides, I doubt that Grandma Abbott is generating a lot of hours, and you've *always* sold to the best bidder." Sebastian shrugs his shoulders and smiles.

"Andrew Industries got awful choppy and illiquid. Who sold him all the stock?" Lawrence asks.

"Yeah, Lawrence, right. As if you don't know," Sebastian says.

🌿🌿🌿

Aaron looks at his watch and meticulously gathers his jacket as he boards the Uber. "1150 North LaSalle, quickly," he says.

"Yes sir," the driver says.

"Drop the visor," Aaron says as he points.

The driver quickly responds. Aaron studies the mirror and combs his hair.

Aaron walks into the offices of Judy O'Brien Public Relations at 11:15 a.m. Judy's fiftyish and very sexy. She has large brown eyes and long brown hair with blond streaks. She's at her desk with her female assistant, Tony. Aaron storms in and startles the women.

"Aaron! You scared me," Judy says smiling.

Judy thinks she knows why Aaron is there but doesn't have the time or the will to pass through that pond.

"How was your trip?" Judy doesn't wait for Aaron to respond and rolls her eyes to the side, looking at an imaginary calendar. "Don't you have the luncheon for the president-elect in fifteen minutes?"

As Aaron often does, he answers her question with a question. "Did you see the article on Andrew Industries?"

"I heard something. What's it got to do with us?"

Aaron stutters, "Us? Nothing, but you-you-you know how the press loves to crucify me. My ex is an heir. They'll try to mix me in the mess somehow."

"Don't sweat the Melissa stuff. Calling off a wedding isn't *that*."

Aaron interrupts. "No, it's not that."

Judy stares at one of the few clients that she wishes would sexually assault her. "Why else should you be mixed into it?"

Aaron's quiet.

"Aaron, skeletons. As CEO of AE, you'll be in the spotlight. I can only protect you from what I know. Clinton's people found out first and eliminated oral sex as a sexual act. I need time to prepare. Got it? I can't protect you from what I don't know."

Aaron removes his hand from his pocket and rubs his forehead.

"What do I have to pull you out of this time?" she asks.

Aaron is offended. "This time?" he asks.

Judy waits for an answer as Aaron's irritation level rises.

"Just do damage control on this Andrew thing. I'll hold up my end." Aaron heads for the door.

"If you *really* want to hold up your end, you should think twice about leaving town to avoid gossip about ex-fiancés."

"It was your idea!"

"I'm an adviser. You and only you are responsible for your actions."

"This is deluxe. I pay for advice; if I don't follow it, you ostracize me. When I do follow it, and it turns out to be bad advice, I'm responsible for my own actions. Can you tell me; *exactly why do I pay you?*"

Judy smiles at him in motherly way. "You pay me because I'm the best at what I do. Now get to the luncheon."

Aaron walks out.

Tony looks at Judy. "That guy should be in the movies."

"If he plays his cards right, someday he'll go from president of AE to president of the country."

"He's a doll. I'd vote for him," Tony says.

"He's our client. You better vote for him," Judy snaps.

ᒪᒪᒪ

Aaron grabs an Uber and gets out in front of the Conrad Hilton. He goes through the revolving door and up the stairs. Sebastian is watching him from below.

At the ballroom entrance, an attractive young girl greets Aaron with a name label. "Hi, Mr. Abbott, can I tag you?"

"Of course," Aaron says, smiling broadly.

A line suddenly forms, and Sebastian butts ahead, almost to the front. He's confronted by Susan, another attractive political aide.

"May I have your name, please?" Susan asks.

Sebastian glances ahead at Aaron. "Sebastian Sherwin," he says loudly.

Susan goes through her file. "I'm sorry, sir. You must be on another list. One moment."

Aaron moves away. Sebastian follows.

"Sir . . . *Sir*," Susan says.

Sebastian looks back. "Don't worry, damn it! I'll send a check."

Sebastian disappears into the crowd. Irritated, Susan looks for backup, but she's by herself and can't leave her post.

The hall is filled with blue-suited men and gorgeous women. There are two long appetizer tables on either side of the room and four bars. Aaron cautiously makes his way through the crowd. He spots Illinois Governor Rauner, who is sixty-seven, but could easily pass for much older. Rauner's surrounded by four people. Aaron reaches his hand in to him.

"Mr. Abbott, good to see you," Governor Rauner says.

"Governor, as always, you can count on AE."

They shake hands. Sebastian barges into the group. His back is to Aaron. He aggressively grabs the governor's hand. "Governor! It's been a while."

"Yes . . . yes it has . . . Mr. . . . ."

"Sherwin, Sebastian Sherwin."

"Oh yes . . . of course . . . Mr. Sebastian."

"Sebastian's my first name."

"But of course, Mr. Sherwin."

6

The governor is completely comfortable speaking to people he doesn't know. There are probably three thousand people in the ballroom, and he might know thirty of them. Of course, it's essential that they write checks; whether he knows them or not is a trivial detail. The governor turns to Sebastian. "This is Aaron Abbott of AE."

Aaron studies Sebastian.

"I know Mr. Abbott," Sebastian replies.

Sebastian reaches for Aaron's hand. Aaron hesitates, then shakes. Sebastian looks at the governor. "We're old friends, Governor."

The governor smiles. "Well, we'll need a lot of old friends to win this one. . . . We all need friends."

"If you only knew, Sir. . . . If *you only knew*," Sebastian replies.

An attractive young woman in a business suit interrupts the group. "Mr. Abbott, you have an urgent call on the house phone."

Aaron smiles. "House phone? I didn't know anyone even used them anymore. Excuse me, Governor. . . . Mr. Sherwin."

"Aaron, I'll be at the bar," Sebastian says.

Aaron is on the verge of blowing Sebastian off.

"We need to speak, Aaron. Something's come out of the closet," Sebastian says.

The governor moves away. Aaron lamely nods at Sebastian.

Aaron follows the woman to the house phone. "Mother, my cell's dead."

"Don't be running around town like some gigolo. It's not good for your image," Ingrid Abbott, Aaron's mother, says.

"I know, Mother," Aaron replies, "and I thank you. I'll find a suitable escort."

"I'm worried, son."

"I know you are worried, Mother. Oh, and Mother . . . have you? Never mind."

Aaron hangs up and walks into the crowd. Sebastian's standing by the packed bar with a drink in his hand. He notices Aaron walking toward him and quickly turns away.

Aaron notices the coy move. He takes Sebastian's shoulder and turns him around. "All right, Sherwin, what gives?"

Sebastian jerks his shoulder under Aaron's hand. "Machiavelli says that generosity can work against you, especially with politicians."

"Cut the bull, Sherwin."

Sebastian looks to both sides. "It's seven years, friend. Seven's a lucky number."

"Yes, Sherwin . . . is that what you wanted to tell me, that seven is a lucky number? I've got things to do."

"We all have things to do Aaron." Sebastian hesitates, searching Aaron's face. "It's a tough break about your engagement."

"Oh? Who's your lucky other half?" Aaron spurns. *"Don't waste my time. What do you want?"*

"It's payback time, Aaron. Funny how things find their way into the papers, and rape's not fashionable in the least. Look at Bill Cosby, they went after him for something that *might* have happened forty years ago."

An amused grin forms across Aaron's face. "I suspected as much. Is that all? Blackmail?"

Sebastian doesn't flinch. "I'm here to help you. There's an imminent leak coming."

"Oh, you're here to remind me about a rape that I had nothing to do with and *help me*? How could you possibly help me?"

"Your star's rising. A rising star needs to protect its path. We wouldn't want you hitting any meteorites." Sebastian hesitates. "A meteorite could blow a rising star into little pieces."

Aaron listens impatiently.

"On the road to progress there are fifty guards to pass. When the dealing gets dirty, and it will, who can you trust? Are you forgetting who I am, Aaron?"

Aaron aggressively moves in closer to Sebastian. "Who you are is of minor importance. What is of major importance is that you don't forget who I am."

The two are interrupted by a stubby, freckled man in glasses. "Looks like Blake Andrew, the CEO of Andrew Industries, overplayed his hand this time," the man says.

Aaron's suspicious. Why did this man decide to talk about Andrew Industries to him? Aaron rapidly scopes the situation. The guy has had a few too many and it's just a coincidence . . . if there is any such thing as a coincidence. Aaron looks sternly into the man's eyes. The man is confused and cowers.

"Blake Andrew is a shrewd player. He'll come out of it. *AI is as solid as a rock*," Aaron says.

The man regains his courage and smiles, looks at Sebastian and then back at Aaron. "So was Pacific Exploration and Production."

Governor Rauner walks up to the three men. "Aaron, my office will call to schedule a lunch."

"That will be fine, Governor." Aaron stares at Sebastian as if he's trying to browbeat him into submission. The freckled man quietly steps back.

"That will be fine, Governor," Aaron repeats.

The governor walks away.

Aaron turns to Sebastian. "My work here is done. Good luck to you, Sebastian."

Aaron walks away. Sebastian is not sure what to do. He moves among the crowd looking somewhat lost. He spots Susan, the political aide. She appears to be looking for him or someone. The appetizers were almost gone when he arrived; there was no way that he was going to write a check.

Chapter 2

Granny's Death Just in Time

Bridgeport is a neighborhood on the South Side of Chicago. It borders Chinatown on the north and the Irish enclave of Canaryville on the South. Bridgeport is the home to the Daley political family on 37th Street and the Italian American Club on 30th Street. At one time the South Side of the neighborhood was predominantly Irish and the North Side predominantly Italian. Today, it's a mixed bag.

Richard J. Daley was mayor from 1955 to 1976, as was his son, Richard M. Daley, from 1989 to 2011. Today, John Daley, Richard M.'s brother, is the Democratic Party Committeeman of the 11th Ward, which encompasses Bridgeport. John and Rich Daley's nephew, and Richard J. Daley's grandson, was the 11th Ward alderman for a few years. Unfortunately for him, he was convicted and imprisoned for lying to federal bank regulators.

Angelo J. LaPietra and his crew ran Bridgeport's North Side. He died in 1999. LaPietra supposedly earned his nickname "the Hook" due to the way he murdered his victims—those that did not, or could not, pay up. He would take his victim—bound and gagged—and hang him on a meat hook (piercing the victim's rib cage) and then torture him to death with a blowtorch. The torch would not actually be the cause of death (that's what the FBI claimed). The Italian American Club on 30th Street and Shields Avenue removed Angelo's picture after his death and today is open to all nationalities.

The power that the Daley and the LaPietra family held in Chicago and particularly in Bridgeport was legendary and absolute. Today, there are still vanishing small pockets of political and outfit influence.

Peter Cerone was named after his father. His friends called him "C." His mother was the granddaughter of Irish immigrants, but C bore no resemblance. He was forty-eight years old, stocky, dark-skinned and balding, with average looks. Rumor had it that he was a relative of Jackie the Lacky Cerone, but C was his own man. He knew a little about a lot of things and was not afraid of investing his time and resources in different ventures, legal or illegal. You could say that about many from Bridgeport.

He's nervously pacing in front of a table for two that is elegantly dressed in the not-so-elegant Franco's restaurant. C's rubbing his hands and slowly breathing in and out.

Benny, a short Italian-looking man of fifty, walks to C with an apron in his hand. "C, do I really have to put this on?"

C picks a fork off the table and pursues Benny with it. "Damn you, Benny! I told you it's *Mr. Cerone*!"

Benny retreats into the kitchen. C throws the fork and it enters the doorway with Benny, about three inches above his head.

"You wouldn't have missed me three years ago!" Benny yells from the kitchen.

C looks at the mirror behind the bar. Benny's right. C had one of the best arms in the neighborhood. He got a scholarship to Arizona and was clocked throwing a ball at 107. The coach said it was a mistake and maybe it was or maybe it wasn't. Anyway, C missed the neighborhood and was back home in less than three weeks.

One day when he and Patty Bo were in Jimbo's, C hurled a shot glass down the bar at Mikey Passarelli. Patty Bo thought that Mikey was a dead man, but the shot glass hit Mikey's beer glass just as he raised it to his lips. Beer flew all over, and Mikey ended up with just a glass rim in his hand. He looked at C and said, "Frig you."

C smiles in the mirror and adjusts his tie. Benny is reentering from C's right.

"Sorry C, I mean Mr. Cerone." Benny begins to fix C's tie. "Jeez, I never seen you like this before."

C stands still. Benny finishes the tie, pats C gently on the chest, nods, and smiles into the mirror.

Benny's troubled that C does not smile back. "Is this the one? Have you finally met Mrs. C?"

C continues to gaze into the mirror; there are tears welled up in his eyes.

"Oh C," Benny says, "I'm so happy for you." Benny hugs C. C shrugs him off.

Benny clears his throat. "Juan! Ramon! Put your aprons on! *Andale!*"

Benny winks and smiles warmly at C and kisses him on the cheek.

"Don't try dat kissy stuff when she gets here."

Benny steps back. "But of course, Mr. Cerone. . . . Don't worry, everything will be perfect." Benny turns and claps his hands. "Move, boys. Everything must be perfect for Mr. Cerone. . . . I'm so happy."

Every patron that enters Franco's nods at or greets C. The small restaurant quickly fills up, but C sits by himself sipping a glass of wine. As the minutes turn into two hours, C's face turns into a stone picture of misery.

Every now and then, Benny looks over at his friend. He doesn't have the courage to ask anything. The neighborhood crowd is smart enough not to dabble, and at 10 p.m. on the dot, C quietly stands and leaves.

$$\mathcal{U} \ \mathcal{U} \ \mathcal{U}$$

The drive to the thirty-thousand-square-foot Abbott Mansion at 7 Fox Hunt Road in Barrington rarely took less than an hour from the Loop in downtown Chicago. Most believed it worth the trip.

The mansion is on a seventy-one-acre lot with a lake, a swimming pool, and all the amenities that one would expect for the home of one of the richest families in the country.

Bradford and Luellyn Abbott, Aaron's grandparents, built the fortress. The atmosphere of the estate is Victorian. Bradford appreciated his lineage to England, even if his people had been in the United States for over four hundred years.

Attached to the manor is a seven-car garage and nestled behind the mansion, invisible from the guard house and gate was the quaint "Cabbage House" where Trisha Abbott, Aaron's twenty-eight-year-old younger sister, lived with Rebecca. Trisha calls her Becky unless Trisha's angry at her.

Rebecca's an Irish imitation of Mammy from *Gone with the Wind*. She always wears a housedress and a handkerchief and speaks with a strong Irish brogue. During the day, Trisha works at Tuesday's Child at 3633 North California Avenue in Chicago. While Trisha is at work, Rebecca cleans, sews, irons, and cooks. In fact, she is happy doting on and caring for Trisha, which has been her only employment for twenty-eight years.

Becky's happily straightening sofa pillows as the morning sun helps itself in through every window in the place.

"Becky! Where's my brown pullover sweater?"

Rebecca raises her hand to her mouth and squints her eyes.

"The one that Rob lent me that he never got ba-ack," (said cutely, almost in song).

Rebecca looks on in confusion and slight concern.

"Is it still in the hamper?" Trisha asks.

Rebecca snaps her fingers and rushes out of the room. Moments later, she knocks on Trisha's bathroom door. It opens a crack, and Rebecca hands the sweater in to Trisha.

Trisha's sweet voice comes from within, a bit muffled by the sound of shower water. "Thanks, Becky. Was it in the hamper?"

"*It's clean*! In twenty-eight years, you never got a dirty sweater from me, Trisha Abbott!"

Trisha takes the sweater and lays it on the bathroom sink. "Thank you, I love you, Becky . . . smells clean to me." As Trisha finishes the sentence, she closes the bathroom door.

Rebecca stands still, grins, and then walks away.

✒ ✒ ✒

At the same time in the Abbott Mansion, Trisha's parents, Howard and Ingrid Abbott, are in the library. The drapery is gaudy, and the mantels are peppered with busts of ancient Romans, Greeks, English, and American statesmen. The rest of the abode, like the library, resembles a history museum.

Howard Abbott is in his late fifties. He's bulky, average height, and resembles the late actor Karl Malden. Ingrid Abbott, his wife of over thirty years, is perfectly beautiful, doesn't have a hair out of place, and could easily pass for thirty-five.

Scorn has become Ingrid's normal tone, especially when speaking to her husband. A day doesn't pass that she does not regret the pact she made with her mother, and then with Howard.

Ingrid's mother may have secured a safety net for the family's fledgling business through Ingrid's marriage to Abbott Electronics, but the arrangement worked for everyone but Ingrid.

Her idiot husband did well. He got his trophy wife, a son, and a daughter. Her mother was able to die in dignity and in financial stability without a stain on the family's crest, but Howard was a mental midget who could not satisfy Ingrid intellectually or any other way. Ingrid loved her children—well, at least Aaron. Trisha had lived so long with Rebecca that sometimes Ingrid forgot what her face even looked like.

Certainly, forgetting her face or most anything about her daughter was simple. After all, Trisha did not have Ingrid's finesse, beauty, charm, or brains. The only suitors that Ingrid recalls for her daughter were beaus at least three tiers lower than their own financial status. The latest was probably the worst of the bunch. He came from an inner-city enclave and went by the name "Hat."

Ingrid turned to Howard and spoke in a contemptuous tone. "This is your fault. You're not a man! You can't control your own son! Now we're ruined!"

13

Howard always spoke calmly to Ingrid. When they were first betrothed, he did so to not lose her. Now, no communication with his wife was minimally effective, so he might as well not aggravate himself.

"You're exaggerating. One of his investments hit the rocks. It happens."

Ingrid throws a vase. Howard calmly moves to the left as it smashes beside him. She picks up another.

"That's a $40,000 Martinuzzi. If it breaks, I'll deduct it from your allowance."

"That's all you have over me. Without your money, you're a void. And even with it, you can't make me love you or even like you." Ingrid moves closer to her husband. He cowers. Her face is within six inches of his own. "You're repulsive," she says sneeringly.

"Thank you for the 'repulsive.' Now get ready. Aaron will be home soon."

Howard smiles but as he turns, his smile drops and he frowns remorsefully. He takes two paces and hears something metallic hitting the wall. He sees their framed marriage picture on the floor. A phone rings. Howard answers. His expression turns mournful. He hangs up and walks into the kitchen. Ingrid sees his expression.

"What?" Ingrid follows him out of the room. "What is it, Howard?"

⚾ ⚾ ⚾

Back in the Cabbage House, Trisha's sandy brown hair falls as she pulls the sweater over her head. She straightens the bottom of the pullover at the top of her boyish jeans. She has a slender frame and moves toward the mirror over the sink. She begins brushing her hair, counting each stroke.

When she arrives at ten, she pulls her head up and gazes at a picture that's stuck to the right side of the mirror. The picture is Trisha in the arms of a man in a baseball uniform. On the bottom corner, it reads: TRISHA & HAT FOREVER.

Trisha counts to fifty and then leaves the bathroom and enters her own bedroom. The room is a tomboy's room with sports items decoratively placed. Her bed is plain, as is the rest of the furniture in her room. On her dresser is a small stack of letters and trinkets.

Trisha picks up and opens the top letter. "Rob, Hat, please answer," she says out loud. She searches the room. She's alone. She reads the letter, cries a little, folds it, and lays it down. She recomposes herself and bounces into the hallway.

Rebecca's waiting at the bottom of the hall stairs. "Did you brush your hair?"

Trisha doesn't respond. She tilts her head in a half nod as Rebecca continues to look on sternly.

"Did you count?"

14

Trisha half nods again.

"You know with the arthritis in my hands, it's hard to brush your hair."

"Yes, I counted."

"Did you count to one hundred?"

Trisha looks at Rebecca. "I counted."

"I didn't ask if you counted. I asked if you counted to one hundred? Will you be home for dinner?"

Trisha grins. "What will you make me?"

"You ain't no colicky baby no more, young lady. You eat what I prepare."

"What will you make me?"

Trisha stares down at Rebecca and smiles.

Rebecca smashes her lips together and looks to the side. "What would you like, honey?

Trisha descends the last stairs and hugs and kisses Rebecca. "Oh, I love you, Becky."

"I love you too, honey. . . . Don't forget I leave for my cousin's tomorrow."

"I know. Two days. I'll try to survive."

Trisha heads to the door with an envelope in her hand. She opens the door and yells back to Rebecca. "Love to find some of that Irish stew! I'll be home about seven."

The door closes and Trisha gets into her ten-year-old Jeep Wrangler.

Trisha's older brother, Aaron, is already in his office at 333 Wacker in the family headquarters. He often slept at the family condo in the Water Tower and did so last night.

The 1986 movie *Ferris Bueller's Day Off* was partially shot at 333 Wacker. It was the building that Ferris's father's office was in. The thing that Aaron appreciated the most about the location was that Nuveen Investments was there. Nuveen had $300 billion under management and were the biggest dogs on the block.

Maps of the Roman empire cover Aaron's wall. The office couch and chairs are made of rough, aged leather. His huge desk is mahogany, and he has a magnificent view of the skyline, river, and lake.

Aaron is standing in his office with Sebastian and would have rather been at the dentist. "It's bull, no one protects us from women who brutalize and humiliate us. The damage can be like that of rape," Aaron says seriously.

"That's all well and good, my friend. I don't disagree." Sebastian prods.

"Once it was scandalous to kiss on the first date. Today's casual sex only becomes rape if you forget to call them the next day," Aaron says.

"Forget all that," Sebastian volleys. "The only important fact is that we'll have trouble if this gets out."

Aaron turns toward Sebastian. "They love playing victims. They run around like bitches in heat and then, when consumed by bitterness and disappointment, blame the richest dog that jumped on for a ride."

Sebastian stares at Aaron, thinking that he could write the next line that Aaron will speak.

"Look at what they did to Bill Cosby," Aaron says. "The guy's a hundred years old, and bitches from thirty-five years ago destroyed his life. After thirty-five years!"

Sebastian was wrong. He was certain that Aaron was going to bring up Mike Tyson being convicted of rape by a woman that voluntarily went to his hotel room in a halter top and shorts at two in the morning.

Sebastian has heard all of this too many times. He is losing his patience. "You're going to be the CEO of a Fortune 500 company. Perry works at the *Reader News*. He's down and out. It'll just be chump change. Closure Aaron, closure," Sebastian says irritably.

Aaron nods. "All right, I understand. Do what has to be done."

Sebastian smiles and leaves. Aaron remains. He sits at his desk and gazes around from item to item on his office mantel.

He stares at pictures of him golfing with George W. Bush, Barack Obama, Bill Clinton, Donald Trump, Joe Biden, and Vladimir Putin.

Aaron looks out the window. The view is indescribably beautiful. He stands, leaves his office, and walks to the Eastman Egg Company. He orders Canadian bacon on egg whites and coffee.

He gets back to his office by 9, and at 9:30, he hits a switch on his phone.

Megan, his secretary, walks in. "Yes, Mr. Abbott?"

"Do I have any calls?"

"No, Mr. Abbott. I would have sent any call through. I know that you are here."

She leaves. Aaron puts his right hand to his chin and hits the switch on his phone, Megan returns.

"Do I have any appointments today?"

"No, Mr. Abbott."

"Would you ask my father if he needs me to attend to anything?"

"He's not here, sir."

"He's not here? Where is he?"

"I don't know, sir. I'm *your* secretary."

Megan leaves. Aaron punches buttons on his Ubiquiti touch screen office phone. Someone picks up on the other end.

"Let me speak to my father, please," Aaron says.

After a pause, his father picks up on the other end.

"D-dad, I need to talk to you."

There's a long pause. Aaron's expression turns to shock.

"Oh my God, Dad. I'm so sorry. Oh, my God. I'll see you at home."

Aaron hangs up and gazes out the window. The anguished look he had speaking to his father passes to relief. He hesitates, stands up, and walks to the door. At the door, he pauses, and gently taps on it. He pushes his head against the wood and takes the door knob in his hand. "Yes," he whispers, "yes, yes, *yes*." Each "yes" becomes more audible.

He quietly opens the door. Megan has her back to him and is speaking with a young man in a suit. "Then he asked me if his father needed him for anything." Megan says sarcastically. "That's a good one."

The suited male notices Aaron. His facial expression freezes. Megan looks curiously at him, turns to see Aaron, and realizes that she's been overheard. Megan attempts to smile and Aaron walks briskly past them.

Chapter 3

Pigs in Suits and Vans

The black limousine pulled up to the Abbott Mansion. One by one, the Abbotts entered. Not a word was spoken for the ten-minute ride. The car came to a stop at the Davenport Funeral Home on Main in Barrington.

Trisha reached for the handle.

"Don't, honey," Ingrid said.

Trisha looked at her mother. At the same time, the chauffeur opened the door from the outside.

"No, no, please. Give us a few moments," Ingrid said to the driver.

The door closed and the four Abbotts were physically closer than they had been in years. Ingrid smiled. She looked at Howard and touched her black lace gloves to his large, wrinkled hands. Howard turned to the side. Ingrid looked at Trisha and smiled. Trisha smiled tightly. Ingrid then looked at her son. Aaron was rarely surprised by his mother. He didn't believe that she'd start surprising him now.

"Son, I know that you did not always get along with your grandmother Luellyn, but I know that you loved her and that she loved you," Ingrid said.

She looked at Howard and Trisha, hoping that they'd pitch in but was disappointed. "Every end is a new beginning. Each loss can be molded into gain," she continued.

"Ingrid, can we get out of the car? People are beginning to arrive," Howard said.

"Yes, yes, we can get out, as a family, strong and unified. Luellyn's death is not pleasant for anyone, but we must use the situation in the best means possible."

Aaron and Howard knew precisely that Ingrid was addressing the family's economic trouble. In fact, Luellyn's inheritance could salvage the situation, maybe.

Aaron nodded to his mother.

"Ingrid, if you don't mind. She was my mother. She was a good woman. We need to get into the funeral home. Others will be mourning her loss as well," Howard said gently.

"Of course, dear, of course, you are so right," Ingrid looked and spoke to him with saintly sentiment.

Howard flinched ever so slightly. Ingrid's kindness was rarely unaccompanied by a thrashing.

His beloved mother Luellyn was dead. Nothing could alter that. However, if Luellyn's death could nudge his wife toward kindness or anything resembling kindness, it would certainly be welcome.

A long line formed to the back of Davenport's. Ingrid, Trisha, Aaron, and Howard are accepting condolences.

An older woman attempts to kiss Aaron. He intentionally moves and shakes her hand instead. "Thank you, Mrs. Rose," Aaron says.

Mrs. Rose coldly passes.

A young woman walks up to Trisha. "How's that boyfriend, Trisha?"

"He's fine, thank you," Trisha responds.

Aaron shoots Trisha a concerned look.

"Is he here this evening? I'd love to get a look at him. I heard he's stunning."

"Yes, he's here, but I don't see him now."

Aaron momentarily stares at Trisha. She doesn't notice.

The young woman leaves, and an elderly couple arrives. The wife looks in Trisha's eyes. "So sorry, first Rob and now your grandmother. Life's not always fair, honey, but do stay strong."

Trisha nods.

Debbie, one of Trisha's childhood classmates is next in line. The friends embrace. "I'm so sorry, Trisha. I know how close you were to your grandmother . . . and it happening so close to Hat, must make it even more devastating."

Debbie cries, hugs, and then releases Trisha.

Trisha looks peacefully at her friend. "Debbie, the ring is only severed temporarily. Eventually it's joined forever."

Trisha smiles; Debbie queerly grins.

Aaron turns to Trisha. "When will the testament be read, Sis?"

Trisha shrugs, smiles tightly, and gently shakes her head.

✿ ✿ ✿

The last of the visitors has left. Aaron, Trisha, Ingrid, and Howard approach the casket.

After a few moments, Aaron turns and nervously whispers to his father. "Dad, I need to talk to you about Andrew Industries."

"This isn't the time."

Aaron's face is momentarily panic-stricken.

Howard puts a hand on Aaron's shoulder. "Son, things will work out for the best."

The black limousine drives the Abbott family home. Their maid, Doris, stands at the door and offers to take each of their garments.

"Come on, kids. Let's have a refreshment, as a family," Howard says as he makes his way into the den.

Ingrid goes directly to the stairs. "A family? Really, Howard." Ingrid scoffs.

Ingrid's kindness in the car had made Howard hopeful. It had been years since he and his wife were intimate. To this day, there was no woman that he had ever met that he would prefer to be with. One's mother only dies once, and he certainly was not above accepting mercy. They had conceived two children together and it surely wouldn't kill her. Of course, having a refreshment is a completely different thing than being intimate.

Ingrid's change of tone was a message to Howard. Each should remain in their own bedroom. "I'm exhausted," she says. "I'm going to bed. We have to escort Luellyn to her final resting ground tomorrow morning."

Ingrid heads up the stairs. Trisha's still holding her jacket. Howard pours himself a drink and offers one to his antsy daughter.

"Dad, why don't you come over to my house?"

"Another time. I'm beat. Why don't you stay here? Spend tomorrow, after the funeral, relaxing."

"I have to work, Dad."

"Your grandmother just died, they can do without you for a day."

Trisha smiles. "No, they actually can't."

Howard looks into his glass and mumbles. "Trish."

Trisha pecks her father on the cheek. "Good night, Dad, Aaron."

After Trisha leaves, Howard takes his drink and sits. Aaron is still standing, impatient and anxious.

"Now, Aaron, son, can't this problem wait? My mother . . ."

Aaron gazes down at his father, shakes his head, and silently exits.

The funeral went off as planned. Luellyn was buried in the Abbott Family Mausoleum next to her husband and another twelve Abbotts in the Evergreen Cemetery.

≠ ≠ ≠

The day after the funeral, Aaron returned to his office. He had to do something to ward off the anxiousness that controlled him while waiting for the will to be read.

He knew that his grandmother had considerable wealth. Always an independent person, she kept just how much to herself. Aaron calculated and had made estimates over the years. He was sure that Grandmother Luellyn's estate was easily north of one hundred million.

He'd control Ingrid's and Howard's share. He hoped that his father would help him convince Trisha to also let him manage her part of the inheritance.

No one any longer doubted that Trisha was unstable. The death of Hat kicked her further off kilter.

Aaron planned to economically support Andrew Industries and get the company back on track. After, he'd merge Andrew Industries into Abbott Electronics and make a killing. The plan would turn out how he had initially planned before he called the wedding off to Melissa Andrew. Of course, for his scheme to work, some critical maneuvers were yet to be made.

Aaron passes an uneventful day at his office and is maneuvering his car out of his reserved spot when Sebastian sprints out of the dark toward Aaron's car.

Aaron slams on the brakes and opens the window. "Jesus H. Christ, Sherwin. Are you trying to scare me to death?"

"Look at this article!" Sebastian screams as he pushes his phone toward Aaron.

"I've already seen it," Aaron says.

"I can do something about it."

"How are you going to do anything about it? It's already out."

"I can make sure that you won't be smeared again. Every writer in the country will fear you."

Aaron distrustfully stares.

"I mean it. This will never happen again."

"And just *how* will you manage that?"

"Aaron, it's true that I abhor religion, but I am Jewish. If you haven't noticed, we have considerable influence in the media." Sebastian smiles broadly. "Leave it to me. OK, boss?"

Aaron looks on, hesitates, and then tightly smiles. "Do you need a lift?"

"No sir, I need to tend to this." Sebastian pockets the phone and reaches his hand out to Aaron.

"I'll bill AE (Abbott Electronics) for my work as legal fees. Deal?"

Aaron hesitates and then shakes Sebastian's hand. "Deal," he says, nodding his head.

Sebastian firmly squeezes Aaron's hand and stares into Aaron's eyes. Aaron momentarily gazes at Sebastian but then looks out the front windshield. After a few seconds, Sebastian releases his grip and Aaron drives away.

When Sebastian no longer hears Aaron's car, he heads for the exit door and jumps into the air. "Yes!"

レレレ

It's early evening at Punchinello's on 31st Street. A fat man named Glum is behind the bar and three customers are scattered in front of him. C walks in. He's wearing sunglasses. His ringed fingers tap on the bar. Glum walks over and whispers in C's ear. At the same time Glum glances and nods toward one of the patrons. The patron's watching television and doesn't notice.

"Hey Jeb," C says.

The sixtyish man looks from the television to C.

"Oh, hey, C." As he looks at C, Jebson's neck twitches nervously. "Didn't see you come in."

"Your Honor's off today, huh?"

Jebson nods.

"How you hittin' 'em?"

"C, I couldn't pick the winner in a one-horse race."

"I got steam at da Glades track."

Jebson strains his eyes. His neck twitches his head back and forth. "I'm all ears, C."

"'Oops He Fall Down,' in the 5th."

Jebson smiles.

C turns to walk away, then turns back. "Oh, and Jeb, pass it to da judge. Tell him dat dere may be sometin' comin.'"

"Got it, C. Thanks, C."

C turns and waves Glum toward the stairs that lead to the basement. C turns back to Jeb. "Hey Jeb."

Jeb squints through the dimly lit bar. "Don't even tink about gettin' it off on our guys. Go hit da online bookies. Lord knows, they can afford it."

Jeb nods his head. His neck twitches simultaneously. In the background one of the customers is going around the bar. "Hey, C!" he yells.

C turns. "Whadda ya want, Porky?"

"It's dark out. Why you wearin' sunglasses?"

"I'm an eternal optimist, jagoff. It's always sunny to me."

Porky nods and C and Glum disappear down the stairs and enter the basement. Glum turns the radio and television volume all the way up. The room is filled with static and garbled noise.

Glum whispers to C. "The Rams saved us."

C nods. "I tought so. Is 26th Street in?"

"Yeah. But C, I tink Bippo's eatin' the long shots again. One out of two of his ponies hit."

"Tell Friar Tuck to make Bippo repent."

"What if it's on the level?"

"It ain't. His daughter just got married. He's short."

Glum reaches under his sweatshirt and hands a manila envelope to C. C winks and walks up the stairs.

Glum turns the television and the radio off, listens for a moment, and then smiles.

"Hey, you sissy faggots, wanna hear someting? Listen to dis."

Glum releases a loud, long fart. "Frig ya's, drink it up."

Glum then heads up the stairs.

Inside the minivan parked down the street from the bar, two FBI agents are wearing headphones and seated in the back.

"Was that human? Did you hear that?" The first agent asked.

"I heard a lot of static and then a flat toot or bull call," the second agent replied.

"It wasn't no bull call. It was a fart. Didn't you hear what they said after? 'Frig ya's, drink it up?'"

"I can't wait to burn these tough guys," the second agent said.

Chapter 4

Maybe It's Not That Easy After All

Aaron walked down the long hall. He rarely looked forward to speaking to the boss, and certainly wasn't up for it now, but there wasn't a choice. Aaron touches the head of Caesar, as the boss had instructed him to do thirty years ago. The boss told him that it would bring good luck. He needed that more now than he could ever remember, in his entire life.

Aaron approached the dark wooden door adorned in gold trim. The door's cracked open, but Aaron knocks anyway.

"It's Aaron. Can I come in?"

A military "*yes*" came back.

Aaron walks in and scans the enormous, mirrored chamber. Ingrid walks out of her wardrobe room holding outfits in front of her. She lays some on a bench next to the bathroom.

"What can I do for you?"

"I wanted to let you know that everything will be all right."

"Oh?" Ingrid says while examining clothes laid on the bed.

Aaron hesitates and then blurts out. "How long will it take to get our inheritance?"

"Your father takes care of those things."

"I didn't want to . . . he's not . . . I think he's upset about Grandma Abbott."

"Hmpf. It doesn't matter to me. I'll get nothing. An Abbott never forgets."

Aaron smiles faintly.

"Damn it! Where is that scarf!" Ingrid screams as she tears through a drawer. "Doris!"

"Was there anything else you wanted?"

"Nothing, Mother. Good night." Aaron walks out.

Aaron approaches a dark mahogany door, opens it, and enters. His room is divided into four parts: the bedroom, bathroom, office, and a foyer. He plops himself in a leather recliner behind his elegant eighteenth-century desk. He unwraps a piece of gum, throwing the wrapper onto the floor. He pushes his head back, closes his eyes, and smiles as he chews the gum. He then takes out a pad of paper and starts writing numbers. He dials on the phone.

"Give me a quote on Andrew Industries shares." He waits for a response. "I know it's illiquid, damn it! Just give me a quote. What's the size of the bid? What's behind it? And the offer?"

He listens while jotting down numbers. He takes the gum out of his mouth and sticks it onto the bottom of the desk. He hangs the phone up, stands and, with his pants and shoes still on, he lies on the bed. He smiles, reaches up, and turns the light off.

⚜ ⚜ ⚜

The following day in Armour Square Park on the South Side of the city, a shiny black Cadillac slows and brakes. The passenger window rolls down.

Armour Park is three miles south of the Loop. The long thin area is twenty-one blocks long and four to five blocks wide. It's wedged between rail lines, expressways, and the South Branch of the Chicago River.

Italians cling to the Armour Park area. African Americans dominate the population to the south; and to the north is the ever-expanding Chinatown.

The Italians strategically call Armour Square Park part of Bridgeport, making them less cognizant of the painful truth that within a few generations, if things continue, it will be Chinese. Armour is a working-class area and the Italian area was the stronghold of Angelo "the Hook" LaPietra and his gang.

The Italian American Club is in Armour Square on 30th and Shields. Other than a few tiny private clubs populated by hoods and wannabe hoods, the Italian American Club is the last standing semblance of a once powerful crime organization dominated by Italians.

Old-timers reminisce about the good old days when there were twenty hits a year. Most speculate that many of the bodies are resting under Palmisano Park between 27th and 29th and Halsted. Rumor has it that Richy Daley, the ex-mayor, had the quarry filled and turned into a park to derail the FBI, who were looking for bodies—including that of Jimmy Hoffa.

"Hey Joey P!"

Joey, a fortyish, short Joe Pesci look-alike, comes to the Cadillac and sticks his head in the window.

"Hey C. What's up?"

"How's Hat's parents?"

"How could dey be? You know, I tink dose WASPs killed him to keep him from pollutin' the money-line."

"You said it. It's not about nationality or race. The wealthy want a closed club. You don't see no Kardashian with no poor dudes."

C throws a toothpick out of his mouth onto the street. "I loved dat kid. You know, I been messin' wit Abbott's ex-fiancée." C proudly grins and nods his head. "It's da least she could do after I got screwed wit her ol' man's company shares."

C looks out his window, shakes his head and looks back at Joey. "If Abbott hadn't shown up, we'd a been sittin' pretty. It would a been my biggest score. Millions, Joey, millions."

"What exactly did Abbott do, C?"

"Joey, it ain't for you. It's complicated."

Joey looks down and blows through pursed lips.

"Get in," C says.

Joey smiles and gets in. The windows roll up and the car pulls to the curb. C starts popping nuts into his mouth.

"Melissa Andrew shows up at the Polack's bank. She's lookin' for cake to bail out her old man. The Polack could never deal in dose numbers but sends her to me like dey do every good-looking broad. She feeds me green grass on her ol' man's company. I start bottom picking Andrew Industries shares. It's not real liquid. Dat's the company name, Andrew Industries."

"Yeah C, I know," Joey says sarcastically.

"When I had fifty thousand shares I sold 'em in blocks, parking blocks."

"Who'd you park 'em wit?"

"I started out wit Edgeview, the Polack's bank, and went out to some of its customers and some offshore accounts."

"I'll bet you dat ol' Polack da owner loves ya for dat."

"He'll get over it. He was gettin' 'em off at a profit. . . . He was my silent partner and smilin' all da way to his own bank. Some of the offshore accounts really cleaned up. Then *super dick* shows up. He wants to merge d' companies as a wedding gift, more or less, and is lookin' for a bargain."

"Super dick's Aaron Abbott?"

"Yeah, Joey. He starts buying every share he can get his hands on, forcin' me to pay higher prices."

"How'd you know it was him?"

"The idiot's a blowhard. He starts braggin' in da clubs and you know most of da places on Rush Street still have ears."

"Maybe he found out you were plowin' his workhorse?"

"Joey, she's sharp."

"I know, C."

"Anyway. She never tol' Aaron about da trouble at da Ponderosa. She sucked me into da hole, hoping her ol' man would find an escape route, selling enough shares to save da ranch."

"She double-crossed ya?"

"Absolutely. She knew about da company headin' down da tubes from her brother or her ol' man's confidant or sometin'."

"Maybe she was lightin' the candles on his birtday cake too."

"Joey, I don' know what she was doin'. I ain't no head doctor. You know dese modern broads. Dey dish it like it's gonna run out someday. It's a wonder anyone marries 'em."

"Yeah, if da milk's free, why buy da cow?"

"Nice, Joey. You and your frickin' euphemisms." C smiles sarcastically.

"So dis chick sucks you in?"

"In more ways den one and when I hear 'bout lover boy's merger idea I get nervous. I ain't no chump. Da G will want their end. Bribin' Janet Hollerin would cost me all my profit. My investors are nervous. They want out."

"Ain't her name Yellen?"

"Hey Joey, Hollerin, Yellen, same god damn ting to me. You wanna hear d' story or edit my monologue?"

Joey stares. C gets aggravated. "What? What!"

"C, turn your monologue into a dialogue."

C ignores the remark. "I start sellin' to ol' lover boy. He don' know who he's buyin' from. He tought he was gettin' a K-Mart blue light special."

C slaps his hands together and shows Joey his palms. "We're almost clean. Da Polack owner's nervous about da G, but I made a few and within a week I won't have a share left."

Joey looks on in admiration.

"Nice C . . . Nice."

A police car beeps. C rolls the window down.

"Hey C, the G's by the park. I'd move on."

"Tanks Nets." C waves and rolls the window up. The police pull away.

"You gonna move?"

27

"Screw him. . . . He just wants to make sure he gets his egg for Easter, the suck ass. What did poor Tony B ever do to get a son to turn to the dark side?"

"It's a shame, C, but it can happen in da best of families."

"I guess. But Tony B's such a great guy. Anyway, Numbnuts finds out dat his girl's been holdin' out on da info."

Joey squints.

"Numbnuts is Aaron Abbott?"

"Of course, but she didn't know he was accumulatin' stock. She wasn't tryin' to do him." C breathes in deeply trying to hide remorse.

"Dames. She's stiffin' me to help her ol' man so she can be wit Abbott."

"Why din't he tell her he was buyin' da ol' man's shares?"

"I tole ya, he wanted to merge his company wit hers. He tought dat it'd be a powerhouse. And da weddin' was still on. Maybe he wanted to announce da merger as a wedding gift."

"In da neighborhood dey just give a few C-notes. An' ol' man Andrew, Melissa's fadder?"

"He was happy. He didn't know why his stock was in play. I tink he unloaded some."

"Which is what the conspirator wanted?"

C stares at Joey.

"Traitor?" Joey eases out.

"Hey Joey, frig you."

"Sorry. An' Big Howard A?"

"I don' know, but when he finds out it'll be a 911 call."

"And da government. What are dey gonna do?"

C looks on sarcastically. "Today's markets are rigged tighter den JFK's assassination and d' weapons of mass destruction. Da G will be fishin' for months. Finally, dey'll find a scapegoat and he'll do a 'Vincent Walkin fuckin' Foster.'"

Joey stares at C. "A Vincent walkin' what?"

"The government had Foster popped in 1993. Our boys were in it. It was beautiful."

"Why didn't you say a Jeffrey fuckin' Epstein?" Joey asks.

"I dint say a Jeffrey fuckin' Epstein because the fuckin' G did its own hit. We had nottin' to do wit it . . . happy now?"

Joey stares out the window. "Yeah, now da government does what dey used to trow us in jail for doin': gamblin', drugs, prostitution, puttin' people to sleep . . ."

"Joey, hey Joey! Pay attention. You know what dey'll do?"

"What?" Joey asks.

"What? What? Why dey'll trow da American flag over it and get praised by da press who are owned by da same guys riggin' da markets, staging phony wars and assassinating people an' calling it suicide. Trump's right, 90 percent of it is fake news."

"Wow, C . . . den Hat, Abbott's soon-to-be brudder-in-law, suddenly dies."

Joey looks out the window, then he looks back at C. "Did somebody ice Hat?"

"Joey, dat poor kid was a little pawn in da game. He an' his broad don' know nuttin'. Dey jus wanned to get married wit da white wicker fence an all dat shit."

C looks confidently at Joey. "An Melissa, she was tryin' to stick me up. I ain' sore, it was a good cause. But I'm gonna stick dat silver spoon of Aaron Abbott's right up his ass and scoop an eyeball."

C gestures to Joey, who opens the car door to get out. "I wanna bury him. Dey'll find his lungs so full of dirt dat the cornerer will have to use a sauce spoon to get to lung tissue."

"Coroner."

C's eyes flare.

Joey raises his hands. "Sorry, sorry." Joey turns back to C. "Oh yeah, I got dat mick alky Danahy on de line if it goes. I been humpin' his shrink's secretary. You got d' good judge. It's spades."

C nods.

"And I know you read de papers." Joey says.

"Yeah. Granny's dead." C's face turns hard. "If dat fag tinks dat he's gonna ride up on some white scallion and swoop Melissa and her ol' man's company from me usin' his granny's inheritance, he's softer den baby shit."

Joey smirks and thinks to himself, *his mudder made pesto sauce with scallions* but he didn't want to push his luck.

Joey takes a step back and puts his head against the roof and his face inside. "C, I like dat Melissa. If it works out, maybe we could swap. You take da shrink's secretary. She smokes a mean pipe."

"Joey, you're hurtin' my feelins. I mean, I would've married dat broad. Who knows, I still might. . . . " C looks to the side and then again fixes on Joey. "What's da shrink's secretary look like?"

Chapter 5

It's Cool for All and Easy for No One

Lawrence Barr almost always missed the boat. He was now in his late sixties and looking forward to retirement. His father was an attorney and his father's father was a law school professor. Lawrence didn't like law but it was the road of least resistance to a comfortable living. He was married with two daughters who were each married off and snug. He was looking for a last big hit to fund his final retreat.

Meeting the Abbott family paved the road to comfort. Chester Chowaniak had been the guy that sealed the deal. Chester got the Abbotts an impossible court delay and helped to flip a bit of Abbott family business to Lawrence.

Chester never won a case, but if you wanted a continuance, he was your man. Once he showed up with forged medical documents for stage four lung cancer to convince a judge to give him an impossible postponement.

Lawrence learned long ago that there is no justice in the law. The winners have the means to pay for victory; hence the contingency lawyers, ambulance chasers, and the like.

August 1st of 2014 pushed Lawrence over the morality cliff for good. "Obama admitted that *some folks* used torture." It wasn't that Lawrence Barr was so against torture. He had been married for decades, but Americans are always criticizing other nations and acting so highfalutin. The least the president could have said was that we'd never do it again. Instead, he glossed over it like it was nothing. "Imagine the stress they were under," Obama said.

Imagine the stress the men and women they were torturing were under, Lawrence thought.

ᛌ ᛌ ᛌ

30

Trisha, Aaron, and Howard are in front of Lawrence Barr and Sheldon Sparks. Sheldon Sparks had done his internship with Barr. To show his gratitude, Sheldon began stealing Barr's clients. Needless to say, they despised each other.

Luellyn Abbott was the last client that Sparks snagged. To compromise, they made a deal that Lawrence would get a 30 percent cut of all the work that Sheldon billed Luellyn for. It wasn't a perfect arrangement, but it kept him in the loop without any effort. Come to think of it, the situation worked quite well.

"Your grandmother went to Mr. Sparks to update her will recently, when I was unavailable," Lawrence announced.

Sheldon smiles insincerely at Lawrence.

"He means that she finally got wise," Aaron whispered under his breath.

Howard looked sternly, yet lovingly at his son and raised his finger to his lips, "Shhh."

Lawrence looks cunningly at Aaron. "I have other clients, Mr. Abbott, I have other very interesting clients."

Aaron wasn't sure what Barr was talking about.

Sheldon wasn't crazy about theatrics. He looked warmly at Howard. "Your mother was quite a woman, Mr. Abbott."

"Thank you, yes she was."

"Before we begin, does anyone want coffee, tea, want to use the restroom or anything?" Lawrence asked.

Everyone shook their heads.

Sheldon smiles faintly. "Mr. Barr, I'd like some water."

Lawrence rolls his eyes and leaves.

Aaron's face is anxious. "Can we just get on with it?"

Lawrence walks back in with a large glass of water. Trisha notices that it is smudged and dirty. Sheldon raises it, barely wets his lips, and lowers the glass to the table. Lawrence rushes a coaster under the simple chalice and grimaces at his younger colleague.

"This is the last will and testament of Luellyn Abbott according to the American Bar Association. Today's date is Friday, June 30th, 2023, and the will was made on Thursday, June 15th of 2023.

"I name Sheldon Sparks to be my executor. I hereby revoke any and all prior wills and codicils I have made, according to the laws of the state of Illinois."

Aaron's phone vibrates. He reads a message and stands. "I'm sorry, is there a way to get to the point here? I have an urgent matter."

Lawrence looks disinterested. Trisha is completely blank.

Howard clears his throat. "Son, I will get you a copy of the will and you can read it later. I'll email it to you."

"It's really not that long, Mr. Abbott," Sheldon says, looking at Aaron.

Aaron's nerves are bare. "Well, can you cut to the chase! I know you're getting paid by the hour, but someone's got to produce the resources to pay all you pen-pushing vultures."

Sheldon smiles. "Of course. I have gone over the document in detail and put simply, Mrs. Abbott blessed a few charities but left everything else to Trisha."

Aaron stares in disbelief.

🖋🖋🖋

Later that evening in Ingrid's bedroom, she's fixing her hair and glances at a news clip on her computer. "Luellyn Abbott, Wife of Founder of Abbott Electronics, Laid to Rest."

"Why aren't you here to straighten things out? You old bat," Ingrid growls at the computer screen.

She hears a knock on the door. "Who is it?"

"Me, Mom . . . Aaron . . . can I come in?"

"Yes, come in."

Aaron enters and scans the room. "Mom, we have to get that money . . . I can't maneuver without it."

As Ingrid scans her handsome son, another knock is heard at the door. "Yes?" Ingrid asks.

"Mum. A guest is arriving. Mr. Abbott wants you to come down," the maid says.

"You tell Mr. Abbott that I'll be down when I'm good and ready. Hmph."

"Yes, Mum."

Aaron looks at his mother. "Trisha's lost it. She's getting letters from the dead."

Ingrid smiles quaintly and nods, "And she'll certainly be giving Grandma's money away. Have the police found the third car in her fiancé's accident?"

Aaron stutters. "Why-why do-do you keep asking me? I don't know anything about it."

"Son, learn from your sister's mistakes. One of the rules of the elite is to marry up. Doesn't matter what religion, race, or breed they are as long as they have more money. If you don't do this, the protection of the elite diminishes."

Aaron raises his hand in an attempt to interrupt. His mother continues steamrolling.

"Learn from the Kardashians. It's no scandal to mate with someone outside your race, as long as they're rich. You don't see any of them marrying common folk. Now that would be a scandal."

"Mom. Please don't start on the Melissa issue again. I screwed up. I—it's over. I told you, my interest is Andrew Industries, not Melissa Andrew."

Ingrid smiles approvingly. "Son, if I'd have followed my instincts, I'd have been another Hillary Clinton, but I'd have won, damn it!" Ingrid slams her hand on the dresser. "I'd have won!"

Aaron stares at his mother.

"Your father always kept me on a leash. He'll see."

"Mom, Sebastian Sherwin, the . . ."

"I remember," Ingrid smiles, "the young man who kept you out of prison."

"Mother, he's the arriving guest," Aaron says.

Ingrid interrupts, "Oh, yes, Sebastian. I hope that he's all that you say. We need to stop your sister effectively. She's our shame."

Aaron looks to the side. "She's our hope."

ℒ ℒ ℒ

By the side of the road, a steel blue BMW with Sebastian sitting inside is parked two hundred feet from the Abbott Mansion entrance. He's grooming his hair and mustache. He smiles into the rearview mirror. The clock reads 6:58. He steps on the gas.

He is waved through the front gate and passes the estate garage where he notices a man dressed as a butler undoing something from one of the limo's fenders.

In the mansion den, Aaron leans on the pool table and his father, Howard, is gazing out the picture window.

"I don't enjoy this," Aaron says. "Do you think that I like to see Trisha losing it?"

"She's mourning, just mourning."

"Please, Dad. There's no hiding from this. Not this time. We can't throw money at it and hope that it disappears."

"How do you envision things working?"

Aaron raises his voice, "Dad, Sebastian's a tactical negotiator." Aaron's hands move. He's speaking with heart. "He's my adviser. He'll cover our backs. It will be over before you know it."

"Aaron, she's not hurting anyone. Can't you let it go?"

Aaron shakes his head, half angered and half annoyed. "She's hurting us, and she's hurting herself!"

"Son, don't let money cloud your head. Someday you'll be my age."

"Dad! Don't you get it? She's sick. . . . She doesn't talk to anyone! She's locked in the Cabbage House when she's not working with those retards." Aaron pauses, moves to his father and shakes his arms. "She's receiving letters from her dead boyfriend!"

"So," Howard responds, just as sternly, "look at the people that are governing our nation and the planet . . . the US government calls a bunch of hooligans a revolution . . . we're shooting down weather balloons to save our sovereignty . . . we're electing mentally challenged folks to Congress . . . we've got a male claiming to be a female serving us as the assistant secretary of health!"

Howard stares into Aaron's eyes and continues. "If your sister, during her grieving, believes that she's receiving letters from the dead . . ."

Howard looks to the floor, hesitates and nods before continuing. "Yes, and there's the money. Could be over a few $100 million," Howard says blankly.

Aaron angers and loses his composure. "That's right, Goddamn it! Could be several hundred million dollars!"

His father turns and looks at his son.

"Sorry," Aaron says.

"Tell me, would we be meeting with this tactical negotiator if there wasn't all that money at stake?"

Aaron, almost crying, begins to stutter. "Dad, you've got-got to-to-to give me a break. I'm doing my best for-for the family, for you. I won't let you dow-down."

"Son, I'd love to believe that." Howard ponders. "The union proceedings cost us dearly."

Aaron stares toward the picture window. "I miscalculated! Must you remind me every day? *It was over a year-year ago!*" Aaron looks gently at his father. "Please . . . I'll come through. No one will get hurt, no court, no mess. I'll take care of everything."

The two are interrupted by the maid. "Sirs, a Mr. Sherwin is at the gate.

"Show him in when he arrives," Aaron says as he pinches the cuff of his father's jacket. "Dad, please."

His father looks to the side and walks away without speaking.

🍃🍃🍃

Rebecca is gazing out the only Cabbage House window that allows a view to the front of the mansion. She watches as Sebastian parks and walks into the estate's front door. She makes a disgusted face and jerks the drape closed.

As Sebastian is being escorted in by the maid, he passes a mirror and adjusts his tie.

"Sirs, Mr. Sherwin," the maid says as she opens the door.

Howard has his back turned. Aaron nods. "Thank you."

Aaron looks at his father's back. "Welcome, Sebastian!" he says in a voice so loud that Luellyn might have heard it.

Aaron and Sebastian walk toward each other. Aaron puts his left hand on Sebastian's right shoulder and guides him.

"Let's have a drink. Dad, do you remember Sebastian?"

Howard remains still, but after ten seconds, which, to Aaron, seems to be the span of a boring baseball game, turns slowly and nods. Sebastian smiles.

"Well, it's been over seven years, Aaron, though your father hasn't changed a bit," Sebastian says.

Everything is momentarily quiet and their attention is drawn by the entrance of Ingrid, who strolls in as if walking into a crowded ballroom.

"Aaron, darling. This must be Sebastian."

Ingrid looks at Sebastian. "I don't recall the beard or mustache, but they do become you."

Sebastian walks to Ingrid and kisses her hand. She blushes.

"What a pleasure, a man of culture," Ingrid says.

"It comes quite naturally, Mrs. Abbott, when facing a woman of such beauty." Sebastian looks in Howard's direction. "You have a lovely wife, Mr. Abbott. I see that you have the best of everything."

"Yes," Howard grumbles, "the best of everything."

ررر

It's Thursday morning. Sebastian unloads a manila envelope onto his desk.

He presses the intercom button as he traces over a letter with a pencil. "Jonathan, get in here."

A pretty woman in her twenties enters, wearing a gray business suit.

Sebastian stares down at his task. "Clear my calendar," he says without looking up.

She appears confused. Sebastian continues to trace. "But you have the Hartford negotiation."

"Screw Hartford. I got AE. Hartford's chicken feed."

Jonathan nods and walks out.

ررر

Aaron Abbott's office, later Thursday morning. The intercom lights up as Aaron's reading at his desk. "Yes?"

"Sir, Mr. Sherwin's here to see you," Aaron's secretary Megan says.

"Wait sixty seconds, then show him in."

Aaron faces a full-length mirror on the back side of the waiting room door. He removes some lint, adjusts his hair, and sits down. After a minute, Megan enters, escorting Sebastian. Sebastian gazes at the oak walls and the marble floors as he walks into Aaron's lair.

"Will that be all, sir?" Megan asks.

"Yes, thank you," Aaron replies.

Sebastian continues to assess his environment as he sits in front of Aaron's desk.

Sebastian finishes his inspection and turns to Aaron. "I expect that you've finished?" Sebastian asks.

"I'm finishing," Aaron says.

Sebastian looks on, almost impatiently. "Negotiations are like arm wrestling. We press, she weakens. When the pain's too much, she drops. Of course . . . there's always court."

Aaron is suddenly aroused. "That's not a consideration. Screw this up, Sherwin, and I'll have your head."

"You may have to reconsider. She needs to feel pressure. She needs to know that we know her little sins. She'll want none of them uncovered."

Aaron stares. Deep inside of his eyes, contempt is burning, a bonfire as large as Lake Michigan.

⚜⚜⚜

It's 3:30 p.m. C and Joey are in racquetball attire. Joey has bracelets on each arm. C has a heavy chain and crucifix around his neck. They're waiting outside a court at the Barrington Golf Racquet Club. Joey combs his hair.

"Ya know, C, it's dangerous in dere. . . . If a guy swings wit de club, dere ain't nobody to stop him. Someone could get killed."

"You golf wit clubs. I told ya, it's a *racquet*."

"At a hundred smackers an hour, you're tellin' me," Joey responds.

"Shut up. He's coming," C says.

"Of course he's coming, dey have de court at 3:30. Dese humps never work?"

"Shut up," C whispers.

Aaron and his opponent walk toward Joey and C.

Aaron smirks. "This is our room at 3:30."

"Oh, the concierge must have made a mistake," C says.

C looks at Joey. "Mr. Pitasi? You did reserve de abode for 3:30, did you not?"

Joey looks confused as if he does not know what to say. "Yeah C . . . I mean I . . ."

C reaches his hand to Aaron. Aaron hesitates and shakes. "Aren't you Mr. Aaron Abbot?" C asks.

"Yes, I am. Do we know each other?"

"No, well not really. I mean, I read about you; I'm an investor."

A bell rings. Two sweaty opponents walk out.

Aaron smiles smugly and takes the door handle in his hand. "The room is ours, Mr. Cerone. Good luck with your investments. And remember the first rule of the market."

C looks on, confused yet interested.

"Don't play out of your league, lowlife." Aaron closes the door. It automatically locks.

Joey looks at C. "I tink he knows who you are."

C stares at Joey and then tugs at the door.

Joey grabs him. "C, don't make a scene. Melissa will find out."

Aaron turns and winks at C through the door's small window.

C again tugs at the locked door. "I'll kill him, I'll kill him," C mutters under his breath.

⚘ ⚘ ⚘

C's car is on the Kennedy Expressway, heading back to Bridgeport from the Country Club. C looks at Joey. "How'd I size up to him?"

Joey squints and grimaces but doesn't answer.

C raises his voice. "How'd you tink it went?" C asks.

"I don' know," Joey replies.

"Whadda ya mean? Dat's why you came. Gimme de skinny. How do I stack up against golden spoon?"

Joey hesitates. "You really wanna know?"

"Of course I really wanna know."

"De truth? You won't get sore?"

"Me? No. I won't get sore."

"Swear on your mudder?" Joey asks.

"Swear," C answers calmly.

"OK. You promise? I don' know how to get back to d' neighborhood from here."

C's knuckles tighten around the steering wheel; his lips are pursed. "I said I promise."

"Swear on your mudder?"

"Yes! Yes! I swear on my mudder!"

Joey smiles. "OK, here goes. He's got you by twenty years and has all his hair. He's fit and is a regular Charlie friggin' Plummer."

C interrupts an uneasy silence. "So. Are you saying I'm ugly? I ain't ugly."

Joey stretches his lips and tilts his head. He hesitates. "No, you're not ugly, C. I din't say dat. Some girls like older balding men. Maybe."

C swerves, slams on the brakes and the car makes a dead stop on the expressway shoulder. C looks at Joey. "Get out."

Joey opens the door and exits. "Good ting you said you wouldn't get mad!" Joey yells.

The passenger car door closes itself as C speeds off.

"You swore on your mudder!" Joey yells, his voice is muffled by passing vehicles.

$$\mathcal{L} \mathcal{L} \mathcal{L}$$

Back in the racquetball court, Aaron is losing badly. He runs toward the wall to return the volley. The ball hits the racquet and ricochets to the floor.

"Damn! Damn!" Aaron yells. He then pauses, tired and sweating.

"Had enough, Abbott?" his opponent asks.

Aaron looks on without saying a word. His opponent picks the ball off the floor and serves it. It's almost a lob. Aaron stares at the lobbed ball and his opponent's back. Aaron swings with all his might. The ball hits his opponent in the middle of the back. The opponent screams in pain as he falls to the floor.

A tinge of remorse barely interrupts the look of satisfaction on Aaron's face as he arrives near his opponent. "Damn it, I'm sorry," Aaron says.

Chapter 6

This Is Going to Fit Just Fine

Sebastian's at his desk with a client on Thursday afternoon. "That's right, sir, that's why you hired me."

"But your fees are preposterous."

"You signed my engagement contract, and it was all spelled out, but for the sake of diligence, let's analyze your statement," Sebastian says kindly.

The client stares.

"You were willing to pay ten. Right?"

"Yes," the client answers.

"And instead, you paid 'eight point five.' Correct?"

"Correct."

"Sir, my fees are more than reasonable."

"Mr. Sherwin, are you sitting here telling me that $500,000 sounds reasonable to you?"

"Would you like to know what it sounds like to me?"

"Yes."

"It sounds like you saved a million. Now of course if you dispute this, I have means to prove my position and if there are any further costs to litigation, it will be on your dime."

The client gets up, slamming the door as he leaves.

Sebastian toggles the intercom. "Jonathan."

Within seconds the door opens and Jonathan walks in.

"Did you finish Abbott's tape?"

"Almost." Jonathan grimaces.

"Almost? Almost? I don't like this, honey."

"Sebastian, Robbin's swamped. I'm her paralegal, too. I'm doing the best I can."

"Do you know how much AE pays in legal fees a year?"

"No."

"Do you care?"

"Well yes, I care but . . ."

Sebastian signals her to shut the door. She closes it.

"Robbin's on her way out. Would you like to go with her?" Sebastian asks snidely.

"No."

"AE will be mine. Do you comprehend?"

Jonathan timidly nods her head.

"Good."

Jonathan's face shows relief. She turns to go.

"And Jonathan."

Jonathan turns back submissively.

"Aaron Abbott likes attractive women," Sebastian says, as he grins and undresses her with his eyes. "Do be a team player; will you?" he smiles.

Jonathan looks blankly.

"Do you know who will be running AE?" Sebastian asks.

"Aaron Abbott?"

Sebastian grins and turns his head slowly side to side. "Ever see a man under pressure?"

"Why . . . yes."

"Have you ever noticed that Abbott stutters?"

Jonathan stares impassively.

"He'll crack under pressure. Do you know who'll be the all-important pressure valve?"

"No."

Sebastian raises his right hand and forms his finger as if they were around a valve. He turns them. "At times of crises, there is *no one* more important or more compensated than the pressure valve." Sebastian grins. "The power of AE will be at *my* fingertips."

Jonathan looks on and slightly nods.

"What name did you put on the file?"

"Abbott Electronics. Should it be Aaron Abbott?"

"No," he begins to sinisterly laugh, "it should be g-g gifts from h-h-eaven. Finish the tape. You've got forty minutes."

"Gifts from heaven, then." She closes the door.

ᘯ ᘯ ᘯ

C and Melissa are sitting together in Café Bionda on 19th and State. C is wearing a blue Armani suit with a red Kiron tie. Melissa is in a black pantsuit that fits her like a just-snug-enough, leather glove.

"Why did you go and see Aaron?"

"I just wanted to size him up. . . ."

"For what? Are you going to eat him?"

"No, I . . . I . . ."

"One of those neighborhood things?" Melissa asked loudly.

People are beginning to stare.

"I told you that I loved him!" Melissa stands up with her napkin in her hand.

Now every single eyeball in the place is on them.

"I told you, I needed time! You make me laugh. You wanted to size him up! You don't want to sleep with me until we're married. . . . What are you, a Neanderthal?"

C turns his head, embarrassed. Melissa continues. "Who said that I wanted to be with you, or sleep with you?"

Melissa stares at C coldly. Silence rushes over the large dining room. After five seconds, she continues to glare. It becomes unbearable to C and he shrugs his shoulders hoping that her eyes will release him.

"Who told you that I ever wanted to sleep with you or be with you?" she screams.

"No one."

"That's right. You give no respect to my feelings. You follow a set of outdated, insane rules." She throws her napkin on the table. "You're a gorilla." She stomps away.

C rolls his eyes and glances over the other patrons. "Waiter! Bring me a banana please."

A few patrons giggle. Of course, C thinks to himself, giggles would be the normal reaction from folks watching a mortally wounded man. . . .

🖋🖋🖋

At the same time, farther north in Gibson's Bar and Steakhouse on Rush, Sebastian and Aaron are sitting together.

"Aaron, I got ten paralegals on this. I'm dedicating all the manpower needed but your notes, your notes . . . they're garbage."

"I gave you what you asked for," Aaron replies.

Sebastian's eyes become slits as he tries to be expressive. "I'm going to put this bluntly. I want to know when she lost her cherry, if she likes women. . . ."

"I don't know these things."

41

"Then make them up. . . . I need a hammer. If we can't settle, we're going to court."

Aaron's face turns white. He stutters excessively, "It, it, it, it can't go to c-c-c-court."

Sebastian gazes strangely at Aaron.

Aaron continues, "I-I-I-I promised my fa-fa-father."

"All right, Aaron. You must understand me. If you don't want to go to court, we need to apply pressure."

"OK. OK," Aaron says.

"Aaron, you've seen tough negotiations. AE's last union debacle, when you guys almost took the tube. . ."

"I-i-i-it was unfair. Our own brass joined the union against us."

"You should've had a better broker."

Aaron hesitates. "I-I-I ran the negotiations."

Sebastian gapes and smirks at Aaron. "Was your sister really colicky?"

Sebastian is interrupted by a call. He answers his phone. His face, angry and nervous. "Yes. . . . I told you to never call me personally." Sebastian hangs up.

Aaron looks anxiously, hoping to please. "Mother moved the nursery to the Cabbage House. Trisha grew up there."

"She grew up separated from your family?"

"Yes, we were in the manor. Trisha and Rebecca Riley were in the Cabbage House."

"This explains some of the things," Sebastian says as he puts his notes away. "I must leave."

Aaron remains as Sebastian rises.

Sebastian turns again to speak. "I want the goods on your sister. Got it?"

Aaron stares, holding his lower lip with his right-hand fingers.

Sebastian's putting on his overcoat. "If she doesn't agonize, she'll never come to the table."

ℒ ℒ ℒ

Sebastian pulls up in front of 11 Lincoln Park on North Clark Street. He pulls into a no-parking zone in front of a fireplug and enters the restaurant with the finesse of a cyclone. Sebastian scans the patrons and quickly notices his brother Ted by Ted's conspicuous, injudicious white yarmulke.

Sebastian rushes to the table not giving Ted time to stand and greet him. "Don't bother standing, Ted. I know why you're here. Every time someone in the family is broke, you come to Chicago for dinner."

"Brother, that's not fair," Ted says mildly. Ted begins to speak in Lithuanian.

Sebastian's face twists. "Stop it, stop it. I don't speak Lithuanian. We're in America."

"Little brother, why are you so bitter? What have we ever done? You know, in Rabbi school they say. . . ."

"I don't care what they say. It's all an excuse to freeload."

The waiter arrives. "Do you want a menu, sir?"

"No, I don't need one, thank you."

The waiter turns to leave.

"Waiter," Sebastian calls. "Waiter, get me the check." He then turns to his brother. "Or would you like to pay it with prayer?"

"I'll pay, I'm tired of this humiliation. I'll never be back here."

"That would be a dream come true," Sebastian says.

Ted stands and heads for the exit.

Sebastian stares at the white yarmulke. After a bit of hesitation he screams, "Aren't you even going to tell me who needs money and how much?"

🌿🌿🌿

C is sitting in the car with Joey later that night. "AE's gonna be another Bed Bat and Beyond, and I'll make a few cigarettes outta de ashes."

"If you're using the correct name, it's 'Bath.' It ends with an 'h.'"

Joey's not worried about getting kicked out of the car. They're in the neighborhood, so he continues to prod. "I'll bet dat Melissa would do de whole park to save her ol' man."

C either didn't hear the comment or pretends to have not heard the comment. "Abbott's lookin' to rob his sister." He pauses. "But de white knight's gonna get shit on his face and have me right up his ass." C moves his groin up and down to the steering wheel.

"Dat a boy, C. Do it for Hat," Joey says.

A hand reaches from the back seat and grabs C's shoulder. "Tanks C." The sniffling voice and hand belong to Hat's brother, Anthony Santis. "Dose rich humps killed my brother," Anthony says.

"We'll take care of 'em for you, Tony," Joey utters.

🌿🌿🌿

Early the next morning, Aaron is pacing in front of the Cabbage House. Rebecca notices him and informs Trisha. Trisha opens the door.

Aaron hears the door opening and turns, seeing Trisha. "Sis, we must talk. I'm not your enemy."

"I didn't say that."

Though he's many galaxies and twenty-five feet away, Aaron attempts to look deep into Trisha's eyes. "Trisha, we only have each other."

"That's not true. You have our mother."

Aaron was hoping to avoid a squabble but more than happy to accommodate. "Yes, and you have Rebecca, that spooky witch."

"This conversation's over, Brother." She turns to leave and then looks back to him. "Aaron, in a short time none of this will matter to me."

Trisha turns again, walks into the house, and closes the door.

🌿🌿🌿

Later that morning Trisha is at work at Tuesday's Child. She's sitting with Kevin, a special needs kid. In the same room, there are other tutors working with children. The room's walls are made of glass.

Trisha's forming sounds with her mouth. "Come on Kevin, you can do it. O, O-pen."

Kevin is sitting on a table. He smiles and tries to repeat. "O-o-open."

"Bravo! Bravo! Bravo!" Trisha takes him in her arms and hugs him.

Outside the glass wall in the hall, two women pass. Liz is thirtyish and heavy. Mrs. Jennings is fiftyish and trim. They're both watching Trisha.

"Liz, she looks quite fine to me," Mrs. Jennings says.

"Poor kid. I hope she gets over it. She's a real sweetheart," Liz says.

"You know, Liz," Mrs. Jennings responds, "she's loaded, I mean filthy rich . . . with her financial possibilities, when she came to work with us you could've knocked me over with a feather."

"Yeah, I think there was a mix-up at the hospital. She's nothing like any Abbott I ever read about. Her brother hired some attorney, Sebastian Sherwin—he's calling, says he wants to talk to me."

"Remember, dear. Words can't be put back into your mouth," Mrs. Jennings says.

"I'll remember."

They continue to walk the hall. "Where are you today?" Mrs. Jennings asks.

"I'm with Tommy Gill. . . . If no other prospects come, I think I'll marry him," Liz says.

Mrs. Jennings smiles with firmness. "Go on, Liz. Have a good day."

Jackie, a secretary, comes from behind Mrs. Jennings. "Mrs. Jennings, a Mr. Sherwin's on the phone. Says it's important. What should I tell him?"

Mrs. Jennings hesitates. "Just take his number."

"Yes, Mrs. Jennings." Jackie leaves.

Mrs. Jennings turns in to another of the therapy rooms.

$$\mathcal{L}\mathcal{L}\mathcal{L}$$

Rebecca is at her cousin Irene's home on Friday morning. Aaron knows this and enters his sister's room. As he quietly goes through the drawers, he finds a letter signed by Hat. Aaron calculates in his mind. The note is dated more than three weeks after Hat's death. Aaron takes a picture of the note with his phone. He puts the note back into the drawer and sneaks out of the house.

Rebecca's at her cousin's kitchen table.

"I'll be fine," Rebecca says, "I've got some money."

"You should've married Duff. He's living well on his police pension," Irene says.

"I wish my family would've stayed in Ireland. I'll never be at home here," Rebecca replies.

"Trisha will not move to Ireland," Irene says.

"Who knows?" Rebecca answers. "With all that's going on, the family may want it as well."

Rebecca stares off. Her cousin fills her teacup.

$$\mathcal{L}\mathcal{L}\mathcal{L}$$

Later that evening, Aaron knocks on the door at the Cabbage House. Trisha answers.

Aaron looks at her warmly. "Trish, I know you hurt. I hurt too after I decided not to be with Melissa. It wasn't easy but life goes on."

"Does it, Aaron? Is this the only life? Is this the important life?"

Aaron stares. "Trisha, I need you to help me, to be on my side."

"I've always been on your side, Brother. Oh, and Aaron . . ."

Aaron gazes at her. Trisha hands him a few letters. "See what your counsel thinks about these."

Aaron stares at his sister. "Letters from the Twilight Zone?" he asks.

Trisha winks. "I'm sure your atheist mercenary will find these useful. . . . I'll see you in court."

Chapter 7

Misguided Destiny

Megan, Aaron's secretary, escorts Jonathan and Sebastian into Aaron's office. Aaron nods authoritatively from his desk, without rising.

"According to our experts, we're talking about expert forgery," Sebastian says.

Aaron looks up and gazes, "Any other possibilities?"

"Maybe Mr. Santis presented a letter saying that it was his son Rob's when it's really him or his wife."

"They love Trish. It's not them," Aaron says.

"I'm waiting for samples from his school," Sebastian says.

Aaron shakes his head gently. "It's got to be something else. They're not like that. They love their son."

Aaron and Jonathan look to Sebastian, waiting for some sort of remedy to the situation.

"All people love their sons. What do you mean by something else?"

Aaron scratches his neck, "I mean, *they really love* their son. Cerones from their area. It's a strange throwback to another time. They're not only about money. . . ."

"Aaron, your Jesus was sold for thirty silver coins. That's about four hundred bucks today. It was all about money then, and it is all about money now. Don't fret, I'll form this situation into a bowling ball and knock your sister on her ass. I can mold this thing how I want. . . . I'm an artist."

Sebastian throws an imaginary bowling ball. "Who's Cerone?"

Aaron completely ignores the question and Sebastian's bowling ball antics. Instead, he concentrates on some unknown object. After a few seconds Aaron nods his head. "Now I remember," Aaron says enthusiastically.

Aaron turns to the window, then back to stare into Sebastian's eyes. "So that's why you want to win so badly!"

Sebastian's truly confused. His face is one big question mark. "What are you getting at, Aaron? You're acting like an insane person yourself . . . maybe it runs in the family, and you're all nuts."

Aaron smiles. "You're an atheist!"

Sebastian stares menacingly back at Aaron. The real motive for his wanting to destroy Trisha has been discovered: If the letters are real, there is afterlife and a God.

Time stops. Centuries pass before Sebastian thaws.

"Did you let her know what she's in for if she doesn't give in? To these delusions?"

"*Yes, I did all of that,*" Aaron says, almost yelling.

"Well? What did she say?" Aaron asks.

Aaron stands and reaches his right hand to the window. He writes on it with his index finger, reaches up to his head with the left hand and runs it over his hair. He sighs. Sebastian is visibly engaged. He walks toward Aaron.

"What did she say? Damn you! What did she say?"

Aaron drops his hands and slowly turns. His face is anguished. It's the end of the world. "She said she'd see us in court."

✌✌✌

Judge Irving Cohen was born and raised in Hyde Park, on the South Side of Chicago in the shadows of Kam Isaiah Israel Synagogue. His father, David Lubuskus, struggled through life as an uneducated Lithuanian. His mother was a housewife. Irving had a younger sister, Sharon, and an older brother, Joel.

Judge Irving Cohen was born and named Irving Lubuskus until Arnold Cohen, the unwed upstairs neighbor, died.

After Arnold's death, Irving's mother went through Cohen's mail. In one of the envelopes was a letter of acceptance to work for the US Post Office.

David Lubuskus had been out of work for a long while. He changed his name to Arnold Cohen and his entire family took the surname of Cohen. Arnold accepted the job and eventually retired from the US Post Office.

Irving Lubuskus, Arnold's son, became Irving Cohen. Irving Cohen became an attorney and soon found himself involved in Chicago politics, a contact sport. His friend, Eddy Vrdolyak, believed that Cohen would make an outstanding judicial candidate and Irving became a judge in the late nineties.

Becoming a judge in Chicago was a fascinating endeavor, especially before Operation Greylord. At the time, Governor Thompson, a Republican, wanted control over who would name judges. Obviously, he preferred it to be the governor and not Chicago and the Cook County politicians who ran the entire state of Illinois.

He convinced the FBI to begin an infiltration/investigation that indicted ninety-three people, including seventeen judges, forty-eight lawyers, ten deputy sheriffs, eight policemen, eight court officials, and Jimmy DeLeo, a state senator.

Of the seventeen judges indicted, fifteen were convicted.

Thompson never got the power he wanted but if it was any solace to him, three defendants committed suicide, including Circuit Court Judge Allen Rosen.

Irving was pragmatic. He believed both Bush and Obama to be war criminals; Bush for the invasion of Iraq and Obama for his assassin drones and the Syrian civil war which he created by attempting to topple Assad in Syria. According to Judge Cohen, both presidents cost the lives of hundreds of thousands of mostly women and children.

Irving tried to hand out justice. He was esteemed among his colleagues as a man who could cut to the chase. The judge was reading the *Tribune* in his chambers on Friday morning. His reading glasses were at the very tip of his nose when Jeb, his clerk, walked in.

"They're trowin' another one at us . . . says it's an emergency . . . told 'em you were full . . ."

The judge turns the page as if he's not heard, then grunts, "Good."

"Some whippersnapper," Jeb says.

The judge turns another page. "Uh huh . . ."

"Some lawyer named Sherwin."

"Sebastian Sherwin?"

"Yep," Jebson answers.

The judge's expression shows that the situation merits his attention. "What's he doin'?"

"It's a whopper. Got the Abbott family as a client. Hearsay says that it'll be a Tarantino movie."

"A Tarantino movie, huh?"

"Oh, and C would take it as a favor if you took it. It's on for a week from Monday."

"It'll never go."

"What will never go?" Jebson asks.

"Sherwin's a negotiator. He makes dates to intimidate."

"Works against himself?"

"Are you kidding? He makes more than a litigator in less time." The judge looks back down at his newspaper. "Jeb, are they ready in there? There ain't a damn thing in this newspaper. I guess I'm going to start reading my news on the internet."

Jeb walks over and cracks the door. "Yeah, they're baked."

The judge walks into the courtroom.

𝓛 𝓛 𝓛

Aaron's tying his tie in a Trump Hotel suite, ten floors above his hairdresser. Taylor, the girl from the salon, is getting herself together.

"I hope we can get some mileage out of this," Aaron says.

"What do you mean? What do you make of us?" Taylor asks.

"Us. What's 'us'? I like you." Aaron looks almost confused. "Why would a man ever settle down?"

"Love," Taylor says.

"In the USA? Over 50 percent of marriages end in divorce, and the court system is politically tilted to the woman's side. The only thing guaranteed to a man who gets married is that someday he'll be raped. And when the court rapes a man for the woman, it's not over in minutes. It can last decades, a lifetime. "Love's only nature's trick to get us to reproduce."

"Well, I don't see why you're worried about getting any mileage out of us. I'm happy to pay down some of my student loan, and you're not horrible looking or boring," Taylor replies.

Aaron heads into the bathroom but abruptly stops. He looks at Taylor and then at the end table next to the bed. While scanning the table, he speaks without looking at Taylor. "Where's it at?"

"Where's what at?"

"You know, come on, hand it over."

Silence cloaks the room as groans had just minutes before. Aaron moves to Taylor and snatches her purse from her hands.

"Hey!" Taylor yells. "You can't do that. My private things are in there."

Aaron pushes his hand into the purse and comes out with a used prophylactic.

"Your private things? Your private things? You were trying to impregnate yourself with my seed."

Taylor's mind is running like a caged rat. It would be useless to say that she wanted it for a souvenir or a sentimental trinket.

Aaron smirks. "This has happened to me more times than I'd like to remember. You're smarter than I thought you were. I like that . . . but please, don't do that again. I have enough economic issues."

Aaron walks into the bathroom. The toilet flushes. Aaron sticks his head out into the bedroom and looks at Taylor. He smiles. "You are gorgeous, but now I have another reason to keep an eye on you."

꧁꧂꧃

Joey and C are driving around the hood in C's car.

"How'd you ever end up wit dat broad?"

"Edgeview Bank likes me? When a cute skirt arrives, they wave me in. She came off da street lookin' for a loan. Edgeview could never deal de numbers she needs, but she was too afraid dat if she went to a big bank dat de word would get out."

"Ole Polack banker likes you, huh?"

"Joey, de big banks got da government to do dere collecting. At our bank when a wise guy don' wanna pay, we can't afford five attorneys and a lawsuit. Dey take care of me and I buy an Armani suit.

Joey looks at C. "Yeah, everyone knows dat an Armani suit is a whole lot cheaper den a lawsuit."

They turn down Shields and pull in front of the Old Neighborhood Italian American Club. C waves at a few guys on the bench in front.

"Well, how is she?" Joey asks.

"She loves dat jerk. She tought dat I could bail out her ol' man's company. Lover boy tinks she's playin' hide da sausage wit me. He canned da wedding. Now he's holdin' her ol' man's funny money . . . an he ain' even got da broad . . . women, dey say we fucked up de planet . . ."

"And Granny's attorney, Lawrence Barr, scoops you?"

"Mr. Barr's gamblin' debts convert into valuable info now and then."

"Dere all so smart wit all dat cake," Joey says.

"Yeah, til dey get dere heads busted. Hey, go talk to China man Chu. He's gettin' cute. He's behind five months and tinks da bank will renegotiate. Tell him he'll be negotiating from da hospital if he don't pay up."

"Done," Joey says.

Joey gets out of the car. He looks back. "Hey C, Cohen sends his regards."

"I don't want his regards. I *want* one of his shoeboxes."

C wheels the car around and parks on Princeton next to Franco's restaurant.

C enters and sits at a table. His eyes are icy.

"Water, Mr. Cerone?" Benny, the waiter asks.

C does not respond. Benny pours the water. Melissa enters. C rises to greet her.

"Hello Melissa. . . . Pasta and broccolis?" Benny asks.

"Thank you, Benny, I won't be eating," Melissa responds.

C's confused.

"Very good ma'am," Benny responds. He then turns and walks away.

C smiles, trying to make light of the situation. "Sit down, Melissa."

Melissa remains standing. "It's over, C."

"Honey . . ." C stands up and tries to take her arm. She jerks away.

"It's over, C! The whole thing's a joke. There's nothing here for us. We're worlds apart."

C tries to talk but Melissa continues. "C, be honest with yourself for once. You know it too." Melissa moves away and walks out.

C looks down at the table. He squeezes a wineglass until it explodes. Blood lets. He swings, breaking everything on the table and tipping it on its side. Benny runs over, arriving with a napkin for C's bleeding hand. Everyone in the restaurant watches, but no one dares say a word.

Benny screams. "Juan, more napkins for Mr. Cerone!"

Benny stares down. C's head slowly turns up. C looks into Benny's eyes. "It's C . . ." C says gently.

ᴇᴇᴇ

It's late Friday afternoon. Aaron is sitting with his elbows on his desk and his head in his hands. Talking comes from the intercom.

"Sir, Melissa Andrew again, line three," Megan says.

Aaron looks at the green blinking light on his phone. He hurls it at the wall. It cracks, and pieces fly all over.

ᴇᴇᴇ

At the same time, Sebastian is on the phone at Hugo's Frog Bar and Fish House. He smiles as he speaks into the mouthpiece. "Yes sir, Tillerson, Bicks, and Sherwin does have a ring to it." He lets out a forced chuckle.

Sebastian spots Aaron Abbott entering. If he gets AE's business, he will clinch the partnership at Tillerson and Bicks. It's a dream come true. Aaron's the meal ticket of a lifetime.

Sebastian looks to the side and then continues speaking into his phone. "Sir, Mr. Abbott has arrived. Yes sir, I can secure all AE's business. . . . Yes sir . . . tonight, then . . . yes, I understand. I'll be at the Airport Hilton, eight sharp."

Sebastian stands, and strongly embraces Aaron's right forearm with his left hand. "I'm sorry for your pain. . . . Do you believe in fate, my brother?

"Fate?" Aaron asks.

"Yes, not God. Fate."

"Well . . ." Aaron begins.

"Aaron, we're not here at the helm of AE by luck." Sebastian looks in Aaron's eyes. "When your own father wanted to hang you, there was no one else but me. That's fate."

Aaron shakes his head. "You're extracting your pound of flesh . . ."

Sebastian nods warmly. "Charles and Prowe were convicted. It was not pretty. Things would have been different. . . ."

Aaron gazes. "I told you then, and I tell you now. I was drunk. They used the pool sticks and if I remember anything . . . I don't want to talk about this."

"Fate. It was fate that you had that investment account," Sebastian says as he looks at Aaron and smiles. "How else would we have found the resources for Charles and Prowe without your old man finding out?"

"They did all right. . . . They got community service and the money . . . best pay they'll ever get," Aaron says.

"You'd have been relegated to the background of AE . . . forever."

"I'm not so sure, Clinton did OK, cigar and all."

"Do you know why we're here? I mean now, today?" Sebastian asks, searching Aaron's face for answers he knows Aaron does not have.

Aaron stares at Sebastian, confidently in his confusion.

"We're arriving together. Man is born with a destiny. Napoleon accepted his. Caesar accepted his. Will you accept yours?"

Aaron's eyes light up. He preens and smirks with a bit of conviction.

"Do you accept?" Sebastian becomes anxious. "*Do you?*"

"Yes," Aaron responds half-heartedly.

Sebastian's glare works like a floodlight. Aaron's thoughts slowly convince his lips to move and show some teeth. "I accept," he says firmly.

"Do you know who John Tillerson is?" Sebastian asks.

"Secretary of State Tillerson?"

"I've been offered a partnership position in his brother's law firm." Sebastian looks very hard at Aaron.

"Those contacts are essential for us. Imagine having the secretary of state as your guardrail. . . . You'd be able to drive AE without any speed limits."

Sebastian grabs Aaron's lapel and smiles. "They got more power than the CIA."

Aaron smirks. "Can Goldman Sachs bother them?"

"Are you kidding? Tillerson is untouchable. The government's the real syndicate. If it gets uncomfortable, someone commits suicide in Central Park. They protect each other. Once I'm head counsel for AE, I'm . . . we're in."

"But my father is still in charge," Aaron says meekly.

Sebastian purses his lips.

Aaron raises his hand. "But once I have Trish's assets, the banks will fall in line, and the Andrew Industries mess will work to our benefit. I'd be in charge, and we'll be in."

Sebastian's stone face etches itself into a smile. "Together, who could stop us?" Sebastian asks.

"Yes. . . . I hope that we're not marching to Waterloo."

⚘ ⚘ ⚘

Monday morning, Sebastian's closing drawers in his desk. Countless pages are open on the computer screen in front of him. The phone rings. He picks it up. "Yes? . . . I know it . . . because I'm busy . . ." Sebastian's face gets angrier and angrier. "I'm preparing a case against a lunatic. You should take it over. . . . You'd be an expert!"

Sebastian places the phone on the receiver. It falls off the desk. While he reaches for it, Jonathan walks in.

Infuriated, Sebastian gazes at her. "If another partner calls . . . I'm walking out."

Jonathan makes a gesture with her hand.

"OK, but . . ."

"But what?"

"It's Mr. Mullen," Jonathan says softly.

"Oh? What's the old pervert want?"

"He wants to pursue his age-discrimination suit. And the partners . . ."

"Oh, the partners, what do they want?" Sebastian asks snidely.

"They want to remind you that Mullen paid almost four million in legal fees last . . ."

Sebastian raises his hand. Jonathan hushes.

"Jonathan," Sebastian says soothingly.

Jonathan looks at him strangely and hesitates. "Yes?"

"Do you know what the suit's about?"

Jonathan shrugs her shoulders. "Age discrimination?"

Sebastian smiles sweetly. "Mullen says that the law discriminates. Fourteen-year-old boys can legally cuff thirteen-year-old girls, but he can't."

Jonathan thinks for a moment. "What should I tell the partners?"

"Tell them to send Mullen Viagra and a box of prophylactics. Money buys justice!" Sebastian slams his hand on his desk. "Look at OJ! With Mullen's money, he's untouchable! Tell him to go at it!"

Jonathan nods. She half closes the door, putting her body on the outside holding the door with her hands. "Should I really tell them that?"

Sebastian lines his phone at the door. Jonathan closes it just in time. From the outside, Jonathan hears Sebastian scream. "Word for word! Half of them should be put on as co-suitors and later as codefendants!"

Chapter 8

You Broke My Dollhouse

Inside the mansion den, the following Friday afternoon, Aaron's standing with a goblet in his hand. Ingrid is on the leather sofa.

"Son, gossip destroys. First the Union debacle . . . this Andrew thing can ruin you."

Aaron looks at his mother as she gazes off. "Mom. Did you ever love? I mean really love?"

"Don't scare me, son. Love's a daft game."

"A daft game?" Aaron softly inquires.

"Yes, son, when the players think they've won, that is precisely the time they're incurably lost."

🌿🌿🌿

Maxine, Sebastian's law office receptionist, approaches Jonathan. Jonathan is deep into what's on her computer screen. "There's someone to see Mr. Sherwin."

Without looking up, Jonathan responds. "Mr. Sherwin can't see anyone now. He's preparing for court on Monday morning."

"I already told her that he was busy," Maxine says.

"Well?" Jonathan asks crossly.

"She insists that he'd see her."

"Really? What's her name?" Jonathan asks arrogantly.

"Trisha Abbott."

🌿🌿🌿

Early Friday evening Sebastian is swerving, speeding, and talking on the phone.

"Aaron! She came to my office with two letters and a physical from . . ." Sebastian tries to read the letter. "From Dr. Brabec. Who is he? The family doctor? . . . Well, reel him in!"

Sebastian almost hits an oncoming car. The driver shouts. Sebastian flips him off. "I'm going to see Cohen at a JDL Dinner, if I don't get myself killed . . . and if that should happen, then we'll both be dead!"

Sebastian pulls up in front of the Marriott on Michigan Avenue. He jumps out of the car and accepts the ticket from the valet parker. He walks into the hotel and takes the elevator to the Grand Ballroom.

The event's full and speckled by yarmulkes. Sebastian stands at the stairs and touches his own yarmulke, frowns, and steps into the crowd. He walks to the hors d'oeuvre table, takes a plate, and picks his eyes up to a smiling face.

"Sebastian . . . Sebastian Sherwin?"

Sebastian smiles insincerely. "Rabbi . . . Rabbi Schultz?"

"Wait for me. I'll come over to your side."

Sebastian nods. The rabbi arrives with Judge Cohen. "I thought you two might like to rub cases."

Sebastian and Judge Cohen shake hands as the rabbi smiles in the background.

"I see that we may see each other," the judge says.

Sebastian nods. "Yes, it's sad. Abbott girl thinks she receives letters from the dead."

"You know the rules, Counselor."

"Of course, Your Honor, of course. I apologize," Sebastian smiles and the judge turns to leave.

"Sir, sir. I'd like a pre-court. I could use your wisdom on this one."

"If your counterpart agrees, contact my office."

"Yes, sir," Sebastian responds.

The judge curtly turns and leaves.

Back in the Abbott Mansion den, Aaron's on the phone, Ingrid's sitting on the sofa, dressed to kill. Howard's looking out the picture window.

The maid walks in. "Pardon me, sir . . . Mr. Sherwin's at the gate."

Aaron covers the phone mouthpiece. "Please show him in when he arrives."

Aaron goes back to talking on the phone. Ingrid rises to look in the mirror then sits back down. Howard is "working on his phone," playing *Tomb Raider*.

The maid knocks. The door opens. Sebastian walks in and goes directly to Ingrid. As he bends to kiss her hand, she slaps him. Sebastian stands erect.

"You venom! What are you doing to my son?"

Sebastian looks around. No one's paying attention.

Aaron speaks loudly into his phone, "I have to go. . . . There's nothing to talk about." Aaron hangs up, looks to his father, then winks at Sebastian. "We're due in court Monday afternoon."

Sebastian nods. "Yes, if you'd allow me?"

Aaron nods and puts the chess king in his hand. Ingrid turns.

"Sebastian, join me in a game," Aaron says.

As they're setting the pieces up, Sebastian speaks, "Judge Cohen's a personal friend of mine."

Ingrid angrily turns. "My son never wanted to go to court."

The chess pieces are in order and Aaron takes the first move. "*Mother*," Aaron says assertively.

Aaron looks back at Sebastian, "As you were saying, friend."

Aaron and Sebastian take a few quick moves.

"We were together earlier. I've never lost a case before him; this one will be no different. It's actually better this way . . . check," Sebastian says.

"What do you mean, better?"

Aaron moves a chess piece.

"If we pre-settle, things will get complicated. Our hands will be tied. Check."

"What rubbish," Ingrid slithers.

Aaron is losing patience with the woman whose womb carried him. He looks at his father and then back at her with a cold icy stare. "If Sebastian gets us through this, our family will be forever indebted."

Aaron looks back in his father's direction. His father has vanished.

⚜ ⚜ ⚜

Late Friday evening, in a parking lot, Joey's wearing a yellow hooded raincoat. C's dressed in a suit holding a wad of money in his hands. Rain is dripping off both of them.

Joey waves in a BMW with two couples in it. The window opens. "How much?" the driver asks.

Joey rolls his eyes. He's irritated. "Dere's a sign. . . . A double sawsky." Joey points at the sign.

"What?" the driver asks.

"It's twenty," Joey impatiently answers.

"Will fifteen do it?" the driver asks.

Joey wipes the rain off his face and looks the car over. "Nice car. BMW 750i?"

"Yeah," the driver says, smiling proudly.

"About 120 grand?" Joey reaches in and grabs a twenty from the driver.

"Hey. What will fifteen get me?"

"A busted head. Go park it."

Joey's speaking to himself. "The more these idiots got, the more they want."

The BMW 750i pulls away and Joey hears screeching tires. A Land Rover SUV is coming full speed toward C, whose back is turned.

"C!" Joey screams.

C turns and moves, being barely missed. The SUV swerves and turns.

"Joey. Da piece!" C yells.

"Frig!" Joey runs toward C. The truck is heading back.

"C! C! Run! I'm naked!"

C looks at Joey. The truck's twenty feet away. C's ready to meet his maker. At the last instant, the SUV swerves, barely missing him. The window opens. "Mr. Businessman, you should've stuck to parking cars and scalping tickets!"

C stares. Aaron's face evolves into a warm smile. "Try selling AI now," Aaron says softly. He then laughs loudly and speeds away.

C looks at the ground for a moment and then starts to kick the side of the car nearest to him. The owner of the car runs back, and Joey grabs him.

"Let it go. Your insurance will cover this. It's much safer."

C continues kicking the car. Joey watches the SUV drive out of the lot, heads for C, and attempts to pull him away from the car.

"C, C, let's go get a beef sandwich."

C slumps on the car putting his forearms and head on the hood. The rain continues to soak him and mixes in with his sweat and maybe a few tears. Of course, he wouldn't admit that.

$$\text{⚘ ⚘ ⚘}$$

Trisha's on her knees planting flowers outside the Cabbage House on Saturday. Aaron arrives. "Hello."

"Hello," Trisha says in a friendly tone.

"Can we talk?" Aaron asks.

Trisha looks at Aaron. "Sure."

Aaron smiles gently. "Can we go inside?"

Trisha moves to one knee. Her brother gives her a hand and she rises. They enter the house and walk into the kitchen. Trisha goes to the sink and washes her hands.

Aaron smiles, acting brotherly, "The place looks great. Remember when I helped you paint? Mom had a fit. 'The Cabbage House is not my daughter's home!'"

"Aaron, if you've come about my inheritance, it's too late."

Aaron gently shakes his head and looks concerned, "I'm worried about you, Trish."

"You show it in a funny way."

The room is silent.

Rebecca enters. "Oh, excuse me," she says.

Rebecca looks unkindly at Aaron who returns an impatient stare. Rebecca goes into the front part of the house.

"Aaron, remember my big dollhouse?"

"Yes."

"Do you know why I loved it?"

"I don't know," Aaron says uncomfortably.

"It housed my dream family. . . . It housed my dream family. It was a refuge from the meanness and the arguing." Tears come to Trisha's eyes.

Aaron notices. He's irritated. "It was just a toy dollhouse! You had your dear Rebecca. I had no one!"

"No, you were busy trying to get what Father had and he was running toward Mother to get away from her. None of you seemed to care then and *by your behavior*, it's hard to believe that you care now."

"That-that was almost twenty years ago. I was just a k-k-kid, searching for my-my-myself, my-my-my pl-pl-place," Aaron stutters.

"That's right, Aaron."

Trisha stares, further disorienting Aaron.

"And now you've found it. You're an ornament in Mother's hell. Isn't that who and where you are?"

Trisha's crude appraisal pushes Aaron into a bizarre confidence. "No!" he screams. Aaron charges and his face is within a centimeter of his sister's face.

Aaron continues with the violent verbal blows. His stuttering has disappeared. "And the question is not who I am! But who you are! Are you so sure that you are better than us because you teach retards? You don't live here! You hide here! You hide here from who you truly are!"

Trisha studies Aaron's face. "And who's that supposed to be?"

"You're an Abbott! You should be helping me build Abbott Electronics! You selfish, spoiled coward!"

"What would we have? More money? More power?"

"That's right! Abbott Electronics would be respected, feared! Like General Electric! You're de-de-destroying this family and that's what you've al-always wanted!"

The eye has passed. The sea calms.

Trisha steps back and speaks softly. "Aaron, remember when you considered Aunt Agatha an arrogant shrew?"

Aaron nods, concentrating and sure. He will not allow her to confuse him.

"Today as you see her, is she a shrew or a refined lady?"

Aaron studies Trisha's face, looking at her lips, as if wanting to confirm the origination of her words. "I came for p-p-peace. But you're really crazy!"

"Am I, brother? Let me tell you, the letters are as real as your anger. But admit it, all you really want to discuss is how to get my piece of the pie."

"Be care-careful or the p-p-p-pie will be smashed! . . . In your face!"

Aaron slams his hand palm down on the table.

Rebecca reenters. "You get out of this house!" Rebecca screams. She picks up a broom and chases Aaron. "This is Trisha's house! Leave her alone, you vulture!"

Aaron retreats to the doorway. He looks at Rebecca, daring her to swing the broom at him. He looks at Trisha, and then regaining his nerve, he again, calmly shifts his gaze to Rebecca. "Why, you old leech. You purposely made her crazy so you could sponge off us all for life. Well, you're done freeloading."

He slams the door shut.

🌿🌿🌿

Saturday afternoon, Joey and C are in C's car.

"It's fixed. Danahy'll get da case," Joey says.

"Stay on Barr for info. I'm gonna bury Abbott." C takes a hundred-dollar bill from his pocket. "Get me an eggplant wit sweet and hot."

"Gimme a sawbuck."

"I ain' got one," C says.

"No you got twenty of 'em. You know Bones won't take anyting bigger than a ten from us. You like makin' him nuts."

C laughs, "Remember when we unloaded $5,000 in counterfeit C-notes on him, tellin' him it was a settlement?"

"Yeah, I remember, so does he. Gimme a sawsky."

C smiles and gives Joey a ten-dollar bill.

℘ ℘ ℘

Ingrid remained in her bedroom, all day and evening Saturday, constantly calling the same phone number. Howard was sealed in his den going through documents and memories.

Ingrid knocks. "Howard, it's Ingrid. I need to speak to you."

"The door's not locked."

Ingrid enters. Howard can feel the breeze as she sweeps in. It carries her scent, not the scent of her Tom Ford Black Orchid. He feels light-headed. It was his father and mother who taught him about unconditional love, marrying the same woman forever. Damn them.

"Could this disaster affect our family life?" Ingrid asks coldly.

"I guess you mean your *lifestyle?*"

"Could it?"

"It could," Howard hesitates and looks at the only love of his existence. "It could drastically change things—ruin, scandal, bankruptcy."

Tears begin flowing from Ingrid's eyes. "Enough! I won't take this anymore!"

Ingrid runs to the gun rack. She takes a pistol in her hands. She moves to the bureau and rummages through the drawers.

"They're in the top drawer on the right," Howard says calmly.

Ingrid tries to open the drawer, but it's locked. "You think I won't! I'd rather die than . . ."

Howard throws keys. They land in front of her.

Ingrid's face turns to an incredulous shock. "I will not face humiliation!"

She fumbles with the keys and opens the drawer.

Howard pours a drink. "Your choice."

Ingrid screams loud screeches. She tries to load a bullet in a chamber. The first bullet falls, as well as the second. She loads the third into the chamber.

"You know, Ingrid. I fantasized about us as a pair of swans, mating for life. Instead, we're black vultures." He pours himself a little more elixir. "And when one is no longer monogamous, death is the lone answer."

Ingrid points the gun to her head.

Aaron rushes in. "Mother!"

"Leave her!" Howard yells.

Aaron looks at Howard, then at Ingrid. His father has a drink in his hand and his mother a gun to her head. It's all so dreamlike. The gun falls to the ground. Ingrid blubbers.

Howard raises his chalice. "We weren't much good in a life of grace. Maybe we'll do better in a life of disgrace."

Howard finishes his drink and calmly walks out. Aaron runs to Ingrid.

Chapter 9

Things Could Have Been Simpler, My Girl

It is Saturday, close to midnight in the Cabbage House. The house is dark, except for a tiny, faded light in the kitchen. Rebecca's painstakingly copying from a letter onto a piece of paper. She hears a noise and quickly looks in that direction. She stands, stuffs everything into the bread box and walks up the stairs. She stops at Trisha's room and moves her ear to the door.

"Be calm, my love, it won't be long," Rebecca hears in a clear male voice.

"Oh Hat," Trisha sighs.

Rebecca remains and hears Trisha giggling. She waits a few more seconds and then walks away.

ᒫ ᒫ ᒫ

Sunday morning, Ingrid bursts through the front door of the Cabbage House. She throws an icy stare at Rebecca, who is sewing buttons on a shirt.

"Where's my daughter?" Ingrid screams.

Rebecca looks over her glasses without responding.

"I said, *where is my daughter?*" Ingrid repeats in a low sinister voice.

Rebecca's eyes communicate intimidation and confusion. "Please leave. Can't *you's* leave her alone?"

Rebecca stands and Ingrid looks at her in disbelief.

"Please leave this house!" Rebecca says.

Ingrid flies at her and knocks Rebecca onto the couch. "Your days are numbered. You ruined my daughter! You'll pay! You leech! You criminal! You sham!"

Ingrid runs up the stairs and swings the door open to Trisha's room. Trisha has headphones on and is writing a letter.

"Take those things off!"

Trisha smiles and lays them on the desk. "Hello, Mother. I've been expecting . . ."

"Don't be insolent!"

"Sorry . . . what may I do for you?"

"Stop this! You will stop inflicting pain on this family! That is what you may and *will* do for me!"

"I didn't pull anyone into court."

Ingrid's face angelically transforms. "Do you agree that Aaron was unjustly cut out of his inheritance?" she asks tenderly.

"It's Grandmother's money, I won't speak for her."

"Fine. It's a financial matter, your father will handle it. I'm glad that's out of the way. Now, can we agree that the dead don't communicate with the living?"

Ingrid stares at her daughter. Trisha smiles back.

"What are you smiling at, young lady?"

"I guess you're saying that the whole Christian faith is based on a con."

Ingrid looks seriously in Trish's eyes. "I said no such thing! I am a Christian! I stayed with a man that I despise because I took a solemn oath! As a Christian! . . . And today! Not many Christians do that! Now, if you continue . . . if you d-dare show up on Monday . . . I'll divorce y-your father."

"Mother, you're beginning to stutter like Aaron."

Ingrid stares at Trisha, not believing what her daughter has just said to her.

"Mother . . . know what Hat says?"

Ingrid gapes, concentrating and squinting.

"What happens after you're gone just happens."

"You've never cared about anyone but yourself and that old maid! She has warped you! But you will now. I mean it, you will now. Oh! I can't wait to be away from your father and you! I mean it with every drop of blood in my body!"

Ingrid opens the door and slams it as she leaves.

$$\mathcal{L}\ \mathcal{L}\ \mathcal{L}$$

C's playing cards at the Adriatic Club on 30th and Wells. Joey's next to him on a high barstool.

"Would Barr scam us? It all sounds kinda goofy," Joey says.

"Nah. Dere's nuttin' in it for him . . . and he knows better," C answers.

"If Barr, a trusted confidant of the grandmother, testifies that the old girl was off her rocker . . . and you know he'd sell out in a minute . . . I mean if Aaron gets Sis's cake, he may save da company and da broad. Dey'll live happily ever. . . ."

"Dat guy ain't gonna have another happy day in his life if I got anyting to say about it."

≠≠≠

Sebastian is cruising alone through the manicured roads of Barrington. His phone rings.

"Hello," Sebastian says.

Sebastian listens for about thirty seconds. "Yes, Doctor Behren, as planned." Sebastian smiles. "I knew I could count on you, Doctor."

Sebastian pauses, "Oh, and Doctor, if you deliver, you can shred my firm's bill."

Sebastian swerves trying to run a squirrel over. "Yes, Doctor, it's that important."

In the Abbott Mansion den, Aaron's on the phone and dressed to impress. Ingrid enters. Aaron holds his finger to his mouth. He hangs the phone up.

"You're acting queerly, hope she's worth it . . . I need to talk," Ingrid says.

"Talk. No one could ever stop you from doing that."

"Son, we're so close. . . and so much alike."

Tears instantly form in Aaron's eyes.

He looks away from his mother as she continues. "Through the Melissa scandal I defended you. I knew . . . Andrew Industries was in trouble. *I want to hear what they say now.* You're smart, son. You knew when to leave."

A tear rolls down Aaron's cheek.

"Son, I've done my best. Your father . . ."

"Mother, please get to the point."

"I need a million dollars to hold me over until I can get a divorce. . . ."

Aaron stares through her.

"Don't look so surprised. . . . You know everything's wrapped up tight, but when I get it, it's all yours."

"Mother, I have a plate f-f-full. Let me get through it. If it goes well, we'll t-t-talk. Otherwise, I can't help you."

"Son, I'm counting on you."

Ingrid hears a slight noise and looks toward the den door. Howard's walking away. He arrives at the front entrance door and slams it as he leaves. Ingrid looks at Aaron, who blankly stares back.

≠≠≠

Sunday afternoon in the Cabbage House, Rebecca's asleep with knitting needles and yarn on her lap. Trisha is writing a letter. There's a gentle rap at the door. Trisha quietly opens it. Her dad's waiting in the rain.

"Come in, Dad."

Howard brushes the water from his overcoat. "I'm glad you're home."

Her father looks at Rebecca sleeping on the chair. He smiles. Trisha hangs up her father's coat.

"Let's go in the kitchen, I'll make some tea," Trisha whispers.

As they walk into the kitchen, Rebecca opens her eyes and watches.

Trisha and Howard are at the kitchen table drinking tea. Her father looks away. "I'll protect you. I'll call Aaron off. Things aren't what they seem. Aaron's assault is not born of greed, but of desperation. . . ."

Howard nervously looks at her. He then looks inside the hall.

"Dad, what's wrong?"

"Trish, your brother's in trouble and I can't help him. . . . *All* empires finally fall." Howard smiles. "If I could . . . I'd live in a house like this."

"Dad, it's never too late."

"It is for me. . . ."

Howard finishes his tea and kisses his daughter's forehead. He walks through the front room and glances at Rebecca sleeping in the same position in the chair. He gets to the door and turns suddenly, as if trying to catch Rebecca feigning sleep. Rebecca's unmoved. He turns again and quietly leaves. As soon as the door is shut, Rebecca's eyes open.

Trisha cleans the teacups and quietly trots to her room. Rebecca hears Trisha close her door. After a few minutes, Rebecca goes to Trisha's room and puts her ear to the door. Everything's quiet. Rebecca walks back down to the kitchen, removes something from the bread box, and goes to her room.

$$\textit{↙ ↙ ↙}$$

Late in the evening, Sebastian is driving. Aaron is in the front passenger seat.

"Aaron, in our justice system, honesty becomes an option when all else fails."

"I'm not comfortable," Aaron says.

"The Santis family wants to defraud her," Sebastian says.

Aaron runs his hands through his hair as he gazes emptily out the window. "This whole thing is getting to me. I need to know the truth."

"My brother, at this moment, truth is a pricey commodity. You *need* the $100 million. And I need to size them up. They're too close to the flame to be disinterested. They'll want to hear what you have to say. The truth can come later."

"What do I say to them?"

"Nothing."

⚜ ⚜ ⚜

In the Cohen family's front room at the same time, Irv is reading the book *Embraced by the Light*. Mary, his wife, is in a chair looking at wallpaper samples.

"Irv, I still like the rose."

"Then get the rose." Irv turns the page in his book.

"Is the Scalise trial still up?"

"It closed Friday."

"What's next?"

"Something with the Abbott family."

"You mean the Abbott family from Abbott Electronics?"

"Bingo."

The phone rings. Mary picks it up. "Hi, Marva, just a minute." It's our daughter, the soon to be counselor," Mary tells her husband.

Irv smiles and takes the phone. "Yes, honey, it's a full day. . . . You may have met him, his name's Sherwin. He's representing a brother who's trying to grab his sister's inheritance. . . . I don't know. He says that she wants to donate it to charity. . . . I think so, too. But there's some other particulars. . . . I agree. . . . But she also claims that she speaks to the dead. It may not go. Sherwin rarely litigates."

Mary glances at Irv. "I love you, too. Call me on my cell at about 2:30–3:00."

Irv sets the phone down. His wife continues to look at him. He looks back at his book but feels her eyeballs all over his face. He turns and raises his head. "Well?"

"Greed. The world's just full of it. You know Gandhi said, 'The world has enough for man's need but not enough for man's greed.' I think it's a worse disease than cancer."

Irv nods and goes back to his book.

"I'm coming in with you tomorrow," Mary says emphatically.

"As you wish."

⚜ ⚜ ⚜

Sebastian's car pulls down a block rowed with bungalows. "Your sister liked slumming. You have to pass through the jungle to get in here and when you're here, the jungle's not so unappealing."

The car passes a gang of teenage boys. Two of them are slap boxing, and one comes close to the car as it's turning the corner. Sebastian hits the brakes as the youth runs in front of the car. "Punk," Sebastian says under his breath.

"There it is, 3219," Aaron says.

They drive to the corner, park the car by Armour Square Park on 33rd Street, and start to walk. They pass Turtles, a bar on the corner. Two Chinese women pass them.

They pass 3235, 33, 31. "Relax," Sebastian says, "you've met these people before." Sebastian knocks.

The door is opened by a rough-looking man in his fifties, Mr. Dominic Santis. "Come in," he says.

They follow Mr. Santis up the hallway.

"She's suffered enough," Mr. Santis says.

Sebastian nods. "We totally agree."

They get to the top of the stairs and turn into the front room and then the kitchen where Mrs. Georgia Santis is making coffee. Sebastian studies every detail.

Mr. Santis looks at Sebastian. Sebastian doesn't feel the warmth.

Sebastian asks generic questions about Trisha and Hat. They speak about their school, their future plans, how they met, and how they got along. Mr. Santis remains civil for the benefit of his wife but does not understand where Sebastian is going with his line of questioning.

"We'll do anything to help Trisha," Mr. Santis says, "and we'll do anything to protect her."

Aaron shrugs his shoulders as if someone just pulled something off his back.

"Well, it's late," Sebastian says, "and we appreciate everything."

They stand, and led by Mr. Santis, walk through the house. Sebastian looks for every detail as they leave.

They reach the exit. Mr. Santis abruptly grabs Aaron's lapel. "I don't know what happened to my son or what you're doin' to your sister. But don't come back here."

"S-s-s-ir, I can as-s-s-sure you that we only . . ." Aaron sputters.

"S-s-sir, I can as-s-ssure you that another trip here will be dangerous to your h-h-health," Mr. Santis mocks.

Sebastian and Aaron quietly walk back to the car. They pull onto the expressway at 31st Street. Sebastian looks in the rearview mirror as if he was expecting to be followed.

After a few minutes, Sebastian blows out slowly. "Great. He's a hothead, and the mother will be our star . . . the voodoo lady. Did you see all those statues? Great work, Aaron."

Aaron gazes out the window as if he hadn't heard a thing.

Chapter 10

Crazy Baby

Monday morning, Sebastian passes the gate and drives to the front of the Abbott Mansion.

Rebecca approaches Sebastian's car. He stops and smiles. "Good morning," he says.

"It was until now," Rebecca returns.

Sebastian smirks. "Can I do something for you?"

"Yes, but you won't."

"Oh?"

Rebecca concentrates. "Do you know who Saint Sebastian was?"

"Excuse me?"

"Saint Sebastian was a Roman official. He persecuted Christians. . . . In the end, he became one."

Sebastian looks at her, half smirking, half confused. "What's this?"

"That's right." Rebecca looks on slyly and nods her head. "Saint Sebastian was an atheist."

"And what happened to our hero? Pray tell."

"He rejected his atheistic beliefs and the Romans put him to death. They executed him with a bow and arrow."

"Really?" Sebastian asks sarcastically as he pulls away.

Sebastian parks the car and walks up the stairs to the front foyer. The maid is waiting and opens the door for him. He quietly hands her his coat and enters, showing himself to the den.

Aaron is waiting along with the chess board revealing an unfinished game. He's sipping Japanese whiskey, Ichiro Malt, Six of Hearts.

"A little early for drinking, isn't it?" Sebastian asks.

"I don't like this," Aaron says. "Finish the game. It's your move."

"It's in the bag. You're in check."

"I saw that Rebecca stopped you."

"Yeah."

"What did she want?"

"Nothing."

Aaron looks out the window and raises the drink to his chest. "She scares me. She's got some sort of power, some sixth sense. . . ."

Sebastian's holding on to every word.

"When I was a kid and went looking to aggravate or torment my sister . . ." Aaron shakes his head and downs his drink. "She always knew. I'd sneak. I'd hide . . . but she always caught me . . . like she could see through walls . . . like she could read my mind. *That's why I did it.* I wanted to prove to myself that she didn't possess some superpower."

Sebastian puts a chess piece down while staring at Aaron. He's mesmerized. "That's why you did it? That's why you did what?"

"I wrecked the dollhouse," Aaron said.

"See, Trisha's mystical lady-in-waiting isn't infallible," Sebastian says.

Aaron continues to stare out the window. His silence unsettles Sebastian.

"Aaron. Earth to Aaron."

Aaron turns and smiles. "I found out later that she wasn't even home."

Sebastian looks to the side with concerned eyes. He then moves a chess piece. "That's mate."

🌿🌿🌿

It's Monday morning, Joey and C are driving around with Impallaria doughnuts and coffee.

"Barr says dat she still ain't got no lawyer. Danahy will be put on," C says.

"He'll play for us like a pinball. He's into us for eight and likes da sauce."

Joey flicks his fingers like he's playing pinball. C smiles.

🌿🌿🌿

Inside Tuesday's Child on Monday morning, Liz waves to Trisha, who's working with a young developmentally disabled girl. Trisha stands, and the eyes of the girl follow her to the door.

Trisha opens the door and exits. "What is it, Liz?"

"Trish, I really like you. I get along better with you than I get along with anyone here," Liz says.

Trisha looks confused. "Sure, Liz. I like you too. What's wrong?"

"I've got a big mouth," Liz says.

Trisha continues to be confused.

Liz pauses and then begins again. "Some attorney, Sherwin, called me. Said he wanted to help you. He asked me if you seemed OK. He seemed real nice and everything. . . ."

Trisha watches Liz's eyes as she speaks. "Go ahead."

"I said you talked to yourself. I thought I was helping you. I can tell him that you were singing." Liz erupts into sobs. "I'm so sorry."

"Don't worry. I know you were trying to help."

Now it's Liz's turn to be confused.

"You're not mad that . . . that I got a mouth bigger than the Grand Canyon?"

"No."

"That I got a mouth bigger than the planet earth?"

"No." Trisha smiles, the smile turns solemn. "You know Liz, some things are true whether we believe them or not. . . ."

It's 9:30 Monday morning the following week in the Cook County Probate Court. Irv smiles down from the bench. On his left are Sebastian Sherwin and Aaron. Ingrid's behind them. On his right is Trisha. Two rows behind her is Mary, Irv's wife. In the back of the court is a street person and an older man.

"Young lady. Is your attorney running late?"

Trisha looks at the judge. "May I speak, sir?"

"Of course, when you're addressed by the court you're obligated to do so."

Aaron is whispering in Sebastian's ear. The judge looks sternly. Sebastian brushes Aaron off.

"Sir. I didn't think I needed an attorney."

Aaron whispers to Sebastian. The judge again looks on harshly.

"Young lady, you're here today without counsel?"

"Yes, sir."

"I assume that it's not a problem of funds."

"I just didn't think that I needed one . . . I really don't know any attorneys."

"Miss, this hearing could have serious ramifications. I insist you be represented."

"She's stalling," Sebastian whispers to Aaron. "Why didn't you tell me that she didn't have an attorney for the hearing?"

Aaron looks blankly. "I never even thought about it."

"Sir, if you'll be kind enough to recommend one," Trisha says.

Sebastian jumps up, "Your Honor, Miss Abbott is trifling. . . ."

Irv shoots a hostile stare at Sebastian. "Counselor. I agree that it's irregular."

Irv looks down at Trisha very fatherly. "Are you trifling with this court, young lady?"

"Why no, Your Honor, of course not."

Irv looks down on his desk. "The Court reconvenes Thursday morning. Young lady, get your attorney's name and address from the clerk."

The judge points at Jebson, raps his gavel, and stands up.

Aaron's enraged. He looks at Sebastian. "What can we do? Do you know what she can do in three days?"

Aaron charges the bench. "Your-your-Your Honor, please, she's crazy, a lunatic."

The judge looks sternly down on Aaron. "Young man. Court's adjourned."

Irv continues to walk away. Aaron approaches his sister. "You'll never get away with this!"

Aaron angrily points as Sebastian's pulling him away. Aaron's face is tortured and disfigured. "One of us will be destroyed! You wanted it this way! Well, it won't be me!"

Trisha's face is tranquil with the slightest traces of impudence.

ᛋᛋᛋ

Patrick Danahy's average in every sense of the word. He walks into his shabby, average office on an average Monday afternoon.

Molly Deere, a heavy woman of forty, is on the phone and doing her nails. "Hold on, Teresa." Molly covers the mouthpiece and looks at Patrick. "You have a case Thursday morning."

"A recommendation?"

"How would I know? I wouldn't recommend you."

"Well, can you tell me how you know about the case?" Patrick asks.

"A court appointment, Jebson called."

"I probably won't get paid."

"Don't complain, the daughter of Howard Abbott's your client."

"Are you drunk?" Patrick asks.

"I don't drink," she says, "but you ought to try it."

Patrick walks into his office and grabs the Pepto-Bismol bottle off the file cabinet. He swigs what's left of it. "Get some Pepto-Bismol today! We're out again," Patrick yells in to Molly.

"Hold on, Teresa." Molly covers the mouthpiece. "I can get you Imodium at the dollar store for a buck. Pepto costs eight bucks."

"I'm a Pepto man."

"Pepto man, I haven't been paid in a month, and you owe me $2,000."

⚘ ⚘ ⚘

Ingrid's in her bedroom Monday afternoon writing in her diary. There's a knock at the door.

"Who is it?"

"It's me, Aaron."

"Oh good, come in."

Aaron enters.

Ingrid has a pencil to her mouth. "What did I wear when the president of Friends of the Opera came to dinner?"

"Mother, we have other things to discuss. Your costume diary can wait."

"I've kept this journal for over thirty years. I want to pass it on to my granddaughter." She looks distastefully at Aaron. "If there ever is one . . . one child's a lunatic, the other a gigolo."

"Mother, I'm not a gigolo."

"You should come with me more often. A Kennedy heir attended the museum gala. She was cute . . . a little pudgy, but cute."

"Mother, we only have two days . . . Sebastian's on the way."

"You can't remember the outfit?"

"Mother, I can't do this all by myself! Trisha has Rebecca. Who do I have?" He slams the door.

A clock slides off the bureau and smashes on the floor.

Ingrid looks at it reflectively. "Yes, of course. The Big Ben dress. Honey, I remember, I'll be there shortly!" Ingrid yells.

⚘ ⚘ ⚘

Later Monday afternoon in Danahy's office, Molly's sipping the straw of a quart cup. Patrick's in his office.

74

"Are my clothes at the cleaners?"

"I'll take them tomorrow."

"I told you to take them today."

"Court's not until Thursday."

Patrick stands and moves to the door. "I meet with Trisha Abbott tomorrow morning. Clean up this office, water the plants, dust."

Patrick Danahy watches as Molly rolls her eyes.

"Don't you understand? This is it. We could be set. It's Abbott Electronics!"

Molly returns to concentrating on a crossword puzzle.

"What must I do to make you respond?"

"Try paying me."

"When this is over I'm gonna pay you every dime I owe you. Then I'll fire you, cousin or not."

"Promises, promises."

ƚƚƚ

Patrick's dressed in a suit surrounded by a small crowd Monday evening at Kelly's bar in Canaryville, the Irish neighborhood just south of Bridgeport. The bar is filled with typical neighborhood drinkers. Mush is the bartender. In his day, Mush, a seventy-year-old man, was the toughest guy in Canaryville. Even today, he's built like a fit twenty-year-old with the facial features of a forty-year-old.

"I heard you got AE on the hook," Mush says to Danahy.

"Mush, that's reserved information," Patrick says as he tilts his glass and takes another swig.

"If you want reserved information, you should change secretaries."

Mush smiles. Everyone laughs.

"Another round, Counselor Danahy?" Mush asks.

Patrick is gazing much farther than the end of the bar. "Yeah . . . yeah! Get everyone!"

The bar erupts into a celebration.

ƚƚƚ

Inside the basement of Punchinello's Tuesday morning, Joey and C are throwing papers into the basement furnace. The stereo and television are blasting.

C leans over and whispers in Joey's ear. "Joey, I need dis."

75

Joey nods and then whispers in C's ear. "Relax, it's in da bag. Cohen's da judge. Danahy's da counsel, he'll use Arnold da shrink. I'm pounding da good doctor's assistant for information. Get it? Pounding her for information?" Joey laughs.

C looks at Joey with a disgusted face. "Yeah, yeah I get it."

"What an organization," Joey whispers, "C, what kinda CEO do you tink I'd make?" Joey smiles. C throws a wad of paper at him.

"Hey, here's a scoop to feed da press. Sherwin took care of Hat and is writin' dose letters?"

"C, you watch too many movies," Joey whispers.

𝕃 𝕃 𝕃

At Doctor Arnold's rundown office Tuesday morning, Doctor Arnold's secretary, Eve, is on the phone. She's thirty and cute. "Dr. Arnold, Psychiatrist" is painted on the windows around the second floor above the clothing store Rainbow on 47th and Ashland.

"Yes, I know, but Dr. Arnold was called for an emergency . . . yes, Mrs. Rath, I'll tell him."

Eve gently puts the phone down and dials another number. There's a buzzer noise, and Eve covers the phone, flips a switch, and talks into a small microphone on the desk. "Yes."

"Trisha Abbott for Dr. Arnold."

"Take the stairs to the top, turn right, I'll buzz you in."

Dr. Arnold's office desk is filled with files, magazines, notes, and random paper. An hour later, Trisha and attorney Patrick Danahy are in front of him. "Miss Abbott, it's late. . . . Let's recap. Rob, let's call him Rob and not Hat. It's more official."

Trisha nods.

"Rob proposed at Christmas, you were supposed to be wed now, in May?"

Trisha nods.

"He was in his last year of architecture school. He worked construction in the summer and bartended on the weekends."

Trisha nods.

"You met at school in September. He's Italian. His mother was teaching you how to cook, and you were converting to Catholicism."

Trisha nods.

"Your family didn't share your enthusiasm. Your brother became hostile when you bought a transmission for Rob's 2012 Chevy."

Doctor Arnold looks at her, "It was a Christmas present," he adds.

Trisha again nods.

"Rob died in a car accident on Saint Valentine's day. You've received letters that he sent . . . *that he sent you after his death.*"

Danahy takes his glasses in his hand and looks sternly at Trisha. "Young lady, those letters will be subpoenaed by the court."

"I don't think so," Trisha says meekly.

"Huh! You're in for a big surprise. They most certainly will!"

Trisha shakes her head.

"And, why wouldn't they?" The doctor asks.

"They already have them," Trisha answers simply.

"They do? And just how did they get them?"

"I gave them to my brother's attorney."

The doctor puts his glasses on, closes his eyes, and rubs his head.

"You gave them to him." Doctor Arnold says, mumbling more to himself than Trisha.

☙ ☙ ☙

Joey's in the fridge at Eve's apartment on Tuesday evening.

Eve's on the couch; the TV's on low. "I'm tired. It's been crazy. That Abbott girl's taking up hours and hours . . . are you listening?"

"Yeah, of course, I'm listening. Didn't you have some beer?"

"I had to bite my tongue. The more people have, the nastier they are. . . . Don't you think?"

"Absolutely." Joey reenters smiling. He kisses Eve on the forehead.

"But Trisha Abbott's kind. She apologized for screwing up the schedule. No one ever . . ."

Joey's eyes narrowed. "What was dat about Abbott?"

"Trisha Abbott, she apologized. . . ."

"Relax honey, I'll give you a massage."

"Joey, you're too good to me. But I shouldn't talk shop."

"Yeah, I am too good to ya. Now keep talkin' or I'll belt ya."

Joey begins massaging her back. Eve laughs. "Her family wants to put her in an institution or something."

"What else, baby?" Joey whispers.

Chapter 11

There Is No God

It's late. C's playing cards in the Italian American Club. Joey walks in. Baby-face is standing next to C. Baby-face looks like the Loki mask Jim Carrey wore in the film *The Mask*, except that Baby-face's skin is not green.

"Hey Baby-face, take my hand. And keep yours above the table," C says.

C stands up. Baby-face smiles and sits down. Joey and C meet in the middle of the room.

"C, dat broad really believes dat da letters are from Hat. She's shot."

C looks at Joey. "Serious?"

"Serious as leukemia."

C looks at the floor.

After a few seconds, Joey also looks at the floor. "What are you looking at C? Is der a roach down der?"

"I'm focusing, ya jerk."

"On what?"

C blows a breath. "Joey, Joey."

"Yeah, Joey, Joey. C, you been sayin' dat since we robbed d' trains when we was ten years old."

C claps his hands and nods. He leans into Joey. "Feed it to da funnies."

"Are you sure?"

C nods.

"OK, but don't get sore at me if it turns bad. You know once it's out der, we lose control. You remember when Tounch got fired from the CTA? You told me to get it out there and they did an investigation and fired anudder four neighborhood guys."

Joey heads out the door of the club and goes to his car in the parking lot. He shuts the door and dials. He bites his tongue and at the same time looks in the mirror. "Answer. Damn it."

78

A man answers. "Joey, this is Lou Sherman and this better be good."

"Oh, it's better than good. This will be front-page news for days to come. You'll be reporter of the year."

"OK. Give it to me."

"AE," Joey says.

"AE, as in Abbott Electronics?" Lou asks groggily.

"Daughter Trisha is cuckoo, and loving brudder's trying to lock her up and take her cake."

"Hold the horn, let me get a pen," Lou says as he turns on the light in his bedroom and reaches into the dresser drawer next to his bed.

ℒℒℒ

Patrick's half drunk, in his boxers and on the phone in his apartment. "Lauren, please let me talk to Patrick . . . I know, baby. But that's all changed now. You know that if I had the cash I'd have sent it to you. . . . I swear it . . . I can't remember the last drink I had."

Patrick covers the mouthpiece and belches. "Please let me talk to him. . . . Oh that's right, how are his grades? . . . Well tell him that, that I, I love him and that I've changed," he rushes out. Really . . . I mean that for you too . . . No, it's ten-thirty in California, isn't it? I'm still in the office working on the Abbott Electronics case. I hope it won't be like this when I'm their head counsel. . . . No, baby, I told you I quit."

Patrick hears a male voice in the background. "Oh, oh should've known. Still gold diggin', huh? Can Grandpa still walk? Wait . . . wait, don't hang up. I didn't mean it. I still . . ."

Dial tone.

In agony, Patrick leans his head against the refrigerator. He moves his hand down the side feeling for the door handle, reaches in, grabs a beer bottle, and pops it open on the bottle opener nailed to the door. With all of the tears running out of his eyes, even if he was watching what he was doing, it's unlikely that he would have been able to see. He violently shakes his head as a lion would to shake the water off his mane. The tears fly and splatter. He looks up at the ceiling and guzzles the beer.

ℒℒℒ

Lou's in his room talking on the phone. "Yeah, the source is good . . . I don't care how late it is. I want a two liner in the gossip column. . . ."

✍ ✍ ✍

It's 9 a.m. on Wednesday morning. Trisha is in Dr. Arnold's waiting room.

Patrick enters reading a newspaper. He looks at Trisha and motions for her to rise with his hand. "Arnold's here, isn't he?"

Eve doesn't like anyone on her turf. She clears her throat. "Dr. Arnold is expecting Attorney Danahy."

"That's me," Patrick says.

Eve rises and knocks on the doctor's door. She opens it a crack. "Doctor, Attorney Danahy and Miss Abbott are now both here."

Danahy turns to Trisha. "There's a leak."

"A leak?" Trisha queries.

"Yep. You're in the rag," Patrick says.

"The rag?"

"You're in the *Chicago Tribune* gossip column."

"Oh, wonderful," Trisha says sarcastically.

"Attorney Patrick Danahy, Miss Trisha Abbott, Dr. Arnold will see you now," Eve says.

Patrick puts his arm around Trisha as they walk into Dr. Arnold's office.

Just before entering, Patrick whispers in Trisha's ear. "The deck is stacked against you, kid. Change your story, and I can hold the dogs off."

Trisha immediately stops. Dr. Arnold and Eve are observing the attorney/client episode.

Trisha looks into Danahy's bloodshot eyes. "Patrick, you don't believe me?"

Patrick doesn't respond. Trisha and Patrick walk into Arnold's room. The office door closes. Eve waits a moment and then leans her ear against the door, carefully listening. After almost fifteen minutes she sits at her desk and calls her apartment.

Joey turns the television off and answers the phone, "Hello, love of my life. Give me the scoop."

Joey listens, hangs up, and leaves. He pulls a cell phone out of the trunk and gets inside his car.

✍ ✍ ✍

At the same time, Lou Sherman's assistants, two average-looking, middle-aged females, Susan and Kathy, are sitting around him in his office. Lou's sixty-ish with the looks of a retired marine. There's a big "No Smoking" sign over his head. He's puffing on a long-ass cigar. He answers the phone and waves his hands for quiet.

"Hello, Joey. Hello."

Lou winks at the girls and continues to listen. "Great tip, Joey . . . Yeah, yeah, I'm listening . . . you don't say? You don't say? Good. Good. . . . And Joey, I paid for the exclusive. I want my colleagues to read about it like everyone else."

Lou hangs the phone up.

"What's goin' on, boss?" Susan asks.

"We got a story. That broad ain't backing down."

"You mean she is nuts," Kathy says.

Lou hesitates before speaking. He stares into space. "Well, she ain't backing down."

"That takes guts," Kathy says.

"Maybe she's got faith," Susan says looking at Lou and Kathy.

"Oh yeah?" Kathy says, "What's faith?"

Susan focuses on Kathy's face. "Faith's believing when common sense tells you not to."

ᒻᒻᒻ

Across town at 333 Wacker, Aaron's sitting behind his desk speaking with Blake Andrew, the CEO of Andrew Industries. Blake is sixty-ish and well-groomed with white-silver hair.

"AE's got the politicians. But liquidity is key to avoid bankruptcy while we merge AI into AE," Aaron says.

"It's brilliant . . . Son . . . I like how it feels," Blake Andrew says.

Aaron smiles. "Get your hands on all the cash you can, we'll need every dime. The unions will behave, there's a lot of jobs at stake here."

"And you'll be the white knight," Blake Andrew retorts.

Aaron gazes away. "Yes . . . to some, I'll be the white knight."

ᒻᒻᒻ

The courthouse parking lot is already filled. Lou swerves in and then backs out. He'd drive over to the *Tribune* building but just doesn't have the time. All the legal spots are filled on the street, and stories like this don't come around often. He parks in front of a fire hydrant, jumps out of the car, and throws his cigar onto the pavement.

Lou fixes himself as he runs to the elevators, which are more crowded than usual. The halls are busier. He hasn't seen this kind of action in the courthouse since the "Hobo street gang trial" in September of 2016.

Lou gets off on the twelfth floor and walks to room 1202. He looks in the slotted door windows. The chamber is full, not an empty chair.

Lou opens the door. The sheriff stops him and whispers, "Lou, you just made it. I'm going to have to lock the doors."

"Oh, come on Jesse, that's not democratic," Lou quips.

Jesse smiles and Lou enters.

Jebson stands and nods to the bailiff. The bailiff addresses the courtroom. "All rise."

Everyone in the room that is not already standing, stands.

Joey tugs on C's sleeve, "Get up, they'll trot you out of here."

"Frig dem, I ain't standin'."

Jesse sees the commotion and walks to the side so he can get a good view of the two "goodfella" fellas. Jesse looks at Joey. Joey grabs harder at C's sleeve. C looks at Joey and catches Jesse's stare. Jesse smiles and motions with his hand for C to stand.

"The Honorable Judge Irving Cohen's court is in session," the bailiff shouts, "please be seated."

Everyone sits.

C, still seated, shrugs his shoulders, and looks at Jesse. Jesse shakes his head and moves to the door where people are still spilling in from the hall.

Judge Irving glances at the new faces in the crowd and grimaces at no one. He looks to his wife, in the second row. She winks. He chisels a smile out of his not-so-jolly mood.

"Your Honor, we move to close the court. There's been a trick played by the defendant."

"Mr. Sherwin, again, keep your tone courteous," the judge says as he menacingly looks around the room. Mary smiles at her husband. He begins to smile back, then stops himself and puts on a hawkish facial expression.

"Are you implying that Mr. Danahy involved the press?" The judge looks squarely at Mr. Danahy then back at Sherwin.

"Your Honor, I don't have any tape-recorded conversations, but someone did." Sebastian motions to the crowd with his hand.

"This decision should include Mr. Danahy and his client. After all it's only fair," the judge states.

Danahy whispers to Trisha.

The judge looks at attorney Danahy. "Mr. Danahy?"

"Your Honor, we're not so motivated," Patrick says.

"But Your Honor, Abbott Electronics is a pillar of our country. This proceeding could create rumbles in the very crust of our nation's economic construction," Sebastian states.

"Attorney Sebastian," the judge says.

"Yes, Your Honor."

"What was your major in college?"

"My major?" Sebastian is thoroughly confused. He looks at Aaron as if he might offer insight.

"My major, Your Honor, I majored in political science."

"And your minor?"

"My minor, why my minor was in architecture."

"Fine, Counselor, now I understand. I think that the homeland's ultimate strength will be able to support the weight strain of these proceedings. I also minored in architecture."

The courtroom erupts into laughter.

The judge waits for silence. "Very well. Counselor Sherwin, you have the floor."

Patrick reaches over and without looking, pats Trisha's hand.

"Only a few days left," Trisha whispers.

Patrick stares. Trisha smiles.

Sebastian stands and addresses the court. He looks over the crowded room and then faces the judge. "Your Honor. I compare Trisha Abbott to a chrysalis, a butterfly slowly emerging from a cocoon."

Sebastian looks back at the crowd. He seems to enjoy having the podium. "Rob Santis was accustoming her to the world."

"Counselor, for someone that wants a private court, you do a lot of showboating," the judge says.

The room again explodes into laughter. Sebastian turns clown-nose red and the judge hits his gavel.

Silence returns and Sebastian continues. "With all due respect. I can find no evidence that someone other than Trisha Abbott wrote these letters. She desperately needs medical treatment. At risk is a fortune that was meant to remain in the Abbott family."

Sebastian seems pleased with his oral argument. He glances at Counselor Danahy. Patrick looks away. Sebastian continues. "Her grandmother, against the better judgment of her esteemed attorney Lawrence Barr, cut Aaron Abbott out of her will. Trisha insists that she will give all the inheritance away."

"There's no law against that," a woman from the packed room states.

The judge hits the gavel. "Sheriff, I will have no interruptions."

"Yes, Your Honor," Jesse says. He looks sternly over at the area where the comment originated.

The room is again quiet.

"Your Honor, I have several witnesses who can testify that Luellyn Abbott meant to change her will before she died. Bradford Abbott, the founder of Abbott Electronics, worked very hard, Your Honor, for the position that his family finds themselves in today. We ask for an immediate injunction."

Sebastian turns, facing Danahy and his client. "Trisha Abbott is not in her right frame of mind, and cannot make sound decisions, economic or other."

Judge Irving looks down at Patrick. Patrick nervously wipes his forehead. Sebastian sits.

Patrick rises. "Your Honor, I've rushed to prepare this case. Trisha Abbott concurs with her family and would like to see this proceeding closed as quickly as possible."

Patrick points to his client. "She's a sensible, upstanding woman and is of no risk to herself or society. I believe that someone else is responsible for writing those letters and that my client is guilty of nothing other than falling for the most cruel and dirty deception."

Trisha's lips mold into an ironic smile.

Danahy continues, the tenor of his voice rises with his confidence. "I believe that someone who has much to gain in this case is the culprit. Several people are suspects. For example, her brother Aaron!"

The courtroom goes wild. Aaron leaps over the rail and takes Patrick by the neck.

Patrick can barely speak. "I wasn't accusing. I was raising . . ."

Sebastian comes from behind Aaron. Backup sheriffs are rushing in from the hallway.

Trisha stands up. She has a horrified look in her eyes. "Stop! Is this what money does? For the love of God, leave me in peace just a little longer!"

Aaron accidentally elbows Sebastian's cheek and knocks him down. Two sheriffs separate Aaron and Patrick.

Sebastian rises to a kneeling position holding his head and cheek. He glares at Trisha. "You fool! These delusions are a part of your sickness! If there is a God, tell him to materialize and take you away from all of this! *He won't!* And you know why? *God does not exist!*"

The courtroom erupts. It's pandemonium. Women and men are screaming. "He said there is no God!" "He's a heretic!" "In the same room you swear on the Bible, he denies it!" "Someone sock him!"

Judge Cohen bangs his gavel. No one pays attention. "I'll have you all arrested!" he screams. The courtroom continues to explode.

The judge looks sternly at Counselors Danahy and Sebastian. "This court will reconvene in the morning. And I remind all of you that this is a court of law! Anyone not conducting themselves appropriately will be promptly arrested."

Trisha's slouched over and weeping into her arms.

🖋🖋🖋

Lou Sherman runs to his car with his phone at his ear. A car swerves to miss him. He arrives and takes the ticket off his windshield and smiles. "That's right. 'There is no God!' I don't care what Editor Zold says! And I want to see it in bold print!" he screams into his cell phone.

🖋🖋🖋

Sebastian and Aaron are playing chess in the Abbott estate den. "That neighborhood's old mob. Hat. What kind of a name is dat?" Sebastian says mockingly. "What the hell did your sister call him?"

Aaron's less amused with the conversation. "Hat, or Rob."

"Why would anyone call someone 'Hat'?"

"I understand that he always wore a hat that his grandfather left him."

"That's ludicrous," Sebastian says.

"Maybe," Aaron says insipidly.

They swap pieces.

"Should've seen the funeral home. The mother was hysterical. Wouldn't let them close the casket until they found her son's hat. It was bizarre, morbid. The mother placed it on the corpse's head. She kissed him a dozen times before Hat's brother and his father dragged her away," Aaron shakes his head. "I've never seen anything like it."

Aaron puts his hand to his chin. "And the hat, it looked like something that came out of *Godfather II*, the mountains of Sicily. It was like one of those those newsboy or big apple caps; grey tweed with little specks of red and black throughout. I've never seen one like it before and hope I never see one like it again."

Aaron reflects on his last sentence. He's confused and startled when Sebastian bangs his hand on the table. A few of the chess pieces fall all over. "Hey. I got it! The mob's behind it. They've got their eyes on your sister's coffers," Sebastian says.

Sebastian fixes the pieces back on the board, purposely putting the queen two spaces to the right.

"Have you ever heard of Peter Cerone of Edgeview Bank?" Aaron asks.

"That's the second time you've said that name. Checkmate. Who is he?"

Aaron looks down at the board in frustration. He rises. "He's behind some of this."

"Really," Sebastian comments. "Is he after your sister's money?"

"It's not only about money," Aaron says, gazing out the window into the darkness. Sebastian stares at Aaron, trying to get his attention. "What does he want?"

"Someone he could never keep."

🖋🖋🖋

It's Thursday evening, and Judge Cohen is at the dinner table with his wife Mary.

"Did you see the evening news, Irving?"

"I don't even want to imagine. Trump says it's all fake news. He's not all wrong."

"Who does he think he is, saying, 'There is no God'?"

Irv raises his hands toward his forehead so Mary does not see him rolling his eyes. "Sherwin was knocked to the ground. Angry people say lots of things they don't mean when they're incensed," Irving said as he glanced across the table.

Mary's face shows her feelings about where she thinks the conversation is going.

"Don't bow to sentiment. . . . It's fortunate you never pursued a legal career. You're far too emotional," Irving comments.

"Well, I certainly would have handled the reprimand differently. What did that poor innocent girl do?" Mary hastily gets up and walks out of the room leaving her dinner on the table.

Irv has a puzzled look on his face. "Menopause," he mumbles to himself.

Chapter 12

We're in the Funnies

In the Abbott Mansion den, Aaron covers the phone as Ingrid enters.

"Did you see the evening news? We're the laughingstock of the country," she says.

Aaron whispers into the phone, hoping that his mother will not overhear, "Melissa, I'll call you later. . . . Yes, me too."

"You're insane as well. She got you into this mess. Her father's ruined. His company's done."

"Where are you going, Mother?"

"I'm going to the Rhodeses'. There's a village meeting. Your father insists on holding his chin up through this fiasco."

"Have fun." Aaron's face becomes pleasant as if he sees something beautiful through his mother.

🌿🌿🌿

Patrick's in Kelly's bar, with another ten patrons. "Mikey, my lad, get everyone another round," Patrick says.

Toad, a guy whose mug resembles one, yells, "Big shot's in the funnies! Now he's a millionaire!"

"Hey, Patty," Mush says, "take it easy . . . I don't know if anyone told you, but it don't look good."

Patrick tips his bottle of beer up and smugly grins. "Why Mush, don't you believe that the dead can write letters?"

"It's not that. Hell, my mother's dead thirty years and I see her in the house all the time. She took a swing at me on Monday."

"Well then, what is it?"

Mush raises his mug of beer which resembles *his* mug. "No offense, laddy, but to me, the nail in her coffin is that she let you represent her. I mean, what sane person would do that?"

⚘⚘⚘

The people in the ballroom at the Rhodeses' estate are dressed in black tie and full. Howard's watching his wife, who's talking to a handsome middle-aged man.

"Excuse me, Mr. Gunther," Ingrid says.

"But of course, Mrs. Abbott."

Ingrid walks to her husband and speaks into his chest. "We're outcasts. The only people that will talk to me are has-beens and no ones."

"It's late," Howard says. "I promised Washington the night off. He's been super nervous lately. I'll have him pull the car up. Go fetch your wrap."

Ingrid looks concerned and then disappears into the crowd.

⚘⚘⚘

Shortly after, Sebastian, Ingrid, and Aaron are in the library, seated at a glass coffee table. The chess pieces are scattered, and Ingrid's still in her evening dress pasting photos in an album.

"She's been under watch. Still, nothing useful has turned up," Sebastian says.

Ingrid looks up. "Either she's nuts or it's that witch. And you, Mr. Artist! I demand that you stop the publicity."

Aaron shakes his head. "We don't have time for this. Rebecca would not hurt Trisha." Aaron looks at Sebastian, "What's tomorrow bring?"

"The calligrapher will report that it's expert forgery. The psychiatrists will testify."

"What about the press?" Aaron asks.

"Cohen won't allow his courtroom to become a circus. They threw their darts; I can't see any further interest."

"I'd like the truth. It's all so strange," Aaron says as he gazes angelically.

Sebastian angers. "The money's essential. The truth's only a distraction. And there's nothing strange! The dead don't write letters. . . . The answer's right in front of your eyes."

Ingrid looks at Sebastian. "I hope the judge sees it so clearly."

"Hard times if he doesn't," Aaron flips.

Ingrid turns her scope to her son. "You and your father are always exaggerating."

"Are we?"

Sebastian's face divulges his concern. "If the judge thinks that someone else wrote those letters he may see her as a victim of fraud, not mental illness."

Ingrid is visibly irritated. "Then what?"

"No, we don't need to go there," Sebastian says. "Just leave it to me. There's more clay."

Aaron puts his head into his hands.

Ingrid rises. "I'm going to bed and leave you master negotiators, bowlers, and artists be. Good night."

The door slams.

⚖︎ ⚖︎ ⚖︎

Later that night, Sebastian is sitting with his brother Ted in Shaw's Crab House.

"That's right! Can you prove that there is? Can anyone?" Sebastian asks.

"Little brother. Just because you can't touch something does not mean that it doesn't exist."

"Huh, well you know what I think, big brother?"

Ted grins. He shakes his head, "no."

"Galileo proved the earth to be round, Einstein the theory of relativity. Sherwin, divine truth."

Ted's grin becomes a smile.

"Little brother, hundreds of brains are operated on every year. No one's ever seen a thought. Would you say that thoughts don't exist?"

Sebastian is completely exhausted from this conversation and this day. Ted and he rise to leave.

Ted turns. "Oh, Sebastian. I almost forgot. My son will be competing at Northwestern University Saturday morning. I can't attend. But he'd love it if you could stand in."

"Oh?" Sebastian queries, "what's the competition?"

"Archery."

⚖︎ ⚖︎ ⚖︎

Trisha rises from the couch in the Cabbage House and lays a magazine down. She stretches and walks. The light's on in the kitchen.

"Becky, are you coming to bed?"

89

Rebecca comes out and meets Trisha. "In a while. You go ahead, I have some things to do."

↙ ↙ ↙

Sebastian's driving at high speed. He doesn't want to go home, but he also doesn't want to be where he is, or anywhere for that matter. He's not comfortable in his own skin. The phone rings. He quickly grabs it, desperately hoping for some sort of news, a reprieve, or even a distraction.

"Yes?" Sebastian says in the friendliest tone he can muster.

Sebastian hears a raspy voice on the other end. "Eventually, good always wins over evil."

Sebastian looks at the caller ID and almost rear-ends a truck. The number is blocked. "Who is this?" he asks.

"Sebastian, you know that we all have to answer someday."

"Who is this? This, this, hoax!" Sebastian is terrified.

The voice continues, "It's unlucky for you that it's not. Life's not a joke. It's a testing ground. Will you pass?"

The car leaps as Sebastian instinctively steps on the gas. "Wrong number, you lunatic!"

Sebastian studies the phone hoping that by some luck, it's not his. He nervously presses the red dot. The home screen appears. It is, in fact, his phone.

↙ ↙ ↙

Irving rolls over and turns off his reading lamp.

"Delusions do not prove insanity, Irving."

"Please Mary, it's tough enough. You've never interfered before."

"Your cases are usually about nonsense."

"Thanks, this one's no different. It's about a sick girl and money."

"How are you so sure that she's sick?"

"Don't be a fool."

"Irv, do you know what a fool is?"

Irv remains complacent.

Mary continues, "A fool is one who substitutes words for deeds." She briskly turns over and shuts off the light.

                    *   *   *

Friday morning the courthouse is busy with people passing through the metal detectors.

Griff, one of the sheriffs, shakes his head and grabs the walkie-talkie.

"Dispatcher Marianne, we need help down here. Why doesn't Cohen lock that Abbott trial down?"

David, another guard checking people, overhears Griff. "Are you kidding? You ever seen a judge turn away publicity?"

                    *   *   *

Near the courthouse on State Street at Gayle's Best Ever Grilled Cheese restaurant, Jimmy and Chucky, two city workers, are sitting in a booth. Jimmy's reading a newspaper.

"What's so interesting?" Chucky asks.

Jimmy continues to read without responding.

"Hey library boy, what's the best seller?"

"That Abbott family from Abbott Electronics got problems," Jimmy mumbles without lowering the paper.

"I'd like to have their problems," Chucky spills.

Jimmy lowers the paper and looks at Chucky. "Really? The daughter's getting letters from some dead guy, the brother's using it as an excuse to grab her dough. And their atheist attorney is showboatin' that there ain't no letters cause there ain't no life after death, cause there ain't no God."

"Hey, screw the Abbotts. Remember what they tried to do to the union?" Chucky asks.

"Yeah, but I feel for the girl. They'll eat her for breakfast."

"What's she look like? Maybe I'll eat her," Chucky rips back.

"Hey Romeo, finish up, I want to stop over there and take a look. . . . And it's your turn to pay."

                    *   *   *

Friday morning, Trisha and Patrick are in a corner in the busy hallway of the courthouse.

Patrick looks kindly at Trisha. "You know, this can only go one way unless you . . ."

Trisha interrupts, "I've only a few days left," then she smiles.

Patrick stares at her.

✿ ✿ ✿

Right under them in a private room, Aaron, Sebastian, and Ingrid are in discussion.

"This is your fault, claiming that there is no God! Had you no idea that we're Presbyterian?"

"I was shoved. I was trying to separate . . ."

Ingrid interrupts him. "What do you care? What does anyone care about you? You're *just another* nonbeliever. But we're the Abbotts, and we're ruined!"

The door opens. Howard Abbott walks in. His face is stern. "This must be resolved now. Nothing is more important. No one moves until this is resolved."

"I'm supposed to leave for Paris. How will that look?" Ingrid asks.

"I'll cut your credit cards. How will that look?" Howard spits back.

"You bastard! I gave you the best years of my life!" Ingrid cries.

"If those were the best years of your life, you should be put out of your misery now," he answers.

Howard looks at Aaron and Sebastian, staring at each one for a few seconds. Unfortunately, he gets no answers. "I'll handle Trisha." Howard leaves.

✿ ✿ ✿

Outside the courthouse, shortly after, Irv and Mary are passing protestors carrying signs.

A dark-skinned man's sign reads "I'm living proof that God exists."

Irv and Mary make their way into the back entrance. Just as they get to the door a woman screams, "There's the judge! Tell 'em, Judge! God exists!"

The courtroom is packed. Trisha is seated next to Patrick. Mary's escorted to a seat behind Trisha. Lou Sherman is seated behind where Sebastian will sit, and artists are busy sketching.

The courtroom explodes with boos and slurs aimed toward Aaron, Ingrid, and Sebastian as they enter.

✿ ✿ ✿

Judge Cohen is in his chambers with Jebson.

"Jebson, tell the sheriffs to get the court under control or I'll cancel today's hearing," Judge Cohen says.

Jebson walks out. He finds Sheriff Jesse and whispers to him. The sheriff nods.

The courtroom becomes quiet, and the bailiff bellows, "Ladies and gentlemen, if there is not complete silence, the judge will cancel this morning's scheduled case."

Most of the people heard him. They become quiet and hush those around them who didn't hear.

Jebson exits from the court chamber and nods to the bailiff.

"All rise! The honorable Judge Irving Cohen presiding," the bailiff yells.

Judge Cohen enters.

"Please be seated," the bailiff chants.

A few spectators whisper. Judge Cohen bangs his gavel. "Order in the court."

The judge nods to Sebastian. Sebastian stands, "Your Honor, I would like to call Dr. Behren to the witness stand."

The bailiff swears Doctor Behren in. Doctor Behren sits.

Sebastian begins. "For the record, will you state your name and occupation?"

"My name is Doctor Samuel Behren. I am a certified psychiatrist."

"Where did you graduate from, Doctor Behren?"

"Stanford University."

"Your Honor, I'd like to note that Stanford is the fourth-rated university for psychiatry in the world."

"Noted," the judge says.

"Doctor, what was your rank in your class?"

"I was ranked at the top of my class."

"Your Honor, I'd like to note that Dr. Behren was ranked at the top . . ."

"Noted," the judge interrupts.

Patrick stands. "Your Honor, we accept that Doctor Behren is an excellent and qualified specialist in the field of psychiatry."

Sebastian looks at Patrick. "Thank you, just one more question about the doctor before we proceed to the more pertinent questioning." Sebastian looks at Doctor Behren. "Doctor, who was valedictorian of your class?"

The doctor attempts to hide his pleasure. "I was."

Sebastian looks at the judge.

"Noted," the judge says.

Sebastian leads the doctor through a maze of questions leading to the final important ones.

"So Doctor, you believe that Trisha Abbott suffers from delusions?"

"I firmly do."

"So, Doctor," Sebastian smiles brotherly at Trisha. "You also believe that Trisha Abbott can be cured of her delusions?

"Yes, completely."

"In your expert opinion, is Miss Trisha Abbott capable of making sound decisions, financial or otherwise?"

"In my expert opinion, no."

ᒪ ᒪ ᒪ

Friday morning, Jonathan is seated next to Sebastian. Howard is seated next to Aaron.

Patrick's examining Trisha's psychiatrist, Doctor Arnold. "Doctor, does Trisha show any signs of violence whatsoever?"

"No."

"Would you say that she's suicidal?"

"Definitely not."

Sebastian stands. "Your Honor, a simple yes or no will suffice."

"Sit down, Counselor Sherwin. Continue, Counselor Danahy," the judge says.

Mary smiles warmly at her husband. Aaron grimaces. A dark-skinned woman in the back of the room screams, "Tell him, Judge!"

The judge smiles at the woman. "Thank you, ma'am, but let's be calm so we can get on with this."

The woman nods. The judges smiles approvingly.

Attorney Patrick Danahy smiles faintly and continues. "So, Doctor, Trisha Abbott presents no threat to the public or herself. Is that correct?"

"Absolutely." The doctor catches himself. "Yes, this is correct, she does not pose a threat to herself or the public."

ᒪ ᒪ ᒪ

Sebastian calls Aaron to the stand. Aaron swears in. They go through the routine questions.

"Mr. Abbott, what is it that you want for your sister?"

"I love my sister; I want her to be well."

"Mr. Abbott, how did you learn about the letters from Hat, her deceased boyfriend?"

"Trisha showed them to me at her home on the day of my grandmother's funeral, after the services."

"Your Honor, this is the first letter. It's dated six days after Mr. Santis's death. It's short. May I?"

The judge nods. The courtroom freezes.

"'Well love, I hope that reading this will make you believe that you'll always be a part of me. Here's the physical proof you wanted. I've told you a thousand times. I will always love you. Death will unite, not separate us. I'll never leave you. Love is one soul in two beings. Love, Hat.'"

Lou Sherman pulls out a handkerchief and blows his nose.

Sebastian places the note next to Jonathan and continues. "Mr. Abbott. Would you say that your sister is astute in business?"

"Well, I don't know how . . ."

Sebastian interrupts. "Let me rephrase." Sebastian smiles warmly at the judge, "Would you say that she has expertise in high finance?"

Aaron smiles. "Sir, my sister wouldn't know Dow Jones from Tom Jones."

There's a burst of laughter. The judge hits the gavel. "Mr. Abbott, please answer clearly."

"Yes sir, Trisha is by no means an expert in high finance."

"Why are you asking to become Trisha's guardian?"

"I handle the bulk of the family's finances, and I will safeguard the inheritance for her until she is in a better situation to make critical decisions for herself."

"Last question. When Trisha *is* well again, what will happen to her funds?"

"They'll be returned to her."

"So, Aaron, this hearing is not about grabbing your sister's money, as the press claims?"

"Absolutely not."

"Thank you, Mr. Abbott, you may take your seat."

The court breaks for lunch.

Sebastian calls Ingrid Abbott. Ingrid stands. She's wearing a costume that one might wear to the Grammy Awards.

"Ms. Abbott . . ."

Ingrid interrupts, "Please call me Mrs. Abbott. Our family does not bow to idiotic language changes dictated by government command."

The courtroom buzzes like a bee's nest.

Sebastian does some facial gymnastics and then recommences. "Noted, Mrs. Abbott. Excuse me. May I continue?"

Ingrid nods, "You may."

"When did you notice that something was drastically wrong with Trisha?" Sebastian asks.

Danahy stands. "Your Honor, Mr. Sherwin is leading the witness."

"Sustained," the judge says.

Sebastian nods. "Mrs. Abbott, have you noticed anything not normal about Trisha?"

"I have."

"When did this happen?" Sebastian inquires.

"Trisha and I were very close until after Santis died. It was a difficult period for her. It was her first and only serious relationship."

"Mrs. Abbott, are you telling me that Trisha had no boyfriends in high school?"

"Mr. Sherwin, we come from good stock. The women in our family are not floozies."

The courtroom erupts with laughter.

"Of course, Mrs. Abbott. Of course."

Mrs. Abbott adjusts herself appropriately.

"Mrs. Abbott, you said that you and Trisha, your daughter, were close until after Santis . . . this is Hat or Rob Santis, is it not?"

Mrs. Abbott nods.

"Mrs. Abbott, please answer yes or no. Our stenographer needs to hear your response," Judge Cohen says.

"Yes, Mr. Santis was Rob Santis and also called Hat. . . ."

"Thank you. . . ." Sebastian says but is interrupted.

Mrs. Abbott continues. "I don't know what society allows people to be referred to as things such as 'Hat,' but it was Trisha's choice . . . certainly not mine."

"So, Mrs. Abbott, after Mr. Santis's death, the relationship between you and Trisha suffered?"

"To say the least, and when her grandmother died she *completely* lost it," Ingrid says blandly.

"I see. Did you do anything to help her?"

"I made an appointment for her with my psychiatrist and went to her home to talk to her." Mrs. Abbott points to Rebecca Riley. "*She* didn't want to let me. I *was not* going to let the hired help forbid me to see my own daughter."

"I see, would you say that Trisha was a normal child?"

"She was timid. . . . Her senior prom was a disaster; a bus came to pick her up."

"Are you close to your daughter?"

96

"She's my only daughter. Yes, I am."

"Do you love your daughter?"

"How vile. Of course, I do."

"Tell us why she confides in Rebecca Riley and not in you."

"That's false! She's just a hired hand, milking my daughter dry."

Sebastian coughs. "Excuse me, Your Honor." Sebastian walks over, sips his water and whispers to Aaron and Howard. "She's going to kill us. We prepped her. These are not the answers we prepared."

Howard's face is turned off.

Aaron rolls his eyes. "Cut it short."

Sebastian turns, smiles at the judge, and approaches Ingrid. "Thank you, Mrs. Abbott."

Patrick stands. "Your Honor, I have a few questions for Mrs. Abbott."

The judge nods.

"Mrs. Abbott, are you a religious woman?"

"I am."

"Are you affiliated or do you belong to any church or religious organization?"

"I, and my family, are among the staunchest supporters of the Barrington Presbyterian Church."

"I see . . . so you believe in God."

Sebastian grimaces, fighting to remain in his seat. Reason loses, and he jumps up. "Your Honor! Where are we going with this nonsensical line of questioning? Everyone says that they believe in God, they're programmed, brainwashed to do so. This does not mean that he or she or it exists."

"I'll allow the witness to answer."

"Thank you, Your Honor," Danahy says. "Mrs. Abbott, do you believe in God?"

"Of course I do," Mrs. Abbott states emphatically.

"I have no further questions, Your Honor," Danahy says.

Sebastian smiles and stands. "Your Honor, I call Rebecca Riley."

Rebecca is wearing the garments that an Irish immigrant would have worn in the sixties. She looks twenty years younger than her real age of eighty-three. The court stirs as she hobbles up and is sworn in.

"How long have you been a nanny to Miss Abbott?"

Rebecca slowly and almost mysteriously raises her head to speak. "Since she was an infant."

"Did you know Rob, Hat Santis?"

"Yes, I did."

97

"Did he ever spend the night at . . ."

Patrick stands. "Objection. Trisha's private life's irrelevant," Patrick says.

"Sir, it is essential to know the background," Sebastian insists.

"Overruled."

Mary grimaces at her husband.

"Thank you, Your Honor. . . . Did Rob Santis ever spend the night at the Cabbage House?"

"No, as long as I live, no man will . . ."

Sebastian smiles faintly. "Never?"

"Never."

Mary Cohen smiles widely.

Sebastian looks at the judge and his audience. He feels a bit more confident after passing through the storm that Ingrid created.

"Cabbage House, Mrs. Riley?"

"Miss," Rebecca corrects.

"Miss," Sebastian smiles. "The Cabbage House has a strange ring. Does its name have anything to do with your heritage or is it just a coincidence?"

"Mr. Sebastian," Rebecca shoots, "your name is Sebastian Sherwin. Your initials are SS. Does this have anything to do with your heritage, or is it just a coincidence?"

The courtroom erupts into conversation, laughter, and obscured murmuring.

The judge hits his gavel. "Mr. Sherwin, stick to pertinent questions."

Sebastian turns back to Rebecca. "When did Trisha begin writing letters to herself?"

Patrick stands. "Your Honor, he's leading the witness."

Sebastian is obviously stung by the SS comment. He tries to smile, but at that moment it would have been easier for him to walk on water.

"Sir, I'd like to finish quickly. We all know where this is going," Sebastian says.

"Rephrase your question, Counselor," the judge says.

"Miss Riley, do you believe that Trisha Abbott wrote those letters? The letters signed by Rob, Hat Santis days and months after his death?"

"Trisha did not write those letters," Rebecca says softly.

"Do you believe that Rob, Hat Santis sent letters from the grave?"

"No."

The courtroom erupts.

The judge bangs the gavel. "Order in the courtroom."

"All right, Miss Riley, then *who* wrote those letters?"

Rebecca looks down. There's complete silence in the room.

"I wrote the letters," she mumbles.

"What?" Sebastian asks meekly.

"I wrote the letters."

The courtroom erupts. The judge bangs his gavel. "Court's recessed until one o'clock."

The journalists scurry to the exit.

Chapter 13

God's Really on Trial

In front of the courthouse, Ingrid, Aaron, and Sebastian are walking, surrounded by private guards and being followed by a mob.

A man yells, "Nazi!"

A woman screams, "You're persecuting an innocent girl!"

A nun screams, "If there's no God, where did you come from?"

A man wearing an Islamic kufi prayer cap yells, "The Lord gave you your health and wealth! You're scheming to get more! Judgment Day is at hand!"

A dark-skinned reverend screams, "Blessed are the meek, for *they* shall inherit the earth!"

The trio are almost to the Atwood restaurant; an egg is thrown. The egg is sailing. . . .

A woman dressed in Hindu garb shouts, "They who give, have all things; they who withhold have nothing!"

The egg lands at the bottom of Sebastian's neck. Sebastian turns in anger. Aaron pulls him into the restaurant.

Inside, the group walks into a rabbi, who is leaving. He looks at Sebastian. "My son, many say that there are two infinite things, the universe and man's stupidity. . . . And I'm not sure about the universe."

The owner greets the group. "Mr. Sebastian, we have your table ready."

The group sits at the table. They don't know, but the table has a hidden microphone attached to the underside of it.

𝓛 𝓛 𝓛

Joey's across town listening to their every word through the bug on the bottom of Sebastian's *regular* table in Atwood.

≝≝≝

Inside Judge Cohen's chamber, Mary and Irving are eating sandwiches.

"She's in no condition to handle her own affairs. . . . I'm afraid . . ." Judge Cohen says. "Eat your sandwich."

"Even if it's true that her house friend wrote those letters . . . Trisha believed that . . ."

"Men! You've got it all figured out."

≝≝≝

Patrick is with Trisha in the office of an attorney friend across the street from the courthouse. Trisha is looking away from him.

"This is our break. Why are you despondent?"

Trisha does not answer. There's a knock at the door. Howard Abbott walks into the room.

"Would you excuse us, Counselor?" Mr. Abbott asks.

"Well, Mr. Abbott, it's . . ." Patrick looks at Trisha, who has still yet to say a word.

"I'll be in the hall," Patrick says impatiently.

≝≝≝

Inside the restaurant the trio are still seated at the dining table in the back room.

Sebastian rubs his hands together. "This is good, folks. The fox has been let loose. Watch me now."

"I thought that you said . . ." Ingrid is interrupted.

"I'll sculpt this into the piece that we wanted from the beginning."

Sebastian is charged because there's no letters from beyond. There is no God. His life is back on course. Sebastian smiles broadly and lifts his coffee, "Aaron . . . to truth, to destiny."

Aaron gazes away. "Yes. To truth," Aaron mumbles.

Sebastian holds his raised cup. Aaron hesitates, and the two toast.

≝≝≝

Patrick is pacing. He looks at his watch. It reads 12:55. The office door opens and shuts. Howard, now wearing sunglasses, walks by silently.

Patrick opens the door. Trisha and Rebecca are both in a tearful embrace. He's utterly confused. He never saw Rebecca enter.

"I love you, little girl," Rebecca blubbers and walks by Patrick without saying a word.

"Is everything OK?" Patrick asks.

Trisha hands him an envelope. "Open this when I nod to do so."

"What is it?"

"Open it when I nod for you to do so." Trisha silently walks by him toward the courtroom.

ℒℒℒ

The courtroom is packed like the final game of the Stanley Cup.

The bailiff reminds Miss Riley that she's still under oath.

Sebastian stands. "Your Honor, if it would please the court, I'd like Miss Riley sworn in again."

The judge looks impatiently.

"Your Honor, she is of advanced years, and if she doesn't mind."

"I don't," Rebecca says. She places her left hand on the Bible and raises her right hand.

"Do you solemnly swear that you will tell the truth, the whole truth, and nothing but the truth, so help you God?" The bailiff asks.

Sebastian hears the word "God" and sneers.

"I do," Rebecca says.

"Rebecca—may I call you Rebecca?" Patrick asks.

"Trisha calls me Becky, but you can call me Rebecca."

"Thank you, Rebecca. How long have you cared for Trisha Abbott?"

"Why, since her birth."

"Who hired you?"

"I was hired by Mr. Abbott."

Rebecca smiles at Howard. He smiles back.

"What did you feel about Trisha's treatment in the Abbott household?"

Sebastian stands. "Your Honor."

The judge quietly motions Sebastian to remain seated.

"I felt that she was neglected," Rebecca says.

Ingrid rises. "How dare you? . . . You . . . you leech!"

Judge Cohen hits the gavel. Ingrid continues to scream. The judge waves for the guards to escort her outside.

Ingrid watches the judge, looks toward the guards and stands. "I'll go myself! This is a zoo! And I'm bored!"

Ingrid exits. The courtroom applauds.

Judge Cohen slams his gavel. "Order in the court . . . and good riddance."

The courtroom erupts with laughter.

Patrick returns to questioning Rebecca, but is interrupted.

"Psst," Trisha beckons. She forms her fingers and mimics ripping open an envelope.

"Oh, yes, yes," Patrick whispers to himself.

Danahy reaches into his suit jacket pocket and produces a tiny packet. Cohen looks on, as Patrick opens the envelope. Sebastian stands.

"Your Honor, this proceeding is . . ."

Keeping his eyes on Patrick, the judge waves a hand at Sebastian, who sits down. Mary smiles approvingly at her husband.

A woman spectator yells, "Sit down, fool!"

Patrick looks at the papers contained in the envelope. He walks to Trisha and whispers in her ear. She whispers back to him.

Patrick stands at attention. "Are you sure?"

Trisha smiles and nods.

"Your Honor, I'd like to ask Rebecca Riley to identify these letters."

Sebastian stands. "Your Honor . . ."

The Judge begins to raise his hand. Mary smiles.

Sebastian nods, "I know. I'll be seated, Your Honor."

A few of the courtroom participants laugh.

"Proceed, Mr. Danahy," the judge says.

Patrick hands one of the letters to Rebecca.

"Miss Riley, please tell the court what the paper in your hand is."

Rebecca looks timidly at the judge.

The judge smiles kindly and nods. "Answer," he says soothingly.

Rebecca looks from the judge to Patrick and then to Trisha. "It's my ABCs."

The judge narrows his eyes. He's extremely interested.

Patrick hands Rebecca another piece of paper. "And this? What is this, Rebecca?"

"It's my paycheck."

"Your Honor?" Patrick walks to the judge and hands him the papers.

The judge studies them, grins, and lays his head in his right hand.

"Miss Riley, did you write the letters dated after the death of and signed by the deceased Rob Hat Santis?"

Rebecca faces the judge. The judge winks at her.

"No."

Sebastian stands, raises his arm, and opens his mouth. The judge pays no attention.

"Sit down, Counselor, please, sit down," the judge says.

Sebastian remains standing. "But Your Honor."

"Sit down, Counselor Sherwin, you're being obnoxious."

The woman from the back yells, "You tell him, Judgey!"

Another attendee joins in. "That's right!"

Another yells, "Sit down clown."

The whole courtroom chants, "Sit down clown! Sit down clown!"

Sebastian looks around the courtroom and finally to the judge, hoping to be thrown a cord to get back to shore. The judge motions for him to sit. Sebastian looks around again, attempting to safeguard even a tenth of an ounce of pride.

The judge nods his head and points to Sebastian's seat. Sebastian smiles a wide frown and sits down slowly, hoping that no one notices.

The crowd simmers. The judge nods to Patrick Danahy.

Danahy continues, "Miss Riley, please tell us why it couldn't have possibly been you who wrote the letters."

Rebecca looks to the judge. The judge smiles reassuringly.

"I can't read or write. Trisha was teaching . . ."

The courtroom blasts out of control. The judge bangs his gavel.

"Order! Order! Guards, escort anyone out who does not maintain order!"

The judge continues to bang his gavel. He stands and screams louder than he has ever screamed, "*ORDER!*"

A blind man with a large metal cross dangling from his neck slams his cane to the floor. "Quiet!"

The court becomes silent.

The judge looks at the blind man. "Thank you."

"No problem, Judgey, anytime," the blind man says.

"Counselor," the judge says, as he looks at Patrick.

Patrick nods and looks kindly to Rebecca. "Miss Riley, who wrote those letters to Trisha?"

The room begins murmuring. Slowly, one by one each participants' eyes are glued to Rebecca's lips. The blind man steps a bit closer. The court becomes silent.

"Miss Riley, who wrote those letters to Trisha?"

Rebecca looks down.

"Miss Riley?"

Rebecca raises her head and looks at Patrick. The world is still. A moth flew around a light in the middle of the room. The wind made by its wings was the only evident sound.

"*Miss Riley,*" Patrick repeats, "*who wrote those letters to Trisha?*"

She stares at him. "Hat . . . Rob Santis."

Utter bedlam takes control of the courtroom. Reporters head for the door.

The courtroom explodes. People are hugging and jumping in the aisles.

"There is a God!" a dark-skinned man yells.

A Roman Catholic priest stands and blesses the room.

A rabbi cants the Shema prayer.

Georgia Santis's head is pressed against her husband Dominic's shoulder. Lou Sherman smiles.

In the court hallway, a reporter is on a headset connected to his cell. "Stop the press! Housekeeper says the letters *are* from Santis!"

Joey goes into the hallway and walks to a tall, dark-skinned guard.

"David, give me your cell."

"Joey, you can't use your cell here."

"I know, it's dead. That's why I need yours."

David frowns and hands the cell phone to Joey.

"Tanks." Joey dials. "Hey C. He ain't gonna get his hands on dat money for months, if ever. Come on over, I'll save you a seat."

Joey clicks off and hands the phone to David.

"Hey man, don't be calling those Eye-talian mafiosa types with my phone."

"David, you shouldn't stereotype."

Soon the hall is overflowing with camera crews from CNN, Fox, ABC, RT, Euro News, and CBS, all vying for position. Joey elbows his way through the crowd.

"I got a seat in dere," Joey yells.

A sheriff allows Joey to pass back into the courtroom.

The judge is standing. "I will shut the public out of these proceedings if you don't all sit down and shut up!"

After ten seconds the murmurs subside.

🌿🌿🌿

Thirty minutes later, Patrick is cross-examining Liz, Trisha's coworker. "Do you believe Trisha to be insane?" Patrick asks.

"No, definitely not."

Sebastian jumps up. "Objection. We have never claimed insanity. We claim that she cannot handle her own financial affairs."

"Sustained," the judge says. "Counselor, rephrase your question."

"Miss Madia, how would you rate Trisha's work?"

"She's the best, most competent worker we have."

"Has she ever caused any problems at work?"

"Not that I know of." Liz smiles tenderly. "Everyone at Tuesday's Child loves her."

"Has any of this changed since Rob Hat Santis's death?"

"No."

"Thank you." Patrick looks to Sebastian. "I have no further questions."

Sebastian adjusts his collar. "Your Honor, I know that I've already questioned the witness, but I have a few other questions."

The judge looks to Patrick.

"She's your witness," Patrick quips.

People, particularly reporters, point as Howard Abbott enters. Howard sits next to Trisha and whispers to Patrick. Sebastian looks at Howard much as the apostles may have looked at Judas Iscariot.

Sebastian turns and faces Liz Madia. It's beyond do or die.

"Have you ever seen Trisha Abbott speaking to herself?" Sebastian asks.

Liz is frozen. Her head is bowed as if she's solemnly praying.

Sebastian looks at the judge. "Your Honor?"

"Repeat the question, Counselor," the honor says.

"*I repeat*, Miss Madia, have you ever seen Trisha Abbott speaking to herself? . . . *You're still under oath*."

Liz looks at Trisha. Trisha winks and smiles.

"I've seen her speaking *by* herself."

"Miss Madia, do not toy with the court. Isn't 'by herself' the same as 'to herself'?"

Liz doesn't answer. The judge peeps at Sebastian.

Sebastian grins thinly. "Let's try it this way. Miss Madia, when you witnessed Trisha speaking *by* herself, was there music on?"

"No, I don't think so."

"Maybe she was singing."

"Is that a question?" Liz asks.

"Yes, was she singing when you witnessed her speaking *by* herself?"

"No, but I sometimes speak to my dad. . . ."

"The court is not interested in who you speak to, Miss Madia. Have you ever asked Trisha who she was speaking to when she was speaking *by herself?*"

Liz is silent. Sebastian looks at the judge. "Your Honor."

The judge looks at Liz. "Answer the question, please."

"Can you repeat the question?" Liz asks.

"Of course," Sebastian says calmly. "When you saw Trisha Abbott speaking *by* herself, who was she talking to?"

"Rob, Hat," Liz says.

The court buzzes.

"And how do you know that, Miss Madia? Did you hear him?"

"Of course not," Liz says.

"Then how do you know that Trisha Abbott was talking to him?"

"She told me."

Sebastian turns and pauses. "Nothing further, Your Honor."

$$\mathcal{L}\,\mathcal{L}\,\mathcal{L}$$

Friday afternoon, Sebastian is cross-examining Detective Perkins.

"So, Detective Perkins, there's been surveillance on the Cabbage House since Rob Santis's death?"

"Yes, Mr. Abbott, Howard, was frightened by the suspicious circumstances surrounding the young man's demise. He feared for his daughter's safety."

"In your professional opinion, is there any way that someone other than the family could have gotten into the Cabbage House to plant those letters?"

"No sir, in my professional opinion, there is no way that a stranger could have gotten into the Cabbage House to place those letters or anything else."

"Could Trisha Abbott have brought them in?"

"Yes, of course."

"Your witness, Counselor." Sebastian gallantly waves Patrick on.

"No questions," Patrick says.

"Very well," Judge Cohen says, "Attorney Sherwin, please call your next witness."

"The plaintiff calls Mrs. Georgia Santis to the stand."

Mrs. Santis stands. She whispers into her husband's ear. He winks at her, and she heads for the witness stand.

The bailiff swears Mrs. Santis in, and Sebastian asks some basic questions in the kindest, most humanly possible manner, for Sebastian.

"Mrs. Santis, how did you and Trisha pass your time together?"

Georgia has the presence of an Italian Edith Bunker. "We would cook Italian meals together. I taught her . . ."

Sebastian interrupts Mrs. Santis. "Thank you, what else?"

"I told her about the saints. We'd say novenas."

"Can you kindly explain to the court what novenas are?"

"They're prayers read from holy cards to saints or the Madonna asking for divine intervention."

"Madonna, the singer?"

"Oh no. Madonna, the mother of Jesus."

"Should I assume that statues are used?"

"Yes, the saint's statue was put on the table . . . if I had it. I don't have . . ."

Sebastian sinisterly grins and cuts her off. "That's enough. So, if I may, Mrs. Santis."

"Oh, please, call me Georgia."

"I'd rather be official; we are in court."

Georgia raises her finger to her mouth as if she understands. "Oh yes, of course."

"So, Mrs. Santis, I am not Catholic and the judge is not Catholic. I'd like to make this clear, especially for him." Sebastian smiles. "Please tell me if I'm making an accurate description."

Georgia nods and smiles at Trisha. Sebastian purposely positions himself between Trisha and Georgia to block any further eye contact.

"You and Trisha would chant over little statues reading from recipe cards."

"Holy cards."

"Yes, I'm sure they're *very* holy . . . Mrs. Santis, your son Rob was called Hat, is that correct?"

"Why yes, since he was a boy."

"Does the name have a religious connotation? Was he named after a holy beret or something?"

"No. My dad and Rob were inseparable. Dom worked two jobs. I worked at the ballpark. We saved for their college. . . . Dom's a fine man." Georgia looks at her husband and smiles.

"I see. It's all very admirable. . . . Could you please answer the question?"

Georgia raises her hand to her mouth trying to recall the question. "Oh yes," she says. "My dad died on May 26th. Rob was twelve. To Rob the world had ended. There would be no more . . ."

"Please, Mrs. Santis, it's all very moving; but please explain to us why your son was called 'Hat,'" Sebastian says impatiently.

"Rob slept with my dad's old hat. He even wore it to school. The kids called him Hat. Father Gondolfo convinced him to leave it at home so he wouldn't lose it. He never lost the hat or the name."

"Tell us, Mrs. Santis, how do you explain the famous letters?"

"Why, it's a miracle."

"Your *wit*-ness," Sebastian said in a "here's Johnny" (Carson) style. Sebastian pretends to putt as he walks back to his chair.

The reporter, Lou Sherman's face is stone. Aaron has his head down. The judge dismissed Georgia, who whispers to Trisha as she passes. Trisha nods and smiles. Sebastian glares meanly.

"It's getting late. Are there any further witnesses?" The judge asks.

Patrick rises. "Sir, I'd like to call Mr. Howard Abbott."

Sebastian leaps out of his seat. "Your Honor, Mr. Abbott's a captain of industry. It would be humiliating to have him testify in this way. It's unnecessary."

"Does he wish to testify, Mr. Danahy?" Judge Cohen asks.

"Sir, it was his idea."

"Counselor Sherwin, I'm sure you don't object, seeing it was Mr. Abbott's own idea."

"Why . . . no." Sebastian responds nervously.

Chapter 14

The Court Calls Howard Abbott

"The court calls Mr. Howard Abbott."

The courtroom hums as Mr. Abbott walks up.

A spectator whispers to another, "He's more powerful than an atom bomb."

The other spectator whispers back, "He's called from the White House before any big industry decision is made."

Howard raises his right hand and puts his left on the Bible.

"I do," he says, loudly and equally proudly.

A few reporters go to the hall to call their papers. "That's right!" one screams, "Ol' man Abbott's taking the stand! Block the space! I got to get back in there!"

The bailiff swears in Mr. Abbott.

Patrick stands.

"Mr. Abbott, I have only one question for you. Do you believe that your daughter Trisha can capably handle her own affairs?"

"I do."

The court buzzes.

"Your witness," Patrick says.

Sebastian asks several general questions about Abbott Electronics and handles Mr. Abbott delicately. "Mr. Abbott, how many employees does Abbott Electronics have?"

Patrick stands up. "Your Honor, we all understand that AE is one of the pillars of American industry. We concur with Mr. Abbott's seriousness, but . . ."

The judge interrupts. "I agree. Mr. Sherwin, it's late. We accept Mr. Abbott to be a serious businessman. Can we proceed?"

Sebastian is losing his patience. "Mr. Abbott, after this case, will your daughter get the best psychological care available?"

"Frankly, I haven't pondered it, though you might consider it . . . for yourself, that is," Mr. Abbott says calmly.

The courtroom spews laughter.

Judge Cohen hits the gavel. "Answer the question please, Mr. Abbott."

"I thought I had."

The judge emits an *it's late, give me a break* expression toward Mr. Abbott.

"I don't believe my daughter requires help, mental or other."

Trisha looks fondly at her father, who looks lovingly back.

"Please, Mr. Abbott. You are aware that Trisha claims to receive letters from Rob Santis?"

"Yes, I am."

"You're aware that the letters are dated after his death?"

"I am."

"Mr. Abbott, handwriting experts have testified that these letters could only be the work of a master forger. Are you aware of this?"

C winks at Joey.

"I am."

"Mr. Abbott. Do you know who this expert forger might be?"

"I don't know any expert forgers."

"That's not the question. Do you know who forged these letters? I remind you that you're under oath!"

Howard suddenly loses his backbone. He seems to become nervous.

"Mr. Abbott! *Who forged these letters?*"

"No one."

"Excuse me, sir? That's impossible!"

"Is it, Mr. Sherwin?"

"Mr. Abbott, I have one last question, and then we can all go home. Who wrote those letters?"

The courtroom is paralyzed.

"Rob, Hat Santis," Mr. Abbott states calmly.

The reporters head out. The judge bangs the gavel. "Court reconvenes Monday morning!"

ピ ピ ピ

It's Friday evening. Aaron's in a suite with Taylor. Aaron stands, looks in the mirror, and adjusts his tie.

"So, the solution is, the children and the companies merge. It's a cure-all."

Aaron finishes tying his tie and turns. Taylor is staring at him in the mirror.

Aaron says, "Don't worry, sweets. I'll find time for us. After all, it's not natural for man to be monogamous. In the Eastern civilizations, it's a part of life. In the West, we're Puritans or hypocrites, wealthy men have mistresses and the johns marry and divorce two or three times."

"Do you love Melissa?"

Aaron runs his hands through his hair.

"Do you love her?"

"She-she-she's a piece in the puzzle."

"What about her? Does she love you, or are you just a piece of a puzzle?"

He looks to the side and breathes deep. He nods. "She loves me."

A tear forms and falls gently from his eye as he looks at the girl.

Taylor looks at Aaron as a mother might. "Do you know what love is?"

Aaron half-smiles and rubs his face. "No, tell me, what is love?"

"It's a tool that we women use to tame a man's wandering heart." Taylor turns. "I shouldn't be here. The money is needed for my education, but I'm still a fool."

"You're no fool." Aaron walks over and hugs her.

"Maybe men aren't monogamous. But I don't believe that a woman can truly give herself to someone that she doesn't believe she can hold," Taylor says.

Aaron walks toward the door.

Taylor stops him. "No, I'll go first. You wait and contemplate."

"Contemplate?" Aaron asks.

"Yes, contemplate this: after passion dies, love is." She gently closes the door.

Friday evening, Mary and Irv are at home in the front room.

"Going to temple or church with me will be a sham if you deny God."

"Don't be foolish. This is about money, not about God."

"You'd make a poor martyr, denouncing God because of popular opinion."

"God is not on trial here!"

"He *is* on trial, and you have a chance to be a guiding light."

"Please. Just tell me when dinner's ready!"

"There's leftovers in the fridge." Mary stands and leaves the room.

🖋 🖋 🖋

Later Friday evening, Aaron's smiling and watching TV in the Abbott Mansion den. His mother enters.

Ingrid is holding a newspaper. "That horrible cartoon is me? I'll sue them!"

"You'd lose; there's a striking resemblance," Aaron responds.

Aaron follows his mother as she huffs into the hall.

"I can't take it! Our life is one big scandal. Your father says that AE may fall."

"What does he? . . ."

Ingrid interrupts, "Your father knows more than you think."

Aaron looks in her eyes and takes her wrists in his hands. "Did you say something to him? What does he know?"

"Aaron, you're hurting my wrists."

"Mother, have you ever lost something that was more important to you than yourself?"

"You're crazy! I demand you let me go!"

"Mother. I'm going to marry Melissa."

"Insanity's rampant in the Abbotts!"

"Do you know why, Mother?" Aaron smiles sinisterly.

"I said to let me go!" Ingrid screams.

"Mother, I'm not like you, and, you know, the other day, the *instant* I realized it . . . was the happiest moment of my life."

His mother glares at him and spits in his right eye. "You're part of me! You can't change that!"

"NO! NO! NO!" Aaron screams.

Ingrid is seriously concerned. Such a display of emotion from a well-to-do man is alarming.

Aaron continues, "*I may be part of you, but I am not like you!*" Tears fall from Aaron's eyes.

Ingrid's face has transformed into that of the Wicked Witch of the West from the *Wizard of Oz.* "Have it your way, Aaron. You'll both be two has-beens!"

Aaron hangs onto his mother's wrists and slouches over, leaning on the back of a leather couch. He's mentally and physically exhausted.

Ingrid looks over at her only son. Though she had hoped that someday he would be strong like her, he is in the end, only an Abbott. She feels a slight bit of pity but is in survival mode. "Aaron, I had hoped to get some funds from you. With the hole you've dug, it wouldn't even be missed."

Ingrid shakes her arms. She could easily unlock his grip but appreciates the irony of the situation. And after all, her son must toughen up. "I have something important to tell you. Let go of my arms."

Aaron looks queerly.

"Washington killed Santis."

"What?"

"That's right, he pushed him with his car into oncoming traffic."

"You're crazy."

"Am I? Ours is the third car."

Aaron is entranced. "But why?"

"Your father wanted to help you. Santis would have eventually challenged you. Your father knew that you'd be no match for his kind."

Aaron releases his mother's hands and stares forward in a trance. Ingrid calmly pours herself a drink.

☙ ☙ ☙

It's 8:10 Saturday morning. Sebastian is writing notes in his office. Jonathan walks in.

Sebastian stares at her. "This is crucial. Can I read this out loud to you?"

"It's my dream come true."

☙ ☙ ☙

Saturday morning, inside the Cohen home, Irving is reading a law book in his front room. The phone rings. He waits and grabs it after four rings. "Marva. How's my girl?"

"Father, you should temporarily appoint an outside trustee until this shakes itself out."

"Why would I appoint an outside trustee? Abbott's more than able."

"Father, there's something not right. Her father . . ."

Irving interrupts, "I admire her father for perjuring himself, it was very touching. But she's acting foolish."

"Are you telling me that you know what is happening? Are you telling me that we should incapacitate every religious person?"

"Well, honey, I'd rather not . . . Honey? Honey?"

Irv looks at the phone and places it back to his ear. "Marva?" There is no response. He hangs the phone up. It rings again. A smile comes to his face as he picks it up. "Marva, the line fell . . ."

"No Father, it was me."

"It was you? Why? You never hung up on me before."

"I did it for your own good, Father. You need to do some soul-searching."

"Well, yes, of course, honey. We all do."

La La La

Back in Sebastian's office, the clock now reads 11:55 a.m. Sebastian is standing, Jonathan is sitting.

"Where was I? Oh, yes. Delusions are a mild form of mental illness with a high cure rate."

Jonathan yawns, picks up a pen, and begins doodling.

Sebastian notices. "You can take notes, no drawing!"

La La La

Irving has not left his home all morning and it's now afternoon. He's pouring a drink. The phone rings. He picks it up. It's his sister, Sharon. Irv smiles into the phone. "Hello Sis . . . Sharon, I'm gonna put you on the speaker, I've had the phone to my ear all day."

Irv places his drink on his desk and sits down.

"We're proud of you, all of us," his sister Sharon says. "Ma always said that you were the chosen one because of your wisdom."

"That's great. Chosen for what?"

"Those atheists are too much. They've become a militant group, like MeToo, LGBTQ, and BLM. They are not solving problems. They are dishing out cruelty and dividing us to gain money and power. Someday God will destroy this pagan planet and start anew," Sharon emphatically states.

"Sharon, really I . . ."

Sharon interrupts. "Brother, I know that it takes courage to be in your position. And I called"—she begins to sniffle—"because I wanted you to know that we're all by your side. We love you, big brother."

La La La

It's Saturday evening in the Abbott Mansion den. Ingrid is sitting. Howard is standing over her.

"You'll hurt yourself in the end," Howard says.

"Will I? Really, Howard, I think you miscalculated."

"Ingrid, what do we have, twenty years? Why not save the savable?"

"It's too late. The ship's far out at sea and sinking. There's nothing left to save."

"It will sink for everyone," Howard says.

"Yes, and you'll get to watch your darling daughter. She will be the first to drown."

🌿🌿🌿

Late Saturday evening, Patrick's in his suit drinking with his friends in Kelly's Bar.

"Hey Patty," Mush says, "I never thought you'd be picked to defend Christ."

"He must be desperate," Mikey, the other bartender, says.

"*Mush*, I embraced this case to fight crony capitalism and atheism, the real rot of our great land. I'll fight until the end. My reward is the honor of carrying His banner."

Someone yells from the back of the gathering. "Amen!"

The rest of the bar joins in. "Amen, amen, amen!"

Toad raises his beer. "Here, here!" he yells. "To Patrick Danahy! The cream of the neighborhood."

Everyone in the bar raises their glasses. "Here, here!" the crowd yells. "To Patrick Danahy."

A teardrop slides off Danahy's cheek and into his beer mug. "It's true," he mumbles to himself, "the road to glory is paved with tears."

Patrick sips his beer and savors the unique taste of long-lost pride. The bar explodes with applause.

🌿🌿🌿

At the same time Trisha's lying on her stomach reading in bed. The door flings open, and Ingrid enters. She grabs Trisha by her hair. "You're getting on a plane, you, you wretched bitch! You play your father, but you'll not play me!"

Trisha whimpers, trying to remove her mother's hands.

"I'm glad Rob's dead! I only wish that I could've killed him with my own hands! You cheap tramp!"

116

Ingrid pulls Trisha to her feet. She looks into her daughter's eyes. "*When you spread your legs, you useless whore, you must be sure to capture something worth catching*!"

"Mother!" Trisha sobs.

Ingrid hears the door open and turns. Rebecca's punch lands accurately, knocking the contempt off of Ingrid's face. On her way down, Ingrid lets go of Trisha's hair.

Rebecca brushes over the Josie Natori Kimono sack. She hugs Trisha with the intent of the south wind in Mayo, Ireland. "You'll soon leave all this, honey." Rebecca squeezes the sobbing Trisha harder. "I promise you. Soon this will all be over."

Rebecca waits until the sobbing's hushed. She stares into Trisha's eyes. "When you leave, darling, don't forget your old Becky."

Trisha weeps. "Becky, I'll come soon. I promise."

Ingrid watches the scene from her throne on the floor. Her eyes sizzle with disdain, disrespect, deprecation, and denigration. Murderous vocal sounds seize the room. "You pathetic, gullible, simpleminded lunatics. I've lived through the winter in my spring, summer, and fall! I command the destiny of your pointless existence!"

Ingrid reaches into her kimono pocket. Rebecca smiles and squarely kicks Ingrid in the ribs. Ingrid grabs her chest and convulses uncontrollably.

Rebecca looks gently at Trisha. "Sorry honey, trick knee."

LLL

It's now 9:10 Saturday evening. Jonathan is sitting on an arm chair in front of Sebastian's desk. Her clothes are wrinkled. Sebastian's tie and jacket are off. He's staring at a small stack of papers. Jonathan studies him.

"She'll return to her devoted family with a clear idea of her life, a free mind to handle her own financial fairs . . . financial *affairs* . . ."

Sebastian grunts, looks at the lit skyscrapers and throws the sheets into the air. He falls to the floor with the sheets, gazing out the window and speaking to the night. "None of this matters! None of this matters! She'll seal her fate when she gets on the stand!"

Tears streak Jonathan's cheeks. Sleep deprivation allows her to land but a weary stare on Sebastian. The sheets of white paper lay beneath them like shreds of fragmented intent. Sebastian laughs uncontrollably.

LLL

C's sitting in the neighborhood club, staring blankly at the bar.

Joey walks up to him. "Hey C. What gives?"

C remains still.

"You should be happy. Did you see da papers? Dat whole family's history," Joey says.

"Yeah," C says halfheartedly.

"Hey, forget that rich broad. We'll do Layla tonight," Joey says.

"I don't want Layla," C says.

"Do you want Leann? Leann's hot and ooh, she knows how to grease the pole."

"Leann would do her father for a twenty-dollar hit," C says, "I don' want dat."

Joey puts his arm around C's shoulder, "Come on buddy, snap out of it."

"She's goin' back to Abbott. I know it. She tinks I'm a jerk."

"Is she goofy? Dat guy's finished. Let her go. Dey deserve each udder. We'll see how long it lasts when his cake's all gone."

"You don' understand Joey, she don' care about de cake. She did and does everyting for love."

"Hah!" Joey yells. "Call a doctor! Johnny Tito, call the ambulance! C says dat dere's a woman dat does something for love."

C rolls his eyes. "Joey, come ear."

Everyone in the club is staring at C. No one has ever seen him so somber. Joey moves next to him.

C puts his arm around Joey's waist, laying his head on Joey's stomach. "Joey, no more letters."

The club becomes quiet.

"Did you hear what I said?" C asks.

Everyone looks at Joey.

"Yeah, yeah, C, I heard what you said."

"What did I say?" C asks.

"You said 'no more letters'."

C pats Joey's back and softly squeezes Joey.

Chapter 15

The Truth?

At the Cohen home, late Saturday evening, Irv's face is drawn and tired. The speakerphone is on and Irv's sitting at his desk. He is listening and, as usual, not doing a whole lot of talking with his older brother Joel.

"And after, my little brother Irving, we'll talk about how the Cohens can contribute to defeat atheists, neo-Nazis, and all the other hate rabble. This could mean a big break for you, for us. It's time that all these idiot, selfish, shortsighted interest groups crawled back into their holes. It's time for decent folk, the real majority, to begin running this country again. You know, that's why Trump won the first time. Girl Boy Scouts, men going into women's bathrooms, men marrying men and women, women. What's next? Soon they'll be marrying their pets, their bicycles!"

Irving's relieved when his brother finally takes a breath. "Are you with me, Irving?"

"Yes," the judge says limply.

"Little brother, these people are a bunch of perverts. I mean, I don't give a damn what they do in their home, in their bedroom, but don't be forcing it down my throat and my kids' throats."

"Yeah, Joel, I'm with you," Irving says.

"You know brother, I can feel the world getting better. I think that Trump will get elected again after his four-year break and stop all these political wars and assassinations like Iraq and Syria. I believe that Russia and Ukraine will settle their border dispute. I believe that the right-wing nuts in Israel will come to their senses, stop stealing others' land, and end their apartheid state. And finally, I believe that morality will return to our great country."

Irving raises his hand to his mouth to cover a yawn.

"You must be tired. I'm sorry, little brother. I love you. I'll let you get some sleep. Give our love to Mary and Marva. Good night, my little brother."

"Good night, Joel."

Irving's finger is almost at the phone to turn it off.

"Oh, and little brother," Joel says.

"Yes?"

"We're all proud of you."

Joel closes the conversation. Irving hits the phone and breathes a sigh of relief.

$$\mathscr{L} \mathscr{L} \mathscr{L}$$

At the same time, in the Abbott Mansion den, Aaron's seated at the desk, his hands behind his neck.

His father's standing in front of him. "You'll be fine. Just let the company fall as it may. No one can control things now."

"Dad, you say it like it's so easy."

"There will be more help than you think." Howard smiles. "You know, son, I was not only a decent *businessman.*"

Aaron looks up at his father.

His father continues. "I was also a decent *man.* AE has done a lot of good for a lot of people. It will not lack supporters."

Aaron wants things to be just as his father says, but internal conflicts, various devils, and perceived reality are raining on his passage.

Aaron stands. "Dad, *there's nothing decent about murder.* And who will catch Mom?"

Aaron moves around the desk in front of his father.

Howard looks in his boy's eyes. "Son, if night falls, I'll absorb the dark."

"But how? You'll have your own problems to battle."

"I have a plan, son. I'll manage. It's my pleasure, and it's my duty." Howard looks warmly at Aaron. "Good night, son."

"Good night, Dad. . . . Dad, I love you." Aaron falls toward the ground, crying, and hugging his father's knees.

$$\mathscr{L} \mathscr{L} \mathscr{L}$$

Sunday morning, Lawrence Barr and Sebastian are sitting at Sebastian's regular table in Atwood's restaurant near Barr's downtown office and the courthouse.

"I sent Tillerson and Bicks our client list. . . . I still think that it's all for nothing," Lawrence Barr says.

"OK, Larry. Watch this." Sebastian takes his cell phone out. "Hello, Mr. Tillerson, Sebastian Sherwin here. Sir, I've instructed Counselor Barr as you asked. . . . I see . . . I see . . . Well, of course, sir . . . Yes, sir . . . Thank you, sir."

Sebastian stares blankly for five seconds.

"Well, are we in?" Lawrence Barr asks.

Sebastian continues to stare in shock.

"Sebastian, I know a lot more than you think, but be honest: Was writing those letters necessary?"

Sebastian does not answer Lawrence Barr's question. Instead, he stands, as if in a trance. "They blew me off."

Barr's eyes move as an elevator would from the second to the first floor and finally to the basement. He couldn't care less about the answer to his question, about the letters, or about anything else.

"That was my last chance," Barr mumbles.

They are absorbed in the wretched situation. Suddenly a light goes off in Barr's head and he begins talking loudly to himself. "That Edgeview Bank used offshore accounts and screwed the IRS while dealing in Andrew Industries stock. That's going to put me into the chips. Our government pays informants generously."

Sebastian hasn't heard a word, but the bug under Sebastian's table did.

Lawrence smiles to himself and then looks at Sebastian. "You know, people say that you'll get with Ingrid Abbott when this ends. . . ."

Sebastian gets up groggily and starts to walk. "She's old and . . ."

Lawrence interrupts, "And rich."

"Go screw yourself, Larry," Sebastian says.

Lawrence tilts his drink glass to his lips as Sebastian walks away.

"Wish I could," Lawrence says, "I wouldn't leave home."

Lawrence is feeling chipper. He orders another drink. Informing to the IRS is the silver lining for him. He grabs his phone and looks up Andrew Schwartz. Not only was Andrew a big guy in the Washington DC office on Constitution Avenue, he was also a distant cousin.

Always fascinated with the law and laws, Lawrence hesitates and ponders the Racketeer Influenced and Corrupt Organization (RICO) ACT, Affirmative Action Laws, Hate Crime Statutes, and the Patriot Act. What we have become . . .

Illinois passed Drew's Law in 2008, allowing hearsay as evidence, and we were now actually rewarded for snitching on one another. The nation was unrecognizable and as a consequence of these and other laws, filled with slimy cowards. And fortunately for him, he would become one of them. . . .

Lawrence downs his drink and walks to the bathroom. Two men in dark clothes follow him. One winks at the waiter who comes and stands at the bathroom door. Punches and grunts are heard. Lawrence's bloodied head falls under the stall door. He's making noise—unconscious, not dead.

"Now go to the IRS. We'll kill you and all of your family."

Lawrence raises his hand. His vision is blurred. He sees fuzz. The men walk out.

✿ ✿ ✿

It's a dark and cloudy Sunday morning. C's in his car, parked between two buildings in the neighborhood. There's a person wearing a hood in the passenger seat. The hood covers almost all of the person's face.

"Now you wanna whack the chauffeur?" C asks. "Look, if dey ain't found him yet, dey ain't gonna find him. Don't get sucked in by all da television. Nobody gets caught. Dey fry twenty-five johns for twenty-five thousand murders a year. Just keep your mout' shut, believe me, the cops don't advertise unsolved murders in Chicago. Last year dere were eight hundred stiffs. You know how many murder convictions dere were? Less den fifty. It'll go away. Your real problem is da bank. . . . Dey won't give you no cake. I'm sorry. Dey say it's too risky."

The passenger's head slowly turns, revealing Ingrid's profile.

"You bastard! I'll go to the police."

"Yeah, take your friend Lawrence Barr wit' ya. He's another guy dat likes to snitch," says C.

Ingrid swings. C smiles and grabs her hair.

"You scum! I've done everything . . ."

"Yeah. Now get outta da car, ya low-life bitch."

Ingrid lunges at C. "You hood! I'm Mrs. Howard Abbott!"

"OK Mrs. Abbott. If dat's da way ya wan' it."

C opens his door and walks around to the other side. The rain is falling from his eyelashes. He drags Ingrid by the hair, and throws her facedown into a puddle. She stops kicking and swinging and begins to cry. C pulls his zipper down.

"Hey Ingrid. You remember ol' one eye?' I don' feel anyting for ya, but he feels sometin.'"

C's urine mixes with the rain falling on Ingrid's hair and face. C zips up, spits on her, and gets in the car and drives away. Ingrid rolls over weeping and again buries her face in the mud.

≈ ≈ ≈

Later that evening, Aaron and Melissa are holding hands across the table in Pizzeria Uno downtown.

"Things will be different," Aaron says.

"I like change," Melissa says.

"You'll be the wife of a struggling businessman. There's a chance that I won't be in on the AI and AE salvage plan.

"Who cares?" Melissa asks. "I don't."

"You know, I actually like pizza," Aaron says.

≈ ≈ ≈

It's early Monday morning. Irv turns over, but Mary's already gone. He holds his stomach and rises.

It's a sunny day, and outside the courthouse, protesters have spilled into the street, blocking traffic. Reporters are interviewing people and noisy helicopters are hovering above.

≈ ≈ ≈

In the Abbott Mansion kitchen, Aaron's drinking orange juice. His mother walks in.

"Aaron . . . about what I said yesterday."

"I didn't hear a thing."

"I'm leaving for good. . . . But before I do, tell me. Why would you let Sherwin convince you to write those letters?" Ingrid asked her son.

"Mother, your question unmasks the truth." Aaron walks out.

≈ ≈ ≈

Atwood's restaurant is packed. Every patron is speaking about the Abbott case.

Jimmy and Chucky are in one of the restaurant booths.

"Trib says that the brother wrote the letters," Jimmy says.

"Oh yeah, I say it was the atheist attorney," Chucky responds.

"Yeah, so does the *Sun-Times*, but when have they ever been right?" Jimmy asks.

"I heard Vegas got odds on it," Chucky says.

"Yeah," Jimmy says, "I'm rooting for the Santis kid to come through."

"Yeah, and bookies have wings," Chucky says.

The two smile at each other.

للل

In the courthouse, Joey and C are let in through an alley door by David the guard. He walks them to the courtroom and escorts them to two taped, empty seats.

Joey looks toward the front of the courtroom at Trisha, who's dressed in a light pastel dress. "She looks like such a sweet kid."

"You know, I . . . I don't know." C shakes his head.

"De mudder, she's da nut. Been goin' to Honest Larry Barr for advice and a divorce for years."

"Larry's not feeling well. He'll be on Tylenol for a few weeks. . . . Hey, de ol' bitch ain't here," Joey says.

"Probably in hiding waiting for da posse," C says.

"Whadda ya mean?," Joey asks.

C continues, "She tinks dat I had her chauffeur whack Hat. Trump's right: not only do the networks lie, but Hollywood, boy do dey got us convinced that right is left."

Joey shakes his head. "People watch too many gangster films."

"I'd kill myself before I'd touch Hat," C says, "and Joey, remember, *no more letters.* To hell wit it all."

Joey's face is a bit cringed and unsure. "You know C, I didn't write dose letters."

"*What?*" C asks loudly.

People turn looking at them.

"I din't. I was happy cause you was happy. You presumed it was me but it wasn't."

C slaps the top of Joey's head with a rolled-up newspaper. "Tell me da trutt."

"I swear on my mudder's grave. May she rot in hell if I'm lyin'."

C looks back at him puzzled, then smiles.

The guards begin to settle the crowd, hushing and scolding people who are talking. Aaron and Melissa make their way down the aisle. A few spectators scoff at Aaron.

Lou Sherman, the *Tribune* reporter, is leaning over behind where Sebastian's seated covering the bench back with his jacket.

The bailiff shouts. "All rise, this court is now in session. The honorable Judge Irving Cohen is presiding."

The judge walks out. "Please be seated."

The people that have a place, sit.

"Counselors Sherwin and Danahy, please approach the bench."

The attorneys rise. The court explodes with laughter. A heart and cross are chalked on the back of Sebastian's navy blue suit jacket. Sebastian, curious about the laughter, turns and looks. The judge sees the design and covers his smile with his hand. Irving looks at Mary. She is beaming.

"Gentlemen, has there been any progress toward a settlement?"

"No, Your Honor," Sebastian says.

"No sir," Patrick says.

"Very well, please take your seats."

The attorneys turn and return to their seats. Cohen looks around Sebastian and spots Lou Sherman. Lou has a childish yet devilish grin on his face. The judge gives him a stern look that turns into a smile.

"Miss Abbott, do you still wish to speak on your own behalf?" the judge asks.

"Yes, Your Honor," Trisha says gently.

"Please approach the bench."

Trisha opens her purse and takes out a folded hat. Georgia gasps.

"Oh my God, it's Rob's hat! Oh my God. I knew it."

"I saw them put dat hat in de coffin. Colletta de stiff director said it was buried wit da kid," Joey says.

"Yeah, it was de family's wish," C said, "and Colletta wouldn't grab a hat. A watch maybe . . ."

The room is silent as everyone tries to hear the conversation between the judge and Trisha.

"Your Honor, I have a request," Trisha says softly.

"Yes?"

"I'd like to make a statement and not be interrupted, if that's possible." Trisha says.

Judge Cohen nods. "That's an easily granted request."

The bailiff arrives. Trisha raises her right hand and swears to tell the truth. Every eye in the nation, in the world, is on Trisha Abbott.

"My family objected profusely to me and Hat. . . . but when Hat left, any hope of happiness left with him. . . ."

Trisha looks at Aaron. "It's not always easy to convince people of things that you feel."

Aaron smiles slightly.

"Hat promised to never leave me. I was upset that he had not kept his promise."

Tears roll over the smile on Georgia's face.

Trisha looks at Sebastian. "Mr. Sherwin, you tried to make it a physical awakening thing."

"I-I-I didn't say . . ." Sebastian stutters.

"Counselor, the lady has the floor," the judge says tenderly.

Trisha smiles at the judge. He smiles back.

"It wasn't that . . . we fit together like two halves of a circle. The night of his funeral, I curled up on a chair in my bedroom. Hail was tapping against the window. The tapping seemed to play a melody. I got up and checked the radio. When I got back, Hat was sitting in my chair. He pulled me into his arms. He told me to stop mourning. He put me in bed, kissed me, and told me that soon we'd be together forever."

Trisha looks in Becky's direction. "I told Becky about it. She told me that I was dreaming." Trisha wipes tears from her eyes and laughs.

Trisha looks back at the judge. "I thought so, too. But the emptiness was gone. I felt that I had something to look forward to. I actually hid my joy at work so that people didn't think I had flipped."

The whole courtroom is mesmerized.

Trisha looks at Becky and continues. "After about a week, I found a letter on my nightstand. Becky was worried. She couldn't understand what was happening. But there's something that she didn't tell you. One night she sat on a chair outside my room. After a while, she heard Hat's voice. She rushed in. He talked to her too."

Becky looks solemnly ahead and nods.

"Hat told her that the rest of her life would be peaceful, that when she was called to leave the feast, she'd do so elegantly."

Patrick wipes his brow. Sebastian is fighting to remain in his seat.

"When Grandmother died, Hat assured me that she was fine. But I never personally spoke to her. We did have a two-day visit a week before. . . . Grandma was a real practical joker."

Aaron looks curiously.

"I told Aaron that I'd donate money to Tuesday's Child. It terrified him. He puts a high value on wealth."

Howard is brushing away tears in the back of the room.

"Hat knew about Aaron's scheming. He asked me to be patient. I'm glad that I can tell you how I felt."

The window shows an ugly rain and gusting wind.

"I'm not here to tell you to become religious fanatics. But it's just not about money."

She takes a hem of her dress in her hand. "This is my wedding dress, simple and elegant at the same time, just like my Rob."

Cohen looks at his wife. Tears are streaming down her face.

The room is growing darker.

"I talked to my grandmother about Hat and Tuesday's Child. She went to an attorney to draw up her will. I promised to keep quiet about it all. It's true that I inherited all her assets. But she had already given everything except her apartment and $100,000 to Tuesday's Child on the stipulation that they give her a generous allowance that ceased to exist the day that she died. This is all legal. It was handled by Sheldon Sparks and Harmon Bicks from Tillerson and Bicks. Grandma's known Mr. Bicks for some time. Says that he's a real card and preferred him to her old attorney, Mr. Barr."

Sebastian's face transforms as Trisha speaks.

"So, we're here to fight over $100,000."

⚜ ⚜ ⚜

People outside the courtroom are taking refuge from flying debris. The sky is black. Wind smashes out one of the courtroom's main windows. The courtroom lights go out. There are screams as people bolt to the door. The lights flicker a few times and then remain on.

Judge Cohen watches Trisha as she calmly walks toward the opening where there was once a window.

"Guards, hold Trisha Abbott!"

Guards run up behind Trisha and grab her. Her body jerks trying to free herself. "Hat! Hat! Please, please! Hat!"

She's held to the ground but continues to struggle and scream. Paramedics race in. One of them prepares a syringe. In the background, other guards have entered and are clearing the room.

Georgia screams, "Rob came for her. *Let her go! Let her go!*"

Sebastian turns to Georgia. He's smiling broadly. "The farce has ended, you old superstitious witch!"

Sebastian turns to his assistant. "Look, Jonathan, I told you! It's all a farce!"

Sebastian turns to the guards and Trisha. "Let her go! What's she going to do? I'll tell you! She'll fall out the window! Let her go," Sebastian says mockingly.

Dominic approaches Sebastian as Trisha's sobs fade into the background.

The judge notices Santis approaching Sherwin. "Mr. Santis, there will be no violence in my courtroom."

Dominic smiles, but he keeps coming. "I'm with him. I don't go for all dis mumbo jumbo. I just want to say sometin'."

127

Dominic reaches to shake. Sebastian hesitates and then clasps his hand. Dominic takes Sebastian's shoulder with his left hand and looks in Jonathan's direction.

"In my neighborhood girls have girls' names. Is she a he-she?"

Sebastian cringes with pain. Dominic lets him go. Sebastian grasps his right hand with his left hand. "Oh, oh my hand, my hand!"

Dominic looks at him and smiles. "That's for my son, Hat."

Two guards walk up behind the Santis family. A crowd forms around the paramedics and Trisha. She's semiconscious and mumbling, "Hat, Hat."

Chapter 16

The For Real

Dominic and his family walk out. The halls are empty and quiet except for a few stragglers and a guy with a transistor radio mopping the hallways.

🌿🌿🌿

A week passes, and Jimmy and Chucky are in Gayle's Restaurant.

Jimmy's reading the newspaper. Chucky is dabbing at his eggs with wheat toast.

"The government's gonna bail out AE and AI," Jimmy says.

"If me and you went broke, they'd send a collection agency," Chucky says.

"There's a lot of jobs at stake," Jimmy replies.

"And the fat cats walk away with the cash," Chucky tosses back.

"It says they'll have to answer to a consumer advisory board," Jimmy says, "that will keep Abbott off the front page of *Fortune* magazine for a while."

"I'm going to cry, let's start a collection," Chucky says.

Jimmy puts a quarter in his glass and jingles it. "Anyone want to help out Howard Abbott and Blake Andrew? We're taking a collection."

A few people laugh.

🌿🌿🌿

It's 7 a.m. at the Chicago-Read Mental Health Center. The hallway is clean and friendly, decorated with various bright paintings.

A middle-aged male nurse is whistling. He pulls a set of keys from his waist. He stops and sticks them into a stainless steel windowed door. He opens it. The room is empty. He inspects the windows. They are locked, closed, and intact.

He looks at the strange hat on the bed and walks out. "Oh my God," he says to himself.

⚘ ⚘ ⚘

Almost a week later, Mary is at home watching ABC local news.

"Today the Department of Industry chose Aaron Abbott as the head of the Andrew Industries–Abbott Electronics restructuring project. But authorities still have no clue on the whereabouts of his sister Trisha Abbott, who disappeared from the Chicago-Read Mental Health Center without a trace five days ago. Just vanished into thin air. The family has no comment and does not suspect foul play."

At the same time Georgia is at home listening to WSFI Catholic Radio.

"This is Radio Maria on WSFI Catholic Radio. Trisha Abbott disappeared on August 15th, the Assumption of the Blessed Mother. Coincidence? We think not."

C and Joey are in C's car by Armour Park listening to K-hits, 104.3.

"Hey C, will dere always be guys like us?" Joey asks.

"Joey, as long as all of da head honchos running da corruptorations are sendin' dere kids four to six years to doze idiot universities, dey'll need guys like us to straighten tings out after dey fuck dem up."

Bo Reynolds, the DJ, comes on. "Well Chicago! Chicago-Read Mental Hospital still can't find their most famous patient, Trisha Abbott. Trisha, here's one for you wherever you are: *It's Your Time* by Patrick Girondi."

It's your time, it can't be wrong
Better learn to sing dat song
Been hurt before, we all have you see
Stung before but still want honey

Don't worry, tomorrow starts in the morning
And he's sporting a new pair of dancing shooooes
That cloud overhead's about done raining
Time to get happy and chase away all of your blues.

Afterword

Where are they today . . .

Aaron and Melissa are married. Melissa's pregnant with their first child. Besides heading the AE/AI reconstruction project, Aaron's on the Board of Directors of Tuesday's Child.

Rebecca died in her sleep at the Cabbage House on September 12th, the feast day of the Blessed Virgin.

Howard Abbott retired and is overseeing construction of a new building at Tuesday's Child.

Sebastian is still wearing a cast on his right arm and is often seen in the company of his rabbi. He's been fired from his firm and is a fervent supporter of his local synagogue.

Ingrid Abbott is always incognito. Her story is no longer important to anyone, and she most certainly is not hiding from shame. But she's definitely hiding. She's not really missed.

For the believers, Trisha and her betrothed were reunited by a miracle that mankind can neither touch nor see nor understand, and for the nonbelievers, no explanation can suffice.

The End.

Blind Faith: Screenplay by Patrick Girondi

INT. WEDNESDAY 10 A.M. ANTHONY'S HAIR SALON—WATER TOWER—CHICAGO

A SHOT FROM ABOVE. ANTHONY'S BUSY YET EXCLUSIVE SALON. MEN AND WOMEN ARE SITTING UNDER DRYERS GETTING THEIR NAILS DONE AND THEIR HAIR HIGHLIGHTED.

THE CAMERA FOCUSES ON A HANDSOME 30ISH GENTLEMAN WHO'S UNDER A DRYER READING THE *WALL STREET JOURNAL*. AARON ABBOTT.

IN THE BACKGROUND ANTHONY, 50, THIN AND BALDING, IS TALKING TO CLIENT, 80.

> ANTHONY
> (Italian accent) Oh Mrs. Stern,
> it's perfect. I told you that red
> was your color.

> MRS. STERN
> Do you really think so? We have
> the opera tonight. I'd just die if
> I didn't look perfect.

> ANTHONY
> Mrs. Stern, when they see you,
> they'll put you on the stage.

She croons as Anthony sails to the next chair.

CLOSE-UP OF PHONE HEADLINE IN AARON'S HAND: ANDREW INDUSTRIES LOSES INVESTOR CONFIDENCE

Anthony arrives at his chair.

> ANTHONY
> Oh Mr. Abbott. You should be done.
> Reading again? (Whispering in
> Aaron's ear) Do you have a tip for

134.

me, Mr. Abbott? The 3 stocks you
gave me are working like a charm.
You're the best.

Aaron mechanically stands up, revealing a slender
figure of 6'1. He's elegantly dressed in a brown
suit with a beige shirt, a large blue tie, and
large gold cuff links. His face is drawn. He looks
through Anthony in shock.

Clients look in his direction. A few whisper.
Anthony notices, he takes out a comb and picks at
Aaron's hair.

                    ANTHONY
          This is your color. These blond
          highlights turn you into another
          Brad Pitt.

Aaron reaches into his pocket and hands something
to the cute brunette (Taylor) who is putting away
the tools and ingredients from his stay.

Aaron creeps forward in a walking coma.

                    ANTHONY
          Please Mr. Abbott, let me finish.
          You still need a cut and style.
          You can't leave looking like this.

Aaron looks back, as if looking for someone, and
then walks out. Anthony watches. Others stare as
Aaron walks out the door. Anthony hurries to Taylor.

                    ANTHONY
          (loudly) He likes you, honey. What
          a catch, he's one of America's
          most eligible bachelors. Abbott
          Electronics is one of the largest,
          best run corporations in the
          state, maybe in the country.

She whispers something to Anthony. His eyes open wide in disbelief. He captures his composure and slaps his hands.

>   ANTHONY
>   Go and pull Miss Pritzker from
>   under the dryer or she'll roast.
>   (under his breath)
>   My own salon and I'm still the
>   last to know the dirt.

INT. WED 10:10 A.M. THE LONG HALL WITH ESCALATORS THAT SPAN TWO FLOORS IN THE WATER TOWER PLACE

Aaron checks his pocket as he approaches the escalator.

AT THE ESCALATORS

Aaron's heading down the escalator in the busy mall. Two old socialites, Mrs. Kittle and Mrs. Albright are coming up on the other side, whispering and looking at Aaron descending toward them. Aaron notices them. He looks away to avoid being spotted. Suddenly one of the women bubbles and waves.

>   MRS. KITTLE
>   (loudly) Aaron, Aaron Abbott.

>   AARON
>   Oh, hi Mrs. Kittle, Mrs. Albright.

Aaron nods his head slightly.

>   MRS. KITTLE
>   (huge, fake smile) Aaron, remind
>   Mum about the CIC Auxiliary
>   meeting on Friday.

> MRS. ALBRIGHT
> And do tell Melissa that we said
> hello.

The pair wave down at Aaron who reluctantly waves
back. Mrs. Kittle turns to Mrs. Albright, speaking
in a low tone.

> MRS. KITTLE
> Didn't you hear? He's not with
> Melissa. He disappeared a few days
> before the wedding.

> MRS. ALBRIGHT
> I know, I just couldn't resist.
> I hope he tells Ingrid, that witch
> of a woman he calls his mother.

> MRS. KITTLE
> He's a cad, and everyone knows it.

Mrs. Kittle and Mrs. Albright turn in to Anthony's
salon.

INT LAWRENCE BARR'S OFFICES, SAME TIME

SEBASTIAN SHERWIN, a neatly dressed 35ish man, lowers
the *WSJ* from his face and smiles widely.

LAWRENCE BARR, neatly dressed and 55ish, takes the
paper from him and lays it on the desk.

> LAWRENCE BARR
> I doubt if Aaron's ol' man knows
> how much of Andrew Industries
> stock Abbott Electronic is holding.

> SEBASTIAN
> It's not something I'd volunteer.
> If it comes back, he's a genius.
> . . . If not, he's an idiot. . . .

Sebastian shakes his head gently.

                    LAWRENCE BARR
          What was he thinking?

                    SEBASTIAN
          The share price kept falling, and
          he kept doubling up.

                    LAWRENCE BARR
          He was engaged to Andrew's only
          daughter. Why didn't she warn him?

                    SEBASTIAN
          That's why he dumped her. He
          thought that her family double-
          crossed him . . .

                    LAWRENCE BARR
          Did they?

                    SEBASTIAN
          I've been waiting for seven
          years . . .

Lawrence looks cautiously.

                    LAWRENCE BARR
          I'm divulging privileged client
          info. How's Abbott's situation
          going to help me?

                    SEBASTIAN
          One hand washes the other. At
          her age, Grandma Abbott won't be
          generating a lot of hours. And
          you've *always* sold to the best
          bidder.

Sebastian shrugs his shoulders and smiles.

                    LAWRENCE BARR
          Who sold him all the stock?

138.

                         SEBASTIAN
          Why do you hate Luellyn so much?
          She must really have you under her
          heel.

                         LAWRENCE BARR
          I'll get mine when she passes.

                         SEBASTIAN
          Yeah, the feisty old hag doesn't
          take counsel from anyone. It's
          a shame that her grandson,
          Aaron, doesn't have some of her
          astuteness.

EXT. WATER TOWER PLACE, MICHIGAN AVE 10:30 A.M.

Aaron waves down a cab, looks at his watch, and
meticulously gathers his jacket as he's getting in
the door.

                         AARON
               1150 North La Salle. Quickly.

The meter starts and cab takes off. Aaron fixes his
hair.

INT. OFFICES OF JUDY O'BRIEN PUBLIC RELATIONS 11:15 A.M.

Judy's 50ish. She's sexy with large eyes and streaked
hair. She's at her desk with a female assistant,
Tony, who's standing about 10 feet away.

Aaron storms in.

                         JUDY O'BRIEN
               (surprised) Aaron! How was your
               trip? Hey, don't you have the
               luncheon for the president elect
               in fifteen minutes?

                    AARON
Did you see the article on Andrew
Industries?

                  JUDY O'BRIEN
I heard something. What's it got
to do with us?

                    AARON
(stutters) Us? Nothing, but you
know how the press loves to
crucify me. My ex is an heir.
They'll try to mix me in somehow.

                  JUDY O'BRIEN
You're still worried about Melissa
talk? Aaron, calling off a wedding
isn't *that*—

                    AARON
(stutters) No, it's not that.

                  JUDY O'BRIEN
Why else should you be mixed in?

Aaron's quiet.

              JUDY O'BRIEN (CONT'D)
Aaron, skeletons. As CEO of AE
you'll be in the spotlight. I can
only protect you from what I know.
Clinton's people found out first
and eliminated oral sex as a
sexual act. I need time to
prepare. Got it? I can't protect
you from what I don't know.

Aaron removes his hand from his pocket and rubs
his forehead.

              JUDY O'BRIEN (CONT'D)
What do I have to pull you out of
this time?

                          AARON
              (offended) This time?

Judy waits for an answer as Aaron gets visibly
irritated.

                     AARON (CONT'D)
              Just do some damage control on
              this Andrew thing. . . . I'll hold
              up my end.

Aaron starts to walk out.

                     JUDY O'BRIEN
              If you really want to hold up your
              end, you should think twice about
              leaving town to avoid gossip about
              ex-fiancées. It was your idea!

              I'm just an adviser. You're still
              responsible for your own actions.

As Aaron is walking out . . .

                     AARON
              That's what I pay you for!

Tony, Judy's assistant, watches him leave.

                     TONY
              That guy could be in the movies.

                     JUDY O'BRIEN
              He plays his cards right, he'll go
              from president of AE to president
              of the country.

                     TONY
              He's a doll. I'd vote for him.

                     JUDY O'BRIEN
              He's our client, you'd better vote
              for him.

INT. STAIRS LEADING TO THE CONRAD HILTON BALLROOM, NOON

Aaron is bouncing up the stairs. Sebastian is watching him from below.

INT. BALLROOM

An attractive young girl greets Aaron with a name label.

> POLITICAL AIDE
> Hi Mr. Abbott, can I tag you?

> AARON
> Of course.

Sebastian butts ahead in the line almost to Aaron. He's confronted by another attractive political aide.

> SUSAN, ANOTHER POLITICAL AIDE
> May I have your name, please?

Sebastian glances ahead at Aaron.

> SEBASTIAN
> (loudly) Sebastian Sherwin.

The aide goes through her file.

> SUSAN
> I'm sorry sir. You must be on another list. One moment, please.

Aaron moves away. Sebastian starts to follow.

> SUSAN (CONT'D)
> Sir . . . Sir. (louder)

Sebastian looks back.

                    SEBASTIAN
          Don't worry, damn it! I'll send a
          check.

Sebastian scans and disappears into the crowd as
the aide looks around for backup.

INT. BALLROOM, CON'T

The room's filled with men in business suits and
scattered gorgeous female assistants. There are
two long tables on either side of the room with
appetizers and four bars.

Aaron walks around the crowded room cautiously. He
spots Governor Rauner who is 70ish and overweight.
He's surrounded by four people. Aaron reaches his
hand in to him.

                    GOVERNOR
          Mr. Abbott, good to see you.

                    AARON
          Governor, as always you can count
          on AE.

They shake hands.

Sebastian barges into the group. His back's to
Aaron, and he aggressively grabs the governor's
hand.

                    SEBASTIAN
          Governor! It's been a while.

                    GOVERNOR
          Yes . . . yes it has . . .
          Mr. . . .

                    SEBASTIAN
          Sherwin, Sebastian Sherwin.

                    GOVERNOR
      Oh yes . . . Of course . . .
      Mr. Sebastian.

                    SEBASTIAN
      Sebastian's my first name.

                    GOVERNOR
      But of course, Mr. Sherwin. This
      is Aaron Abbott of AE.

The governor turns. Aaron looks at Sebastian. He
hesitates.

                    AARON
      I know Mr. Sherwin.

Sebastian reaches for Aaron's hand. Aaron hesitates, then shakes. Sebastian looks at the
governor.

                    SEBASTIAN
      We're old friends, Governor . . .

The governor smiles.

                    GOVERNOR
      Well, we'll need a lot of old
      friends to win this one. . . .
      We all need friends.

                    SEBASTIAN
      If you only knew, Sir . . . *If you
      only knew.*

A young attractive woman in a suit interrupts the
group.

                    POLITICAL AIDE 3
      Mr. Abbott. You have an urgent
      call on the house phone.

144.

> AARON
> Excuse me, Governor . . .
> Mr. Sherwin.

> SEBASTIAN
> Aaron, I'll be at the bar.

Aaron is on the verge of blowing Sebastian off.

> SEBASTIAN (CONT'D)
> We need to talk, Aaron.
> Something's come out of the
> closet.

The governor moves away. Aaron lamely nods at
Sebastian.

INT BALLROOM HALL WEDNESDAY 12:30

Aaron's on the phone.

> AARON
> Mother, my cell's dead. . . .
> I know, Mother, I know. And
> I thank you. I'll find a suitable
> escort . . . I know you do,
> Mother. Oh and Mother . . . have
> you? . . . never mind.

He hangs up.

BALLROOM MOMENTS LATER

Sebastian's by the crowded bar with a drink in
his hand. He notices Aaron walking toward him and
quickly turns.

> AARON
> All right Sherwin, what gives?

Sebastian turns.

                    SEBASTIAN
          Remember Machiavelli, generosity
          can work against you, especially
          with politicians.

                    AARON
          Cut the bull, Sebastian.

Sebastian looks to both sides.

                    SEBASTIAN
          It's seven years, friend. Seven's a
          lucky number.

                    AARON
          Yes Sherwin. I've got things to do.
          Don't waste my time.

                    SEBASTIAN
          We all have things to do,
          Aaron. . . . It's a tough break
          about your engagement.

                    AARON
          Oh? Who's your lucky other half?

Sebastian's eyes narrow.

                    SEBASTIAN
          Your attitude's changed. . . . Once
          I was quite important to you.

                    AARON
          Don't waste my time. What do you
          want?

                    SEBASTIAN
          It's payback time Aaron, baffling
          how things find their way into the
          funny papers. . . . Rape's not
          fashionable.

An amused grin forms across Aaron's face.

                         AARON
              Oh, is that all? Blackmail?

Sebastian doesn't flinch.

                       SEBASTIAN
              I'm here to help you.

                         AARON
              Oh? How could you possibly help me?

                       SEBASTIAN
              Your star's rising. Every rising
              star needs someone to protect its
              path.
              We wouldn't want you hitting any
              meteorites. . . . They could blow
              you into little pieces. . . .

Aaron looks on impatiently.

                   SEBASTIAN (CONT'D)
              On the road to progress there are
              fifty guards to pass. . . . When
              the dealing gets dirty . . . and
              it will . . . who can you trust?
              Are you forgetting who I am, Aaron?

Aaron aggressively moves in closer to Sebastian.

                         AARON
              Who you are is of minor
              importance. What is of major
              importance is that you don't
              forget who I am.

The two are interrupted by a stubby freckled man
in glasses.

                          MAN
              Looks like Blake Andrew, the CEO
              of Andrew Industries overplayed
              his hand this time.

>   AARON
>   I don't know, he's a shrewd
>   player . . . he'll come out of it.
>   AI's as solid as a rock.

The man smiles, then looks a bit confused.

>   MAN
>   So was Silicon Valley Bank.

The governor walks up to Aaron.

>   GOVERNOR
>   Aaron, my office will call to
>   schedule a lunch.

>   AARON
>   That will be fine, governor.

The governor walks away. Aaron turns to Sebastian.

>   AARON (CONT'D)
>   My work here is done. Good luck to
>   you, Sebastian.

He walks out. Sebastian is among the crowd looking
lost.

He sees the girl that he promised a check to and
ducks out.

INT RESTAURANT IN NEIGHBORHOOD EARLY EVENING

C is 45ish, balding with average looks. He's nervously pacing in front of a table for two that is
elegantly dressed in the not-so-elegant restaurant.
C's rubbing his hands and puffing.

A short man of about 50 walks to C with an apron
in his hand.

>   BENNY
>   C, do I really have to put this on?

C picks up a napkin and pursues Benny with it.

                    CERONE
          Damn you, Benny! I told you it's
          Mr. Cerone!

He hits Benny over the head and Benny blocks the
napkin.

                    BENNY
          Sorry C . . . sorry . . . Jeez,
          I never seen you like this before.

C stops and gazes. Benny looks on and smiles.

                BENNY (CONT'D)
          Is this the one? Have you finally
          met Mrs. C?

C looks at Benny. There are tears welled up in his
eyes.

                BENNY (CONT'D)
          Oh C. I'm so happy for you.

Benny hugs C. C shrugs him off. Benny clears his
throat.

                    BENNY
          Juan! Ramon! Put your aprons on!
          Andale!

Benny winks and smiles warmly at C. He tries to
embrace him. C puts his arms out.

                    CERONE
          Don't try dat kissy stuff again.

Benny steps back.

                    BENNY
          (in an imitated Italian) But
          of course-a Mr. Cerone . . .
          Everything will be-a perfect.

Benny turns and claps his hands.

                    BENNY
          Move boys. Everything must be
          perfect for Mr. Cerone. . . .
          I'm so happy.

EXT. ABBOTT MANSION-CABBAGE HOUSE EARLY FRIDAY
MORNING

THE DRIVE RUNS UP TO A CLASSICALLY SOUTHERN-LOOKING
MANSION. FOUR HUGE PILLARS SUPPORT THE OVERHANGING
ROOF. NEXT TO THE MANSION IS A SEVEN-CAR GARAGE.
NEXT TO THE SEVEN-CAR GARAGE IS A TINY BRICK HOME
(THE CABBAGE HOUSE).

INT. CABBAGE HOUSE

Rebecca is an Irish imitation of Mammy from *Gone
with the Wind*. She's wearing a housedress and a
handkerchief. She's happily straightening out sofa
pillows. A yell comes in from another part of the
house.

                    TRISHA
          Becky! Where's my brown pullover
          sweater?

Rebecca raises her hand to her mouth and squints
her eyes.

                    TRISHA (CONT'D)
          You know. The one that Rob lent me
          that he (said-cute singsong) never
          got ba-ack.

Rebecca looks on in confusion and slight concern.

                    TRISHA (CONT'D)
        Is it still in the hamper?

Rebecca snaps her finger and rushes out of the room.

INT. CABBAGE HOUSE FRONT ROOM MOMENTS LATER

THE CAMERA FOLLOWS REBECCA UP INTO A HALLWAY.

Rebecca knocks on a door. It opens a crack, and
Rebecca hands in the sweater. A voice comes from
within, the shower's on.

                    TRISHA
        Thanks, Becky. Was it in the
        hamper?

                    REBECCA
        It's clean. In twenty-eight years
        you never got a dirty sweater from
        me, Trisha Abbott!

INT. ABBOTT MANSION FRIDAY, SAME TIME

THE CAMERA MOVES INTO THE LAVISHLY FURNISHED HOME
PEPPERED WITH BUSTS OF ANCIENT ROMANS. THE DRAPERY
IS GAUDY, AND THE HOUSE RESEMBLES A HISTORY MUSEUM.

A woman's yelling. A MAID panics out of the kitchen
door.

THE CAMERA MOVES FARTHER TOWARD THE KITCHEN.

Howard Abbott's in his 50s. He's bulky and resembles Karl Malden. He's standing half in and half
out of the doorway.

THE CAMERA MOVES FARTHER IN

Ingrid Abbott could pass for 35. She's perfectly
beautiful and doesn't have a hair out of place.

                    INGRID
          (scornfully) He what? This is your
          fault. You're not a man! You can't
          control your own son! Now we're
          ruined!

                    HOWARD
          (calmly) You're exaggerating. One
          of his investment's hit the rocks.
          It happens.

She throws a vase. Howard calmly moves to the left
as it smashes beside him. She picks up another.

                    HOWARD (CONT'D)
          (calmly) That's a 40,000 dollar
          Martinuzzi. If it breaks, I'll
          deduct it from your allowance.

                    INGRID
          That's all you have. Without your
          money, you're a void. Even with it
          you can't make me love you. . . .
          (scornfully) You're repulsive.

                    HOWARD
          (calmly) Thank you for the
          repulsive. Now get ready. Aaron
          will be home soon.

Ingrid remains still. Howard smiles and turns away.
His smile drops, and he frowns remorsefully. As he
walks away there is the sound of something metallic hitting the wall.

A phone rings. Howard answers. His expression turns
mournful. He hangs up and walks into the kitchen.
Ingrid sees his expression.

                    INGRID
          What?

INT. CABBAGE HOUSE BATHROOM MOMENTS LATER

Trisha pulls sweater over her head

She's in her mid-20s with sandy blonde hair and a
slender boyish figure. She brushes her hair over the
sink, counting each stroke.

                    TRISHA
          8,9,10.

She pulls her head up and gazes at a picture that's
stuck to the mirror.

THE CAMERA TAKES IN THE PICTURE

Trisha in the arms of a man in a baseball uniform.
On the bottom corner it reads: TRISHA & HAT FOREVER.

INT. TRISH'S ROOM MOMENTS LATER

The room is a tomboy's room. There are sports items
decoratively placed. Her bed is plain. In a neat
pile on her dresser are a small stack of letters
and trinkets.

THE STACK OF LETTERS

She enters, picks up and opens the top letter.

                    TRISHA
          Rob . . . Hat . . . Please answer.

She searches the room, then reads the letter, cries
a little, folds it, and lays it down. She composes
herself and bounces into the hallway. Rebecca's
waiting at the bottom of the stairs.

                    REBECCA
          Did you brush your hair?

Trisha doesn't respond. She tilts her head in a half nod as Rebecca continues to look on sternly.

>   REBECCA (CONT'D)
>   Did you count?

Trisha half nods again.

>   REBECCA (CONT'D)
>   You know with the arthritis in
>   my hands it's hard to brush your
>   hair.

>   TRISHA
>   Yes, I counted.

>   REBECCA
>   Will you be home for dinner?

Trisha grins.

>   TRISHA
>   What will you make me?

>   REBECCA
>   You ain't no colicky baby no
>   more, young lady. You eat what I
>   prepare.

>   TRISHA
>   What will you make me?

>   REBECCA
>   (melting) What would you like,
>   honey?

Trisha descends the last stairs and hugs and kisses Rebecca.

>   TRISHA
>   Oh I love you, Becky.

> REBECCA
> I love you too, honey. . . . Don't
> forget I leave for my cousin's
> tomorrow.

> TRISHA
> I know, two days, I'll try to
> survive.

Trisha heads to the door with an envelope in her hand. She opens the door and yells back to Rebecca.

> TRISHA (CONT'D)
> Love to find some of that Irish
> stew! I'll be home about 7.

The door closes.

AARON'S OFFICE FRIDAY MORNING

Maps of the Roman empire cover the wall. The couch and chairs are rough aged leather. His desk is mahogany and huge. He has a magnificent view of the skyline and the lake.

Aaron is speaking very seriously to Sebastian.

> AARON
> It's bull, no one protects us from
> women who brutalize and humiliate
> us. The damage can be very similar
> to that of rape.

> SEBASTIAN
> That's all well and good but . . .

> AARON
> Once it was scandalous to kiss on
> the first date. Today's casual sex
> only becomes rape if you forget to
> call them the next day.

                    SEBASTIAN
     Forget all that . . . we've got
     trouble if this gets out.

                    AARON
     They love playing victims. They
     run around like bitches in heat
     and then want to blame the last
     dog that jumps off.

                    SEBASTIAN
     (impatiently) You're going to be
     the CEO of a Fortune 500 company.
     Perry works at the *Reader News*.
     He's down and out. It'll just
     be chump change. Closure Aaron,
     closure.

Aaron nods, Sebastian leaves. Aaron remains seated
gazing around from item to item on his office mantel.

PICTURES OF AARON GOLFING WITH GEORGE W. BUSH.

Aaron hits a switch. Aaron's secretary, Megan,
walks in.

                    MEGAN
          Yes, Mr. Abbott.

                    AARON
          Do I have any calls?

                    MEGAN
          No, Mr. Abbott.

She leaves. There's a pause. Aaron hits the switch
and she returns.

                    AARON
          Any appointments?

                    MEGAN
          No, Mr. Abbott.

AARON
Would you ask my father if he
needs me to attend to anything?

MEGAN
He's not here, sir.

AARON
He's not here? Where is he?

MEGAN
I don't know sir, I'm *your*
secretary.

Megan leaves. Aaron punches buttons on the phone.
Phone to his ear, someone picks up on the other
end.

AARON
Let me speak to my father please.

After a pause, his father picks up on the other
end.

AARON (CONT'D)
D-dad, I need to talk to you.

There's a long pause. Aaron's expression turns to
shock.

AARON (CONT'D)
When is the funeral?

He hangs up, gazes out the window with a look of
relief. He hesitates, opens the door, and walks out.
His secretary has her back to him and is speaking
with a young man in a suit.

MEGAN
Then he asked me if his father
needed him for anything . . .
that's a good one.

The suited male notices Aaron and quickly walks away. The secretary looks and attempts a smile. Aaron walks past them.

INT. FUNERAL HOME NEXT DAY

Crowded. Aaron, Trisha, and Howard are accepting condolences. An elderly woman attempts to kiss Aaron. He takes her hand and shakes it.

                    AARON
          Thank you, Mrs. Rose.

The woman passes. A young woman walks up to Trisha.

                    YOUNG WOMAN
          How's that boyfriend, Trisha? I'd
          love to get a look at him. I heard
          that he's stunning. Where's he at?

                    TRISHA
          He's fine, but I don't see him now.

The woman smiles and moves on. Aaron shoots his sister a concerned look. A young woman approaches Trisha.

                    YOUNG WOMAN 2
          So sorry, first Rob and now your
          grandmother. Stay strong.

                    TRISHA
          Debbie, you know the ring is only
          severed temporarily. Eventually
          it's joined forever.

Trisha smiles, Debbie grins queerly. Aaron turns to Trisha.

                    AARON
          When will the will be read, Sis?

She annoyingly shrugs. Aaron, Trish, Ingrid, and Howard approach the casket. After a few moments Aaron nervously turns to his father.

                    AARON
          (whisper) Dad, I need to talk to
          you about Andrew Industries.

                    HOWARD
          This isn't the time . . .

Aaron shows concern. Howard puts a hand on his shoulder.

                    HOWARD (CONT'D)
          Son, things will work out for the
          best.

ABBOTT MAUSOLEUM, CROWD DISPERSING AFTER THE FUNERAL

EXT. ABBOTT ESTATE LATER

The four Abbotts walk in the front door. The maid, Doris, collects their coats.

                    HOWARD
          Come into the den, kids. Have a
          refreshment with us . . . as a
          family.

Howard makes his way into the den.

                    INGRID
          A family? Really Howard. All
          people have relatives. Very few
          have families.

Howard stares. He's not used to philosophical Ingrid.

                    INGRID (CONT'D)
The beginning of the end for the
weak, like you, was that Whitney
Houston song, "The Greatest Love,"
love for yourself. . . . It was
liberating for people like me.
Family?

Ingrid heads up the stairs. Trisha turns down the
maid's offer to take her coat.

INT. DEN   22

Trisha and Aaron follow Howard. Howard pours himself a drink and offers one to an antsy Trish.

                    TRISHA
        Dad, why don't you come over to my
        house?

                    HOWARD
        Another time. I'm beat. Why don't
        you stay here tonight? Spend
        tomorrow relaxing.

                    TRISHA
        I have to work, Dad.

                    HOWARD
        Your grandmother just died; they
        can do without you for a day.

                    TRISHA
        No, they can't, actually.

                    HOWARD
        Trish . . .

                    TRISHA
        Good night, Dad, Aaron.

Trisha leaves. Howard takes his drink and sits while Aaron is standing and waiting patiently.

> HOWARD
> Now, Aaron. Can't this problem wait?

EXT PARKING GARAGE MONDAY MORNING

Sebastian runs to Aaron's car with an opened magazine in his hand. Aaron opens the window and looks down at the article.

> AARON
> I've already seen it.

> SEBASTIAN
> I can do something about it.

> AARON
> It's too late. It's already out.

> SEBASTIAN
> I can make sure that you won't be smeared again. Every writer in the country will fear you.

> AARON
> How will you manage that?

> SEBASTIAN
> Aaron, it's true that I abhor religion. . . . But I am Jewish, we have considerable influence in the media . . .

Sebastian smiles broadly.

> SEBASTIAN (CONT'D)
> Leave it to me . . . OK boss?

Aaron looks on, hesitates, and then smiles.

                    AARON
        Do you need a lift?

                  SEBASTIAN
        No sir, I need to tend to this.

Sebastian raises the paper and reaches his hand
out to Aaron.

              SEBASTIAN (CONT'D)
        I'll bill AE as legal fees . . .
        Deal?

Aaron hesitates then takes Sebastian's hand.

                    AARON
        Deal.

Aaron drives away. Sebastian heads for the exit
door.

                  SEBASTIAN
        Yes!

INT NEIGHBORHOOD BAR WEDNESDAY MORNING

There's a fat man (Glum) behind the bar. Three
customers are scattered in front. C walks in wearing sunglasses. His ringed fingers tap on the bar.
The bartender walks over and whispers in his ear
glancing at one of the patrons who's watching television.

                    CERONE
        Hey Jeb.

The 60ish man looks from the television to C.

                    JEBSON
        Oh . . . Hey C . . .

Jebson's neck twitches nervously.

                    JEBSON (CONT'D)
          Didn't see you come in.

                         CERONE
          Your Honor's off today huh?

Jebson nods.

                    CERONE (CONT'D)
          How you hittin' em?

                         JEBSON
          C, I couldn't pick the winner in a
          one-horse race.

                         CERONE
          I got steam at da Glades track.

Jebson strains his eyes, and his neck twitches.

                         JEBSON
          I'm all ears, C.

                         CERONE
          "Oops He Fall Down," in the 5th.

Jebson smiles.

C turns to walk away, then turns back.

                    CERONE (CONT'D)
          Oh, and Jeb, give it to da
          judge . . . tell him dat dere may
          be sometin' comin.'

                         JEBSON
          Got it, C. Thanks, C.

C turns and waves the bartender toward the stairs
that lead to the basement. He turns back to Jeb.

> CERONE
> Hey Jeb.

Jeb squints through the dimly lit bar.

> CERONE (CONT'D)
> Don't even tink about gettin'
> it off on our guys. Go hit the
> Off Track Betting guys. Wit dis
> frickin' mayor, Lord knows dey can
> afford it.

Jeb nods his head, his neck twitches simultaneously. C and Glum head toward the stairs. In the
background one of the customers (Porky) is going
around the bar. Once behind, he yells to C.

> PORKY
> Hey, C!

C turns.

> CERONE
> Whadda ya want, Porky?

> PORKY
> It's dark out. Why you wearin'
> sunglasses?

> CERONE
> I'm an eternal optimist, jagoff.
> It's always sunny to me.

C AND FAT GLUM DISAPPEAR DOWN THE STAIRS.

They enter the basement. Glum turns the radio and
television on. Only loud static is heard. He whispers to C.

> GLUM
> The Rams saved us.

                    CERONE
          I thought so. Is 26th Street in?

                    GLUM
          Yeah, I tink Bippo's eatin' the
          long shots again. One out of two
          of his ponies are hittin.'

                    CERONE
          Tell Friar Tuck to make Bippo
          repent.

                    GLUM
          What if it's on the level?

                    CERONE
          It ain't. His daughter just got
          married. He's short.

The bartender reaches under his T-shirt and hands
a manila envelope to C, who winks and walks up the
stairs.

The bartender turns the television and the radio
off. He listens for a moment. Then he smiles.

                    GLUM
          Hey you sissy faggots wanna hear
          something? Listen to dis.

The bartender lets out a loud long gasser.

                    GLUM (CONT'D)
          Frig ya's, drink it up.

The bartender heads up the stairs.

INT MINIVAN PARKED DOWN THE STREET FROM THE BAR.

Two AGENTS with headphones are listening.

                    MAN 1
     I never heard anything like
     that. . . . Was that human? You
     get anything?

                    MAN 2
     Only static, a flat toot and the
     "frig ya's" drink up thing.

                    MAN 1
     I can't wait to burn these tough
     guys.

INT. ABBOTT MANSION DAY

ART PIECES AND THE HEAD OF CAESAR IN THE HALL.

HALLWAY CONTINUOUS. AARON APPROACHES A DOOR

The door's cracked open. Aaron knocks.

                    AARON
     It's Aaron. Can I come in?

                    INGRID
     Yes.

INT. INGRID'S ROOM SHORTLY AFTER

Enormous with one mirrored wall. Ingrid's walking
in and out of her wardrobe room holding outfits in
front of her. She lays some on a bench next to the
bathroom.

Aaron walks in and scans the room.

                    INGRID
     What can I do for you?

                    AARON
     I wanted to let you know that
     everything will be all right.

                    INGRID
          Oh?

Ingrid looks at her clothes.

                    AARON
          (stutters) Mom, if Andrew
          Industries falters . . .

Ingrid pays no attention to her son.

                    AARON (CONT'D)
          Mom, how long will it take to get
          our inheritance?

                    INGRID
          Your father takes care of those
          things.

                    AARON
          I didn't want to bother him. He's
          not . . . I think he's upset,
          about Grandma Abbott.

                    INGRID
          Hmpf. It doesn't matter much to
          me. I'll get nothing. An Abbott
          never forgets . . .

Aaron faintly smiles.

                    INGRID (CONT'D)
          Damn it! Where is that scarf?

She tears through a drawer.

                    INGRID (CONT'D)
          Doris! . . . Was there anything
          else you wanted, son?

                         AARON
                Nothing, Mother. Good night.

Aaron walks out.

HALLWAY

Aaron approaches a dark mahogany door, opens it,
and enters.

INT. AARON'S ROOM MOMENTS LATER

The room's divided into four parts: the bedroom,
bathroom, an office, and a foyer. He plops himself
in a leather recliner behind his elegant eighteenth-century desk.

He takes and unwraps a piece of gum, throwing the
wrapper onto the floor. He pushes his head back,
closes his eyes and smiles as he chews the gum. He
then takes out a pad of paper and starts writing
numbers. He dials a number on the phone.

                         AARON
                Give me a quote on Andrew Industry
                shares. I know that I can look
                on the computer, but I want the
                real market depth . . . how much
                do you think is offered at that
                level? . . . 10 cents higher?

He listens while jotting down numbers. He takes the
gum out of his mouth and sticks it onto the bottom
of the desk. He gets up. With his pants and shoes
still on, he lies on the bed. He smiles, reaches
up, and turns the light off.

EXT. PARK IN WORKING CLASS NEIGHBORHOOD NEXT DAY

A Cadillac slows and brakes. The passenger window
rolls down.

                    CERONE
          Hey, Joey P!

Joey Pitasi (short and 40ish) comes and sticks his
head in the window.

                     JOEY
          Hey C. What's up?

                    CERONE
          How's Hat's parents?

                     JOEY
          How could dey be? You know, I tink
          dose fag WASPs killed him.

                    CERONE
          I loved dat kid. Dose blue bloods
          sure didn't wanna pollute da
          line . . .

                     JOEY
          You said it. It's not about
          nationality or race. The wealthy
          want a closed club. You don't see
          no Kardashian with no poor dudes.

C throws a toothpick from his mouth.

                    CERONE
          You know, I been messin' wit
          Abbott's ex-fiancée.

Joey proudly grins and nods his head.

                CERONE (CONT'D)
          It's da least she could do after
          I got screwed wit her ol' man's
          company shares.

C looks out his window, shakes his head and looks
back.

                    CERONE (CONT'D)
If Abbott hadn't shown up we'd a
been sittin' pretty. It would a
been my biggest score. Millions,
Joey, millions.

                    JOEY
What did he exactly do, C?

                    CERONE
Joey, it ain't for you. It's
complicated . . .

Joey looks down and blows through pursed lips.

                    CERONE (CONT'D)
Get in, Joey.

Joey smiles and gets in. The windows roll up and
the car pulls to the curb. C starts popping nuts
into his mouth.

                    CERONE (CONT'D)
Melissa Andrew shows up outta
nowhere. She's feedin' me green
grass on her ol' man's company.
I start scoopin' Andrew Industry
shares. That's the company name.

                    JOEY
Yeah C, I know.

                    CERONE
When I had 50 thousand shares I
sold 'em to one buyer. It's called
parking blocks.

                    JOEY
Who'd you park 'em wit?

                         CERONE
          Relax. I started out wit Edgeview
          Bank and went out to some of its
          customers.

                          JOEY
          I'll bet you dat ol' Polack da
          owner loves ya for dat.

                         CERONE
          He'll get over it . . . I was
          gettin' 'em off at a profit every
          time . . . He was my silent
          partner and smilin' all da way to
          his own bank. Den super dick shows
          up . . .

                          JOEY
          Super dick's Aaron Abbott?

                         CERONE
          Yeah, Joey.

                          JOEY
          Maybe he found out you were
          plowin' his workhorse?

                         CERONE
          Joey, she's sharp. I mean, she's
          one of the few women I know who
          looks better with her clothes off.

                          JOEY
          Dey all look better wit dere
          clothes off to me.

                         CERONE
          Anyway. She never told Aaron about
          da trouble at da Ponderosa. She
          sucked me into da hole so her ol'
          man could escape.

                    JOEY
She double crossed ya?

                    CERONE
Absolutely. She knew about da
company headin' down da tubes
from her brudder or her ol' man's
confidant or sometin'.

                    JOEY
Maybe she was lighting the candles
on his birthday cake too.

                    CERONE
Joey, I don' know what she was
doin' . . . I ain't no head
doctor. . . . You know dese modern
broads. Dey dish it like it's
gonna run out some day. It's a
wonder anyone marries 'em.

                    JOEY
Yeah, if da milk's free, why buy
da cow?

                    CERONE
Nice Joey. You and your frickin'
euphemisms.

C smiles sarcastically.

                    JOEY
So dis chick sucks you in?

                    CERONE
In more ways den one.

                    CERONE (CONT'D)
Well, when I hear about lover
boy's merger idea I get nervous.

                    CERONE (CONT'D)
I ain't no chump. Da G will want
their end. Bribin' Janet Hollerin
would cost me all my profit. My
investors are nervous . . . Dey
want out.

                    JOEY
Ain't her name Yellen?

                    CERONE
Hey Joey, Hollerin, Yellen, same
damn ting to me. Wanna hear d'
story or edit my monologue?

Joey stares. C gets aggravated.

                    CERONE (CONT'D)
What? What?

                    JOEY
C, turn your monologue into a
dialogue.

C ignores the remark.

                    CERONE
I start sellin' to ol' lover boy.
He don' know who he's buyin' from.
He tought dat he was pickin' up a
K-Mart blue light special.

C slaps his hands together and shows Joey his
palms.

                    CERONE (CONT'D)
We're clean. Da Polack owner's
nervous about da G but I made a
few. Within a week I won't have a
share left.

Joey looks on in admiration.

                    JOEY
          Nice C . . . Nice.

A police car beeps. C rolls the window down.

               POLICE OFFICER
          Hey C, the G's by the park. I'd
          move on.

                  CERONE
          Tanks Nets.

C waves and rolls the window up. The police pull
                    away.

                    JOEY
          You gonna move?

                  CERONE
          Screw him. . . . He just wants
          to make sure he gets his egg for
          Easter, the suck ass. What did
          poor Tony B ever do to get a son
          to turn cop?

                    JOEY
          It's a shame, C . . . but it can
          happen in da best of families.

                  CERONE
          I guess. But Tony B's such a
          great guy . . . anyway, it ain't
          over . . . Numbnuts finds out dat
          his girl's been holdin' out on da
          info.

Joey squints.

                    JOEY
Numbnuts is Aaron Abbott?

                   CERONE
Of course, but she didn't know dat
he was accumulatin' stock. She
wasn't tryin' to do him . . .

C breathes in deeply. He's remorseful but tries to
hide it.

               CERONE (CONT'D)
Dames. She's stiffin' me to help
her ol' man so she can be wit
Abbott.

                    JOEY
Why din't he tell her he was
buyin' da ol' man's shares?

                   CERONE
I dunno, he wanted to merge his
company wit hers. He tought dat
it'd be a powerhouse. And da
weddin' was still on. Maybe he
wanted to announce da merger as a
wedding gift.

                    JOEY
In da neighborhood dey just give
money . . . an' ol' man Andrew,
Melissa's fadder?

                   CERONE
He was happy. He didn't know why
his stock was active. I tink he
unloaded some.

                    JOEY
Which is what the conspirator
wanted?

C stares at Joey.

> JOEY
> Traitor?

> CERONE
> Hey Joey *fo guck yourself.*

> JOEY
> An' Big Howard Abbott?

> CERONE
> I don' know, but when he finds out
> it'll be a 911 call.

> JOEY
> And da government? What are dey
> gonna do?

Cerone looks on sarcastically.

> CERONE
> Today's markets are rigged tighter
> den JFK's assassination and d'
> weapons of mass destruction.
> Da G will be fishin' for months.
> Finally they'll find a scapegoat.
> He'll do a Vincent Walkin'
> fuckin' Foster.

Joey stares at C.

> JOEY
> A Vincent walkin' what?

> CERONE
> D' government had Foster popped in
> 1993. Our boys were in on it. It
> was beautiful.

JOEY
Why didn't you say a Jeffrey
fuckin' Epstein?

CERONE
I dint say a Jeffrey fuckin'
Epstein because the fuckin' G did
its own hit. We had nuttin' to do
with it . . . happy now?

Joey stares out the window.

JOEY
Yeah, now the government does
what dey used to trow us in
jail for doing; gambling, drugs,
prostitution, puttin' people to
sleep. . .

CERONE
Joey, hey Joey! Pay attention. You
know what dey'll do?

JOEY
What?

CERONE
What? What? Why dey'll trow da
American flag over it and get
praised by da press who are
owned by da same guys rigging
da markets, staging phony wars
and assassinating people an'
calling it suicide. Trump's right,
90 percent of it is fake news.

JOEY
Wow C . . . Den Hat, Abbott's
soon-to-be brudder-in-law, suddenly
dies.

Joey looks out the window, then he looks back at C.

                    JOEY (CONT'D)
Did somebody ice Hat?

                    CERONE
Joey, dat poor heart-throbbed kid
was a little pawn in da game. He
an' his broad don' know nuttin'.
Dey jus wanned to get married wit
da white wicker fence an all dat
shit. . . .

C looks confidently at Joey.

                    CERONE (CONT'D)
An' Melissa, she was tryin' to
stick me up. I ain' sore, it was
for a good cause an' all. But
I'm gonna stick dat silver spoon
of his up his ass and clean an
eyeball out.

C gestures to Joey, who opens the car door to get
out.

                    CERONE (CONT'D)
I wanna bury him. Dey'll find his
chest so full of dirt dat the
cornerer will have to use a sauce
spoon to get to lung tissue.

                    JOEY
    Coroner?

C's eyes flare. Joey raises his hands.

                    JOEY
Sorry. Sorry. I got dat mick alky
Danahy on de cuff if it goes
and I been humpin' his shrink's
secretary. . . . You got de good
judge . . . It's spades. . . .

C nods.

                    JOEY (CONT'D)
          And I know you read de
          papers . . .

                    CERONE
          Yeah. Granny's dead.

C's face turns hard.

                    CERONE (CONT'D)
          If dat fag tinks dat he's gonna
          ride up on some white scallion and
          swoop Melissa and her ol' man's
          company from me usin' his granny's
          inheritance, he's softer den baby
          shit.

                    JOEY
          C, I like dat Melissa. If it
          works out, maybe we could
          swap. . . . You try de shrink's
          secretary . . . she smokes a mean
          pipe.

                    CERONE
          Joey, you're hurtin' my feelins.
          I mean, I would've married
          dat broad. Who knows, I still
          might. . . .

C looks to the side.

                    CERONE (CONT'D)
          What's the secretary look like?

INT LAWRENCE BARR'S LAW OFFICE AFTERNOON

Trish, Aaron, and Howard are in front of Lawrence
Barr and Sheldon Sparks, a middle-aged lawyer.

                  LAWRENCE BARR
        Your grandmother went to Mr.
        Sparks to update her will recently
        when I was unavailable.

Sheldon smiles insincerely at Lawrence.

                  AARON
        (whispered) He means that she
        finally got wise.

                  HOWARD
        Shhh . . .

                  SHELDON
        Your mother was quite a woman,
        Mr. Abbott.

                  HOWARD
        Thank you, yes she was.

                  LAWRENCE BARR
        Before Mr. Sparks begins, does
        anyone want coffee or anything?

Everyone shakes their heads to decline.

                  SHELDON
        Mr. Barr. I'd like some water.

Lawrence rolls his eyes and leaves the room. Aaron's face is anxious. Lawrence reenters and hands a
smudged glass filled with water to Sheldon. Sheldon
sneers. He ain't drinking it.

                  AARON
        Can we just get on with this?

                    SHELDON
        (Clears throat) Put simply.
        Mrs. Abbott blessed some charities
        and left everything else to
        Trisha.

AARON'S STARING IN DISBELIEF.

INT THE ABBOTT MANSION IN INGRID'S BEDROOM WED
EVENING

Ingrid's fixing her hair and glancing at a news
clipping: WIFE OF FOUNDER OF ABBOTT ELECTRONICS
DIES

                    INGRID
        Why aren't you here to straighten
        things out? You old bat.

Knock on the door.

                    INGRID
        Who is it?

                    AARON
        Me, Mom, can I come in?

                    INGRID
        Yes, come in.

Aaron walks in and scans the room.

                    AARON
        Mom, we have to get that
        money . . . I can't maneuver
        without it.

Another knock on the door.

                    INGRID
        Yes?

All images are original paintings for *Blind Faith* by Megan Euker,
Acrylic on Board, 25 × 30 cm, 2023
Photo credit: Luigi Porzia

Rebecca Riley

Anthony Cristiano's salon

Hat's car crash

Patrick Danahy

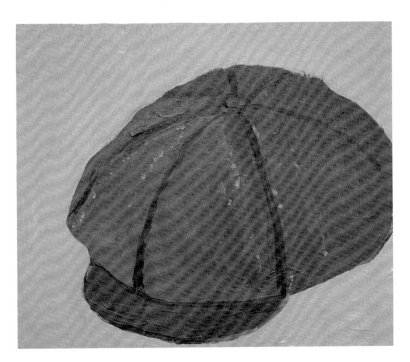

Hat's hat

Sebastian Sherwin at Abbott Family trial

Ingrid Abbott

Press outside of the courthouse during the Abbott family trial

Washington

C

Italian American Club, Chicago

Punchinello's Chicago

Abbott family mansion

The Cabbage House

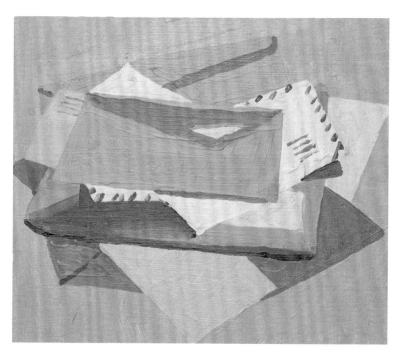

Trisha Abbott's letters

Georgia Santis

                    MAID
    Mum. A guest is arriving shortly.
    Mr. Abbott wants you to come down.

                    INGRID
    You tell Mr. Abbott that I'll be
    down when I'm good and ready.
    Hmph.

                    MAID
    Yes, Mum.

Aaron looks at his mother.

                    AARON
    Trisha's lost it. Giving all of
    Grandma's money away . . . letters
    from the dead . . .

                    INGRID
    Have the police found the third
    car in her fiancé's accident?

                    AARON
    (stutters) Why do you keep asking
    me? I don't know anything about it.

                    INGRID
    Son, learn from your sister's
    mistakes. One of the rules of
    class is to marry up. Doesn't
    matter what religion, race,
    breed they are as long as they
    have more money. If you don't do
    this, the protection of the elite
    diminishes.

Aaron raises his hands. His mother continues steamrolling.

                INGRID (CONT'D)
    Learn from the Kardashians. It's
    no scandal to mate with someone

outside your race, as long as
they're rich. You don't see any of
them marrying common folk. . . .
Now that would be a scandal.

> AARON
> (stutters) Mom. Please don't
> start on Melissa again. I screwed
> up. I-it's over. I told you, my
> interest is Andrew Industries, not
> Melissa Andrew.

Ingrid smiles approvingly.

> INGRID
> Son, if I'd have followed my
> instincts, I'd have been another
> Hillary Clinton. But I'd have won,
> damn it! I'd have won!

Aaron stares at his mother.

> INGRID (CONT'D)
> Your father always kept me on a
> leash. He'll see . . .

> AARON
> Mom, Sebastian Sherwin . . .

> INGRID
> I remember, the young man who
> kept you out of prison.

> AARON
> Mother, he's the arriving guest.

> INGRID
> Oh yes, Sebastian Sherwin.
> I hope that he's all that you
> say. We need to stop your sister
> effectively. She's our shame. . . .

AARON
She's our hope.

E/I BY THE SIDE OF THE ROAD WEDNESDAY EVENING

A STEEL BLUE BMW. SEBASTIAN'S SITTING INSIDE.

He's grooming his hair and mustache. He smiles in
the rearview mirror. The clock reads 6:58. He steps
on the gas.

HE PASSES THE ESTATE GARAGE WHERE A MAN DRESSED
AS A BUTLER IS UNDOING SOMETHING FROM ONE OF THE
LIMO'S FENDERS.

INT THE ABBOTT MANSION IN THE DEN SHORTLY AFTER

Aaron's hands are on the pool table. Howard is gazing out the picture window.

AARON
I don't enjoy this. Do you think
that it makes me happy to see
Trisha losing it?

HOWARD
She's mourning, just
mourning . . .

AARON
Please Dad. There's no hiding from
this . . . not this time. We can't
throw money at it and wait for it
to disappear.

HOWARD
How do you envision things
working?

AARON
(raised voice) Dad, Sebastian's a
strategic negotiator.

Aaron's hands move. He's speaking with heart.

                    AARON (CONT'D)
          He's here as my adviser. He'll
          cover our backs. It will be over
          before you know it.

                    HOWARD
          Aaron, she's not hurting anyone.
          Let it go.

Aaron shakes his head, half angered, half impatient.

                    AARON
          She's hurting herself! She's
          hurting us.

                    HOWARD
          (lovingly) Son, don't let money
          cloud your head. Someday you'll be
          my age. . . .

                    AARON
          Dad! Don't you get it? She's
          sick. . . . She doesn't talk
          to anyone! She's locked in the
          Cabbage House when she's not
          working with those retards. . . .
          She's receiving letters from her
          dead boyfriend!

                    HOWARD
          Look at the people that are
          governing our nation and the
          planet . . . The US government
          calls a bunch of hooligans a
          revolution . . . We're shooting
          down weather balloons to save our
          sovereignty . . . we're electing
          mentally challenged folks to
          congress . . . We've got a male
          claiming to be a female, serving

us as the assistant secretary for
health!

Howard stares into Aaron's eyes.

> HOWARD (CONT'D)
> If your sister, during her
> grieving, believes that she's
> receiving letters from the
> dead . . .

Howard looks at the floor, hesitates and nods before
continuing.

> HOWARD (CONT'D)
> And there's the money. Could be
> over a few hundred million . . .

Aaron is angry and losing his composure.

> AARON
> (stutters) That's right, could be
> several hundred million dollars,
> goddamn it! . . . Sorry.

There's a pause and then his father turns to look
at him.

> HOWARD
> Tell me, would we be meeting with
> this strategic negotiator if there
> wasn't all that money at stake?

> AARON
> (Almost crying, stuttering) Dad,
> you've got to give me a break. I'm
> doing my best for the family, for
> you. I won't let you down.

> HOWARD
> Son, I'd love to believe
> that. . . .

Howard ponders.

> HOWARD (CONT'D)
> The union proceedings cost us
> dearly.

> AARON
> I miscalculated! Must I be
> reminded every day of my life?
> It was over a year ago!

Aaron looks gently at his father.

> AARON (CONT'D)
> Please . . . I'll come through.
> No one will get hurt, no court,
> no mess. I'll take care of
> everything.

The two are interrupted by the maid.

> MAID
> Sirs. A Mr. Sherwin is at the
> gate.

> AARON
> Show him in when he arrives.

Aaron walks over to his father.

> AARON (CONT'D)
> Dad . . .

> HOWARD
> OK Aaron.

His father looks to the side and walks away without
speaking.

E/I OUTSIDE THE MANSION, SAME TIME

THE CAMERA'S ON THE CABBAGE HOUSE. REBECCA IS GAZ-
ING OUT A WINDOW.

She looks as Sebastian parks and walks into the mansion. She makes a disgusted face and jerks the drape closed.

INT THE ABBOTT MANSION IN THE DEN WEDNESDAY 18:10

SEBASTIAN IS BEING ESCORTED IN BY THE MAID.

He passes a mirror and adjusts his tie. The camera follows them into the den.

                    MAID
          Sirs, Mr. Sherwin.

Howard has his back turned. Aaron looks on.

                    AARON
          Thank you. Welcome, Sebastian.

They walk toward each other. Aaron puts his left hand on Sebastian's right shoulder and guides him.

                    AARON
          Let's have a drink. . . . Dad, do
          you remember Sebastian?

Howard turns slowly. Sebastian smiles in his direction. Howard looks solemnly and nods.

                    SEBASTIAN
          Well it's been over seven years,
          Aaron, though your father hasn't
          changed a bit.

It's quiet. Their attention is drawn by the entrance of Ingrid. She strolls in as if walking into a crowded ballroom.

                    INGRID
          Aaron, darling. This must be
          Sebastian.

Ingrid looks at Sebastian.

> INGRID (CONT'D)
> I don't remember the beard or
> mustache . . . but they do become
> you.

Sebastian walks to Ingrid and kisses her hand. She blushes.

> INGRID
> What a pleasure, a man of
> culture . . .

> SEBASTIAN
> It comes quite naturally,
> Mrs. Abbott.

Sebastian looks in Howard's direction.

> SEBASTIAN (CONT'D)
> You have such a lovely wife,
> Mr. Abbott. I see that you have
> the best of everything.

> HOWARD
> (grumbles) Yes, the best of
> everything.

INT SEBASTIAN'S OFFICE THURSDAY MORNING

Sebastian unloads a manila envelope onto his desk. He presses the intercom button as he traces over a letter with a pencil.

> SEBASTIAN
> Jonathan, get in here.

A pretty woman (Jonathan) in her 20s walks in wearing a gray business suit. Sebastian's head's down at his task.

                    SEBASTIAN
          Clear my calendar.

She appears confused. Sebastian continues to trace.

                    JONATHAN
          But you have the Hartford
          negotiation . . .

                    SEBASTIAN
          (Still with his head down) Screw
          Hartford. I got AE. Hartford's
          chicken feed.

Jonathan nods and walks out.

AARON ABBOTT'S OFFICE LATER THURSDAY MORNING

The intercom lights up as Aaron's reading at his
desk.

                    AARON
          Megan . . .

                    MEGAN
          Sir, Mr. Sherwin's here to see you.

                    AARON
          Wait sixty seconds, then show
          him in.

Aaron looks into a full-length mirror on the back
side of the door. He removes some lint, adjusts his
hair, and sits down.

Megan escorts Sebastian in. Sebastian gazes at the
oak walls and the marble floors.

                    MEGAN
          Will that be all, sir?

                         AARON
             Yes.

Sebastian continues to assess. At the same time he
sits in front of Aaron's desk. Aaron's observing
him.

                       SEBASTIAN
             I expect that you've finished?

                         AARON
             I'm finishing.

Sebastian looks on almost impatiently.

                       SEBASTIAN
             Negotiations are like arm
             wrestling. We press, she weakens.
             When the pain is too much, she
             drops. . . . Of course, there's
             always court.

Aaron is suddenly aroused.

                         AARON
             (stutters) That's not a
             consideration. Screw this up,
             Sherwin, and I'll have your head.

                       SEBASTIAN
             You may have to reconsider. . . .
             She needs to feel pressure, she
             needs to know that we know her
             little sins. She'll want none of
             them uncovered.

Aaron stares. Inside burns a bonfire the size of
Lake Michigan. Closes with Aaron gazing on Sebastian.

INT SUBURBAN TENNIS AND RACQUETBALL CLUB THURSDAY
3:30 P.M.

C and Joey are in racquetball attire. Joey has bracelets on each arm. C has a heavy chain and crucifix around his neck. They're waiting outside a court. Joey combs his hair.

> JOEY
> Ya know C . . . it's dangerous in dere. . . . If a guy swings wit de club, dere ain't nobody to stop him. Someone could get killed.

> CERONE
> You golf wit clubs. I told ya, it's a *racquet*.

> JOEY
> At a hundred smackers an hour, you're tellin' me.

> CERONE
> Shut up. He's coming.

> JOEY
> Of course he's coming. I told you, dey have de court at 3:30. Dese humps ever work?

> CERONE
> Shut up. (whispered)

AARON AND HIS OPPONENT ARE WALKING TOWARD JOEY AND C.

Aaron smirks at Joey and C.

> AARON
> This is our room at 3:30.

> CERONE
> Oh, the garcon must have made a mistake.

C looks at Joey.

CERONE
Mr. Pitasi? You did reserve de
abode for 3:30, did you not?

Joey looks confused as if he does not know what
to say.

JOEY
Yeah C . . . I mean I . . .

C reaches his hand to Aaron. Aaron hesitates and
shakes.

CERONE
Aren't you Mr. Aaron Abbott?

AARON
Yes, I am. Do we know each other?

CERONE
(Tense) No, well not really. I
mean I read about you, I'm an
investor.

A bell rings. Two sweaty opponents walk out. Aaron
smiles smugly and takes the door in his hand to
enter.

AARON
The room is legitimately ours,
Mr. Cerone. Good luck with your
investments. . . . And remember
the first rule of the market.

C gazes, confused yet interested.

AARON (CONT'D)
Don't play out of your league,
lowlife.

Aaron closes and locks the door. Joey looks at C.

                    JOEY
        I tink he knows who you are . . .

C stares, then he tugs at the door. Joey grabs him.

                 JOEY (CONT'D)
        C, don't make a scene. Melissa
        will find out.

Aaron turns and winks at C.

C tugs at the locked door.

                   CERONE
        (muttered under his breath) I'll
        kill him . . . I'll kill him . . .

INT C'S CAR ON THE EXPRESSWAY RETURNING FROM RAC-
QUET BALL CLUB

                   CERONE
        How'd I size up to him?

Joey squints and grimaces.

               CERONE (CONT'D)
        How'd you tink it went?

                    JOEY
        I don' know.

                   CERONE
        Whadda ya mean? Dat's why
        I brought you. Gimme de skinny.
        How do I stack up against golden
        spoon?

Joey hesitates.

                    JOEY
        You really wanna know?

194.

                    CERONE
        Of course.

                    JOEY
        Da truth? You won't get sore?

                    CERONE
        Me? No. I won't get sore.

                    JOEY
        Swear on your mudder?

                    CERONE
        Yes! Yes! Swear on my mudder.

                    JOEY
        OK. You promise?

C'S KNUCKLES TIGHTENING AROUND THE STEERING WHEEL

                    CERONE
        I said I promise. (lips pursed)

Joey smiles.

                    JOEY
        Swear on your mudder?

                    CERONE
        Swear.

                    JOEY
        OK. You promise? I don't know how
        to get back to d' neighborhood
        from here.

C's knuckles tighten around the steering wheel; his
lips are pursed.

                    CERONE
        I said I promise.

Joey smiles.

> JOEY
> OK. Here goes. He's got you by
> 20 years and has all his hair.
> He's fit and is a regular Charlie
> friggin' Plummer.

Silence as Joey looks at C.

> CERONE
> So . . . are you saying I'm ugly?
> I ain't ugly.

Joey stretches his lips and tilts his head. Hesitation.

> JOEY
> No, you're not ugly, C. I din't say
> dat. Some girls like older balding
> men. Maybe . . .

The sound of screeching tires.

A car swerves not to rear-end C's car

C makes a dead stop on the expressway shoulder.

> CERONE
> (seriously and calmly) Get out.

Joey opens the door and exits.

> JOEY
> Good ting you ain't mad.

The passenger door closes itself as C speeds off.

> JOEY
> You swore on your mudder! (voice
> muffled by passing cars)

196.

INT RACQUET BALL COURT THURSDAY 3:50

AARON IS PLAYING, LOSING BADLY.

Aaron runs toward the wall to return the volley. The ball hits the racket and ricochets to the floor.

                    AARON
          Damn! Damn!

Aaron pauses, tired and sweating.

                    OPPONENT
          Had enough, Abbott?

Aaron looks on without saying a word. His opponent picks the ball off the floor and serves it. It's almost a lob.

THE ANGER IN AARON'S EYES.

A SHOT OF THE OPPONENT'S BACK.

AARON'S EVIL EYES THEN GO BACK TO THE OPPONENT'S BACK.

Aaron swings with all of his might. You hear a yell.

                    OPPONENT
          Damn it! Oh, crap.

THE OPPONENT'S ON THE FLOOR HOLDING HIS BACK. AARON'S FACE DISPLAYS SATISFACTION AND REMORSE.

INT SEBASTIAN'S OFFICE THURSDAY AFTERNOON

Sebastian is at his desk with a client.

                    SEBASTIAN
          That's right, sir, that's why you
          hired me.

                    CLIENT
But your fees are preposterous.

                    SEBASTIAN
You signed my engagement contract,
and it was all spelled out, but
for the sake of diligence, let's
analyze your statement. . . . You
were willing to pay 10. Right?

                    CLIENT
Yes.

                    SEBASTIAN
I got you off for eight point five.
Correct?

                    CLIENT
Correct.

                    SEBASTIAN
Sir, my fees are more than
reasonable.

                    CLIENT
Does five hundred thousand dollars
sound reasonable to you?

                    SEBASTIAN
Would you like to know what it
sounds like to me?

                    CLIENT
Yes.

                    SEBASTIAN
It sounds like you saved a
million. Now of course if
you dispute this, I have the
means . . .

The client gets up and leaves, slamming the door.
Sebastian toggles the intercom.

                    SEBASTIAN
          Jonathan.

Within seconds the door opens and Jonathan walks in.

                    SEBASTIAN
          Did you finish Abbott's tape?

                    JONATHAN
          Almost.

Jonathan grimaces.

                    SEBASTIAN
          Almost? Almost? I don't like this,
          honey.

                    JONATHAN
          Look, Sebastian, Robbin's bogged
          down. I'm the paralegal for both
          of you. I'm doing the best I can.

                    SEBASTIAN
          I don't care about Robbin. Do you
          have any idea how much AE pays in
          legal fees a year?

                    JONATHAN
          No.

                    SEBASTIAN
          Do you care?

                    JONATHAN
          Well yes, I care but . . .

Sebastian signals to shut the door. She closes it.

                    SEBASTIAN
        (snide and low) Robbin is on her way
        out. Would you like to go with her?

                    JONATHAN
        No.

                    SEBASTIAN

        AE will be mine. Do you comprehend?

Jonathan timidly nods her head.

                    SEBASTIAN (CONT'D)
        Good.

Jonathan's face shows relief, and she turns to go.

                    SEBASTIAN (CONT'D)
        And Jonathan.

Jonathan turns back meekly.

                    SEBASTIAN (CONT'D)
        Aaron likes attractive
        women. . . .

Sebastian grins as he undresses her with his eyes.

                    SEBASTIAN (CONT'D)
        Do be a team player, will you?

He smiles. She looks blankly.

                    SEBASTIAN (CONT'D)
        Do you know who will be running AE?

                    JONATHAN
        Aaron Abbott?

Sebastian grins and turns his head slowly side to
side.

                    SEBASTIAN
          Ever see a man under pressure?

                    JONATHAN
          Why . . . yes.

                    SEBASTIAN
          Abbott stutters. He'll crack under
          pressure. . . . Do you know who'll
          be the all-important pressure valve?

                    JONATHAN
          No.

Sebastian raises his right hand and forms his fingers
as if they were around a valve. He turns them.

                    SEBASTIAN
          At times of crises, there is
          no one more important or more
          compensated than the pressure
          valve. . . . The power of AE at my
          fingertips.

Jonathan looks on and slightly nods.

                    SEBASTIAN (CONT'D)
          What name did you put on the file?

                    JONATHAN
          Abbott Electronics . . . Should it
          be Aaron Abbott?

                    SEBASTIAN
          No, (he begins to sinisterly
          laugh) it should be g-g gifts from
          h-h-eaven. Finish the tape, 40
          minutes.

                    JONATHAN
          Gifts from heaven, then.

She closes the door.

INSIDE CAFÉ BIONDA, A FANCY RESTAURANT, THURSDAY
EVENING

C and Melissa are sitting together. C is wearing a
blue Armani suit with a red Kiron tie. Melissa is
in a black pantsuit that fits her like a just-snug-
enough leather glove.

> MELISSA
> Why did you go and see Aaron?

> CERONE
> I just wanted to size him
> up. . . .

> MELISSA
> For what? Are you going to eat
> him?

> CERONE
> No, I . . . I . . .

> MELISSA
> (loud) One of those neighborhood
> things?

People are beginning to stare.

> MELISSA (CONT'D)
> I told you that I loved him!

Melissa stands up with her napkin in her hand.

> MELISSA (CONT'D)
> I told you, I needed time! . . .
> You make me laugh. You wanted
> to size him up! You don't want
> to sleep with me until we're
> married. . . . What are you, a
> Neanderthal?

202.

C turns his head, embarrassed.

                    MELISSA (CONT'D)
          And who said that I wanted to be
          with you, or sleep with you?

She looks coldly at him. Silence. She continues to
stare. C shrugs his shoulders.

                    CERONE
               No one.

                    MELISSA
               That's right. You give no respect
               to my feelings. You follow a set
               of primitive rules.

She throws her napkin on the table.

                    MELISSA (CONT'D)
               You're . . . you're a gorilla.

She stomps away. C rolls his eyes.

                    CERONE
               Waiter! Bring me a banana please.

INT GIBSON'S BAR AND STEAK HOUSE, SAME TIME

Sebastian and Aaron are sitting together.

                    SEBASTIAN
               Aaron, I got ten paralegals on
               this. Your notes are garbage.

                    AARON
               I gave you what you asked for.

SEBASTIAN'S EYES BECOME SLITS AS HE TRIES TO BE
EXPRESSIVE

                    SEBASTIAN
          I'm going to put this bluntly.
          I want to know when she lost her
          cherry and if she likes women.
          I want to know if . . .

                      AARON
          I don't know these things.

                    SEBASTIAN
          Then make them up. . . . Get me a
          hammer to use. If we can't settle
          we're going to court.

Aaron's face turns white.

                      AARON
          (stutters) It c-c-can't go to c-c-
          court.

Sebastian gazes strangely at Aaron.

                  AARON (CONT'D)
          (stutters) I promised my father.
          I—ttt c-an c-aan can't go to
          court.

                    SEBASTIAN
          Then we need to apply pressure.

                      AARON
          O-o-oK. OK.

                    SEBASTIAN
          You've seen tough negotiations.
          AE's last union debacle, when you
          guys almost took the tube . . .

                      AARON
          (stutters) I-i-it was unfair. The
          brass, our own br-br-brass joined
          the union against u-u-s.

                    SEBASTIAN
          You should've had a better broker.

Aaron hesitates.

                      AARON
          (stutters) I ran the negotiations.

Sebastian gazes and smirks at Aaron.

                    SEBASTIAN
          Was your sister really colicky?

A call comes in. Sebastian picks up the phone.
SEBASTIAN'S FACE, ANGRY AND NERVOUS.

                    SEBASTIAN
          Yes . . . I told you to never call
          me personally.

Sebastian hangs up. Aaron looks anxiously, hoping
to please.

                      AARON
          My mother moved the nursery to
          the Cabbage House because of it.
          Trisha grew up there.

                    SEBASTIAN
          She grew up separated from your
          family?

                      AARON
          Yes, we were in the house, Trisha
          and Rebecca Riley in the Cabbage
          House.

                    SEBASTIAN
          This explains some things.

Sebastian puts his notes away.

                    SEBASTIAN (CONT'D)
          I must leave.

Aaron remains as Sebastian rises. Sebastian turns
to speak.

                    SEBASTIAN
          I want the goods on your sister.
          Got it?

Aaron stares, holding his lower lip with his right-
hand fingers. Sebastian's putting on his overcoat.

                    SEBASTIAN (CONT'D)
          If she doesn't agonize, she'll
          never come to the table.

INT ELEVEN LINCOLN PARK RESTAURANT LATE THURSDAY
EVENING

Sebastian's sitting with another man, 40ish with a
yarmulke.

                    SEBASTIAN
          Ted. Every time someone in the
          family's broke, you come to
          Chicago for dinner.

                    TED
          Brother, that's not fair.

Ted begins to speak in Lithuanian. Sebastian's face
twists.

                    SEBASTIAN
          Stop it, stop it. I don't speak
          Lithuanian. We're in America.

                    TED
          Little brother, Why are you so
          bitter? What have we ever done?
          You know in Rabbi school they
          say . . .

                    SEBASTIAN
          I don't care what they say. It's
          all an excuse to freeload.

The waiter passes.

                    SEBASTIAN
          Waiter, get me the check. Or would
          you like to pay it with prayer?

                      TED
          I'll pay. I'm tired of this
          humiliation. I don't think that
          I'll ever be back here.

                    SEBASTIAN
          That would be a dream come true.

Ted gets up and heads for the door.

                    SEBASTIAN
          Aren't you at least going to tell
          me who needs the money and how
          much?

INT C'S CAR THURSDAY LATE EVENING

                     CERONE
          AE's gonna be another Bed Bat'
          and Beyond, and I'll make a few
          cigarettes outta de ashes.

                      JOEY
          If you're using a correct name,
          it's bath, it's not a sports
          store . . . I'll bet dat Melissa
          would do de whole park to save her
          ol' man.

                     CERONE
          Abbott's lookin' to rob his
          sister. . . . But the white

knight's gonna get shit on his
face and have me right up his ass.

C moves his groin up and down to the steering
wheel.

                    JOEY
          Do it for Hat, C.

A hand reaches from the back seat and grabs C's
shoulder.

                    ANTHONY SANTIS
          Tanks, C. (sniffling) Doze rich
          humps killed my brother.

                    JOEY
          We'll take care of 'em for you,
          Tony.

EXT THE CABBAGE HOUSE EARLY FRIDAY MORNING TRISHA'S
DOORWAY.

                    AARON
          Sis, we must talk. . . . I'm not
          your enemy.

                    TRISHA
          I didn't say that.

                    AARON
          Trisha, we only have each other.

                    TRISHA
          That's not true. You have Mother.

                    AARON
          Yes, and you have Rebecca, the
          spooky witch.

                    TRISHA
          This conversation's over,
          Brother. . . .

She turns to leave and then looks back to him.

                    TRISHA (CONT'D)
          Aaron, in a short time, none
          of this will mean anything to
          me. . . .

Trisha walks away.

INT THE TUESDAY'S CHILD FRIDAY EARLY MORNING

TRISHA IS WORKING WITH A BOY. IN THE SAME ROOM
THERE ARE OTHERS WORKING WITH CHILDREN. THE ROOM
HAS A GLASS WALL.

She's forming sounds with her mouth.

                    TRISHA
          Come on Kevin, you can do it.
          O, O-pen.

The boy is sitting on a table. He smiles and tries
to repeat.

                    KEVIN
          O-o-open.

                    TRISHA
          Bravo! Bravo! Bravo!

Trisha takes him in her arms and hugs him.

INT OUTSIDE THE GLASS WALL IN THE HALL

TWO WOMEN ARE PASSING, LIZ IS 30ISH AND HEAVY. MRS.
JENNINGS IS 50ISH AND TRIM. THEY'RE BOTH LOOKING IN
AT TRISHA.

MRS. JENNINGS
Liz, she looks quite fine to me.

LIZ
Poor kid. I hope that she gets
over it. She's a real sweetheart.

MRS. JENNINGS
You know, with her financial
possibilities, when she came to
work with us you could've knocked
me over with a feather.

LIZ
She's a good kid. There was a mix-up
at the hospital. She's nothing like
any Abbott I ever read about. . . .
Her brother's got some attorney,
Sherwin, trying to talk to me.

MRS. JENNINGS
Remember, dear. Once a word leaves
your mouth, it cannot be put back.

LIZ
I'll remember.

They continue to walk the grubby hall.

MRS. JENNINGS
Where are you today?

LIZ
I'm still with Tommy Arthur. . . .
If no other prospects come,
I think I'll marry him.

Mrs. Jennings smiles firmly.

MRS. JENNINGS
Go on, Liz. Have a good day.

From behind Mrs. Jennings comes a girl.

                    JACKIE
          Mrs. Jennings, a Mr. Sherwin's on
          the phone. Says it's important.
          What should I tell him?

Mrs. Jennings hesitates.

                    MRS. JENNINGS
               Just take his number.

                    JACKIE
               Yes, Mrs. Jennings.

Jackie leaves. Mrs. Jennings turns in to a therapy
room.

TRISHA'S ROOM

Aaron knows that no one is home and enters his sister's room. As he quietly goes through the drawers
he finds a letter signed "From Hat."

Aaron calculates in his mind, takes a picture of
the note with his phone, puts the note back into
the drawer and sneaks out of the house

INT REBECCA'S COUSIN'S HOME FRIDAY MORNING

                    REBECCA
          I'll be fine, I've some money.

                    IRENE
          You should've married Duff. He's
          living well on his police pension.

                    REBECCA
          I wish my family would've stayed
          in Ireland. I'll never be at home
          here.

                    IRENE
     Trisha will not move to Ireland.

                   REBECCA
     Who knows? With all she's gone
     through, she just might. The
     family may want it as well.

Rebecca stares off. Her cousin fills her teacup.

LATER THAT EVENING AARON KNOCKS ON THE DOOR AT THE
CABBAGE HOUSE.

Trisha answers. Aaron looks at her warmly.

                    AARON
     Trish, I know you hurt. I hurt too
     after I decided not to be with
     Melissa. It wasn't easy but life
     goes on.

                   TRISHA
     Does it, Aaron? Is this the only
     life? Is this the important life?

AARON STARES

                    AARON
     I need you to help me, to be on my
     side.

                   TRISHA
     I've always been on your side,
     Brother. Oh, and Aaron . . .

Aaron gazes at her. Trisha hands him a few letters.

                   TRISHA
     See what your counsel thinks about
     these.

AARON STARES AT HIS SISTER

                    AARON
          Letters from the Twilight Zone?

                    TRISHA
          I'm sure your atheist mercenary
          will find them useful. . . . I'll
          see you in court.

INT AARON'S OFFICE FRIDAY MORNING

Megan, Aaron's secretary, escorts Jonathan and
Sebastian.

                    SEBASTIAN
          (assertively) According to our
          experts, we're talking about
          expert forgery.

Aaron gazes.

                    AARON
          And other possibilities?

                    SEBASTIAN
          Maybe the Santis family presented
          letters written by Rob that were
          really written by one of them.

                    AARON
          They love Trisha . . . it's not
          them.

                    SEBASTIAN
          I'm waiting for samples from his
          school.

Aaron shakes his head gently.

                    AARON
         There's something else . . .
         they're not like that. They love
         their son. . . .

Aaron gazes. Jonathan watches.

                    SEBASTIAN
         All people love their sons. What
         do you mean "something else"?

Aaron scratches his neck.

                    AARON
         I mean, *they really love* their
         son . . . Cerone's from their
         area . . . they're not about
         money . . .

                    SEBASTIAN
         Aaron, your Jesus was sold for
         30 silver coins. That's about 400
         bucks today. It was all about
         money then, and it is all about
         money now. Don't fret, I'll form
         this situation into a bowling
         ball and knock your sister on her
         ass. I can mold this thing how I
         want . . . I'm an artist.

Sebastian throws an imaginary bowling ball.

                    SEBASTIAN (CONT'D)
         Who's Cerone?

Aaron completely ignores the question and nods his
head.

                    AARON
         Now I remember . . . You're an
         atheist. . . .

Aaron turns to the window, then back to stare into
Sebastian's eyes.

> AARON (CONT'D)
> So you have two reasons to
> win. . . .

> SEBASTIAN
> What are you getting at, Aaron?
> You're acting like an insane person
> yourself . . . maybe it runs in
> the family and you're all nuts.

AARON SMILES

> AARON
> You're an atheist!

SEBASTIAN'S ICY STARE, MOMENTS PASS

> SEBASTIAN
> Did you let her know what she's
> in for if she doesn't give in? To
> these delusions?

> AARON
> (louder) Yes, I did all of that.

> SEBASTIAN
> Well? What did she say?

Aaron reaches his right hand to the window. He
writes on it with his index finger. He reaches up to
his head with the left hand and runs it over his
hair. He sighs. Sebastian is visibly engaged. He
also stands up.

> SEBASTIAN
> What did she say? . . . Damn you!
> What did she say?

Aaron drops both of his hands and slowly turns. His face is anguished. It's the end of the world. He responds without spirit as he gazes through Sebastian.

                    AARON
        She said she'd see us in court.

INT JUDGE COHEN'S CHAMBERS FRIDAY LATE MORNING

The judge is reading a newspaper. His reading glasses are at the very tip of his nose. Jeb, his clerk, walks in.

                    JEBSON
        They're throwin' another
        one at us . . . says it's an
        emergency . . . told em' you were
        full . . .

The judge turns the page as if he's not heard. He grunts.

                    JUDGE COHEN
        Good.

                    JEBSON
        Some whippersnapper.

Turns another page.

                    JUDGE COHEN
        Uh huh . . .

                    JEBSON
        Some lawyer named Sherwin.

                    JUDGE COHEN
        Sebastian Sherwin?

                         JEBSON
              Yep.

The judge's expression shows that he merits the
situation.

                      JUDGE COHEN
              What's he doin'?

                         JEBSON
              It's a whopper. Got the Abbott
              family as a client. They say that
              it'll be like a Tarantino movie.

                      JUDGE COHEN
              A Tarantino movie, huh?

                         JEBSON
              Oh, and C would take it as a favor
              if you took it. It's on for Monday.

                      JUDGE COHEN
              It'll never go.

                         JEBSON
              What will never go?

                      JUDGE COHEN
              Sherwin's a negotiator. He makes
              dates to intimidate.

                         JEBSON
              Works against himself?

                      JUDGE COHEN
              Are you kidding? He makes more
              than a litigator and wastes less
              time.

The judge looks back down at his newspaper.

                    JUDGE COHEN
     Jeb, are they ready in there?
     I said 15 minutes, but there ain't
     a damn thing in this newspaper.

Jeb walks over to the door and looks into the
courtroom.

                    JEBSON
     Yeah, they're baked.

The judge stands up and walks into the courtroom.

INT HOTEL ROOM FRIDAY NOON

Aaron's tying his tie. Taylor, the girl from the
salon, is getting herself together.

                    AARON
     I hope we can get some mileage out
     of this.

                    TAYLOR
     What do you mean? . . . What do
     you make of us?

                    AARON
     Us. What's us? I like you.

Aaron looks almost confused.

                    AARON (CONT'D)
     Why would a man ever settle down?

                    TAYLOR
     Love.

                    AARON
     In the USA? Over 50 percent of
     marriages end in divorce, and the
     court system is politically tilted
     to the woman's side. The only

thing guaranteed to a man who
gets married is that someday he'll
be raped. And when the court
rapes a man for the woman, it's
not over in minutes. It can last
decades, a lifetime. . . . Love's
only nature's trick to get us to
reproduce.

                    TAYLOR
          Well, I don't see why you're
          worried about getting any mileage
          out of us. I'm happy to pay down
          some of my student loan and you're
          not horrible looking or boring.

Aaron heads into the bathroom but abruptly stops.
He looks at Taylor and then at the end table next
to the bed. While scanning the table, he speaks.

                    AARON
          Where's it at?

                    TAYLOR
          Where's what at?

                    AARON
          You know what, now hand it over.

Aaron moves toward Taylor and snatches her purse.

                    TAYLOR
          Hey! You can't do that! It's an
          invasion of my privacy.

Aaron pushes his hand into the purse and comes out
with a used prophylactic.

                    AARON
          Your private things? Your private
          things? You were trying to
          impregnate yourself with my seed.

> AARON (CONT'D)
> This has happened to me more times
> than I'd like to remember. You're
> smarter than I thought you were.
> I like that . . . but please,
> don't do that again. I have enough
> economic issues.

Aaron walks into the bathroom. The toilet flushes.
Aaron sticks his head out into the bedroom and
looks at Taylor. He smiles.

> AARON
> You are gorgeous . . . now I have
> another reason to keep an eye on
> you.

INT C's CAR FRIDAY EARLY AFTERNOON

Joey and C are driving around the hood.

> JOEY
> How'd you ever end up wit' dat
> broad?

> CERONE
> Edgeview Bank likes me? When a
> cute skirt walks in, they wave me
> on. She came walking off da street
> lookin' for a loan. We could never
> deal the numbers she needs.

> JOEY
> Ol' Polack banker likes you, huh?

> CERONE
> Joey, de big banks got da
> government to do dere collecting.
> At our bank when a wise guy don'
> wanna pay, we can't afford 5

attorneys and a lawsuit. They take care of me and I buy an Armani suit. . . . Everyone knows dat an Armani suit is a whole lot cheaper den a lawsuit.

                    JOEY
Well how is she?

                    CERONE
She loves dat moron jerk. She tought dat I could bail out her ol' man's company. Lover boy tinks she's playin' hide da sausage wit me. He canned da wedding. Now he's holdin' her ol' man's funny money . . . an he ain' even got da broad . . . women, dey say we fucked up de planet . . .

                    JOEY
And Granny's attorney scoops you?

                    CERONE
Mr. Barr's gamblin' debts convert into valuable info now and then.

                    JOEY
Dere all so smart wit' all dat cake.

                    CERONE
Yeah, til dey get dere head busted. Hey go talk to dat Chinaman Chu. He's gettin' cute, he's behind five months and tinks da bank will renegotiate. Tell him he'll be negotiating from da hospital if he don't pay up.

                    JOEY
Done.

Joey gets out of the car. He looks back.

                    JOEY
          Hey C. Cohen sends his regards.

                    CERONE
          I don't want his regards. I want
          one of his shoeboxes.

INT FRANCO'S NEIGHBORHOOD RESTAURANT LATER FRIDAY

C's sitting at a table. He is visibly angry.

                    BENNY
          Water, Mr. Cerone?

Benny pours water. C does not respond. Melissa
walks in.

                    BENNY
          Hello Melissa . . . pasta and
          broccoli's . . .

                    MELISSA
          Thank you, Benny. I won't be
          eating.

C'S CONFUSED FACE.

                    BENNY
          Very well, ma'am.

Benny turns and walks away.

C smiles, trying to make light of the situation.

                    CERONE
          Sit down, Melissa.

Melissa remains standing.

                         MELISSA
          It's over, C.

                         CERONE
          Honey . . .

C stands up and tries to take her arm. She jerks
away.

                         MELISSA
          It's over, C! The whole thing's
          a joke. There's nothing here for
          us. . . . We're worlds apart.

C tries to talk.

                         MELISSA
          C . . . You know it too.

Melissa moves away and walks out.

C is still standing looking down at the table.

He squeezes a wineglass until it explodes. Blood
spills. He swings, breaking everything on the table,
and tips it over. Benny runs over with a napkin for
C's bleeding hand.

                         BENNY
          Juan, more napkins for Mr. Cerone.

As Benny says "Mr. Cerone," C's head gently moves
up. C'S kindly looking in Benny's eyes.

                         CERONE
          (gently) It's C . . .

INT AARON'S OFFICE FRIDAY AFTERNOON

Aaron is sitting with his elbows on his desk and
his head in his hands. Talking comes from the
intercom.

                    MEGAN
        Sir, Melissa Andrew again, line 3.

Aaron looks at the phone. GREEN BLINKING LIGHT

He hurls it at the wall. It cracks and pieces fly
all over.

INT DOWNTOWN RESTAURANT LATER FRIDAY AFTERNOON

SEBASTIAN'S WAITING. HE'S ON THE PHONE.

                    SEBASTIAN
        Yes sir (laughs). Tillerson, Bicks
        and Sherwin does have a ring to it
        (laughs again).

                SEBASTIAN (CONT'D)
        Sir, Mr. Abbott has arrived.
        Yes sir, AE comes with me as a
        client. Tonight then . . . yes
        I understand. I'll be at the
        Airport Hilton 8 sharp.

Sebastian stands up and strongly embraces Aaron's
right forearm with his left hand.

                    SEBASTIAN
        I'm sorry for your pain . . .
        Do you believe in fate, my
        brother?

                     AARON
        Fate?

                    SEBASTIAN
        Not God. Fate.

                     AARON
        Well . . .

>   SEBASTIAN
>   Aaron, you're not here at the helm
>   of AE by luck. I'm not by your
>   side by luck.

Sebastian looks in Aaron's eyes.

>   SEBASTIAN (CONT'D)
>   When your own father wanted to
>   hang you, there was no one else,
>   but me. That's fate.

Aaron shakes his head.

>   AARON
>   You're extracting your pound of
>   flesh . . .

Sebastian nods warmly.

>   SEBASTIAN
>   Charles and Prowe were convicted.
>   It was not pretty. Things would
>   have been different . . .

>   AARON
>   I told you then and I tell you
>   now. I was drunk. They used the
>   pool sticks, not me.

>   SEBASTIAN
>   Lucky that you had that investment
>   account.

Looks at Aaron and smiles.

>   SEBASTIAN (CONT'D)
>   How would we have found the money
>   for Charles and Prowe without your
>   old man finding out?

                    AARON
They did all right. . . . They
got community service and the
money . . . best pay they'll ever
get.

                    SEBASTIAN
You'd have been relegated to the
background of AE.

                    AARON
I don't know, Clinton did OK,
cigar and all.

                    SEBASTIAN
Do you know why we're here? I mean
now, today.

Aaron looks confused.

                 SEBASTIAN (CONT'D)
We're arriving together. Man is
born with a destiny. Napoleon
accepted his. Caesar accepted his.
Will you accept yours?

Aaron's eyes light up. He preens and smirks confidently.

                 SEBASTIAN (CONT'D)
Do you accept? . . . (anxiously)
Do you?

                    AARON
Yes, (he smiles) I accept.

                    SEBASTIAN
Do you know who John Tillerson is?

                    AARON
Secretary of State Tillerson?

                         SEBASTIAN
          I've been offered a partnership
          position in his law firm.

Sebastian looks very hard at Aaron.

                      SEBASTIAN (CONT'D)
          Those contacts are essential for
          us. Imagine having them as your
          guard rail? You'd be able to drive
          AE without limits.

Sebastian grabs Aaron's lapel and smiles.

                      SEBASTIAN (CONT'D)
          They got more power than the CIA.

Aaron smirks.

                          AARON
          Can Goldman Sachs bother them?

                         SEBASTIAN
          Are you kidding? Tillerson is
          untouchable. . . . You know
          that the government's the real
          syndicate, the world's true
          criminal organization. If things
          get uncomfortable for them,
          someone commits suicide in Central
          Park. They protect each other.
          Once I'm head counsel for AE
          I'm . . . we're in.

                          AARON
          But my father is still in
          charge . . .

Sebastian purses his lips, Aaron raises his hand
to stop him.

                    AARON (CONT'D)
Once I have control of Trisha's
assets, the banks will fall in
line, the Andrew Industry mess
will work to our benefit. I'd be
in.

                    SEBASTIAN
Together, who could stop us?

                    AARON
Yes . . . I hope that we're not
marching to Waterloo . . .

INT SEBASTIAN'S OFFICE FRIDAY LATE AFTERNOON

Sebastian's closing drawers in his desk. Law books
are spread out in front of him. The phone rings.
He picks it up.

                    SEBASTIAN
Yes? . . . I know it . . . Because
I'm busy . . .

Sebastian's face is getting angrier and angrier.

                    SEBASTIAN (CONT'D)
I'm preparing a case against
a lunatic. You should take it
over. . . . You'd be an expert.

Sebastian closes the phone. It falls off the desk.
While he's reaching for it, Jonathan walks in.
Sebastian gazes angrily.

                    SEBASTIAN
If another partner calls . . .
I'm walking out.

Jonathan makes a gesture with her hand.

                    JONATHAN
          OK, but . . . But—

                    SEBASTIAN
          What?

                    JONATHAN
          (gently) It's Mr. Mullen.

                    SEBASTIAN
          Oh? What's the old pervert want?

                    JONATHAN
          He wants to pursue his age-
          discrimination suit. And the
          partners . . .

                    SEBASTIAN
          Oh, the partners, what do they
          want?

                    JONATHAN
          They want to remind you that
          Mullen's firm paid almost four
          million in fees last . . .

                    SEBASTIAN
          (sweetly) Jonathan?

Jonathan looks at him strangely.

                    JONATHAN
          Yes?

                    SEBASTIAN
          Do you know what the suit's about?

Jonathan looks at Sebastian and shrugs her shoulders.

                    JONATHAN
          Age discrimination?

                    SEBASTIAN
          (sweetly) Mullen says that the law
          discriminates. Fourteen-year-old
          boys can legally cuff thirteen-
          year-old girls, but he can't.

Jonathan thinks for a moment.

                    JONATHAN
          What should I tell the partners?

                    SEBASTIAN
          Tell them to send Mullen Viagra
          and a box of prophylactics.

                    SEBASTIAN (CONT'D)
          Money buys justice, look at
          OJ! With Mullen's money, he's
          untouchable! Tell him to go at it!

Jonathan nods. She half closes the door putting
her body on the outside holding the door with her
hands.

                    JONATHAN
          Should I really tell them that?

Sebastian lines a book at the door. She closes it
just in time. From the inside, she hears. . . .

                    SEBASTIAN
          Word for word! Half of them should
          be put on as co-suitors and
          later as codefendants. Tell them
          to go fuck themselves! Go fuck
          themselves!

INT THE ABBOTT MANSION IN THE DEN FRIDAY LATE
AFTERNOON

Aaron's standing with a goblet in his hand.

                    INGRID
          Son, gossip destroys. First the
          Union debacle . . . this Andrew
          thing can ruin you.

                    AARON
          Mom. Did you ever love? . . .
          I mean really love?

Aaron looks at his mother as she gazes off.

                    INGRID
          Don't scare me, son. . . . Love's
          a daft game.

                    AARON
          A daft game?

                    INGRID
          Yes son, when the players think
          they've won, that's when they're
          incurably lost.

JONATHAN'S DESK FRIDAY LATE AFTERNOON

Jonathan's at her computer screen. Maxine, Sebastian's law office receptionist, arrives.

                    MAXINE
          There's someone to see
          Mr. Sherwin.

                    JONATHAN
          Mr. Sherwin can't see anyone now.

                    MAXINE
          That's what I told her.

                    JONATHAN
          (crossly) Well?

                    MAXINE
        She said that he'd see her.

                   JONATHAN
        (arrogantly) Really? Who is she?

                    MAXINE
        Says her name is Trisha Abbott.

INT SEBASTIAN'S CAR, FRIDAY EARLY EVENING

Sebastian is swerving, speeding and talking on the
phone.

                   SEBASTIAN
        She came to my office with two more
        letters and a physical from . . .

Sebastian tries to read the letter.

               SEBASTIAN (CONT'D)
        From Dr. Brabec. Who is he? . . .
        Reel him in.

Sebastian almost hits an oncoming car. The driver
shouts. Sebastian flips him off.

                   SEBASTIAN
        I'm going to see Cohen at a JDL
        Dinner, if I don't get myself
        killed. . . . If that happens then
        we'll both be dead.

INT MARRIOTT BALLROOM FRIDAY EVENING

The ballroom's full and speckled by yarmulkes.
Sebastian stands at the stairs. He touches his
yarmulke, frowns, and steps into the crowd. He
walks to the hors d'oeuvre table. He takes a plate
and picks his eyes up to a smiling face.

                    RABBI SCHULTZ
          Sebastian . . . Sebastian Sherwin?

                    SEBASTIAN
          Rabbi . . . Rabbi Schultz?

                    RABBI SCHULTZ
          Wait for me. I'll come over to
          your side.

Sebastian nods. The rabbi arrives with Judge Cohen.

                    RABBI SCHULTZ
          I thought you two might like to
          rub cases.

They shake hands as the rabbi smiles in the background.

                    JUDGE COHEN
          I see that we may see each other.

                    SEBASTIAN
          (nodding) It's sad. Abbott girl
          thinks she receives letters from
          the dead.

                    JUDGE COHEN
          You know the rules, Counselor.

                    SEBASTIAN
          Of course, Your Honor, of course.

Sebastian smiles, and the judge turns to leave.

                    SEBASTIAN (CONT'D)
          Sir, sir. I'd like a pretrial. I
          could use your wisdom on this one.

                    JUDGE COHEN
          If your counterpart agrees,
          contact my office.

                    SEBASTIAN
        Yes sir.

    The judge turns precisely and leaves.

INT THE ABBOTT MANSION IN THE DEN LATER FRIDAY
EVENING

Aaron's on the phone, Ingrid's on the sofa dressed
to kill. Howard's looking out the picture window.
The maid walks in.

                      MAID
        Pardon, Mr. Sherwin's at the gate.

Aaron covers the phone mouthpiece.

                     AARON
        Please show him in when he
        arrives.

Aaron goes back to talking on the phone.

INT ABBOTT ESTATE DEN MINUTES LATER

Sebastian walks in and goes to Ingrid. As he bends
to kiss her hand, she slaps him. Sebastian stands
erect.

                    INGRID
        You venom! What are you doing to
        my son?

Sebastian looks around. No one's paying attention.

                     AARON
        (audibly) I have to go . . .
        There's nothing to talk about.

Aaron hangs up, looks to his father, then winks at
Sebastian.

                            AARON
              We're due in court Monday
              afternoon.

Sebastian nods.

                          SEBASTIAN
                Yes, if you'd allow me?

Aaron nods and puts the chess king in his hand.
Ingrid turns.

                            AARON
            Sebastian, join me in a game.

As they're setting the pieces up.

                          SEBASTIAN
            Judge Cohen's a friend of mine.

Ingrid angrily turns.

                           INGRID
              My son never wanted to go to
              court.

The chess pieces are in order, and aaron takes the
first move.

                            AARON
              (assertively) Mother.

He looks back at Sebastian.

                            AARON
              Friend?

                          SEBASTIAN
              We were together earlier. I've
              never lost a case before him, this
              one will be no different. . . .
              It's better this way. Check.

                        AARON
            What do you mean, "better"?

Aaron moves a chess piece.

                        SEBASTIAN
            If we pre-settle, things will get
            complicated. Our hands will be
            tied. Check.

                        INGRID
            What rubbish.

The camera goes to aaron's cold icy stare.

                        AARON
            Sebastian, get us through this,
            and my family will be forever
            indebted.

Aaron looks in his father's direction.

The camera goes to where howard was. There's no one
there.

PARKING LOT FRIDAY LATE EVENING, RAINING

Joey has a yellow raincoat and hood on. C's dressed
in a suit holding a wad of money in his hands. Rain
dripping.

Joey waves in a BMW with two couples in it. The
window opens.

                        DRIVER
            How much?

                        JOEY
            (irritated) Dere's a sign . . .
            A double sawsky.

Joey points at sign.

                         DRIVER
          What?

                          JOEY
          (impatiently) It's twenty.

                         DRIVER
          Will fifteen do it?

Joey wipes the rain off his face and looks the car
over.

                          JOEY
          (calmly) Nice car. BMW 750i series?

                         DRIVER
          (smiling) Yeah.

                          JOEY
          About 75-80 grand?

Joey reaches in and grabs a twenty from the driver.

                         DRIVER
          Hey. What will 15 get me?

                          JOEY
          A busted head . . . Go park it.

The car pulls away.

                          JOEY
          (speaking to himself) The more these
          idiots got, the more they want.

The sound of screeching tires. A Land Rover is
coming full speed toward C whose back is turned.

                          JOEY
          C!

C turns and moves, being barely missed. The car
stops.

                    CERONE
        Joey. Da piece!

                    JOEY
        Frig!

Joey runs toward C. The truck is coming back.

                    JOEY
        C! C! Run! I'm naked!

C looks at joey. He's ready to meet his maker.

The truck swerves, barely missing him. The window
opens.

                    AARON
        Mr. Businessman, you should've
        stuck to parking cars and scalping
        tickets.

C STARES INTO AARON ABBOTT'S EYES

                    AARON (CONT'D)
        (softly) Try selling Andrew
        Industries now.

Aaron laughs loudly and speeds away.

C looks at the ground for a moment and then starts
to kick the side of the car nearest to him.

Joey watches the truck drive out of the lot.

Joey grabs C and attempts to pull him away from
the car.

                    JOEY
        C . . . C . . . let's go get a
        beef sandwich.

The camera pulls away until their figures are small. C slumps on the car putting his forearms and head on the hood.

EXT THE CABBAGE HOUSE SATURDAY MORNING

Trisha's on her knees planting flowers. Aaron arrives.

> AARON
> Hello.

> TRISHA
> (friendly tone) Hello.

> AARON
> Can we talk?

> TRISHA
> Sure.

Trisha looks at Aaron. He smiles gently.

> AARON
> Can we go inside?

Trisha moves to one knee. Her brother gives her a hand, she accepts it and rises.

INT THE CABBAGE HOUSE KITCHEN MOMENTS LATER

Trisha washes her hands, Aaron smiles, acting brotherly.

> AARON
> I love what you did with this
> place. . . . Remember when I
> helped you paint? . . . Mom had
> a fit. "My daughter, living in the
> Cabbage House?"

                    TRISHA
        Aaron, if you've come about my
        inheritance, it's too late.

Aaron gently shakes his head and looks concerned.

                    AARON
        I'm worried about you, Trish.

                    TRISHA
        You show it in a funny way.

There's silence. Becky walks in.

                    REBECCA
        Oh, excuse me.

Rebecca looks unkindly at Aaron, who looks impatiently back. Rebecca exits.

                    TRISHA
        Aaron, remember my big dollhouse?

                    AARON
        Yes.

                    TRISHA
        Do you know why I loved it?

                    AARON
        (uncomfortably) I don't know.

                    TRISHA
        It housed my dream family. It was
        a refuge from the meanness and the
        arguing.

Tears come to her eyes. Aaron notices. He's irritated.

                    AARON
          It was just a toy! You had your
          dear Rebecca. I had no one!

                    TRISHA
          No, you were busy trying to get
          what Father had, and he was
          running away from Mother. None
          of you cared then and by your
          behavior, it's hard to believe that
          you care now.

                    AARON
          (stutters) That . . . that was
          twenty years ago. I was, I was
          just a kid.

                    TRISHA
          That's right, Aaron . . .

She stares. He looks back confused.

                    TRISHA (CONT'D)
          And now you're an ornament in
          Mother's hell. Isn't that who and
          where you are?

                    AARON
          No! And the real question is who
          you are? Are you really better
          than us because you teach retards?
          You don't live here, you hide
          here. I've always looked out for
          the family, the same family that
          bought this home. Instead, you ran
          away from who you are.

                    TRISHA
          And who's that supposed to be?

                    AARON
        You're an Abbott! You should be
        helping me build AE. But you're a
        selfish, spoiled coward.

                    TRISHA
        And what would we have? More
        money? Power?

                    AARON
        That's right! AE would be
        respected, feared! You're
        destroying this family and that's
        what you've always wanted!

                    TRISHA
        Aaron . . . remember when we
        thought Aunt Agatha was an
        arrogant shrew?

Aaron nods, his face confused.

                TRISHA (CONT'D)
        Today as you see her, is she a
        shrew or a refined lady?

                    AARON
        I came for p-p-peace. But you're
        really crazy!

                    TRISHA
        Am I, Brother? The letters are
        as real as your anger. . . . But
        all you want to discuss is how to
        split the pie, Brother.

                    AARON
        Be careful or the p-p-p-pie will
        be smashed! . . . In your face!

Aaron slams his hand on the table, palm down.
Rebecca enters.

                              REBECCA
                You get out of this house!

Rebecca picks up a broom and goes after Aaron.

                         REBECCA (CONT'D)
                This is Trisha's house! Leave her
                alone, you vulture!

Aaron retreats.

                              AARON
                (calmly) You old leech. You
                purposely made her crazy so you
                could sponge off of us for life.
                Well, your freeloading days are
                over.

He slams the door shut.

INT C CAR SATURDAY AFTERNOON

                              JOEY
                It's fixed. Danahy'll get da case.

                             CERONE
                Stay on Barr for info. I'm gonna
                bury Abbott.

C takes a hundred-dollar bill from his pocket.

                         CERONE (CONT'D)
                Get me an eggplant wit sweet and
                hot.

                              JOEY
                Gimme a sawbuck.

                             CERONE
                I ain' got one.

                    JOEY
        No you got 20 of 'em. You know
        Bones won't take anything bigger
        than a 10 from us. You like makin'
        him nuts.

C laughs.

                    CERONE
        Remember when we unloaded 5,000 in
        counterfeit C-notes on him tellin'
        him it was a settlement?

                    JOEY
        Yeah, I remember, so does he.
        Gimme a sawsky.

C smiles and gives Joey a 10-dollar bill.

INT THE ABBOTT MANSION SATURDAY EVENING

Ingrid's standing, and Howard's at his desk.

                    INGRID
        Could this disaster affect our
        family life?

                    HOWARD
        You mean your *lifestyle*.

                    INGRID
        Could it?

                    HOWARD
        Drastically . . . ruin,
        bankruptcy.

Ingrid starts to cry.

                    INGRID
        Enough! I won't take this anymore!

Ingrid runs to the gun rack and takes a pistol
in her hands. She rummages through the drawer in
front of her.

> HOWARD
> They're in the drawer on the
> right.

RIGHT-HAND DRAWER.

Ingrid tries to open it. It's locked.

> INGRID
> You think I won't! I'd rather die
> than . . .

THE KEYS LAND ON THE DESK. INGRID'S SHOCKED FACE

> INGRID
> I will not face humiliation!

She fumbles with the keys. She opens the drawer.

HOWARD POURS A DRINK

> HOWARD
> Your choice.

> INGRID
> (crying) Ahh! Ahh!

Ingrid tries to load a bullet in a chamber. The
first bullet falls, as well as the second.

> HOWARD
> You know, Ingrid. I used to
> fantasize about us as a pair of
> swans, mating for life. Instead,
> we're black vultures.

He tops off his drink.

                    HOWARD (CONT'D)
          And when one is no longer
          monogamous, death is the lone
          answer.

Ingrid loads the third into the chamber. She points
the gun to her head.

Aaron runs in.

                         AARON
          Mother!

                         HOWARD
          Leave her.

AARON LOOKS AT HIS MOTHER THEN AT HIS FATHER,
INGRID HAS THE GUN TO HER HEAD

The gun falls to the ground. She blubbers.

                         HOWARD
          We weren't much good in a life of
          grace. Maybe we'll do better in a
          life of disgrace.

Howard downs his drink and walks out. Aaron runs
to Ingrid.

INT THE CABBAGE HOUSE—DARK SATURDAY MIDNIGHT

THERE'S A TINY LIGHT ON IN THE KITCHEN. THE CLOCK
READS 12:10.

Rebecca's copying from a letter onto a piece of
paper. She puts it all in the bread box and walks
up the stairs. She stops at Trisha's room. She
moves her ear to the door.

                         VOICE
          (a male voice) Be calm, my love,
          it won't be long.

                         TRISHA
              Oh Hat.

Trisha giggles. Rebecca walks away.

INT THE CABBAGE HOUSE SUNDAY MORNING

THE CAMERA'S ON THE FRONT DOOR

It bursts open. Ingrid enters and throws an icy
stare at Rebecca, who is sewing buttons on a shirt.

                         INGRID
              Where's my daughter?

Rebecca looks over her glasses without responding.

                     INGRID (CONT'D)
              (low, sinister) I said. Where is
              my daughter?

CONFUSION AND INTIMIDATION IN REBECCA'S EYES

                         REBECCA
              Please leave. . . . Can't you all
              leave her alone?

Ingrid looks at her in disbelief.

                     REBECCA (CONT'D)
              Please leave this house!

Ingrid flies at Rebecca and knocks her onto the
couch.

                         INGRID
              Your days are numbered. You ruined
              my daughter! You'll pay! You leech!
              You criminal, you sham.

Ingrid runs up the stairs and swings open the door to Trisha's room. Trisha's writing a letter with headphones on.

> INGRID
> Take those things off!

Trisha smiles and lays them on the desk.

> TRISHA
> Hello, Mother. I've been
> expecting . . .

> INGRID
> (grunted) Don't be insolent!

> TRISHA
> Sorry. . . . What may I do for
> you?

> INGRID
> Stop all of this nonsense! You
> will stop inflicting pain on this
> family!

> TRISHA
> I didn't pull anyone into court.

> INGRID
> (softly) Do you agree that Aaron
> was unjustly cut out of his
> inheritance?

> TRISHA
> It's Grandmother's money, I won't
> speak for her.

> INGRID
> Fine. It's a financial matter, your
> father will handle it.

> INGRID (CONT'D)
> Can we agree that dead people
> don't communicate with the living?

Ingrid stares at her daughter. Trisha smiles back.

> INGRID
> What are you smiling at, young
> lady?

> TRISHA
> I guess you're saying that the
> whole Christian faith is based on
> a scam.

She looks seriously in Trish's eyes.

> INGRID
> I said no such thing! I am a
> Christian! I stayed with a man that
> I despise because I took a solemn
> oath! As a Christian! . . . And
> today! Not many Christians do-do
> that! Now, if you continue . . .
> if you dare show up on Monday. I'll
> divorce your father.

> TRISHA
> Mother . . . you're beginning to
> stutter like Aaron.

Ingrid looks, concentrating and squinting.

> TRISHA (CONT'D)
> Know what Rob says? What happens
> after you're gone just happens.

> INGRID
> You've never cared about anyone but
> yourself and that old maid! . . .
> She has warped you! But you will
> now. I mean it, you will now. Oh!

I can't wait to be away from your
father and you! I mean it with
every drop of blood in my body!

Ingrid opens the door, slamming it as she leaves.

INT NEIGHBORHOOD CLUB SUNDAY MORNING

C's playing cards. Joey's next to him on a high
barstool.

                    JOEY
          Would Barr scam us? It all sounds
          kinda goofy.

                    CERONE
          Nah. Dere's nuttin' in it for
          him . . . and he knows better.

                    JOEY
          If Aaron gets Sis's cake, he may
          save da company and the broad.
          Dey'll live happily ever. . . .

                    CERONE
          Dat guy ain't gonna have anudder
          happy day in his life if I got
          anyting to say about it.

                    JOEY
          Dat broad's got you all worked up.

                    CERONE
          Broads, der da most powerful tings
          on da planet.

C stares into space.

                    CERONE (CONT'D)
          Dey bleed a week witout dyin' and
          bust balls witout touchin' dem.

250.

INT SEBASTIAN'S CAR SUNDAY MORNING

Sebastian's driving alone. The phone rings.

                    SEBASTIAN
          Hello. Yes, Doctor Behren, as
          planned.

Sebastian smiles.

                    SEBASTIAN (CONT'D)
          I knew I could count on you,
          Doctor. . . . Doctor, if you
          deliver, you can shred my firm's
          bill.

Sebastian swerves trying to run a squirrel over.

The camera does a close-up of sebastian's deter-
mined face.

                    SEBASTIAN
          Yes Doctor, it's that important.

INT THE ABBOTT MANSION IN THE DEN SHORTLY AFTER

Aaron's on the phone. He's dressed to kill. Ingrid
enters. Aaron holds his finger to his mouth. He
hangs the phone up.

                    INGRID
          You're acting queerly. I hope she's
          worth it. . . . I need to talk.

                    AARON
          Talk, no one could ever stop that.

                    INGRID
          Son, we're so close . . . and so
          much alike.

Tears form in Aaron's eyes. His mother is looking away.

                    INGRID (CONT'D)
          Through the Melissa scandal I
          defended you. I knew . . . Andrew
          Industries was in trouble. I want
          to hear what they have to say now.
          You're smart, Son.
          You knew when to leave.

A tear rolls down Aaron's cheek.

                    INGRID
          Son, I've done my best. Your
          father . . .

                    AARON
          Mother, please get to the point.

                    INGRID
          I need a million dollars to
          hold me over until I can get a
          divorce . . .

Aaron stares through her.

                    INGRID
          Don't look so surprised. You know
          everything's wrapped up tight, but
          when I get it, it's all yours.

                    AARON
          (stutters) Mother, I have a plate
          f-f-full. Let me get through it.
          If it goes well we'll t-talk.
          Otherwise, I can't help you.

                    INGRID
          Son, I'm counting on you.

THE CAMERA GOES TO THE OPEN DEN DOOR.

252.

Howard's walking away. He opens the front entrance
door, slamming it as he leaves. Ingrid looks at
Aaron.

INT THE CABBAGE HOUSE SUNDAY AFTERNOON

Rebecca's asleep with knitting needles and yarn
on her lap. Trisha is writing a letter. There's a
gentle rap at the door. Trisha quietly opens it.

Her dad's waiting in the rain.

                    TRISHA
          Come in, Dad.

Howard brushes the water from his overcoat.

                    HOWARD
          I'm glad you're home. . . .

Her father looks at Rebecca sleeping on the chair.
He smiles. Trisha hangs his coat up.

                    TRISHA
          (whispered) Let's go in the
          kitchen. I'll make some tea.

As they walk into the kitchen rebecca is watching

INT TRISHA'S KITCHEN MOMENTS LATER

Trisha and Howard are at the kitchen table drinking tea. Her father looks away.

                    HOWARD
          I'll protect you. I'll call Aaron
          off. It's got to stop. Things
          aren't what they seem. Aaron's
          assault is born of desperation.

He nervously looks at her. He then looks inside the
hall.

                        TRISHA
            Dad, what's wrong?

                        HOWARD
            Trish, your brother's in trouble
            and I can't help him. . . . *All*
            empires finally fall.

Howard smiles.

                        HOWARD
            If I could . . . I'd live in a
            house like this.

                        TRISHA
            Dad, it's never too late.

                        HOWARD
            It's too late for me. . . .

INT TRISH'S FRONT ROOM

Howard kisses Trisha's forehead, walks through the
front room, and glances at Rebecca sleeping. At the
door, he turns suddenly, trying to catch Rebecca
feigning sleep. Rebecca's unmoved. He turns again
and quietly leaves.

Rebecca's eyes open.

Trisha cleans the teacups, passes Rebecca solemnly
sleeping in her chair, and retires.

Shortly after, Rebecca rises, goes to Trisha's room
and puts her ear to the door. Everything's quiet.

She walks down to the kitchen, removes something
from the bread box, and retires.

I/E SEBASTIAN'S CAR NIGHT LATE EVENING

Sebastian is driving, and Aaron is in the front
seat.

                    SEBASTIAN
          Aaron, honesty becomes an option
          when all else fails.

                    AARON
          I'm not comfortable.

                    SEBASTIAN
          The Santises want to defraud her.

Aaron runs his hands through his hair as he gazes
emptily.

                    AARON
          I need to know the truth.

                    SEBASTIAN
          At the moment the truth is a
          pricey commodity. It can wait. You
          need your grandmother's money.
          And I need to size them up.
          They're too close to the flame to
          be disinterested. They'll want to
          hear what you have to say.

                    AARON
          What do I say?

                    SEBASTIAN
          Nothing.

INT JUDGE COHEN'S HOME FRONT ROOM, SAME TIME

The judge is reading a book. Mary, his wife, is in
a chair looking down on wallpaper samples.

                    MARY
          Irv, I still like the rose.

                    JUDGE COHEN
          Then get the rose.

Irv turns the page in his book.

                      MARY
          Is the Scalise trial still up?

                    JUDGE COHEN
          It'll close tomorrow.

                      MARY
          What's next?

                    JUDGE COHEN
          Something with the Abbott family.

                      MARY
          You mean the Abbott family from
          AE?

                    JUDGE COHEN
          Bingo.

The phone rings. Mary picks it up.

                      MARY
          Hi honey, just a minute. . . . It's
          soon-to-be counselor Marva.

Irv smiles and takes the phone.

                    JUDGE COHEN
          Yes honey, it's a full day . . .
          you may have met him, his name's
          Sherwin. He's representing a
          brother who's trying to wrestle an
          inheritance from his sister. . . .
          I don't know. I think she wants
          to donate it to charity . . .
          Yes, I think so too. But there's
          some other particulars . . . I

agree . . . but she also claims
that she speaks to the dead.
It may not go. Sherwin rarely
litigates.

Mary glances at Irv.

                    JUDGE COHEN
          I love you too, honey. Call me on
          my cell at about 2:30-3:00.

Irv sets the phone down. His wife is watching. He
looks back at his book. He turns and raises his
head.

                    JUDGE COHEN
          Well?

                    MARY
          Greed. The world's just full of it.
          You know Gandhi said, "The world
          has enough for man's need but not
          enough for man's greed." I think
          it's a worse disease than cancer.

Irv nods and goes back to his book.

                    MARY
          I'm coming in with you tomorrow.

                    JUDGE COHEN
          As you wish.

I/E SEBASTIAN'S CAR SHORTLY AFTER

The car pulls down a block rowed with bungalows.

                    SEBASTIAN
          Your sister liked slumming. You
          got to pass the jungle to get in
          here and when you're here, the
          jungle's not so unappealing.

The car passes a gang of teenage boys. Two of them
are slap boxing, and one comes close to the car as
it's turning the corner. Sebastian hits the brakes
as the youth runs in front.

                    SEBASTIAN
          (under his breath) Punk.

                      AARON
          There it is—3219.

EXT IN FRONT OF 3219 SHORTLY AFTER

                    SEBASTIAN
          Relax. You've met these people
          before.

Sebastian knocks. The door is opened by a rough-looking 55ish man, Dominic Santis.

                    MR. SANTIS
          Come in.

They follow Mr. Santis up the hallway.

INT SANTIS KITCHEN A FEW MINUTES LATER

Mrs. Santis is up refilling coffee cups.

                    MR. SANTIS
          She's suffered enough.

                    SEBASTIAN
          We totally agree.

Mr. Santis looks suspiciously at Sebastian.

                    MR. SANTIS
          We'll do anything to help
          Trisha. . . . We'll do anything to
          protect her. . . .

Aaron shrugs his shoulders.

                    SEBASTIAN
          (stutters) Well, it's late. We
          appreciate every-everything.

They stand and walk through the house led by
Mr. Santis.

The house is lined with holy statues.

They reach the exit. Mr. Santis abruptly grabs
Aaron's lapel.

                    MR. SANTIS
          I don't know what happened to my
          son or what you're doin' to your
          sister. But don't come back here.

                    SEBASTIAN
          (stutters) Sir, I can as-s-sure you
          that we o-o-nly . . .

                    MR. SANTIS
          (mockingly) S-s-sir, I can assure
          you that another trip here will be
          dangerous to your h-h-health.

INT SEBASTIAN'S CAR EVENING SUNDAY MINUTES LATER

                    SEBASTIAN
          Great. He's a hothead, and the
          mother will be our star.

                    SEBASTIAN (cont'd)
          Did you see all those
          statues? . . . the voodoo lady.
          Great work.

Aaron's gazing out the window.

EXT THE ABBOTT MANSION MONDAY MORNING EARLY

Rebecca approaches Sebastian's car. He stops and smiles.

                    SEBASTIAN
          Good morning.

                    REBECCA
          It was until now.

Sebastian smirks.

                    SEBASTIAN
          Can I do something for you?

                    REBECCA
          Yes, but you won't.

                    SEBASTIAN
          Oh?

                    REBECCA
          Do you know who Saint Sebastian
          was?

                    SEBASTIAN
          Excuse me?

                    REBECCA
          Saint Sebastian was a Roman
          official. He persecuted
          Christians. . . . In the end he
          became one.

Sebastian looks at her, half smirking, half confused.

                    SEBASTIAN
          What's this?

                    REBECCA
          That's right.

Rebecca looks on slyly and nods her head.

                    REBECCA
          Saint Sebastian was an atheist.

                    SEBASTIAN
          And what happened to our hero?

                    REBECCA
          He rejected his atheistic beliefs
          and the Romans put him to death.
          They executed him with a bow and
          arrow.

                    SEBASTIAN
          Really?

INT THE ABBOTT MANSION IN THE DEN SHORTLY AFTER

                    SEBASTIAN
          A little early for drinking, isn't
          it?

                    AARON
          I don't like this. Finish the
          game, it eases me. It's your move.

                    SEBASTIAN
          It's in the bag. You're in check.

                    AARON
          I saw that Rebecca stopped you.

                    SEBASTIAN
          Yeah.

                    AARON
          What did she want?

                    SEBASTIAN
          Nothing.

Aaron looks out the window and raises his drink to
his chest.

                     AARON
          She scares me. She's got some sort
          of power, some sixth sense . . .

Sebastian's holding on to every word.

                     AARON
          When I was a kid and came looking
          to aggravate or torment my
          sister . . .

Aaron shakes his head and downs his drink.

                  AARON (CONT'D)
          She always knew. I'd sneak. I'd
          hide . . . but she always caught
          me . . . like she could see
          through walls . . . like she could
          read my mind . . . that's why I
          did it.

Sebastian puts a chess piece down while staring at
Aaron.

                    SEBASTIAN
          (mesmerized) Did what?

                     AARON
          I wrecked the dollhouse.

                    SEBASTIAN
          See . . . her mystical lady-in-
          waiting isn't infallible.

                     AARON
          Right . . . she wasn't home.

Sebastian moves a chess piece.

                    SEBASTIAN
          That's mate.

Sebastian looks to the side with concerned eyes.

INT C CAR MONDAY MORNING

Joey and C are driving around with Impallaria
donuts and coffee.

                    CERONE
          Barr says dat she still ain't got
          no lawyer. Danahy will be put on.

                    JOEY
          He'll play for us like a pinball.
          He's into us for eight, likes da
          sauce.

Joey flicks his fingers (playing pinball). C smiles.

TUESDAY'S CHILD MONDAY MORNING

Liz waves to Trisha, who's working with a young
developmentally disabled girl. Trisha gets up. The
eyes of the girl follow Trisha to the door.

                    TRISHA
          What is it?

                    LIZ
          Trish, I really like you. I get
          along better with you than I get
          along with anyone here.

Trisha looks confused.

                    TRISHA
          Sure, Liz. I like you too. What's
          wrong?

                         LIZ
          I've got a big mouth.

Trisha looks confused again. There's a pause.

                         LIZ
          Some attorney, Sherwin, called
          me. Said he wanted to help
          you. He asked me if you seemed
          OK. He seemed real nice and
          everything. . . .

                       TRISHA
          Go ahead.

                         LIZ
          I said that you talk to yourself.
          I thought I was helping you.
          I can tell him that you were
          singing . . . (sobbing) I'm so
          sorry.

                       TRISHA
          Don't worry. I know you were
          trying to help.

Liz looks confused.

                         LIZ
          You're not mad that . . . that I
          got a mouth bigger than the Grand
          Canyon?

                       TRISHA
          No.

                         LIZ
          That I got a mouth bigger than the
          planet Earth?

                       TRISHA
          No.

Trisha smiles, the smile turns solemn.

                    TRISHA
          You know Liz, some things are
          true whether we believe them or
          not. . . .

INT COURTROOM MONDAY AFTERNOON

Irv smiles down from the bench. On his left are
Sebastian Sherwin and Aaron. Ingrid's behind them.
On his right is Trisha; two rows behind is Mary,
Irv's wife. In the back of the court is a street
person and an older man.

                    JUDGE COHEN
          Young lady. Is your attorney
          running late?

Trisha looks at the judge.

                    TRISHA
          May I speak, sir?

                    JUDGE COHEN
          Of course. When you're addressed
          by the court you're obligated to.

AARON IS TRYING TO WHISPER IN SEBASTIAN'S EAR.

The judge looks sternly. Sebastian brushes Aaron
off.

                    TRISHA
          Sir. I didn't think I needed an
          attorney.

Aaron whispers to Sebastian. The judge looks on
sternly.

                    JUDGE COHEN
          Young lady, you're here today
          without counsel?

                    TRISHA
          Yes sir.

                    JUDGE COHEN
          I assume that it's not a problem
          of funds.

                    TRISHA
          I just didn't think that I needed
          one . . . I really don't know any
          attorneys.

                    JUDGE COHEN
          Miss, this hearing could have
          serious ramifications. I insist you
          be represented.

                    SEBASTIAN
          (whispers to Aaron) She's
          stalling.

                    TRISHA
          Sir, if you'll be kind enough to
          recommend one.

                    SEBASTIAN
          Your Honor, Miss Abbott is
          trifling . . .

Irv looks sternly at Sebastian.

                    JUDGE COHEN
          Counselor. I agree that it's
          irregular.

Irv looks down at Trisha very fatherly.

                              TRISHA
            Are you trifling with this court
            young lady?

                              TRISHA
            No, Your Honor, of course not.

Irv looks down on his desk.

                           JUDGE COHEN
            Court reconvenes Thursday morning.
            Young lady, get your attorney's
            name and address from the clerk.

The judge points at Jebson. He raps his gavel and
stands up. Aaron's crazed. He looks at Sebastian.

                              AARON
            What are we going to do? Do you
            know what she can do in three
            days?

Aaron charges the bench.

                         AARON (CONT'D)
            (stutters) Y-y-Your Honor, please,
            she's crazy, a lunatic.

The judge looks strangely down on Aaron.

                           JUDGE COHEN
            Young man. Court's adjourned.

Irv continues to walk away. Aaron approaches his
sister.

                              AARON
            You'll never get away with this!

Aaron angrily points at Trisha. Sebastian pulls him
away.

AARON'S FACE

                    AARON
          One of us will be destroyed! You
          wanted it this way! Not me!

TRISHA'S FACE IS TRANQUIL WITH A TRACE OF IMPUDENCE.

PATRICK DANAHY'S OFFICE MONDAY AFTERNOON

The office is shabby. A heavy woman of 40 is on the
phone and doing her nails.

                  MOLLY DEERE
          You have a case Thursday
          morning. . . . How would I know?
          I wouldn't recommend you. . . .
          A court appointment, Jebson
          called . . . Don't complain, the
          daughter of Howard Abbott's your
          client . . . I don't drink . . .
          You ought to try it.

She hangs the phone up.

INT THE ABBOTT MANSION, INGRID'S BEDROOM MONDAY
AFTERNOON

Ingrid is writing in a diary. There's a knock at
the door.

                    INGRID
          Who is it?

                    AARON
          It's me, Aaron.

                    INGRID
          Oh good, come in.

Aaron enters. Ingrid has a pencil to her mouth.

                    INGRID
          What did I wear when the president
          of Friends of the Opera came to
          dinner?

                    AARON
          Mother, we have other things to
          discuss. Your costume diary can
          wait.

                    INGRID
          I've kept this diary for over
          thirty years. I want to pass it on
          to my granddaughter.

She looks distastefully at Aaron.

                    INGRID
          If there ever is one. One child's
          a lunatic, the other a gigolo.

                    AARON
          Mother, I'm not a gigolo.

                    INGRID
          You should come with me more
          often. One of the Kennedy heirs
          attended the museum gala. She was
          cute . . . a little pudgy, but
          cute.

                    AARON
          Mother, we only have two
          days . . . Sebastian's on the way.

                    INGRID
          You can't remember the outfit?

                    AARON
          I can't do it all by myself!
          Trisha has Rebecca. Who do I have?

He slams the door. A clock slides off the bureau and smashes on the floor. Ingrid looks at it reflectively.

                    INGRID
          Yes, of course. The Big Ben dress.
          Honey, I remember, I'll be ready
          shortly.

INT PATRICK'S OFFICE LATER MONDAY AFTERNOON

Molly's sipping the straw of a quart cup. Patrick's in his office.

                    PATRICK
          Are my clothes at the cleaners?

                    MOLLY DEERE
          I'll take them tomorrow.

                    PATRICK
          I told you to take them today.

                    MOLLY DEERE
          Court's not until Thursday.

Patrick comes to the door.

                    PATRICK
          I meet with Trisha Abbott tomorrow
          morning. Clean up this office,
          water the plants, dust.

Molly rolls her eyes.

                    PATRICK
          Don't you understand? This could
          be it. We could be set. It's AE!

Molly's concentrating on a crossword puzzle.

                        PATRICK
        What must I do to make you
        respond?

                        MOLLY DEERE
        Try paying me.

                        PATRICK
        When this is over, I'm gonna pay
        you every dime I owe you. Then
        I'll fire you . . . cousin or not.

                        MOLLY DEERE
        Promises, promises.

INT KELLY'S BAR MONDAY EVENING

Patrick is dressed in a suit surrounded by a small
crowd. Mush is a seventy-year-old regular.

                        MUSH
        I heard you got AE on the hook.

                        PATRICK
        Mush, that's reserved information.

                        MUSH
        If you want reserved information,
        you should change secretaries.

Mush smiles. Everyone laughs.

                        MUSH
        Another round, Counselor Danahy?

Patrick is gazing much farther than the end of the
bar.

                        PATRICK
        Yeah . . . yeah! Get everyone!

INT NEIGHBORHOOD CLUB BASEMENT TUESDAY MORNING

Joey and C are throwing papers into the basement furnace.

                    CERONE
          Joey, I need dis.

                    JOEY
          Relax, it's in da bag. Cohen's
          da judge. Danahy's da counsel,
          he'll use Arnold the shrink. I'm
          pounding da good doctor's aide for
          information. Get it? Pounding her
          for information?

                    CERONE
          Yeah, yeah I get it.

                    JOEY
          What an organization. Hey C, what
          kinda CEO do you tink I'd make?

Joey smiles. C throws a wad of paper at him.

                    CERONE
          Hey, here's a scoop to feed da
          press. Sherwin took care of Hat
          and is writin' dose letters?

                    JOEY
          C, you watch too many movies.

INT DOCTOR ARNOLD'S OFFICE TUESDAY MORNING

His aide, Eve, is 30ish and cute. She's on the phone in the rundown office. "Dr. Arnold, Psychiatrist" is painted on the windows.

                    EVE
          Yes I know, but Dr. Arnold was
          called for an emergency . . . Yes,
          Mrs. Rath, I'll tell him.

Eve gently puts the phone down and dials another number. There's a buzzer noise, and Eve covers the phone, flips a switch, and talks into a small speaker on the desk.

                    EVE
          Yes?

                  TRISHA
          Trisha Abbott for Dr. Arnold.

                    EVE
          Take the stairs to the top of the
          hall, turn right, I'll buzz you in.

INT DR. ARNOLD'S OFFICE NOON

He has pages of notes on the desk. Trisha is in front of him.

                  DR. ARNOLD
          Miss Abbott, it's late. . . . Let's
          recap. Rob proposed at Christmas,
          you were supposed to be wed now,
          in May?

Trisha nods.

                  DR. ARNOLD
          He was in his last year of
          architecture school. He worked
          construction in the summer and
          bartended on the weekends.

Trisha nods.

                  DR. ARNOLD
          You met at school in September.
          He's Italian. His mother was
          teaching you to cook and you were
          converting to Catholicism.

Trisha nods.

                    DR. ARNOLD
Your family did not share your
enthusiasm. Your brother became
hostile when you bought a
transmission for Rob's 2012 Chevy.

                    TRISHA
It was a Christmas present.

                    DR. ARNOLD
Yes . . . Rob died in a car
accident on Saint Valentine's
day. You've received letters and
trinkets that he sent to you after
his death.

He takes his glasses in his hand and looks sternly
at Trish.

                    DR. ARNOLD
Young lady. Those letters will be
subpoenaed by the court.

                    TRISHA
(meekly) I don't think so.

                    DR. ARNOLD
Huh! You're in for a big
surprise. . . . They most
certainly will.

Trisha shakes her head.

                    DR. ARNOLD
And why wouldn't they? (smiling)

                    TRISHA
They already have them.

                    DR. ARNOLD
They do? . . . How did they get them?

                        TRISHA
            I gave them to my brother.

He puts his glasses on, closes his eyes, and rubs
his head.

                      DR. ARNOLD
            (mumbles) You gave them to him?

INT EVE'S APARTMENT TUESDAY EVENING

Joey's in the fridge. Eve's on the couch, the TV's
on low.

                         EVE
            I'm tired. It's been crazy. That
            Abbott girl's taking up hours and
            hours. . . . Are you listening?

                        JOEY
            Yeah. Didn't you have some beer?

                         EVE
            I had to bite my tongue. The more
            people have, the nastier they
            are. . . . Don't you think?

                        JOEY
            Yeah.

Joey comes in smiling. He kisses Eve on the forehead.

                         EVE
            But Trisha Abbott's kind. She
            apologized for screwing up the
            schedule. No one ever . . .

Joey's eyes narrowed.

                        JOEY
            What was dat about Abbott?

                    EVE
     Trisha Abbott, she
     apologized . . .

                    JOEY
     Relax, I'll give you a massage.

                    EVE
     Joey, you're too good to me. But
     I shouldn't talk shop.

                    JOEY
     Yeah, I am too good to ya. Now
     keep talkin' or I'll belt ya.

Joey begins massaging her back. Eve laughs.

                    EVE
     Her family wants to put her in an
     institution or something.

                    JOEY
     (whispered) What else, baby?

INT NEIGHBORHOOD CLUB TUESDAY LATE EVENING

C's playing cards. Joey walks in.

                    CERONE
     Hey Baby-face, take my hand. And
     keep yours above the table.

Joey and C meet in the middle of the room.

                    JOEY
     Dat broad really believes dat da
     letters are from Hat. She's shot.

                    CERONE
     Feed it to da funnies.

INT JOEY PITASI'S CAR TUESDAY NIGHT

He bites his tongue and at the same time looks in the mirror.

> JOEY
> Answer. Damn it, answer.

A man answers.

> LOU SHERMAN
> This better be good.

> JOEY
> AE.

> LOU SHERMAN
> (groggily) AE . . . Abbott Electronics?

> JOEY
> Daughter Trisha is cuckoo, and loving brudder's trying to lock her up and take her cake.

> LOU SHERMAN
> Hold the horn, let me get a pen.

INT PATRICK DANAHY'S APARTMENT TUESDAY LATE

Patrick's on the phone.

> PATRICK
> Lauren, please let me talk to Patrick. . . . I know, baby. But that's all changed now. You know that if I had the cash, I'd have sent it to you. I swear it . . . I can't remember the last drink I had . . . please let me talk to him . . . oh that's right, how are his grades? . . . Well tell him that, that I, I love him . . .

(said rushed) and that I've
changed.

> PATRICK (CONT'D)
> Really . . . I mean that for you
> too . . . no, it's ten thirty in
> California, isn't it? I'm still in
> the office working on the Abbott
> Electronics case. I hope it won't
> be like this when I'm their head
> counsel . . . no, baby, I told you
> I quit.

A male voice is heard in the background.

> PATRICK (CONT'D)
> Oh, oh should've known. Still
> gold diggin', huh? Can Grandpa
> still walk? Wait. . . . Wait,
> don't hang up. I didn't mean it. I
> still . . .

Dial tone.

Patrick leans his head against the fridge (agoniz-
ing). He reaches down feeling for the door handle,
reaches in the fridge, grabs a beer bottle, and
pops it open on the bottle opener nailed to the
fridge (all without looking). Tears run down his
cheeks as he looks up and guzzles the beer.

INT LOU SHERMAN'S BEDROOM TUESDAY NIGHT

Lou's talking on the phone.

> LOU SHERMAN
> Yeah, the source is good . . . I
> don't care how late it is. I want
> a two-liner in Joan Coullane's
> column . . . We'll go from
> there . . .

INT PATRICK'S OFFICE WEDNESDAY MORNING

Trisha looks at her watch—9 A.M. Patrick enters
reading a newspaper. Molly's doing her nails at her
desk.

> PATRICK
> There's a leak.

> TRISHA
> A leak?

> PATRICK
> Yep. You're in the funnies.

> TRISHA
> The funnies?

> PATRICK
> You're in Coullane's column.

> TRISHA
> (sarcastically) Oh wonderful.

He puts his arm around Trisha as they walk into
his office.

> PATRICK
> Change your story, and I can hold
> the dogs off.

The camera zooms to trisha's eyes.

> PATRICK (CONT'D)
> The deck's stacked against ya,
> kid . . .

> TRISHA
> Patrick, you don't believe
> me . . .

The office door closes. Molly puts her ear to the door.

I/E EVE'S APARTMENT WEDNESDAY AFTERNOON

Joey puts his cell to his ear as he runs down the stairs.

INT LOU SHERMAN'S OFFICE WED, SAME TIME

Lou is 60ish with the looks of a retired marine. Sitting around him are two average-looking middle-aged women and a man in his late 20s.

                    LOU SHERMAN
          Hello Joe. Hello.

Lou is smoking a cigar. There is a big "No Smoking" sign over his head. He waves his hands for quiet.

                    LOU SHERMAN
          Great tip . . . Yeah, Yeah I'm
          listening . . . you don't say?
          You don't say? Good. Good . . .
          and Joey . . . I paid for the
          exclusive. I want my colleagues to
          read it in the paper like everyone
          else.

Lou hangs up the phone.

               MALE ASSISTANT TO LOU SHERMAN
          What's up, boss?

                    LOU SHERMAN
          We got a story. That broad ain't
          backing down.

               MALE ASSISTANT TO LOU SHERMAN
          You mean she is nuts?

Lou hesitates before speaking. He stares into space.

                    LOU SHERMAN
          Well she ain't backing down . . .

                  FEMALE ASSISTANT 1
          She's got guts.

                  FEMALE ASSISTANT 2
          Maybe she's got faith.

                    MALE ASSISTANT
          Faith . . . hah. . . . What's
          faith?

Camera Focuses on the face of one of the female
assts.

                  FEMALE ASSISTANT 2
          Faith's believing when common
          sense tells you not to.

                    LOU SHERMAN
          Then she's got blind faith.

INT AARON'S OFFICE WEDNESDAY AFTERNOON

Aaron is sitting behind his desk speaking with
Blake Andrew. Blake is 60ish. He has white-silver
hair and is well groomed.

                      AARON
          AE's got the politicians. But
          liquidity is key to avoid
          bankruptcy and merge AI into AE.

                    BLAKE ANDREW
          It's brilliant . . . Son . . . I
          like how it feels.

Aaron smiles.

                         AARON
          Get all the cash you can. . . .
          The unions will behave, there's a
          lot of jobs at stake.

                      BLAKE ANDREW
          And you'll be the white knight.

Aaron gazes away.

                         AARON
          Yes . . . to some I'll be the
          white knight.

I/E PARKING LOT OF COURTHOUSE THURSDAY EARLY AFTER-
NOON

Lou Sherman is fixing himself as he runs to the
elevators.

INT COURTROOM THURSDAY SHORTLY AFTER

Court is in session. There are 40-50 newcomers.

                        JEBSON
          The Honorable Irving Cohen. Please
          be seated.

The judge glances at the new faces and grimaces.

                      JUDGE COHEN
          Would you like to begin,
          Counselor?

He is looking directly at Sebastian.

                      SEBASTIAN
          Your Honor, we move to close
          court. There has been a trick
          played by the defendant.

                         JUDGE COHEN
                Mr. Sherwin, again. This is a
                civil suit. There is no defendant.

The judge menacingly looks around the room.

Mary smiles at her husband; he starts to smile
back.

                         JUDGE COHEN
                Are you implying that Mr. Danahy
                involved the press?

He looks squarely at Mr. Danahy then back to Sherwin.

                         SEBASTIAN
                Someone did.

                         JUDGE COHEN
                This decision should include Mr.
                Danahy and his client. After all,
                it's only fair.

Danahy whispers to Trisha.

                         JUDGE COHEN
                Mr. Danahy.

                         PATRICK
                Your Honor, we're not so motivated.

                         JUDGE COHEN
                Very well. Counselor Sherwin, you
                have the floor.

PATRICK REACHES OVER AND, WITHOUT LOOKING, PATS
TRISHA'S HAND.

                         TRISHA
                (whispered) Only a few days left.

Patrick stares as Trisha smiles widely. Sebastian addresses the court.

                    SEBASTIAN
          Your Honor. I compare Trisha
          Abbott to a chrysalis, a butterfly
          slowly emerging from a cocoon.
          Rob Santis was bringing her out
          into the world . . . with all due
          respect.

Sebastian clears his throat.

                    SEBASTIAN (CONT'D)
          I can find no evidence that someone
          other than Trisha Abbott wrote
          these letters and bought these
          gifts. She desperately needs
          medical treatment. At risk is a
          fortune that was meant to remain
          in the Abbott family. . . . Her
          grandmother, against the better
          judgment of her attorney Lawrence
          Barr, cut Aaron Abbott out of
          her will. Trisha insists that she
          will give all of the inheritance
          away. . . . I have several
          witnesses who can testify that
          Luellyn Abbott meant to change the
          will before she died. . . . She
          was the wife of Bradford Abbott,
          the founder of Abbott Electronics.
          He worked very hard, Your Honor,
          for the position that his family
          finds themselves in today. . . .
          We ask for an immediate
          injunction. . . . Trisha Abbott is
          not in her right frame of mind,
          and cannot make sound decisions,
          economic or other.

Irv looks down at Patrick, who nervously wipes his forehead. Sebastian sits, and Patrick rises.

>   PATRICK
>   Your Honor, I've rushed to prepare
>   this case. Trisha Abbott concurs
>   with her family and would like
>   to see this proceeding closed
>   as quickly as possible. She's
>   a sensible, upstanding woman.
>   She is of no risk to herself or
>   society. I believe that someone
>   else is responsible for writing
>   those letters and leaving the
>   gifts at her home. . . . My client
>   is guilty of nothing other than
>   falling for the most cruel and
>   dirty deception. I believe that
>   someone who has the most to gain
>   in this case is the culprit.
>   Several people are suspect. For
>   example, her brother Aaron. . . .

The courtroom becomes noisy, and Aaron leaps over
the rail and takes Patrick by the neck. Patrick can
barely speak.

>   PATRICK
>   I wasn't accusing. I was
>   raising . . .

Sebastian comes from behind to stop Aaron. Guards
are rushing in from the hallway. Trisha stands up.
She has a horrified look in her eyes.

>   TRISHA
>   Stop! Is this what money does? For
>   the love of God, leave me in peace
>   just a little longer!

Aaron's elbow pokes Sebastian's cheek and knocks
him to the ground. The guard separates Aaron and
Patrick. Sebastian rises to a kneeling position
holding his head and cheek. He glares at Trisha.

                    SEBASTIAN
          You fool! These delusions are a
          part of your sickness! If there is
          a God, tell him to materialize and
          take you away from all of this! He
          won't! And you know why? God does
          not exist.

Judge Cohen bangs his gavel and looks sternly at
all parties.

                    JUDGE COHEN
          This court will reconvene in
          the morning. And I remind all of
          you that this is a court of law!
          Anyone not conducting themselves
          appropriately will be promptly
          arrested.

Trisha is slouched over and weeping into her arms.

INT LOU SHERMAN'S OFFICE LATER THURSDAY AFTERNOON

He is on the phone.

                    LOU SHERMAN
          That's right. "There is no God!"
          I don't care what Zold says! And
          I want to see it in block.

INT ABBOTT ESTATE DEN EARLY EVENING

Sebastian and Aaron are playing chess.

                    SEBASTIAN
          That neighborhood's old mob. Hat.
          What kind of a name is dat? (said
          "dat" mockingly) What did your
          sister call him?

                         AARON
          Hat.

                       SEBASTIAN
          Why would anyone call someone
          "Hat"?

                         AARON
          He wore a hat that his grandfather
          left him.

                       SEBASTIAN
          That's ludicrous.

They swap pieces.

                         AARON
          Should've seen the funeral home.
          The mother was hysterical.

Aaron pauses.

                     AARON (CONT'D)
          Wouldn't let them close the casket
          until they found the hat to put in
          with him. It was bizarre.

                       SEBASTIAN
          Hey. I got it!! The mob's behind
          it. They've got their eyes on your
          sister's coffers.

                         AARON
          Have you ever heard of Peter
          Cerone of Edgeview Bank?

                       SEBASTIAN
          That's the second time you've said
          that name. Checkmate. Who is he?

Aaron is frustrated and he rises.

AARON
He's behind some of this.

SEBASTIAN
What does he want?

AARON
Someone he could never keep.

INT JUDGE COHEN'S HOME THURSDAY EVENING

The Cohens are at the dinner table.

MARY
Did you see the evening news?

JUDGE COHEN
I don't even want to imagine.
Trump says it's all fake news. He's
not all wrong.

MARY
Who does he think he is, saying,
"There is no God"?

Irv rolls his eyes. Mary does not see.

JUDGE COHEN
(irritated) Sherwin was knocked to
the ground and angry. Don't bow
to sentiment. . . . It's fortunate
that you never pursued a legal
career. You're too emotional.

MARY
You should have handled the
reprimand differently. What did
that innocent girl do?

Mary hastily gets up and walks out of the room. Irv
has a puzzled look on his face.

> JUDGE COHEN
> (under breath) Menopause.

INT THE ABBOTT MANSION IN THE DEN THURSDAY EVENING

Aaron covers the phone as Ingrid enters.

> INGRID
> Did you see the evening news?
> We're the laughingstock of the
> country.

> AARON
> Melissa, I'll call you later. . . .
> Yes, me too.

> INGRID
> You're insane as well. She got
> you into this mess. Her father's
> ruined. His company's done.

> AARON
> Where are you going, Mother?

> INGRID
> I'm going to the Rhodeses'. There's
> a village meeting. Your father
> insists on holding his chin up
> through this fiasco.

> AARON
> Have fun.

Aaron's face is pleasant as if he sees through his
mother.

INT KELLY'S BAR THURSDAY EVENING

Patrick is at the bar with another 10 patrons.

> PATRICK
> Mikey, get everyone another round.

Toad, a guy who got his nickname from his face, smiles at Patrick.

> TOAD
> Big shot is in the funnies. Now
> he's a millionaire.

> MUSH
> Hey Patty, take it easy. . . . I
> don't know if anyone told you, but
> it don't look good.

Patrick tips his bottle of beer up and smugly looks on.

> PATRICK
> Why, Mush, don't you believe that
> the dead can write letters?

> MUSH
> It's not that. Hell, my mother's
> dead thirty years and I see her in
> the house all the time. She took a
> swing at me Monday.

> PATRICK
> Well, what is it then?

Mush smiles and raises the mug to his face.

> MUSH
> No offense, but to me the nail
> in the coffin is that she let you
> represent her. I mean, what sane
> person would do that?

INT THE RHODESES' ESTATE THURSDAY EVENING

The room is black tie and full. Howard's watching his wife, who is talking to a handsome middle-aged man.

> INGRID
> Excuse me, Mr. Gunther.

                    MR. GUNTHER
          But of course, Mrs. Abbott.

Ingrid walks to her husband. She speaks closely to
him.

                    INGRID
          We're outcasts. The only people
          that will talk to me are has-beens
          and no ones.

                    HOWARD
          It's late anyway. I promised
          Washington the night off. He's
          been so nervous lately. . . .
          He'll pull the car up. Go get our
          coats.

Ingrid looks concerned and then disappears into
the crowd.

INT THE ABBOTT MANSION IN THE DEN SHORTLY AFTER

Sebastian, Ingrid, and Aaron are seated at a glass
coffee table. The chess pieces are scattered.

Ingrid is in her evening dress and pasting photos.

                    SEBASTIAN
          She's been under watch. Nothing
          useful has turned up.

                    INGRID
          Either she's nuts or it's that
          witch. And you, Mr. Artist!
          I demand that you stop the
          publicity.

                    AARON
          We don't have time for this.
          Rebecca would not hurt

Trisha. . . . What does tomorrow
bring?

                SEBASTIAN
The calligrapher will report
that it's expert forgery. The
psychiatrists will testify.

                AARON
What about the press?

                SEBASTIAN
Cohen won't allow his courtroom to
become a circus. They threw their
dart. I can't see any further
interest.

                AARON
I'd like the truth. . . . It's all
so strange.

Aaron gazes angelically. Sebastian angers.

                SEBASTIAN
The money is essential. The truth
is only a distraction. And there
is nothing strange! The dead don't
write letters. . . . The answer's
right in front of our eyes.

                INGRID
I hope the judge sees it so
clearly.

                AARON
Hard times if he doesn't.

                INGRID
You and your father are always
exaggerating.

                        AARON
            Are we?

Sebastian looks at them strangely.

                      SEBASTIAN
            If the judge thinks that someone
            else wrote those letters, he may
            see her as a victim of fraud, not
            mental illness.

Ingrid is visibly irritated.

                       INGRID
            Then what?

                      SEBASTIAN
            Just let me be. There's more clay.

Aaron puts his head into his hands and turns his
head.

                       INGRID
            I'm going to bed. Good night.

The door slams.

THE DOOR.

INT RESTAURANT LATE THURSDAY EVENING

Sebastian is sitting with his brother Ted.

                      SEBASTIAN
            That's right! Can you prove that
            there is? Can anyone?

                        TED
            Little Brother . . . Just because
            you can't touch something does not
            mean that it doesn't exist.

                    SEBASTIAN
        Galileo proved the earth to be
        round, Einstein the theory of
        relativity. Sherwin, divine truth.

                      TED
        My friend is a brain surgeon. He
        has worked on hundreds. He has
        never seen a thought. Would you
        say that thoughts don't exist?

Sebastian and Ted rise to leave.

                      TED
        Oh, Sebastian. I almost forgot.
        My son David will be competing at
        Northwestern University Saturday
        morning. I can't attend. But he'd
        love it if you could stand in.

                    SEBASTIAN
        Oh? What's the competition?

                      TED
        Archery.

INT THE CABBAGE HOUSE THURSDAY NIGHT

Trisha rises from the couch and lays a magazine
down. She stretches and walks. The light is on in
the kitchen.

                    TRISHA
        Becky, are you coming to bed?

Rebecca comes out and meets her.

                    REBECCA
        In a while. . . . You go ahead, I
        have some things to do.

INT SEBASTIAN'S CAR THURSDAY NIGHT

Sebastian is driving at high speed. The phone rings.

                    SEBASTIAN
          Yes?

                    VOICE
          (raspy voice) Eventually good
          always wins over evil.

                    SEBASTIAN
          Who is this?

                    VOICE
          Sebastian, you know that we all
          have to account someday.

                    SEBASTIAN
          Who is this? This—this is a hoax!

SEBASTIAN'S TERRIFIED FACE

                    VOICE
          It's unlucky for you that it's not.
          Life is not a joke. It's a testing
          ground. . . . Will you pass?

                    SEBASTIAN
          Wrong number, you lunatic!

He looks at the phone before nervously hanging it up.

INT IRV COHEN'S HOME IN THE BEDROOM THURSDAY LATE
NIGHT

Irv rolls over and turns off his reading lamp.

                    MARY
          Delusions do not prove insanity.

                    JUDGE COHEN
          Please, it's tough enough. You've
          never interfered before.

                    MARY
Your cases are usually nonsense.

                 JUDGE COHEN
Thanks, this one is no different.
It's about a sick girl and money.

                    MARY
Are you so sure that she's sick?

                 JUDGE COHEN
Don't be a fool.

                    MARY
Irv, do you know what a fool is?

Irv remains complacent.

                MARY (CONT'D)
A fool is one who substitutes
words for deeds.

She briskly turns over and shuts the light.

INT COURTHOUSE FRIDAY MORNING EARLY

Busy with people passing the metal detectors. Guard
1 shakes his head. Then he grabs the walkie-talkie.

                  GUARD 1
We need help down here. Why
doesn't Cohen lock that Abbott
trial down?

Guard 2 is listening.

                  GUARD 2
Are you kidding? You ever seen a
judge turn away publicity?

INT RESTAURANT ACROSS FROM COURTHOUSE FRIDAY MORNING

Two men (Jimmy and Chucky) are sitting in a booth.
One is reading a newspaper.

>   CHUCKY
>   What's so interesting?

Jimmy just continues to read.

>   JIMMY
>   That Abbott family that owns
>   Abbott Electronics got problems.

>   CHUCKY
>   I'd like to have their problems.

>   JIMMY
>   Really. The daughter is getting
>   letters from some dead guy, the
>   brother is using it as an excuse
>   to grab her dough. And their
>   atheist attorney is showboatin'
>   that there ain't no letters cause
>   there ain't no life after death,
>   cause there ain't no God.

>   CHUCKY
>   Hey screw 'em all. Remember what
>   they tried to do to the union?

>   JIMMY
>   Yeah, but I feel for the girl.
>   They'll eat her for breakfast.

>   CHUCKY
>   What's she look like? Maybe I'll
>   eat her.

>   JIMMY
>   Hey Romeo, pay. I want to stop
>   over there and take a look.

INT COURTHOUSE HALLWAY FRIDAY MORNING

Trisha and Patrick are in a corner. The hallway is
busy.

> PATRICK
> This can only go one way unless
> you . . .

> TRISHA
> I only have a few days left.

She smiles widely. Patrick stares at her.

INT COURTHOUSE IN A PRIVATE ROOM, SAME TIME

Aaron, Sebastian, and Ingrid are in discussion.

> INGRID
> This is your fault, claiming that
> there is no God! Had you no idea
> that we're Presbyterians?

> SEBASTIAN
> I was shoved. I was trying to
> separate . . .

> INGRID
> What do you care? What does
> anyone care about you? You're just
> another nonbeliever. But we're the
> Abbotts, and we're ruined!

The door opens. Howard Abbott walks in. His face
is stern.

> HOWARD
> Ingrid, no travel until this is
> resolved.

> INGRID
> I'm supposed to leave for Paris.
> How will that look?

> HOWARD
> I'll cut your credit cards. How
> will that look?

> INGRID
> You bastard! I gave you the best
> years of my life!

> HOWARD
> If that's so, you should be put
> out of your misery now. I'll
> handle Trisha.

EXT STREET OUTSIDE THE COURTHOUSE SHORTLY AFTER

Irv and Mary are passing protestors carrying signs.

A dark-skinned man's sign reads "i'm living proof that god exists".

Irv and mary make their way into the back entrance. Just as they get to the door, a woman screams.

> WOMAN
> There's the judge! Tell 'em, judge!
> God exists!

INT JUDGE COHEN'S COURTROOM FRIDAY MORNING

The court is packed. Mary is escorted to a seat behind trisha. Lou sherman is behind where sebastian will sit. There are artists busy sketching. Trisha is seated next to patrick.

Sebastian, Aaron and Ingrid enter, there's commotion, the crowd boos. Cohen hits the gavel.

> JUDGE COHEN
> Order in the court.

INT JUDGE COHEN'S COURTROOM LATER

Sebastian is standing, Dr. Behren is on the witness stand.

> SEBASTIAN
> Do you believe that Miss Abbott can be cured of her delusions?

> DR. BEHREN
> Yes, completely.

> SEBASTIAN
> In your expert opinion, is Miss Abbott capable of making sound decisions, financial or otherwise?

> DR. BEHREN
> In my expert opinion, no.

INT JUDGE COHEN'S COURTROOM FRIDAY MORNING

Patrick is questioning Doctor Arnold.

> PATRICK
> Doctor, does Trisha show any signs of violence whatsoever?

> DR. ARNOLD
> No.

> PATRICK
> Would you say that she's suicidal?

> DR. ARNOLD
> Definitely not.

INT JUDGE COHEN'S COURTROOM FRIDAY SHORTLY AFTER

Aaron is being questioned by Sebastian.

> AARON
> I just want to see her well.

                    SEBASTIAN
          Mr. Abbott, how did you learn
          about the letters?

                    AARON
          She showed them to me at her home
          after my grandmother's funeral.

Jonathan is seated next to sebastian's seat.

Howard is seated next to where aaron's seat is.

                    SEBASTIAN
          Your Honor, this is the first
          letter. It arrived 6 days after Mr.
          Santis's death. It's short. May I?

The judge nods. The courtroom is completely silent.

                    SEBASTIAN (CONT'D)
          "Well Love, I hope that reading
          this will make you believe that
          you'll always be a part of me.
          Here's the physical proof you
          wanted. I've told you a thousand
          times. I will always love you.
          Death will unite, not separate us.
          I'll never leave you.
          Love is one soul in two beings.
          Love, Hat."

Lou sherman pulls out a handkerchief and blows his
nose.

                    SEBASTIAN (CONT'D)
          Mr. Abbott. Would you say that
          your sister is astute in business?

                    AARON
          Well, I don't know how . . .

                    SEBASTIAN
          Let me rephrase. Would you say
          that she has expertise in high
          finance?

Aaron smiles.

                    AARON
          Sir, my sister wouldn't know Dow
          Jones from Tom Jones.

There's a burst of laughter. The judge hits the
gavel.

                    JUDGE COHEN
          Mr. Abbott, please answer clearly.

                    AARON
          Yes sir. Trisha is by no means an
          expert in high finance.

                    SEBASTIAN
          Is your father requesting to
          position himself as financial
          guardian for Trisha?

                    AARON
          My father is concerned about
          Trisha. I handle the bulk of the
          family finance.

                    SEBASTIAN
          Last question. When Trisha is
          again well, what will happen to
          her funds?

                    AARON
          They'll be returned to her.

INT JUDGE COHEN'S COURTROOM AFTER

Sebastian is questioning Ingrid.

                         SEBASTIAN
          When did you notice that something
          was drastically wrong with Trisha?

                          INGRID
          We were close until after Santis
          died. When her grandmother died,
          she *completely* lost it.

                         SEBASTIAN
          Did you do anything to help her?

                          INGRID
          I went to her home to talk to her
          and made an appointment with my
          psychiatrist.

     She points to Rebecca Riley.

                          INGRID
          She didn't want to let me in. I
          wasn't going to let the hired help
          forbid me to see my own daughter.

                         SEBASTIAN
          I see. Mrs. Abbott, would you say
          that Trisha was a normal child?

                          INGRID
          She was timid. . . . Her senior
          prom was a disaster, a bus came to
          pick her up.

                         SEBASTIAN
          Are you close to your daughter?

                          INGRID
          Yes I am.

                         SEBASTIAN
          Do you love your daughter?

                    INGRID
        How vile. Of course I do.

                  SEBASTIAN
        Tell us why she confides in Rebecca
        Riley and not in you?

                    INGRID
        That's false! She's just a hand
        who's milking my daughter dry.

                  SEBASTIAN
        Thank you, Mrs. Abbott.

INT JUDGE COHEN'S COURTROOM LATE FRIDAY MORNING

                  SEBASTIAN
        Your Honor, I call Rebecca Riley.

The court stirs as Rebecca hobbles up and is sworn
in.

                  SEBASTIAN
        How long have you been a nanny to
        Miss Abbott?

She slowly and almost mysteriously raises her head
to speak.

                   REBECCA
        Since she was an infant.

                  SEBASTIAN
        Did you know Rob Santis?

                   REBECCA
        Yes I did.

                  SEBASTIAN
        Did he spend the night ever
        at . . .

                    PATRICK
          Objection. Trisha's private life's
          irrelevant.

                    SEBASTIAN
          Sir, it is essential to know the
          background.

                    JUDGE COHEN
          Overruled.

                    SEBASTIAN
          Thank you, Your Honor. . . . Did
          Rob Santis ever spend the night?

                    REBECCA
          No.

                    SEBASTIAN
          Never?

                    REBECCA
          Never.

Mary cohen smiles widely.

                    SEBASTIAN
          The Cabbage House has a strange
          ring. Does its name have anything
          to do with your heritage or is it
          just a coincidence?

                    REBECCA
          Mr. Sebastian, your name is
          Sebastian Sherwin. Your initials
          are SS. Does this have anything
          to do with your heritage or is it
          just a coincidence?

The courtroom erupts into conversation, laughter,
and obscured murmuring. The judge hits the gavel.

                    JUDGE COHEN
          Mr. Sherwin, stick to pertinent
          questions.

                    SEBASTIAN
          When did Trisha begin writing
          letters to herself?

                    PATRICK
          Your Honor.

                    SEBASTIAN
          Sir, I'd like to finish quickly.

                    JUDGE COHEN
          You may answer, Miss Riley.

                    REBECCA
          Trisha did not write those letters.

                    SEBASTIAN
          Do you believe that Hat Santis
          sent letters from the grave?

Rebecca looks down and there's complete silence in
the room.

                    REBECCA
          (mumbled) I wrote the letters.

                    SEBASTIAN
          (meekly) What?

                    REBECCA
          I wrote the letters.

The courtroom explodes. The judge bangs his gavel.

                    JUDGE COHEN
          Court is in recess until one
          o'clock.

EXT IN FRONT OF THE COURTHOUSE, NOON

Guarded, Ingrid, Aaron, and Sebastian being followed by a mob.

> PERSON 1
>
> Nazi!

> PERSON 2
>
> You're persecuting an innocent
> girl!

> NUN
>
> If there's no God, where did you
> come from?

> PERSON 3
>
> The Lord gave you health and
> wealth! You're scheming to get
> more! Judgment Day is at hand!

> DARK-SKINNED REVEREND
> Blessed are the meek for theirs
> shall be the kingdom of heaven.

The trio are almost in the restaurant, an egg is
thrown.

The egg is sailing.

> PERSON 4
>
> Wrath will be mine, says the Lord
> your God!

The egg splatters on the back of Sebastian's head.
Sebastian turns in anger. Aaron pulls him through
the restaurant door.

INT JUDGE COHEN'S CHAMBER

Mary and the judge are seated eating sandwiches.

                    JUDGE COHEN
          She's in no condition to
          handle her affairs. . . . I'm
          afraid . . .

                       MARY
          Eat your sandwich. . . . Men!
          You've got it all figured out.

INT COURTHOUSE PRIVATE ROOM LUNCHTIME

Patrick is with Trisha, who is looking away from
him.

                     PATRICK
          This is our break. Why are you
          despondent?

Howard Abbott walks into the room.

                     HOWARD
          Would you excuse us, Counselor?

                     PATRICK
          Well, Mr. Abbott, it's . . .
          (impatient) I'll be in the hall.

INT RESTAURANT SHORTLY AFTER

The trio are seated at a dining table in a back room.

                   SEBASTIAN
          This is good, folks. The fox has
          been let loose. Watch me now.

                     INGRID
          I thought that you said . . .

                   SEBASTIAN
          I'll sculpt this into the piece
          that we wanted from the beginning.

                              AARON
            Sebastian is charged because
            there's no letters from
            beyond . . . Had me spooked too.

A big smile comes to Sebastian's face.

                            SEBASTIAN
              Aaron . . . to truth, to destiny.

AARON GAZES AWAY

                              AARON
                (mumbled) Yes. To truth.

Sebastian raises a glass. Aaron hesitates, and the
two toast.

INT COURTHOUSE OUTSIDE THE PRIVATE ROOM, SAME TIME
PATRICK IS PACING AND LOOKING AT HIS WATCH. 12:55

The door opens. Howard is wearing dark sunglasses.
He walks silently by Patrick, who stares and enters.
Trisha and Rebecca are both in a tearful embrace.

                            REBECCA
              I love you, little girl.

Rebecca blubbers and walks by Patrick without saying a word.

                            PATRICK
              Is everything OK?

Trisha hands him an envelope.

                            TRISHA
            Open this when I nod my head.

                            PATRICK
            What is it?

Trisha silently walks by him toward the courtroom.

PATRICK'S FACE.

INT COURTHOUSE FRIDAY AFTER LUNCH

Rebecca is being questioned by Patrick.

                    REBECCA
         I felt that she was neglected.

Ingrid rises.

                    INGRID
         How dare you? You . . . leech!

Judge hits the gavel.

                  JUDGE COHEN
         Guards, escort Mrs. Abbott
         out . . .

                    INGRID
         I'll go myself! This is a zoo! I'm
         bored!

Patrick turns back to Rebecca then to Trisha.

                    TRISHA
         Psst.

Trisha forms her fingers and mimics ripping open an
envelope.

                    PATRICK
         (whispered) Oh, yes, yes.

Cohen looks on as Patrick opens the envelope.
Sebastian stands.

                   SEBASTIAN
         Your Honor, this proceeding
         is . . .

Keeping his eyes on Patrick, the judge waves a hand
at Sebastian, who sits down.

MARY SMILES APPROVINGLY AT HER HUSBAND.

Trisha waves Patrick over and whispers in his ear.

> PATRICK
> Are you sure?

Trisha smiles and nods.

> PATRICK
> Your Honor, I'd like to ask Rebecca
> Riley to identify these letters.

> SEBASTIAN
> Your Honor . . .

> JUDGE COHEN
> Please be seated. Proceed, Mr.
> Danahy.

> WOMAN
> Sit down, fool!

The courtroom erupts. The judge hits the gavel.
Patrick hands one of the letters to Rebecca.

> PATRICK
> Miss Riley, please tell the court
> what the paper in your hand is.

Rebecca looks timidly at the judge.

> REBECCA
> It's my ABCs.

THE JUDGE NARROWS HIS EYES, EXTREMELY INTERESTED.

> PATRICK
> And this?

                    REBECCA
          It's my paycheck.

                    PATRICK
          Your Honor?

The judge nods. Patrick walks over to the judge and
hands him the papers.

THE JUDGE STUDIES THE PAPERS, GRINS, AND RAISES HIS
HEAD.

                    PATRICK
          Miss Riley, did you write the
          letters Trisha claims came from
          Hat Santis?

REBECCA FACES THE JUDGE. THE JUDGE WINKS AT HER.

                    REBECCA
          No.

Sebastian stands, raises his arm, and opens his
mouth. The judge pays no attention.

                    JUDGE COHEN
          (calmly) Sit down, Counselor.

Sebastian remains standing.

                    SEBASTIAN
          But Your Honor!

                    JUDGE COHEN
          Sit down, you're being obnoxious.

                    WOMAN
          You tell him, Judgey!

Sebastian looks around, smiles a phony smile, and
sits down.

> PATRICK
> Miss Riley, please tell us why it
> couldn't have possibly been you
> who wrote the letters.

Rebecca looks to the judge. The judge smiles reassuringly.

> REBECCA
> I can't read or write. Trisha was
> teaching . . .

The courtroom explodes. . . . The judge bangs his
gavel.

> JUDGE COHEN
> Order! Order! Counselor.

> PATRICK
> Miss Riley, who wrote those
> letters to Trisha?

Again the courtroom becomes silent.

> REBECCA
> Hat . . . Rob Santis.

Pandemonium breaks out. Reporters are heading for
the door.

GEORGIA'S HEAD IS PRESSED AGAINST DOMINIC'S SHOUL-
DERS. LOU SMILES.

INT COURTHOUSE HALLWAY FRIDAY AFTERNOON

A reporter is on a headphone set connected to his
cell.

                    REPORTER
          Stop the press! Housekeeper says
          the letters *are* from Santis!

Joey goes into the hallway and walks to a tall,
dark-skinned guard.

                     JOEY
          David, give me your cell.

                    DAVID
          Joey, you can't use your cell
          here.

                     JOEY
          I know. That's why I need yours.

David frowns and hands over the cell phone.

                     JOEY
          Tanks.

Joey dials a number.

                     JOEY
          Hey C. He ain't gonna get his
          hands on dat money for months, if
          ever. See you tonight.

He clicks off and hands the phone to David.

                    DAVID
          Hey man, don't be calling those
          mafiosa humps with my phone.

                     JOEY
          David, you shouldn't stereotype.

Soon the hall is overflowing with camera crews from
CNN, Fox, ABC, RT, Euro News, and CBS, all vying for
position. Joey elbows his way through the crowd.

INT COURTROOM FRIDAY AFTERNOON

Patrick is questioning Liz Madia.

> PATRICK
> Do you believe Trisha to be
> insane?

> LIZ
> No, definitely not.

> SEBASTIAN
> Objection. We have never claimed
> insanity.

> JUDGE COHEN
> Sustained. Rephrase your question.

> PATRICK
> Miss Madia, how would you rate
> Trisha's work?

> LIZ
> She's the best, most competent
> worker we have.

> PATRICK
> Have there ever been any patient-
> related problems caused by her?

> LIZ
> Not that I know of. (smiling) They
> love her.

> PATRICK
> Has this changed since Rob, Hat
> Santis's death?

> LIZ
> No.

                    PATRICK
        Thank you.

Patrick, pleased with himself, imitates a golf putt
and waves Sebastian on.

                    PATRICK
        Counselor.

Sebastian adjusts his collar.

Reporters point as Howard Abbott enters and whispers to Patrick.

INT COURTROOM FRIDAY AFTERNOON

The cross between Sebastian and Liz is already
under way.

                    SEBASTIAN
        I repeat. Have you ever seen
        Trisha Abbott speaking to
        herself? . . . You're under oath.

Liz looks at Trisha and smiles.

                    LIZ
        I've seen her speaking by herself.

                    SEBASTIAN
        Was there music on? Could she
        have been singing, a speakerphone
        maybe?

                    LIZ
        No, but I sometimes . . .

                    SEBASTIAN
        Who was she talking to? . . . Your
        Honor.

> JUDGE COHEN
> Miss, answer the question please.

> LIZ
> Hat, Rob . . .

There's murmur in the court.

> SEBASTIAN
> How do you know that Trisha Abbott
> was talking to him?

> LIZ
> She told me.

Sebastian turns, pauses.

> SEBASTIAN
> No further cross, Your Honor . . .

INT COURTROOM FRIDAY AFTERNOON

Sebastian is cross-examining a detective.

> DETECTIVE
> No sir, there is no way that
> someone got into the Cabbage House
> to place trinkets or letters.

> SEBASTIAN
> Could Trisha have brought them in?

> DETECTIVE
> Yes, of course.

> SEBASTIAN
> Your witness, Counselor.

Sebastian gallantly waves Patrick on.

INT COURTROOM LATER

Sebastian is crossing Georgia Santis.

                    SEBASTIAN
          Mrs. Santis, how did you and
          Trisha pass your time together?

Georgia has the presence of an Italian Edith Bunker.

                    GEORGIA
          We would cook Italian meals . . .
          I taught her . . .

                    SEBASTIAN
          Thank you, what else?

                    GEORGIA
          I told her about the saints. We'd
          say novenas.

                    SEBASTIAN
          Can you explain what novenas are?

                    GEORGIA
          They're prayers read from holy
          cards to saints or the Madonna
          asking for divine intervention.

                    SEBASTIAN
          I assume that statues are used.

                    GEORGIA
          Yes, the saint's statue was put
          on the table . . . If I had it.
          I don't have . . .

Sebastian sinisterly grins.

                    SEBASTIAN
          That's enough. So, if I may, Mrs.
          Santis?

                    GEORGIA
          Oh, please call me Georgia.

                    SEBASTIAN
          I'd rather be official, we are in
          court.

Georgia raises her finger to her mouth as if she
understands.

                    GEORGIA
          Oh yes. Of course.

                    SEBASTIAN
          Tell me if I'm making an accurate
          description.

Georgia nods and smiles at Trisha. Sebastian purposely positions himself to block any further eye
contact.

                    SEBASTIAN
          You and Trisha would chant over
          little statues of people reading
          from recipe cards?

                    GEORGIA
          Holy cards.

                    SEBASTIAN
          Yes, I'm sure they're *very*
          holy. . . . Mrs. Santis, your
          son Rob was called Hat, is that
          correct?

                    GEORGIA
          Why yes, since he was a boy.

                    SEBASTIAN
Does the name have a religious
connotation? Was he named after a
holy beret or something?

                    GEORGIA
No. My dad and Rob were
inseparable. Dom worked two jobs.
I worked at the ballpark. We saved
for their college. . . . Dom's a
fine man.

Georgia looks at her husband and smiles.

                    SEBASTIAN
I see. It's very admirable. . . .
Could you please answer the
question?

                    GEORGIA
My dad died on May 26th. Rob was
12, to Rob the world had ended.
There would be no more . . .

                    SEBASTIAN
(impatiently) Please, Mrs. Santis,
it's moving. Why was your son
called Hat?

                    GEORGIA
Rob slept with my dad's old hat.
He even wore it to school. . . .
The kids called him Hat. Father
Gondolfo convinced him to leave it
at home so he wouldn't lose it. He
never lost the hat or the name.

                    SEBASTIAN
Tell us, Mrs. Santis, how do you
explain the famous letters?

                    GEORGIA
          Why it's a miracle.

                   SEBASTIAN
          ('Here's Johnny' flow) No further
          questions.

Sebastian pretends to putt and clenches his fist as
he walks back to his spot.

LOU SHERMAN'S FACE IS STONE. AARON HAS HIS HEAD
DOWN.

Georgia descends. She whispers to Trisha as she
passes her. Trisha nods and smiles. Sebastian
glares meanly.

                  JUDGE COHEN
          It's late. Are there any further
          witnesses?

                    PATRICK
          Sir, I'd like to call Mr. Howard
          Abbott.

                   SEBASTIAN
          Your Honor, Mr. Abbott's a
          captain of industry. It would be
          humiliating to have him testify in
          this way. It's unnecessary.

                  JUDGE COHEN
          Does he wish to testify, Mr.
          Danahy?

                    PATRICK
          Sir, it was his idea.

                  JUDGE COHEN
          Do you object?

SHERWIN IS STARING INTO SPACE

                    JUDGE COHEN
          Counselor Sherwin? Do you object?

                    SEBASTIAN
          (nervously) Why . . . no.

                    JUDGE COHEN
          The court calls Mr. Howard Abbott.

The court hums with whispers as Howard Abbott
walks up.

                 COURT SPECTATOR 1
          He's more powerful than the atom
          bomb.

                 COURT SPECTATOR 2
          (whispers) He's called from the
          White House before any big
          industry decisions are made.

Howard raises his right hand and puts his left on
the bible.

                     HOWARD
          I do. (proudly and vocally)

INT COURTHOUSE HALLWAY FRIDAY AFTERNOON

Reporter's on his cell.

                    REPORTER
          That's right! Ol' man Abbott's
          taking the stand. . . . Get it in!
          I got to get back in there.

INT JUDGE COHEN'S COURTROOM LATER FRIDAY

Sebastian is gently questioning Howard.

                    SEBASTIAN
          How many employees does AE have?

Patrick stands up.

                     PATRICK
          Your Honor, we all understand that
          AE is one of the premier American
          success stories. We stipulate to
          Mr. Abbott's seriousness, but . . .

                   JUDGE COHEN
          I agree. Mr. Sherwin, it's late. We
          accept Mr. Abbott to be a serious
          businessman.

Sebastian looks impatient.

                    SEBASTIAN
          Mr. Abbott, after this case,
          will your daughter get the best
          psychological care available?

                     HOWARD
          Frankly, I haven't pondered it,
          though you might consider it . . .
          for yourself, that is.

The courtroom erupts in laughter. Judge Cohen hits
the gavel.

                   JUDGE COHEN
          Answer the question please,
          Mr. Abbott.

                     HOWARD
          I don't believe my daughter
          requires help, mental or
          otherwise.

TRISHA LOOKS FONDLY AT HER FATHER WHO LOOKS PROUDLY
BACK.

SEBASTIAN
Are you aware that Trisha claims
that she receives letters from
Hat, Rob Santis?

HOWARD
Yes.

SEBASTIAN
You're aware that they're dated
after his death?

HOWARD
I am.

SEBASTIAN
Mr. Abbott, handwriting experts
have testified that these letters
could only be the work of master
forgery. . . . Are you aware of
this?

HOWARD
I am.

SEBASTIAN
Mr. Abbott. Do you know who this
expert forger might be?

HOWARD
I don't know any expert forgers.

SEBASTIAN
That's not the question. Do you
know who forged these letters? I
remind you that you're under oath!

HOWARD'S NERVOUS FACE.

SEBASTIAN (CONT'D)
Mr. Abbott! Who forged these
letters?

                         HOWARD
               No one.

                         SEBASTIAN
               Excuse me? That's impossible!

                         HOWARD
               Is it, Mr. Sherwin?

                         SEBASTIAN
               Mr. Abbott, who wrote those
               letters?

The courtroom is paralyzed.

                         HOWARD
               Rob Hat Santis.

The reporters head out. The judge is banging his
gavel.

                         JUDGE COHEN
               Court reconvenes Monday morning!

INT HOTEL ROOM FRIDAY EVENING

Aaron is adjusting his tie while looking in the
mirror.

                         AARON
               The children and the companies
               merge.

He turns and sees Taylor staring.

                         AARON
               I'll find time for us . . . It's
               not at all natural for man to
               be monogamous. In the Eastern
               civilizations it's a part of
               life. In the West we're Puritans

or hypocrites, wealthy men have
mistresses, and the johns marry
and divorce two or three times.

                    TAYLOR
          Do you love Melissa?

Aaron runs his hands through his hair.

                    TAYLOR
          Do you love her?

                    AARON
          (stutters) She's a piece in the
          puzzle.

                    TAYLOR
          What about her puzzle? Are you
          just a piece or does she love you?

He looks to the side and breathes deep. He nods.

                    AARON
          She loves me.

A TEAR FALLS GENTLY FROM HIS EYE AS HE LOOKS AT
THE GIRL

                    TAYLOR
          Do you know what love is?

Aaron half-smiles and rubs his face.

                    AARON
          No . . . what is love?

                    TAYLOR
          It's a tool that we women use to
          tame man's wandering heart.

Taylor turns.

                    TAYLOR
        I shouldn't be here. I'm a fool.

                    AARON
        You're no fool.

Aaron walks over and hugs her.

                    TAYLOR
        Maybe men aren't monogamous. But
        a woman can't give herself to
        someone that she can't hold.

Aaron walks toward the door.

                    TAYLOR
        No, I'll go first. You wait, and
        contemplate this: after passion
        dies, love is.

She gently closes the door.

INT COHEN HOME FRIDAY EVENING

Mary and Irv are in the front room.

                    MARY
        Going to temple or church with me
        will be a sham if you deny God.

                    JUDGE COHEN
        This is about money, not God. Stop
        being idiotic.

                    MARY
        You'd make a poor martyr,
        denouncing God because of popular
        opinion.

                    JUDGE COHEN
        God is not on trial here!

> MARY
> He is on trial, and you have a
> chance to be a guiding light.

> JUDGE COHEN
> Please. Just tell me when dinner's
> ready!

> MARY
> There's leftovers in the fridge.

INT THE ABBOTT MANSION IN THE DEN LATER FRIDAY
EVENING

Aaron is watching the TV and smiling. His mother
enters.

> INGRID
> That horrible cartoon is me! I'll
> sue them!

> AARON
> You'd lose, there's a striking
> resemblance.

Ingrid huffs out and stops in the hall. Aaron follows her.

> INGRID
> I can't take it! Our life's become
> one big scandal. Your father says
> that AE may fall.

> AARON
> What does he? . . .

> INGRID
> Your father knows more than you
> think.

Aaron looks in her eyes and takes her wrists in
his hands.

                         AARON
          Did you say something to him? What
          does he know?

                         INGRID
          Aaron, you're hurting my wrists.

                         AARON
          Mother, have you ever lost
          something that was more important
          to you than yourself?

                         INGRID
          You're crazy! I demand you let me
          go!

                         AARON
          Mother. I'm going to marry
          Melissa.

                         INGRID
          Insanity's rampant in the Abbotts!

                         AARON
          Do you know why, Mother?

Aaron sinisterly smiles.

                         INGRID
          I said to let me go!

                         AARON
          Because . . . I'm not like
          you . . . when I realized it . . .

AARON STARING INTO INGRID'S EYES.

                    AARON (CONT'D)
          It was the happiest day of my
          life.

Ingrid glares, jerks, and spits in Aaron's face.

                    INGRID
    You're part of me! You can't change
    that!

                    AARON
    (stutters) No! No! It's not true!

TEARS FALL FROM AARON'S EYES.

                    INGRID
    (wickedly) You'll be two has-
    beens . . . I had hoped to
    get funds from you. With the
    hole you've dug, it wouldn't be
    missed . . . I have something to
    tell you. Let go of my arms.

Aaron looks queerly.

                INGRID (CONT'D)
    Washington killed Rob.

                    AARON
    What?

                    INGRID
    That's right . . . he pushed him
    into oncoming traffic.

                    AARON
    You're crazy.

                    INGRID
    Am I? Ours is the third car.

                    AARON
    (as if in a trance) But why?

                    INGRID
    Your father wanted to help you.
    Santis would've challenged you.

Your father knew that you'd be no
match for his kind.

Aaron releases her and stares as she calmly pours
a drink.

INT SEBASTIAN'S OFFICE SATURDAY MORNING CLOCK SHOWS
8:10

Sebastian writing notes. Jonathan walks in.

                    SEBASTIAN
          It's crucial. Can I read this out
          loud to you?

                    JONATHAN
          It's my dream come true.

INT THE COHEN HOME DEN EARLY SATURDAY MORNING

Irv is reading a law book. He grabs the phone after
four rings.

                    JUDGE COHEN
          Marva. How's my girl? . . .
          Why would I appoint an outside
          trustee? Abbott's more than able.
          I admire her father for perjuring
          himself, it was very touching. But
          she's acting foolish . . . Well,
          honey, I'd rather not. Honey?

Irv looks at the phone and hangs it up. It rings
again.

A smile comes to his face as he picks it up.

                    JUDGE COHEN
          Marva, the line . . . You hung up
          on me? But why?

INT SEBASTIAN'S OFFICE SATURDAY THE CLOCK READS
12:00

Sebastian is standing. Jonathan is sitting.

> SEBASTIAN
> Where was I? Oh yes. Delusions are
> a mild form of mental illness with
> a high cure rate.

Jonathan yawns. She picks a pen up and starts to
doodle.

> SEBASTIAN
> You can take notes, no drawing!

INT THE COHEN HOME SATURDAY EARLY AFTERNOON

Irv is pouring a drink. The phone rings. He picks
it up.

> JUDGE COHEN
> Hello, Sis . . . Sharon, I'm gonna
> put you on the speaker, I've had
> the phone to my ear all day.

Irv reaches down and flicks on the speaker box.

> SHARON
> We're all proud of you. Ma says
> you were chosen for your wisdom.

> JUDGE COHEN
> That's great. Sharon, I've
> got . . .

> SHARON
> Those atheists are too much.
> They've become a militant group,
> like MeToo, LGBTQ and BLM. They
> are not solving problems. They are
> dishing out cruelty and dividing

us to gain money and power.
Someday God will destroy this
pagan planet and start anew.

                JUDGE COHEN
Sharon, really, I . . .

                SHARON
We're all by your side. 'Night, big
brother. We love you, and we're
all by your side.

INT THE ABBOTT MANSION IN THE DEN SATURDAY EVENING

Ingrid is sitting and Howard is standing over her.

                HOWARD
You'll hurt yourself in the end.

                INGRID
Will I?

                HOWARD
What do we have, twenty years?
Let's save the savable.

                INGRID
It's too late, Howard. The ship's
sinking. There's nothing to save.

                HOWARD
It will sink for everyone.

                INGRID
(calmly) Yes, and your darling
daughter will be the first to
drown.

INT KELLY'S BAR LATER SATURDAY EVENING

Patrick is in his suit drinking with his friends.

                    MUSH
Hey Patty. I never thought you'd
be picked to defend Christ.

                  BAR CLIENT
He must be desperate.

                   PATRICK
(loudly) Mush, I embraced this
case to fight corruptorations and
atheism, the real rot of our great
land. I'll fight until the end. My
reward is the honor of carrying
His banner.

Someone yells out from the back of the crowd.

                    YELLER
Amen!

                   EVERYONE
Amen, amen, amen!

                  BAR CLIENT
He was always the cream of the
neighborhood.

A teardrop slides off Danahy's cheek and into his
beer mug.

                   PATRICK
(mumbling to self) It's true, the
road to glory is paved with tears.

Patrick sips his beer and savors the unique taste
of long-lost pride. The bar explodes with applause.

INT TRISH'S ROOM SAME TIME

Trisha is inside reading. The door flings open.
Ingrid enters and grabs Trisha by the hair.

                    INGRID
         You're getting on a plane, you
         paltry bitch! You play your father
         but you'll not play me!

Trisha is whimpering and trying to remove her
mother's hands.

                    INGRID (CONT'D)
         I'm glad Rob's dead! I only wish
         that I could've killed him with my
         own hands!

INGRID'S EYES

                    INGRID
         When you spread your legs, you,
         useless whore, you must be sure to
         capture something worth catching!

                    TRISHA
         (sobbing) Mother.

The door opens. Ingrid turns, Rebecca punches her
in the face. Ingrid falls. Rebecca hugs Trisha.

                    REBECCA
         You'll soon leave all this. Don't
         forget old Becky.

                    TRISHA
         (sobbing) Rebecca, I'll come soon.
         I promise.

INGRID WATCHES THE SCENE FROM HER THRONE ON THE
FLOOR. HER EYES SIZZLE WITH DISDAIN, DISRESPECT,
DEPRECATION, AND DENIGRATION.

                    INGRID
         (murderous) You pathetic,
         gullible, simpleminded lunatics.

> I've lived through the winter
> in my spring, summer, and fall!
> I command the destiny of your
> pointless existence!

Ingrid reaches into her kimono pocket. Rebecca smiles and squarely kicks Ingrid in the ribs. She then looks gently at Trisha.

                    REBECCA
        Sorry honey, trick knee.

INT SEBASTIAN'S OFFICE SATURDAY EVENING 9:10

THE CLOCK, 9:10. JONATHAN IS SITTING GLARING AT SEBASTIAN.

                    SEBASTIAN
        She'll return to her devoted
        family with a clear idea of her
        life, a free mind to handle her
        financial fairs . . . financial
        affairs . . .

He looks at the lit sky scrapers, turns and throws the sheets up. He stumbles as they fall to the ground.

                    SEBASTIAN
        None of this matters! She'll seal
        her fate when she gets on the
        stand (he laughs).

THE DOORWAY WITH ALL OF THE SHEETS OF PAPER IN HIS TRACKS.

INT THE NEIGHBORHOOD CLUB SATURDAY NIGHT

C's sitting and staring blankly. Joey walks up to him.

                         JOEY
          Hey C. What gives? You should be
          happy. Did you see da papers? Dat
          whole family's history.

                        CERONE
          Yeah.

                         JOEY
          Forget dat broad. We'll do Layla
          tonight.

Joey puts his arm on C's shoulder.

                    JOEY (CONT'D)
          Come on buddy, snap out of it.

                        CERONE
          She's goin' back to Abbott. Says
          I'm a jerk.

                         JOEY
          She's goofy? Dat guy's finished.

                        CERONE
          Hey Joey, no more letters.

INT THE COHEN HOME SAT NIGHT

The speaker phone is on. Irv's sitting at the desk.

                         JOEL
          And after, big brother, we'll
          talk about how the Cohens can
          contribute to defeat atheists,
          neo-Nazis, and all the other
          special interest hate rabble.

                     JUDGE COHEN
          (impatiently) Yeah Joel,
          thanks . . . great idea.

IRV REACHES DOWN AND DISCONNECTS THE PHONE

INT THE ABBOTT MANSION IN THE DEN, SAME TIME

Aaron is seated at the desk, his hands behind his
neck. His father is standing in front of him.

>   HOWARD
> You'll be fine. Just let the
> company fall as it may. No one can
> control things now.

>   AARON
> Dad, you say it like it's so easy.

>   HOWARD
> There will be more help than you
> think. . . . You know son, I was
> not only a *business*man. I was also
> a *decent* man. AE has done good for
> a lot of people. It will not lack
> supporters.

>   AARON
> There's nothing decent about
> murder. And Mom, who will catch
> her?

>   HOWARD
> If night falls, I'll absorb the
> dark.

>   AARON
> How? You'll have major problems.

>   HOWARD
> I've a plan. I'll manage . . . It's
> my duty. Good night son.

>   AARON
> Good night Dad . . . Dad, I love
> you.

Aaron falls crying to the ground and hugs his father's knees.

INT RESTAURANT SUNDAY MORNING

Lawrence Barr and Sebastian are sitting at a table.

> LAWRENCE BARR
> I sent Tillerson and Bicks our client list . . . I still think that it's all for nothing.

> SEBASTIAN
> OK, Larry. Watch this.

Sebastian takes his cell phone out.

> SEBASTIAN (CONT'D)
> Hello, Mr. Tillerson. Sebastian Sherwin here. Sir, I've instructed Counselor Barr as you asked . . . I see . . . I see . . . Well of course sir . . . Yes sir . . . Thank you sir.

Sebastian stares blankly for 5 seconds.

> LAWRENCE BARR
> I told you . . .

Sebastian continues to stare in shock.

> LAWRENCE BARR (CONT'D)
> There will be other chances . . . But be honest. Was writing those letters necessary?

> SEBASTIAN
> They blew me off. (in a trance)

> LAWRENCE BARR
> People say that you'll marry Ingrid Abbott when this ends . . .

Sebastian gets up groggily and starts to walk.

                    SEBASTIAN
          She's old and . . .

                    LAWRENCE BARR
          And rich.

                    SEBASTIAN
          Go screw yourself, Larry.

Lawrence tilts his drink glass to his lips. Sebastian walks.

                    LAWRENCE BARR
          Wish I could, I wouldn't leave
          home.

Lawrence downs his drink and walks to the bathroom. Two men in suits follow him.

One winks at the waiter, who comes and stands at
the bathroom door. Punches and grunts are heard.

INT RESTAURANT BATHROOM MOMENTS LATER

The two men walk out. Lawrence's bloodied head
falls under the stall door. He's making noise,
unconscious, not dead.

INT C'S CAR—EMPTY PARKING LOT SUNDAY NOON RAINY
DARK

HOODED HEAD OF PASSENGER AND C'S FACE

                    CERONE
          Now you wanna whack the chauffeur?
          Look, if dey ain't found him yet
          dey ain't gonna find him. Don't get
          sucked in by all da television.
          Nobody gets caught. Dey fry
          twenty-five johns for twenty-five

thousand murders a year. Just
keep your mout shut, believe me,
Washington won't advertise. It'll
go away. Your real problem is da
bank. . . . Dey won't give you no
cake, say it's too risky.

THE BACK OF THE HEAD OF THE PASSENGER SLOWLY TURNS,
REVEALING INGRID'S PROFILE.

                    INGRID
          You bastard! I'll go to the police.

                    CERONE
          Yeah, take your friend Lawrence
          Barr wit ya. He's another guy dat
          likes to snitch.

Ingrid swings. C smiles and grabs her hair.

                    INGRID
          You, scum! I've done
          everything . . .

                    CERONE
          Yeah. Now get outta da car,
          lowlife.

Ingrid lunges at C. C grabs her arms.

                    INGRID
          You hood! I'm Mrs. Howard Abbott!

                    CERONE
          OK Mrs. Abbott. If dat's da way ya
          wan it.

He opens his door. The rain is falling from his
eye lashes. He drags her face down into a puddle.
She stops kicking and swinging and begins to cry.
C pulls his zipper down.

                    CERONE
          Hey Ingrid. You remember ol' 'one
          eye'? I don feel anyting for ya
          but he feels sometin'.

The sound of urine becomes more audible than the
rain. C gets back in the car and drives away.

INGRID LYING DOWN WITH HER HEAD IN HER HANDS IN
THE RAIN.

INT PIZZERIA SUNDAY EVE AFTERWARDS

Aaron and Melissa sitting holding hands across the
table.

                    AARON
          Things will be different.

                    MELISSA
          I like change.

                    AARON
          You'll be the wife of a struggling
          businessman. . . . There's a
          chance that I won't be included in
          the plan to salvage AE and AI.

                    MELISSA
          Who cares? I don't.

                    AARON
          You know, I actually like pizza.

INT IRV COHEN'S BEDROOM MONDAY EARLY MORNING

Irv turns over. Mary's gone. He holds his stomach
and rises.

EXT THE COURTHOUSE MONDAY EARLY MORNING SUNNY

Protesters are spilling into the street blocking
traffic. Reporters are interviewing people on the
street outside.

INT THE ABBOTT MANSION IN THE KITCHEN, SAME TIME

Aaron is drinking orange juice. His mother walks
in.

                    INGRID
          Aaron . . . About what I said
          yesterday.

                    AARON
          I didn't hear a thing.

                    INGRID
          I'm leaving for good . . . But
          before I do, tell me. Why would
          you let Sherwin convince you to
          write those letters?

                    AARON
          Mother, your question unmasks the
          truth.

Aaron walks out.

INT RESTAURANT ACROSS FROM COURTHOUSE MONDAY MORNING

The same two guys (Jimmy and Chucky) in the restaurant are eating.

                    JIMMY
          Trib says that the brother wrote
          the letters.

                    CHUCKY
          I say it was the atheist attorney.

                    JIMMY
          Yeah so does the *Sun-Times*.

> CHUCKY
> I heard you can get odds on it.

> JIMMY
> Yeah. I'm rooting for the Santis
> kid.

> CHUCKY
> Yeah, and the bookies have wings.

The two smile at each other.

COURTHOUSE ENTRANCE SHORTLY AFTER

Joey and C are walking to the courtroom. David escorts them to two empty seats. Joey looks at Trisha, who's dressed in a light pastel dress.

> JOEY
> She looks like such a sweet kid.

> CERONE
> You know, I . . . I don't know.

C shakes his head.

> CERONE
> De mudder, she's da nut. Been
> goin' to Honest Larry Barr for
> advice and a divorce for years.

> JOEY
> Larry's not feeling well. He'll be
> on Tylenol for a few weeks. . . .
> Hey, the ol' bitch ain't here.

> CERONE
> Probably in hiding waiting for da
> posse.

> JOEY
> Whadda ya mean?

                    CERONE
          She tinks dat I had her chauffeur
          whack Hat. She watches too many
          gangster flicks.

Joey shakes his head.

                    JOEY
          I'd kill myself before I'd touch
          dat kid.

                    CERONE
          Yeah, me too . . . No more
          letters, Joey. To hell wit it all.

JOEY'S FACE A BIT CRINGED AND UNSURE.

                    JOEY
          You know C, I didn't write dose
          letters.

                    CERONE
          (loudly) What?

People are turning and looking at them.

                    JOEY
          I din't. I was happy cause you was
          happy. You presumed it was me, but
          it wasn't.

C slaps the top of Joey's head with a rolled-up
newspaper.

                    CERONE
          Tell me da trutt.

                    JOEY
          I swear on my mudder's grave. May
          she rot in hell if I'm lyin'.

C just looks back at him puzzled. Then he smiles.
THE JUDGE SEES THE RUCKUS

                    JUDGE COHEN
          Order in the court.

AARON AND MELISSA ARE MAKING THEIR WAY DOWN THE
AISLE.

A few spectators sneer at Aaron. Judge Cohen hits
the gavel.

                    JUDGE COHEN
          Order. Order.

LOU IS LEANING OVER BEHIND WHERE SEBASTIAN'S SEATED

Lou's covering the bench back with his jacket.

                    JUDGE COHEN
          Counselor Sherwin and Counselor
          Danahy, please approach the bench.

They rise. The court explodes with laughter as
Sebastian, who has a navy blue suit on, has a
chalked cross inside a heart on the back of his
jacket. Sebastian turns to look. The judge sees the
design and covers his smile with his hand. He looks
to Mary, who is openly smiling.

                    JUDGE COHEN
          Has there been any progress toward
          a settlement?

                    SEBASTIAN
          No, Your Honor.

                    PATRICK
          No, sir.

                    JUDGE COHEN
          Very well.

The attorneys leave. Cohen looks around Sebastian
and spots Lou Sherman.

LOU HAS A CHILDISH YET DEVILISH GRIN ON HIS FACE.

The judge gives him a stern look that turns into a smile.

> JUDGE COHEN
> Miss Abbott, do you still wish to speak on your own behalf?

> TRISHA
> Yes, Your Honor.

> JUDGE COHEN
> Please approach the bench.

Trisha opens her purse and takes out a folded hat.

GEORGIA GASPS.

> GEORGIA
> It's Rob's hat! Oh my God. I knew it.

> JOEY
> I saw them put that hat in de coffin. Colletta de stiff director said it was buried with the kid.

C stares at Joey.

> JOEY (CONT'D)
> Colletta wouldn't rob no hat. A watch maybe . . .

> TRISHA
> Your Honor, I have a request.

> JUDGE COHEN
> Yes.

> TRISHA
> I'd like not to be interrupted, if that's possible.

Judge Cohen nods.

                    JUDGE COHEN
          That's an easily granted request.
          Go ahead.

                    TRISHA
          My family objected profusely to
          me and Hat. But when Hat left,
          any hope of happiness left with
          him. . . . My family objected
          profusely.

She looks at Aaron.

                    TRISHA (CONT'D)
          But you can't convince people of
          things that you feel.

Aaron smiles slightly.

                    TRISHA (CONT'D)
          Hat promised to never leave me. I
          was upset that he had not kept his
          promise.

TEARS AND A SMILE ON GEORGIA'S FACE.

Trisha looks at Sebastian.

                    TRISHA
          Mr. Sherwin, you tried to make it
          a sexual awakening thing.

                    SEBASTIAN
          I didn't say . . .

                    JUDGE COHEN
          Counselor, the lady has the floor.

Trisha smiles at the judge, who smiles back.

                        TRISHA
            It wasn't that . . . We fit
            together like two halves of a
            circle. The night of his funeral
            I curled up on a chair in my
            bedroom. Sleet was tapping against
            the window, and the tapping
            seemed to play a melody. I got
            up and checked the radio. When I
            got back, Rob was sitting in my
            chair. He pulled me into his arms.
            He told me to stop mourning, put
            me in bed, kissed me, and told
            me that soon we'd be together
            forever.

Trisha looks in Becky's direction.

                        TRISHA (CONT'D)
            I told Becky. . . . She told me
            that I was dreaming.

Trisha wipes tears from her eyes and laughs.

                        TRISHA (CONT'D)
            I thought so too. But the
            emptiness was gone. I felt that
            I had something to look forward
            to. I actually hid my joy at work
            so that people didn't think I had
            flipped. After about a week, I
            found a letter on my nightstand.
            Becky thought that I was having
            delusions. But there's something
            that she didn't tell you. One
            night she sat on a chair outside
            my room. When she heard Rob's
            voice she rushed in. He talked to
            her too.

BECKY IS LOOKING SOLEMNLY AHEAD

TRISHA (CONT'D)
Hat told her that the rest of her
life would be peaceful, that when
she was called to leave the feast
she'd do so elegantly.

PATRICK WIPES HIS BROW. THE ROOM IS COMPLETELY
SILENT.

TRISHA (CONT'D)
When Grandmother died, Hat assured
me that she was fine. I never
personally spoke to her. Though we
did have a two-day visit a week
before . . . Grandma was a real
practical joker.

AARON LOOKS CURIOUSLY.

TRISHA (CONT'D)
I told Aaron that I'd donate all
of the money to Tuesday's Child.
It terrified him. He puts a high
value on wealth.

HOWARD BRUSHING AWAY TEARS IN THE BACK OF THE ROOM.

TRISHA (CONT'D)
Hat knew about Aaron's scheming.
He asked me to be patient. I'm
glad that I can tell you how I
felt.

THE WINDOW SHOWS AN UGLY RAIN AND WIND GUSTING

TRISHA (CONT'D)
I'm not here to tell you to become
religious fanatics. But it's just
not about money . . .

She takes a hem of her dress in her hand.

> TRISHA (CONT'D)
> This is my wedding dress.

Judge cohen looks to his wife mary. Tears are streaming down her face.

The room is growing darker.

> TRISHA (CONT'D)
> I talked to my grandmother about
> Hat and Tuesday's Child. She went
> to an attorney to draw up her
> will. I promised to keep quiet
> about it all. It's true that I
> inherited all of her assets. But
> she had already given everything
> except her apartment and one
> hundred thousand dollars to
> Tuesday's Child on the stipulation
> that they give her a generous
> allowance that ceased the day
> that she died. This is all legal.
> It was handled by Bicks from
> Tillerson and Bicks. Grandma knew
> Mr. Bicks for some time. Said that
> he was a real card. She preferred
> him to her old attorney, Mr. Barr.

SEBASTIAN'S FACE.

> TRISHA (CONT'D)
> So we're really here to fight over
> a hundred thousand dollars.

EXT PEOPLE OUTSIDE TAKING REFUGE DEBRIS FLYING-DARK

INT JUDGE COHEN'S COURTROOM, SAME TIME

One of the windows bursts, and a pane of glass smashes on the wall. The courtroom lights go out. There are screams as people bolt to the door. The lights flicker a few times and then remain on.

Trisha calmly walks toward the window.

Judge cohen looks to trisha.

OPEN WINDOW

> JUDGE COHEN
> Guards, hold Trisha Abbott!

Guards run up behind Trisha and grab her. She jerks, trying to free herself.

> TRISHA
> Hat! Hat! Please, please! Hat!

In the struggle she falls onto the floor sobbing. Trisha continues to struggle and scream.

TRISHA'S FACE

Paramedics run in. One of them prepares a syringe. In the background other guards have entered and are clearing the room.

> GEORGIA
> Rob came for her. Let her go! Let her go!

Sebastian turns to Georgia.

> SEBASTIAN
> The farce is ended! (mockingly) Let her go! Where, to fall out the window?

Dominic approaches Sebastian as Trisha's sobs fade into the background.

> JUDGE COHEN
> Mr. Santis, there will be no violence in my courtroom.

Dominic smiles, but he keeps coming.

>   MR. SANTIS
>   I'm with him. I don't go for all
>   of dis mumbo jumbo. I just want to
>   say sometin'.

Dominic reaches to shake. Sebastian hesitates and then clasps his hand. Dominic takes Sebastian's shoulder with his left hand and looks in Jonathan's direction.

>   MR. SANTIS
>   In my neighborhood, we give girls
>   girls' names. Is she a he-she?

Sebastian cringes with pain. Dominic lets him go. Sebastian grasps his right hand with his left hand.

>   SEBASTIAN
>   Oh, oh my hand.

Dominic looks at him, and he smiles.

>   MR. SANTIS
>   That's for my son Hat.

Two guards walk up behind the Santis family. There's a crowd around Trisha. She's semiconscious.

TRISHA'S FACE

>   TRISHA
>   (mumbling) Hat . . . Hat . . .

Her voice fades off.

Dominic and his family walk out. The halls are empty and quiet except for a few stragglers and the guy cleaning the barrier glass who listens to a transistor radio.

                    RADIO ANNOUNCER
        Today the Department of Industry
        chose Aaron Abbott as the head of
        the AE-AI restructuring.

INT COURTHOUSE RESTAURANT MORNING

The same two patrons. Jimmy is sitting at the table
reading a newspaper. Chucky is dabbing at his eggs.

                    JIMMY
        The government's gonna bail out AE
        and AI.

                    CHUCKY
        If me and you went broke, they'd
        send a collection agency.

                    JIMMY
        There's a lot of jobs at stake.

                    CHUCKY
        And the fat cats walk away with
        the cash.

                    JIMMY
        They'll have to answer to a
        consumer advisory board.

Jimmy lowers the paper.

                    JIMMY (CONT'D)
        That will keep 'em off of the
        front page of *Fortune* magazine for
        a while.

                    CHUCKY
        I'm going to cry, let's start a
        collection.

Jimmy puts a quarter in his glass and jingles it

                    JIMMY
        Anyone want to help out Aaron
        Abbott and Blake Andrews? We're
        taking a collection.

A few people laugh.

INT CHICAGO-READ MENTAL HOSPITAL EARLY MORNING

The hallway is clean and friendly, decorated with
various bright paintings. The clock reads 7 A.M.

A middle-aged male nurse is whistling. He pulls on
a set of keys from his waist.

He stops and sticks them into the stainless-steel
windowed door. He opens it. The room is empty. He
looks over the room.

The windows are closed and intact. The hat on the
desk.

He turns to walk out.

                    NURSE
        (whispered to himself) Oh my God.

Picture freezes. Camera goes outside and takes a
shot of the busy street in front of the courthouse.
Radio announcer is talking in the background.

                RADIO ANNOUNCER
        Today the Department of Industry
        chose Aaron Abbott as the head
        of the AE-AI restructuring. But
        authorities still have no clue
        on the whereabouts of his sister
        Trisha Abbott. . . . Her family
        has no comment.

She disappeared from the Chicago-
Read Mental Hospital without a
trace five days ago. Just vanished
into thin air . . .

                SISTER BRENDA
This is Radio Maria. Trisha
Abbott disappeared on August
15th, the feast of the Assumption.
Coincidence? We think not.

                RADIO ANNOUNCER
Here's one for you Trisha,
wherever you are.

Music "It's Your Time" by Patrick Girondi

It's your time, it can't be wrong
Better learn to sing dat song
Been hurt before, we all have you see
Stung before but still want honey
Don't worry, tomorrow starts in the morning
And he's sporting a new pair of dancing shooooes
That cloud overhead's about done raining
Time to get happy and chase away all of your blues.

A still picture rolls down of Aaron and Melissa.

Afterword

Written: *Aaron and Melissa are married. Melissa's pregnant with their first child. Besides heading the AE-AI reconstruction project, Aaron is on the board of directors of Tuesday's Child.*

Picture of Rebecca. Written: *Rebecca died in her sleep at the Cabbage House on September 12th, the feast day of the Blessed Virgin.*

Picture of Howard in a hard hat. Written: *Howard Abbott is retired and is overseeing the building at Tuesday's Child.*

Picture of C and Joey P. The picture comes to life. Joey P, "Hey C, will dere always be guys like us?" C, "Joey, as long as all of da honchos are sendin' dere kids four to six years at da university dere'll be guys like us to straighten tings out."

Picture of Sebastian. He's wearing a yarmulke and has a cast on his right hand. He's in the company of a rabbi. Written: *He's been fired from his firm and is a fervent supporter of his local synagogue.*

Picture of Ingrid wearing sunglasses. Written: *Ingrid is always incognito. Her story is no longer important to anyone, and she most certainly is not hiding from shame. But she's definitely hiding. She's not really missed.*

Followed by a still picture of Trisha. Written: *For the believers, Trisha and her betrothed were reunited by a miracle that mankind can neither touch nor see nor understand, and for the nonbelievers, no explanation can suffice.*

The End

Pictured Above: Robert F. Kennedy Jr. with Patrick Girondi
Photo credit: Deborah Suchman Zeolla

Other books by Patrick Girondi, published by Skyhorse:

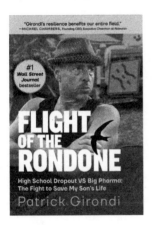  

Coming Soon:

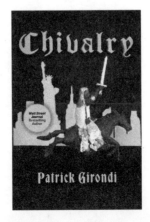